WITCHING AFTER FORTY

VOLUME THREE

LIA DAVIS

L.A. BORUFF

A Wedded Midlife

© Copyright 2022 Lia Davis & L.A. Boruff

Published by Davis Raynes Publishing

PO Box 224

Middleburg, FL 32050

DavisRaynesPublishing.com

Cover by Glowing Moon Designs

Formatting by Glowing Moon Designs

DavisRaynesPublishing.com

Witching After Forty follows the misadventures of Ava Harper – a forty-something necromancer with a light witchy side that you wouldn't expect from someone who can raise the dead. Join Ava as she learns how to start over after losing the love of her life, in this new paranormal women's fiction series with a touch of cozy mystery, magic, and a whole lot of mayhem.

A Ghoulish Midlife
Cookies for Satan (Christmas novella)
I'm With Cupid (Valentine novella)
A Cursed Midlife
Birthday Blunder (Olivia Novella)
A Girlfriend For Mr. Snoozerton (Novella)
A Haunting Midlife
An Animated Midlife
Faery Odd-Mother (Novella)
A Killer Midlife
A Grave Midlife
A Powerful Midlife
A Wedded Midlife
A Newly-Webs Midlife
An Inherited Midlife: Coming Soon!

A GRAVE MIDLIFE

WITCHING AFTER FORTY BOOK 11

Dedicated to Cheryl Johnson-Sorrell, a beautiful fan and wonderful person. May your life be blessed with an Alfred. At the very least, a Snoozer. If NOTHING else, a Lucy-Fur, but fair warning, she's kind of a jerk.

1

AVA

It was gigantic, long, and proud. And a little intimidating.

I bet you thought I was talking about something else. Double entendre completely intended.

It was pretty hard to intimidate me, considering I was a powerful necromancer. One of the most powerful necros in decades, according to Drew and my father. It all boiled down to me being the last female in my bloodline, blah blah. You get the picture. I had a lot of juice.

Enough about me and back to the intimidating mystery sword Dad and I had found in the cave, along with a large power stone, also known as the chasm.

It'd been almost a week since we found the sword, and we still knew little about it other than it looks Norse. That discovery only added to the number of questions we all had.

By we, I meant the whole chaotic menagerie: Olivia, my best friend; Sam, my lifelong best friend; Drew, my hunky boyfriend; Mom and Dad, recently back from the sort-of dead; Winnie, recently back from the literal dead; Owen, my friend, and necro-mancer mentor; Liv's older kids with her first husband, Jess and Devan; Liv and Sam's young son, Sammie; Wally, my son and his girlfriend, Michelle; Uncle Wade, my dead husband's uncle, who is now a vampire and under my care; Luci, our next-door neighbor, who is also the literal devil and his girlfriend Phira, who is also Olivia's mom, and do I need to remind you that Luci is her dad? Yeah, drama. And then there are my seven ghouls: Alfred, Mr. Snoozerton, Lucy-Fur, Zoey, Larry, and my mother and aunt who are also technically ghouls under my care.

Well, maybe not all seven ghouls had questions. The cats seemed to not care one way or another. Little Sammie only cared about play-ing. And Jess and Devan's focus was on their father, who was miss-ing. That was another mystery we had kind of pushed to the back burner. Not that we didn't care whether Carter was really missing. Olivia just wasn't sure. Plus, she was a little bitter because the SOB had turned his back on his kids when they needed him the most.

"Alfred, why do you enjoy cooking and cleaning for Ava?" Dad asked, drawing my attention from the sword over to Alfred.

I glanced at Dad, noting how his attention was divided between the sword and my ghoul. Everyone at the kitchen table, including me, Mom, Dad, Winnie, and Olivia, was captivated by the sword. I wasn't sure if it was the strange low pulse of power coming from it or the mystery of not knowing anything about it. Probably both. We hadn't figured out a darn thing about it, and that added to the frus-tration and curiosity.

But now, everyone seemed to be waiting for Alfred to answer Dad's question.

Alfred smiled his stiff-lipped smile. "I've always enjoyed cooking. Ava has done so much for me in our short time together. It's the least I can do to thank her." Alfred's high-pitched voice was a little squeakier than usual. Was he maybe a little emotional? How sweet.

I didn't sense a lie, but the way he quickly set the breakfast plates on the table and rushed back into the kitchen told me he didn't want to talk about it. I also noted how he purposely avoided the sword. There was a story there, I was sure of it. However, I wasn't the type of person to call people out in front of others unless they were harming my family and friends. Whatever it was about the weapon, it made Alfred supremely uncomfortable.

To take the spotlight off of Alfred, I asked, "Has anyone found *anything* on the sword? Even a whisper of a rumor?"

Olivia shook her head as she fixed her plate. "Phira took a look at it and confirmed it's not from the fae realm. She too seems to think it's Norse."

Yeah, we'd already come to that conclusion. I'd even searched the internet with no luck. There were plenty of swords used in various mythologies. Norse had several. It was hard to narrow it down. A historical researcher, I was not. A writer? Yes, well, maybe every other Tuesday and twice on Sundays, but a researcher, most definitely not. I'd been hoping Phira might have some knowledge of it.

The sword wasn't my only worry. Mom and Winnie still wanted to find human bodies so they could be actually alive and their biggest hope was that their magic would return. It irked them that they couldn't use magic to help me.

Then there was a minor problem called the vampire council. A group of elder vamps had been holding necromancers hostage and recently tried to kill me. I'd sent them a message not to mess with me or mine again, but I wasn't hopeful they would listen. That message had come in the form of a new power of mine that was sure to motivate the council to increase their number of assassins or find a new alliance of some kind. They weren't the type to take my threat lying down. We were going to have to prepare for another attack.

I voted to bring it on. I was pretty dang powerful, and my friends were no chumps. I mean, Olivia's dad, my next-door neighbor, was the *literal* devil! We could handle it.

But first, we needed to prioritize our magical to-do list. 'Cause it was long.

Tabling the sword for the moment, I fixed my gaze on Mom. "Any luck on finding bodies?" They'd been volunteering at the hospital a few towns over. The ideal body would be someone with no family to miss them, and they had to be beyond all hope of a cure. Their souls had to have moved on already. We wouldn't risk putting Mom or Winnie in a body that had another sentient being in it. That was how the Alfred-Winnie fiasco had happened, though that hadn't been intentional.

Mom shook her head while Winnie said, "It'll be better if we look outside of Maine. The farther out, the better."

That was true. "Yeah. That way, if you find a body without a soul, if there *is* any family around, you'll be less likely to run into them here in Shipton." However, that idea wasn't a new one. It was a nudge for them to leave again and continue their search. But where? I didn't want to just send them off anywhere. Their powers were tied to the stones we'd excavated from the chasm now, rather than being tied directly to me, which meant they could travel virtually anywhere. The thought of them being alone in a strange city without me there to help them if something happened to their stones. What if they were in the middle of New York or some other city and they turned back to ashes? They'd just blow away, and I'd never see them again. It had to be somewhere I could still keep an eye on them.

Then an idea hit me. "Would Philadelphia be far enough away?" If they went to Philly, they could potentially stay with Hailey, the woman who bought my house. She'd been turned into a vampire right after buying it. The vampire leader of the whole United

States, Jaxon Parsons, lived in a nondescript house across the street, and if we sent them there, Wade could go with them and maybe get in a bit more vampire training with Jax. It would help us out tremendously. Although I didn't see much in it for Hailey, I'd hope she'd be amenable to opening her home to a few fellow supernatural creatures.

Mom nodded thoughtfully while Winnie said, "Yes, I think it is. If we find live bodies there and bring them back here, we'd be fairly well sheltered from running into any of their relatives."

Hopefully, they were right. "Great. I'll give Hailey a call and see if you guys could stay with her." I took a bite out of my eggs, then sipped my coffee. One thing checked off the list. Did that mean I could take a break now?

Then Olivia asked, "Would Yaya know about the sword?"

Nope. No breaks for me. I started to shake my head, but then reconsidered. "If she did, we would have no way of contacting her. I'm not going back into the Inbetween to hunt down her soul either." Not to mention, I was pretty sure she was already past the Inbetween and on to peace.

"What about the mirror?" Olivia asked, shoveling food into her face.

That was a good idea. It could work, except I was pretty sure we'd exhausted all the magic Yaya had put in the little mirror.

Winnie stared at me with wide eyes. So I explained. "We found an old hand mirror that Yaya had placed an imprinting spell on. It was her way of saying bye. Wallie got to meet her that way. But the magic is used up because the spell was only meant to last a short time."

My aunt grinned like she had the best idea ever. "You can do the spell and we can ask her."

I could? I wasn't so sure. Then again, it turned out I could shoot electricity from my hands, which was another thing to add to my list—learn to control the light.

Mom added, "We could go to the cave with the chasm before we leave and use that as a booster."

That would probably work. At least, it would give me some peace of mind that they wouldn't suddenly *poof* and be gone forever.

I waved a hand, and the family grimoire appeared on the table behind my plate. While I finished my breakfast and everyone moved around the kitchen, eating and getting ready for the day, I magically flipped the pages, looking for the imprinting spell. Our grimoire was a collection of family spells and recipes that went back hundreds of years. When I was little, I used to read all the spells, so I was pretty sure I remembered it being in there.

After studying the spell for a few minutes, I bobbed my head. "Looks like we're taking a trip to the chasm cave. I think with the power from the crystal, I can make the imprint permanent."

Maybe. We'd soon see. I was about to call out for Owen when he appeared in the archway of the kitchen. He seemed to do that a lot. I studied him for a second. "You always know when I need you." He'd also shown up in town exactly when I'd needed him, and I'd thanked my lucky stars for him more than once.

He smiled and crossed his arms. "I'm intuitive."

Apparently.

I glanced around the table, thinking of who else was missing. I'd become used to having so many people in the house, I didn't keep track of them all. Wallie, Jess, and Devon were all back at their colleges. Or at least getting settled into starting classes in a few weeks. Luci, aka Lucifer, had created portals for each of them to use to pop back home whenever they wanted. Wallie's was located in his bedroom upstairs. Jess's and Devon's were in their rooms at Luci's house.

Little Sammie—Liv and Sam's too-cute-for-words five-year-old—had said he wanted his own portal. Olivia had told him he could have one when he went to college. Now Sammie couldn't wait to go to college. No one had the heart to tell him he had a very long time to wait.

Putting my attention back to Owen, I asked, "Have you eaten?"

"Earlier, before you got up." He sat across from me and smiled expectantly.

He was a morning person. I wasn't, nevertheless, I'd been up this morning earlier than normal. Was it weird that I was a little proud of that? "Will you come to the cave with us?" I asked. "I might need help."

He chuckled and glanced at my dad. "I'm sure you won't, but yes, I'll come."

His confidence in me was touching. "Great. I just need a few minutes to get dressed and grab the mirror."

As I rinsed my plate in the sink, a telltale sound reached my ears, and I, like all cat owners in the world, braced for impact. "I hear a cat puking!" I yelled. "Lucy, Snoozer, get off the rugs!"

Owen, Dad, Alfred, Winnie, Mom, and I went running. Footsteps sounded all over the house. When we cleared the first floor, I sprinted up the stairs to see if the sound had come from up there.

I flung my bedroom door open just in time to find Lucy walking slowly off of my bedroom rug. "Don't worry," she said dismissively, the tip of her tail twitching up in the air as she sauntered by. "I made it to the rug before I horked."

Dismayed, I looked into my room to see a giant, slimy hairball on the very edge of my carpet. An inch to the right and she would've puked on the hardwood, where it was much easier to clean up.

"Thanks a lot," I muttered with a voice full of sarcasm.

Which was totally lost on Lucy. She stopped in the doorway and sat, delicately licking one paw. "My pleasure."

2

AVA

I CHANGED into a pair of jeans and a comfy, oversized sweatshirt that belonged to Drew. I'd warned him that once he started moving things in, his clothes were now mine, especially his shirts.

I didn't have to take the time to shower because Mr. Hottie Sheriff had woken me up in the best way possible this morning before he left for work. We'd showered afterward, and then I'd put on a clean pair of PJs and went back to sleep. What was the point of working for myself and from home if I couldn't sleep in?

Even still, Drew had my sleep schedule all out of sorts, thanks to the frequent interruptions. But, hey. We all make sacrifices in the name of love, don't we?

Love! I never thought I'd fall for another man after Clay died. Here I was, in love and engaged. Well, we were one step further than engaged. We were a bonded pair. Essentially, we'd been forced to bond when I kept getting ill. It'd been a curse placed by a rogue fae at the request of the vampire council, but at the time, we'd all thought I was sick. Drew had volunteered to bond with me so that I would be bolstered by his hunter strength. It had worked... until it didn't. Drew and I both ended up in a weird coma and in this strange, ghostly realm. It'd been a mess, but finally, we got it all sorted and the fae prince in question was now in a prison world.

The vampires who'd ordered the hit were another matter. And they were on the to-do list. The silver lining had been Drew's and my engagement!

Oof. That gave me one more thing to add to the list. Plan a wedding —in two months! Boy, oh, boy, was I glad I had Olivia. She loved planning parties and organizing things. All the more power to her. If I had my way, I'd give her full reins and just show up on the day.

I wasn't so lucky as to get away with that, though, was I? No. After cleaning the cat puke off of the carpet, which came up fairly easily with a little bit of the old razzle-dazzle, I put my tennis shoes on and grabbed the hand mirror from my vanity, then trotted downstairs.

Everyone, including the two immortal cats, Snoozer and pukey-butt Lucy-Fur, waited by the front door. Lucy saw me and said, "It's about time."

Glaring at the little diva, I considered and rejected several hateful responses. "I'd have been a lot faster if I hadn't been cleaning up *your* mess," I said.

She simply sniffed and turned her head away. It didn't do any good to remind her that there was a cat door at the bottom of the back door, and she was welcome to use it at any time. I knew it wouldn't do any good because I'd told her that many, many times. She never used it.

"I'm ready," I said, still glaring at the female feline.

Olivia opened the front door and exited. Mom and Winnie followed her out while my dad and Owen waited for me to step outside. Of course, no shock here, the cats darted out at the same moment I did, twining around my feet and almost tripping me.

Dad grabbed my elbow to steady me.

I grinned up at him. "Thanks. It's not like they couldn't have gotten out on their own and met us there." I spoke loud enough that they'd hear me.

Lucy twitched her tail as she strolled beside Snoozer, just ahead of us. Then she stopped and lowered her belly to the ground. Then came the butt-wiggle. Ah, she was on the prowl. There was no telling what she was about to pounce on. We kept walking as the cats moved deeper into the field between our house, Winston, and Luci's house next door.

"We need to book a flight to Milan soon," I said as we strolled, the anger at nearly being murdered still pretty fresh in my mind. Not to mention they'd held my father hostage for literally decades. That was pretty infuriating.

Dad shook his head. "We shouldn't move too rashly."

Pfft. He was far more patient than me. He'd had a lot of years to plan his revenge, too. If I were him, I'd be chomping at the bit to go back and destroy all of those... those effers. "Listen, the last thing I need is for them to send more assassins out for me. I need to worry about planning my wedding. I should be thinking about flower arrangements and dress hems, not the frikkin' vampire council." The thought of the vampire council wanting me dead put my mood into a downward spiral, and I felt my newfound electrical magic bubbling within. "Who do they think they are? I mean, half the supernatural world thought vampires were extinct. Now I'm inclined to tell everyone of their existence, despite the danger to Wade and Jax."

Dad's magic flared as if he didn't like the thought any more than I did. He took a breath and said, "I'm right there with you, but we should figure out the sword first and have a really good plan in place before we go to Milan."

Oh, I had a good plan, all right. Fire them all. Okay, that was a little extreme, but I wasn't one to sit by and let crazy, power-hungry vamps run me into hiding. They got the wrong necromancer. "A plan is good, but I want it taken care of before my wedding in September."

"Noted." Dad smiled at me before taking the path down to the beach and the cave entrance. I followed quietly, thinking about how good it would feel to let this raging power out against those responsible for the years of separation between us. It would be sweet, sweet revenge.

The power and depth of my anger against these creatures surprised even me. I was *hot*.

The spray of the ocean took my attention for a moment, and I breathed in the salt and moisture, calming with every uneven, sandy step. Once we got to the entrance of the cave, I'd calmed down enough, so I turned to Dad and Owen. "Should we do it inside the cave?" It was a little overwhelming in there as the chasm held a significant amount of power.

Dad shrugged. "We could get a small piece of the quartz and bring it out here. That way, the rest of us can form a circle around you."

Good idea. Sometimes I felt like such a newbie at being a witch-necro hybrid. In a way, I was. I'd tried to suppress my powers for all those years. "Alrighty then, let's do this."

Dad and I slowly entered the dark cave. To light the passage, I formed a glowing orb to float beside us as we walked. Melanie, my right hand in leading the coven, had taught me how to do that trick, and it'd come in handy more than once.

The gigantic cave that held the quartz and power chasm glowed with an unearthly blue light. The quartz went down and down the massive split in the rock, down to who knew where? Before Luci, I might've said down to Hell, but Hell was more of a dimension, less a place in the center of the Earth.

I didn't know much about the power here. Luci had told me it was also a ley line, which was another subject on my list to research. I wanted to know all I could learn about them.

Just like the last time, I sat down in front of the quartz, feeling the need to explain myself to the immense power. "Hi, again. It's me, Ava. I'm back to ask for a little bit of power so that I can power a mirror that houses the imprinted memory of my grandmother. Would you mind?"

I waited a few seconds, then with a sliver of power, I circled the tip of a piece of beautiful quartz and squeezed. It broke off easily, a very small piece, no bigger than a quarter. Just enough to press into the mirror's handle. "Thank you," I whispered. I got no response, but somehow, I knew the power here heard me, and appreciated my asking.

We stepped back out of the cave and walked a few feet from it so we'd have plenty of room. Mom, Winnie, Olivia, and Owen formed a circle around me and Dad. I handed the crystal to Dad. "Hold that, and I'll see what I can do."

The imprinting spell had already been done, but the power Yaya had used to charge it had faded. She'd had to put a piece of her own magic in the mirror for it to work, not having access to this quartz. Well, she'd had access. She just hadn't known it.

Focusing on the metal around the mirror, I pushed the stone against it until the magic melted the metal, though I felt no heat.

Magic was so cool.

When the quartz was firmly seated in the metal at the base of the glass and the top of the handle, I sighed and held it up to my face.

The mirror rippled like water, then smoothed out again right before Yaya's face appeared. She frowned and asked, "What are you guys doing?"

I couldn't help but grin at her. "It's wonderful to see you, Yaya. We need to talk with you."

"Hello, sweet girl." Her eyes sparkled, and if she wasn't so small, I would've tried to reach out and touch her. She looked so real.

Winnie and Mom crowded in behind me, and Yaya exclaimed in delight. "Girls! How are you here?"

Handing over the mirror, I let them tell their stories about how I'd brought them back—Mom from the Inbetween and Winnie from the dead... and then from Alfred.

When they wound down their stories, I gently took the mirror back. "There's a lot that's happened, Yaya." I started with the chasm, telling her about finding it and how it helped reactivate the mirror. "Now the spell is permanent."

"Chasm? Oh, you mean the power source the house draws from." She looked around as if trying to see who was all there. "I didn't know it could be used in the manner you described, though."

That made two of us. "I'm learning as I go. Do you know anything about Norse swords?"

"No, why?"

Well, crap. "When we found the cave the chasm is in, we found what looks to be a Norse sword, and we're trying to dig up information."

My mom tugged at my sleeve. "Give it back."

I handed the mirror to Mom and motioned for everyone to head back to the house. Mom and Winnie walked shoulder to shoulder while talking to Yaya in the mirror. My heart filled with love at the happy little reunion.

When we reached the house, I decided to enter through the conservatory while my family and friends hung out on the patio with the mirror. I'd have some time with Yaya later. And when Wallie stopped by for sure.

In my kitchen was Satan himself, Luci. He sat at the table with a plate full of food, stuffing his face with Alfred hovering. Luci was slowly growing on me, but I still didn't totally trust him. How could I?

I stopped beside him and took a slice of bacon from his plate. "I need a favor," I said around the salty goodness.

"Anything for my daughter's best friend." He grinned at me, but when Olivia entered the kitchen, his features softened, and his grin morphed into a smile.

"Can you take Mom, Winnie, Dad, and Wade to Philly?" I asked. I still needed to call Hailey, but I was banking on her saying yes. Maybe a bit presumptuous of me. But if we had to, we could pay for a hotel room.

He grunted and swallowed. "Of course, but not tonight. I have a hot date with a fae princess. I'll take them tomorrow just before sun-up."

"That works, thanks. I'll call Hailey to see if it's okay."

Everyone sat back down in the kitchen to talk to Yaya. Even Luci got in on the conversation.

I excused myself and grabbed my cell, settling down on the front porch in the breeze. I dialed Hailey's number. The last time I'd called them to warn them about the council, it'd been Jax I called. This time, I hit the button for Hailey. And belatedly remembered she was a vampire when she answered with a groggy, "Lo?" Like Uncle Wade, she'd likely been sound asleep.

"Oh, Hailey, I'm so sorry. I didn't think about it being late morning and you most likely being sound asleep."

"It's okay," she whispered. "I'm just talking quietly, so Jax doesn't wake up."

"I'm already awake," he said groggily.

"Sorry," I called through the line as I pushed off with my toe and got the rocking chair going. "I can call back."

"No," Hailey said. "What's going on?"

"Would it be possible for me to ask a humongous favor?" I paused and waited with bated breath.

"It depends on the favor, I suppose," she said, still sounding like she was mumbling half asleep.

"I was hoping my mom and dad, Aunt Winnie, and Uncle Wade could come to stay for a week or two," I said, hurriedly moving into the rest of the explanation. "Uncle Wade could use some more training from Jax and his crew, but the rest of them are searching for new bodies."

"Bodies?" she asked, far more clearly. "What do you mean, new bodies?"

"They are seeking bodies without souls to inhabit so they'll be back in living bodies. It sounds icky, but they're being very careful to find people who are truly no longer in healthy bodies."

She sighed. "That could be Luke."

"What do you mean?" I asked.

"My brother was shot," she said. "And we nearly lost him. I wondered before he was saved if maybe his soul had already moved on."

"Well, my father can sense if the soul is departed, or lingering, or still fully attached. And if the soul is fully departed, Mom and Winnie have a spell they can use to inhabit the body and no longer be ghouls in reincarnated, still-dead, magical bodies."

Hailey chuckled and murmured something between her and Jax. "Send them on," she said. "I'm interested in learning more about this. I wonder if a vampire's body can be inhabited."

"I never thought about it, but it'd be fun to try," I said with a snort. "And that's a subject I never in a million years imagined I'd want to explore more fully."

After a good laugh, we banged out the details and hung up. We were a go for Operation Philly.

It worked out fine for us that Luci couldn't take everyone to Philly until the next day. Mom, Dad, and Winnie had time to pack, and we got to say goodbye. Alfred made a nice dinner and the whole family hung out. We even called Wallie home to eat with us, which he happily did, bringing Michelle with him through the handy new portal.

By the time they left early the next morning, before dawn for Wade's sake, I was calm and ready to say goodbye. They had power, they were intelligent, and if things went wonky, they had Dad. He could handle animating both of them.

It was going to be okay.

3

OLIVIA

THANK THE GODS FOR FRIDAY. It wasn't just any Friday. This was Friday the 13th. My second favorite day out of the year. The first was Halloween.

Tonight, Ava was holding an informal coven meeting. Really, we were going to talk about the sword for a bit and then watch some Friday the 13th movies. It was more of a girls' night than a real coven meeting, and I was looking forward to it. Not so much girls' night if some of the men from the coven turned up, but I didn't care. It felt like a girls' night.

Both Sam and Drew were working. Little Sammie was at Sam's parents' house for the night. They begged us for him so often I had to tell them no half the time. My adopted parents were at Devan and Jess's apartment, helping them get settled in for school. I was companionless and free to have a great time!

About halfway through my walk from Luci's gothic mansion to Ava's old Victorian, my phone rang. When I looked at the screen, my heart dropped to my feet. This wasn't happening. Not today! My ex-in-laws were calling.

After taking a calming breath, I answered. "Hello?"

Carter's mother didn't waste a second on pleasantries. "Where is Carter? Did you even know he was missing?"

Don't be rude. Don't be rude. "Hello, Joan. Are you well? Yes, Jess told me he was missing, and we are doing everything we can to find him."

Well, not at the moment, but it was in the plans. We honestly had tried everything we could think of. Scrying and the like. Besides, Carter wouldn't care one whit if I went missing, and judging from the way he'd spoken to our kids when he found out they had magic powers, I doubted he'd bother to look for them either. So, I wasn't in that much of a hurry to find him. Although I had promised my kids I would try, and try I had.

"Obviously you're not. He's not returning my calls." She sniffed. The last thing I needed was Carter's parents getting involved.

That makes the two of us not receiving phone calls. I clamped my jaw down tight and counted to three before I replied. "I'm sure he's just taking a vacation or something. He hasn't called the kids either, but there's no reason to think there was any foul play or anything like that." I took a deep breath and held the phone a little tighter as I crossed Ava's yard to her house. "The police went to his house and couldn't find anything that suggested he'd left under duress. He's a grown man, and as best we can tell, he chose to leave."

By police, I meant Sam and Drew. We hadn't contacted the Portland police because I wasn't convinced that Carter was actually missing. After he discovered that Jess and Devan were magical fae, he just took off. Probably because of all the stress and shock of the whole thing. He was a turd anyway. If I thought he was in danger, I'd do something, but he was just being a big freaking baby, like always.

I wasn't a peach during our marriage. I was a different person then, but thankfully, I'd gained some self-awareness and made strides to change myself into a better person.

Carter had no such drive to improve himself. If anything, he'd gotten worse since our divorce.

"It's not like him to just run off without telling me," his mother continued, apparently not listening to anything I was saying. "We're going to come down and get Jessica and Devan."

"No!" My voice was a little louder than I'd intended. I didn't need my ex-in-laws to come sniffing around. I had enough to deal with. And what did they think, that I couldn't be here for my pretty-much-grown children? "Do not come here. I have everything under control. Plus, the kids are in school."

Well, getting ready to go back to school. They spent half their time at their dorms thanks to the handy portal.

"Why are they in school while their father is missing? What kind of mother would make them go in this situation?" Joan let out a huff, and I heard her husband Chad in the background mumbling, but I couldn't make out what he said. The mean words died on my lips as I reminded myself that I was a *good person*. I would not sink to her level.

"It was their choice to return to school. Plus, they can't miss too many days, or they flunk." I didn't need to explain myself or my kids to this woman. I entered Ava's house through the back door and the floorboards started shaking as I moved through the conservatory. Winston, the house, didn't like me much. Ava said he was just messing with me, but I wasn't so sure. I ignored his attempts to rile me up. He was too late. Carter's mother had beat the old house to it.

"I have to go," I said to Joan. "I'll call when I know something."

I hung up before she had another chance to bash my parental abilities again. Like mother, like son. "Shove it, Winston. I'm not in the mood."

The kitchen was empty, so I continued to the living room, where I found Ava using her magic to clean and decorate for the coven meeting-slash-party. She glanced at me and frowned. She knew me well enough now to know at first glance I was upset. "What's wrong?"

I held up my phone. "Carter's mother called. I think they might be planning to visit, even though I told her not to." It would be just like them to barge in up here, no matter my protests. Carter didn't even live in Shipton anymore! No doubt they'd come anyway.

"It is odd that he hasn't contacted his mother." Ava flicked her wrist, opening the window so a cloud of dust could float outside.

I shrugged and plopped down on the couch. "I just think Carter is off pouting somewhere. He's got plenty of money to go sit on an island if he wanted to. Hell, he could retire and buy the dang thing." I set my phone on the coffee table and glanced around to see if there was anything I could do. "Can I help?"

She shook her head. Oh, well. I could go for blowing a few things up right about now. Instead, I changed the subject. "Are you going to tell the coven about your new lightning powers and the sword tonight?"

She let the dust tornado drop into the garbage can and sighed. "Yeah, it's time I put some real trust in my coven. After all, I am their fearless leader." She rolled her eyes, then frowned. "Although Melody does more than I do."

"Why don't you hand over the reins to her?" I suggested and moved over to the bookcase that held the DVDs. It looked like Wallie, Larry, or Zoey had added to the collection. Maybe all three had.

Ava didn't watch much TV. "I mean, you don't need to leave the coven. The two of us needed their support."

She pursed her lips and cocked her head at me. "That's a good idea. I'd been thinking about it already. I have so much going on right now. This new power of mine brings a truckload of uncertainties. I'm hoping someone knows something and they can help, but I don't have to be the official leader for them to be able to help, or for me to help them if they need it."

I wished I could help my friend out, but this magic stuff was still new to me. "I'm sure someone in the coven can help."

"I'm hoping so." She sighed. "So far, it's been all one-sided, them coming to my aid. Hopefully, I'll be able to return the favors someday."

I snorted. "No, hopefully, their lives won't be so dramatic that they need any help."

We both laughed at the truth in that statement. A knock on the door interrupted our laughter. Winston echoed the knock throughout the house in his way. Ava chuckled and said, "He acts like we can't hear the door when it's right over there."

4

AVA

With a genuine smile on my face, I opened the door and greeted my coven. Well, at least five of them anyway. Melody, my right hand, was front and center. She studied me for a moment before asking, "Everything all right?"

Bless her. She was so intuitive. I chuckled. "That depends." When she drew her brows together and looked like she wanted to ask another question, I moved to the side and motioned them to enter. "Come on in. I'll explain once everyone is settled."

She nodded and entered the house, then drew in a deep breath. "Good evening, Winston." Her voice was formal, almost reverent.

The house shuddered happily, and I huffed while rolling my eyes. Figures the house loved Melody more than me. I didn't baby him like she did. Turning to our other guests as they entered, I greeted each of them. There were only four more besides Melody.

The twins, Ben and Brandon Stamp. They were a quiet pair and mostly stayed to themselves. They'd been super creepy at first, but it was their witchy-twin bond. That thing was strong and caused them to be a little introverted. It didn't help that they had a strong case of RBF, so every time they looked at anyone, it was a glare. Maybe for me it would be RWF. Resting Witch Face. Heh.

Leena and Mai were next. Leena was a fount of local history. As the local high school history teacher, she'd made it her mission to know as much about Shipton Harbor as possible, especially the witchy part.

Mai was quiet and stuck close to Leena most days, but I felt like there was something under the skin there. A hidden power or something. Only time would tell. "Hello," I greeted her warmly. She brushed her black hair over her shoulder and nodded her head without speaking, but her smile was pleasant. The lady just didn't speak often.

Before shutting the door, I asked, "Is anyone else coming?"

Our coven wasn't huge, but we had more than the seven of us here now. Melody looked a little worried as she said, "I didn't think it was a mandatory meeting."

"Oh, no, it's not." I'd been so closed off from every member that I was hoping they all came, especially since I planned a full disclosure speech for the evening. But the five members that were here would have to do. They'd fill everyone else in.

"I do want to talk about some things before we start the fun." After motioning for them to have a seat, I gave them a slight bow. "Be right back."

I walked into the kitchen. Alfred was there cooking up some snacks for movie night. I didn't know what I'd do without him if he ever left me. I'd grown far too dependent on his love of being in the kitchen. "Our guests are here. I'm going to ask them about the sword."

He nodded and paused, stirring something on the stove, his gaze skirting to the sword in the corner. Then he quickly turned to plate some of tonight's snacks. When I went to the sword, I debated on picking it up or using my magic to float it into the living room. The float would be awfully dramatic. Kind of cool, really.

Alfred said, "I wouldn't use magic or directly touch it."

Yeah, maybe he was right. I felt the small amount of power coming off it. Since none of us knew much about it, it was safer to not touch it. So I conjured one of my large, luxurious bath towels and wrapped the sword in it.

When I walked back into the living room, carrying the towel-wrapped sword, a few of the coven members watched me with raised brows. Carefully, I set it on the coffee table and unfolded the towel to reveal the sword.

Leena scooted forward on the couch. "Wow," she breathed. "Where did you get this?"

Hope soared in my breast. "Do you know what it is?"

She nodded slowly, completely entranced by the weapon while hovering her hand over it. I knew she was a history buff, and she knew more than just about anyone about local witch lore. I was thankful she'd come tonight. I hoped she could tell me something about the sword.

"It looks to be Viking."

"Viking?" Olivia and I asked at the same time. We'd already suspected that ourselves, or Norse, at least, just based on its style.

Leena nodded. "There was a Viking cave discovered here several years ago. It's only known about in the magical community because it seemed to be the tomb of a shaman but there were no remains or body in there. And no record of it in any historical texts. Believe me, I searched like mad. And that sword looks like a shaman's sword. It's the right style." She moved closer and peered at the hilt without touching it, but her nose was a hair's breadth away from pressing against the metal. "It's possible it belonged to whoever was in that tomb."

That was interesting. A shaman. That would make sense if he were a true Viking witch. Of course, there were all sorts of legends about them, but most humans assumed it was all down to fantastical retellings and the ignorance of the age. "Do you know anything else about it?"

Leena shook her head. "No, but I'll be happy to head up a small team to research the burial ground, tomb, and sword." She looked positively giddy. "We can start tomorrow."

That was a fantastic idea. "Please and thank you."

Leena's face brightened as if I'd just told her she won the lottery. That made me feel good. At least it was making her happy.

"I'd like to be on that team," Ben said, but Brandon shuddered.

"Brother, in this particular subject, you are nuts," Brandon said. "I'll sit this one out."

Ben chuckled. "Even warlock twins can't do *everything* together."

Well, it was good to know they weren't alike in every way. "Now on to the second thing I wanted to discuss." I sucked in my bottom lip and glanced at Olivia. She gave me a nod of encouragement. I wasn't used to being so open to so many people at once. I'd spent my entire adult life hiding my witchy side, only fully embracing it in the last ten months or so. "I have a new magical ability that surfaced when I faced off with vampires a few weeks ago."

Everyone gasped. Melody leaned forward. "Really?" she asked in an excited voice.

"Yeah." I grimaced. "So, essentially, the vampire council has spent decades, maybe longer, keeping necromancers suppressed."

Owen wandered in and sat down, nodding at the coven and giving me his attention. "Go on," he mouthed.

I smiled and sucked in a deep breath. "My father was with them, imprisoned and forced to do their bidding, from the time I was a baby until just a short few weeks ago when we rescued him." I nodded toward Olivia. "Liv did, really."

She preened and smiled at the group. "Happy to."

"Well, when they caught wind of how powerful I am, they made a deal with Olivia's uncle, a Fae, to kill me."

"Don't worry," Liv cut in. "He's been sent to a prison world to pay for his crimes. He can't hurt us now."

The crowd's gazes whipped back to me. It was almost comical, watching them watch us. "Now, I'm going to have to deal with the vampires. Once the Fae assassination attempt failed, they sent a group of vamps to kill me, but I dispatched them with ease. They had to do as I said, since all dead things are the dominion of the necromancer." I shrugged as if to say I couldn't help it... 'cause I couldn't.

"While I was dealing with the little group of vamps, well... It might be easier to show you." I took in a breath and raised my hand to demonstrate my new gift. My fingertips sparked with pale blue light, then with little effort from me, the electricity shot across the living room and blew a softball size hole in the wall. Oops.

The lights blinked, then went out as Winston groaned. Alfred squeaked from the kitchen and dropped a plate or something. Whatever it was, it shattered into a million pieces. A few seconds later, the lights come back. I sighed and said, "Thanks, Winston."

The floor rumbled under my feet, and I assumed it was him telling me I was welcome.

"I'll get whatever broke in the kitchen," Olivia said. "I've been practicing that." She hurried to the kitchen to repair the broken item.

Ben narrowed his eyes at me, the shock written all over his face. "That is ancient magic and tied to earth witches. Only the oldest witch bloodlines have it. Our great aunt had a similar power."

Brandon added, "Not many have it anymore because the hunters killed them off because they were considered too powerful."

Huh, that was interesting. I would be asking my hunter-soon-to-be-husband about that little tidbit. Was I now too powerful as both a necromancer *and* an earth witch? As if I didn't have a big enough target on my back.

5

AVA

It was almost midnight before Drew made it home. The party had ended about an hour ago, and I'd retreated to my office to get some writing done while I waited for Drew.

One thing was bugging me about what Brandon and Ben had said about the witches with electrical powers. Something that Drew should have mentioned when my new magical gift surfaced. I hoped he hadn't deliberately withheld information from me. But just in case, I had the truth stone out and had it displayed on the corner of my desk.

When I heard the front door open and felt Drew's presence as he entered the house, I touched the stone and activated it.

"Ava?" he called quietly. "You in your office?"

"Yeah," I said. "Come on in."

He walked in and stopped short when he saw the truth stone out on my desk. "Why's that out? Did something happen?" He looked around like he was about to take on some attacker in my office.

"No, not like you're thinking." I nodded toward the chair across from my desk. "Have a seat."

His demeanor changed, as if he could now tell I was miffed at him. Should I have waited to get aggravated until I asked him about the power? Probably. But I hadn't waited, and I was already pissed off. "I was told that my new power was an old earth witch power and had been fiercely eradicated by the hunters in an attempt to rid the world of the power."

He stared at me, then the stone, then back at me. "I didn't say anything because I knew you were stressed from recent events. Plus, this is my territory. The hunters know that and wouldn't dare come here."

"Bull!" I yelled. "You should've told me."

"It's not bull," he said through his teeth. "I was trying to protect you, and you have enough to worry about already."

I threw my hands up in the air. "I don't need protection. I'm damn near all-powerful, aren't I?" Maybe I was being a little cocky.

Drew snorted. "You sure needed protecting when you were passed out cold and in another realm."

"You're one to talk," I said with my voice raised. "You were right there with me in that realm"

"Yeah," he shot out. "Because I was *protecting* you."

I snarled at him, nearly a growl. "You are the most infuriating man at times!"

"Fine," he said. "I'm going to go home and cool off. But just so you know, you didn't have to use that truth stone. If you'd asked me, I would've told you the truth."

He was right. He would've. The truth stone had been overkill. I instantly regretted it but was far too prideful to admit it yet.

Instead, I watched him stomp out of the house with a rock in my gut, wishing I had gone about this entirely differently.

I'd really made a mess of things. Drew was gone, and it was all my fault.

It had been a few hours since Drew left, and I felt absolutely sick. How could I have let him walk out without resolving this? Whatever *this* was.

I'll tell you what it was. It was our first freaking fight.

It wasn't going to be the last. I was sure of that. Both of us were headstrong, independent people. We were going to butt heads a few times over the next hundred or so years. More than a few times.

Witches typically lived a little longer than humans, and since Drew was bonded to me, so would he. Besides, at the rate I was going with all the new abilities, I wouldn't be surprised if I lived longer than the average witch. Wouldn't that be nice? Plus, with Drew being a hunter, they were a hardier bunch, anyway.

But I wasn't going to think too much about that. There were more important things, like finding Drew and telling him I didn't want to be mad and that I was sorry for how I approached the situation.

I jumped up from my desk chair and conjured my purse and keys, then marched straight out of the house and to my car. There was no way I would get any sleep until Drew and I resolved our little tiff. He'd been in the wrong, sure, for not telling me what he knew about my new powers, but I could've handled his misstep with *way* more grace.

I'd just turned off of Main Street toward his house when I felt him. Drew's emotions filled me, nearly overwhelming me. He was as heartbroken as I was. *And* he was heading straight for me. I stopped my car in the middle of the road and killed the engine, waiting for him so we didn't end up passing each other on the road.

By the time he put his truck in park in front of my car, I was at his door, waiting for him to get out. As soon as he did, we lunged for each other at the same time. He kissed me like he thought he'd never get to again. I returned the kiss with the same urgency. I hated fighting and unresolved things.

When he broke the kiss, we both said, "I'm sorry."

Then he kissed me again while grabbing my bottom and lifting me off the ground. My body obeyed him without any hesitation. Our emotions entwined, sending a cyclone of regret and desire crashing through me. "I did it all wrong, I'm sorry," I mumbled against his lips.

"No, it was me," he replied. At least, I thought that was what he said. The kisses interrupted it all. "I should've told you the truth."

He pulled me closer, or at least tried. I wasn't sure how much closer we could get. Nor did I care. All I wanted was him, every inch of him.

The back door to his SUV opened and he moved to put me inside. I broke the kiss to slide across the backseat. I hadn't had sex in a vehicle in *years*. A thrill shuddered through me as Drew crawled in and shut the door behind him.

When he sat on the seat next to me, I reached for him, and he pulled me to straddle him while claiming my mouth in another toe-curling kiss. The tip of his tongue floated around my lips, teasingly. I let out a moan as he planted small kisses down to my neck, then toward my ear.

"I love you. I want you," he whispered.

"I love you, too." I truly did, with everything in me. "Stop talking and take me already. I need to feel all of you."

Without another word, he unbuttoned my shirt, then worked on undoing my jeans. Standing as much as I could in the back of an SUV, I pushed my jeans and panties down, wishing I'd worn a skirt. Why didn't I wear more skirts? I was getting online and ordering a dozen skirts as soon as I got home.

Drew leaned forward to help pull my leg out. "Shoes," I said, while trying not to fall onto the floorboard. He lifted my foot when I wasn't ready for it, but when I fell, he caught me.

"You caught me," I whispered and pressed a kiss to the side of his mouth, which was all I could reach.

Drew's voice deepened and he looked down into my eyes. The moonlight shone through the window, illuminating us just enough for me to see the emotion in his eyes. "I'll always catch you."

"Daaaamn," I drawled. "That was smooth."

He dropped his face to my chest and laughed from deep in his chest.

Wheezing, I said, "This isn't working."

"No, I guess it's not." He moved me to sit on the seat.

I pulled my pants all the way up. "We're too old for this. Or at least, we're too old and too dressed."

He chuckled and kissed me quickly. "I'm sorry." The look in his eyes proved his sincerity. "I should have told you more about what the hunters know. I just worked so hard to separate myself from that life. I just don't want to think about it or talk about it."

That didn't excuse him, though I wasn't furious at this point, just needed to settle this. "I have no clue what I'm doing. This isn't about me opening up to my powers and discovering myself anymore. It feels like the more I learn and the stronger I get, the less I understand the world around me. I need you to help me. We're in this for a very long time." My chest tightened and for a microsecond, I feared he'd change his mind about staying with me. I pushed that thought away quickly. There was no room for doubt. "The main problem, though, is that you knew that this is a trait the hunters try to eradicate, which puts me in danger. You must tell me any dangers that could come our way." I sucked in a breath to keep going, but he cradled my face in his hands.

"From now on, we will be more open with each other." The very corners of his lips curved up, and he continued, "I'll be more open with you. I promise."

Warmth spread across my stomach. "Yes. And we will ask for help when we need it."

"Deal." He kissed me with all the passion of a few minutes ago but without the urgency.

I groaned and deepened the kiss, ready to do whatever it took to get him inside me.

A tap on the window jerked us apart and terror shot through me. For a second, electricity crackled in my fingertips, but I suppressed it. We looked out the window to find Sam staring at us with one eyebrow arched, aiming a flashlight beam through the window. He kept it low enough that it didn't blind us. I giggled. "Uh-oh. We're busted."

Drew opened the door as he laughed. "Hello, officer."

Sam rolled his eyes. "What are you two doing?"

I grinned and said, "Making up. We had our first fight."

With a groan, Sam lowered the flashlight. "You guys are the worst."

Drew and I roared with laughter as Sam walked back to his cruiser.

"Come on," I said. "My place or yours?"

"Yours," Drew growled. "It's closer."

I ran to my car and headed home, Drew hot on my tail.

In the future, I may have to plan to pick more fights, on account of how delicious making up could be.

6

OLIVIA

"I WANT the crust cut off mine."

I lifted a brow and looked over at my precious five-year-old, who was currently using his magic to make the salt and pepper shakers do some kind of waltz on the countertop in front of him. He'd been going to Carrie's a few times a week to practice his fae magic. I'd hoped a little positive nature-based magic would balance out everything that had been going on around us lately, and Sam had agreed. Being non-magical, he was at a loss, but he'd been a good sport about it all. It helped that he'd grown up with Ava and her family.

Carrie's little sessions seemed to be paying off. Then again, he'd been far more receptive to being a magical being than I had. He was like his father that way. Laid-back and took things as they came. Bless that wonderful man.

Carrie and I had even talked about homeschooling Sammie for the next year or two. I hadn't given it much thought before, but so much had happened during the summer. Homeschooling felt like the safest thing for Sammie right now. He had me, Carrie, Phira, and Luci to help with his academics and magical lessons. Plus, no doubt Ava would chip in if we needed it.

"Since when do you like no crust?" He'd never been a picky eater, a fact I thanked my lucky stars for regularly. Jess and Devan both had been the most persnickety eaters in the world. Sometimes still were.

He shrugged and said, "Grammy Fee cuts them off. She even cuts the bread into shapes."

Well then, if Grammy Fee did it, who was I to argue? I smiled and cut the crust off of his bread before assembling his sandwich, then called out to Sam in a sickly-sweet voice, "Honey, do you want your crust cut off too?"

He entered Luci's massive kitchen and walked around the island to place a kiss on my cheek. "No. I like the crust." He nuzzled my neck and asked, "Where are Luci and Phira?"

"I'm not sure. They left about an hour ago like a couple of love-struck teens." I *so* didn't want to know what they were doing. A shudder went through me at the thought. It was bad enough having my adoptive parents out there in the world and knowing they might do naughty things at any given moment. Now I had to have the knowledge of my biological parents in the back of my mind, too.

Sam laughed and picked up a slice of ham and shoved it into his mouth. Just then, a pulse of magic drifted in the air as a shimmer of soft light flashed from behind the pantry door. A second later Jess emerged from the small room.

"Hi, hon," I said, pleased to have her home. "Do you want lunch?"

Jess stopped next to Sammie and ruffled his hair. "Hi, Little Man." Then she answered my question. "Yes, please. But cut the crust off like Fee does."

Just like a grandmother. Phira was already spoiling my kids. That thought made me smile. They deserved a little spoiling, especially lately. My happy smile died as my daughter said, "University orientation is in a week, Mom. Dad needs to be there. I want him there. You need to find him."

Ugh. Why was it my responsibility to hunt down my ex-husband when he'd chosen to take off? He didn't want anything to do with us anymore, and that was my fault.

I studied my only girl, instantly recognizing my younger, sassier self in her. The snobby rich kid that got whatever she demanded. That was something we'd have to work on now that she was solidly back in my life. "You know, Miss Ma'am, if you ask for things a little nicer, then you just might get them. You can't go through life thinking everyone owes you something. Believe me, it doesn't work that way."

I'd found that out the hard way. The day Carter had told me wanted a divorce, and he was taking the kids was a massive wake-up call for me. Even so, it wasn't until Sam and I started dating that I truly wanted to change. At that point, it was too late to reconcile with Jess and Devan, because their father had already fed them with a bunch of lies that turned them against me. Not to mention the true stuff. I hadn't been the best mom.

That was all in the past. We were at a point now that they knew it and hopefully trusted the new me.

Even if Carter was missing, and *if* we found him in time, I wasn't sure he'd attend orientation at all. He'd rejected both kids when he found out they were magical. And that made all this my fault. Whatever. I personally didn't want to find him. He could rot wherever he was.

However, Jess and Devan loved him, and I loved them, so I'd find the horrible man for my kids.

Jess sighed, and I could see her physically fighting herself not to roll her eyes before she said through clenched teeth, "*Please* ask Luci if he can do a spell or something to find Dad?"

I smiled and covered her hand. "See, that wasn't so hard."

She gave in to her impulse to roll her eyes at me. I started to say something, but Sam kissed my temple and whispered, "Give it time. She's struggling right now."

He was right. We were all stressed. I reached across the island and took Jess's hand in mine. "Let me finish making lunch, then if he's not already back, I'll summon Luci to see if he can do a locating spell or whatever he does to find people."

Jess nodded and the tension left her shoulders as she settled on the barstool next to Sammie. Her face relaxed a little and the smile she shot at her little brother was less worried and happier.

When I finished making our simple lunch and got Sammie settled with eating, I moved to the living room to summon Luci. Only, I didn't get too far before he and Phira walked in the back door. Phira had a leaf in her hair, and her clothes were disheveled.

I scrunched up my face as I watched them act like a couple of teens. On one hand, it was nice that they'd found each other again. On the other hand, I knew exactly what they'd been doing out in the woods. Then I shuddered at the thought and sent Sam a look that made him laugh. Luci and Phira didn't gross him out the way they did me. He covered up his laugh by coughing and leaving the house.

"I gotta go," he muttered as he dashed out of the kitchen. Some help my husband was.

"I was about to summon you," I said brightly, ignoring Phira as she adjusted the buttons on her shirt.

Luci smirked at me. "Good thing you hadn't, or you might—"

"Nope." I held up my hand and said, cutting him off, "Do not finish that sentence." I moved on as fast as possible. "I wanted to ask you to do a locating spell on Carter. It's not like him to not answer the kids or his parents."

As I said that, I hoped I was right. Even though he got bent out of shape about them being magical, he should have gotten over it by now. Maybe he really was missing?

Nah, probably not.

Luci gave a short nod and a one-shoulder shrug. "Sure." He walked to the kids at the kitchen island and placed a hand on Jess's shoulder. He closed his eyes and, after a few seconds, he frowned. "That's strange."

Dread sank inside me like a rock. Something *was* wrong, and I'd dismissed it. I moved closer and Luci turned to me, a serious expression on his face. "He's being magically blocked."

"What does that mean?" A small amount of panic squeaked out with my words. For Devan's and Jess's sake, I wanted him to be safe.

Luci stole a chip from Jess's plate and turned to me. "It could mean a few things." At least he didn't sound too concerned. "He could have learned magic and is blocking us himself. Or he is somewhere that has a spell that blocks locating spells. Or he could be dead."

Jess gasped and shot off her stool, rushing to Luci and clawing at his shirt. "He's not dead. He can't be!"

I reached out for her just as Luci wrapped her in a hug. When I stepped closer to them, Jess pulled me into their hug, too. "Please, do something," she begged.

This was nicer than I'd expected it to be, being hugged by Luci. It was nice to have my daughter in my arms again.

Too bad I didn't want to find him as much as she did. But interesting that Carter being missing wasn't a human thing. That was worrisome. Where in the world could he have been? "I'll go see again if Ava can find him, though we have tried already," I said, to try to comfort Jess. At least Ava would be able to tell me if he was dead or not. I kept that little tidbit to myself.

Luci glared at me like he was offended by my suggestion to ask Ava to try. Whatever, I didn't have time to soothe his hurt ego. The hug was nice, but my loyalties were always with Ava. He had to learn it wasn't a competition.

He waved me off and walked Jess back to the counter and her half-eaten lunch. "Go on and ask your BFF. But if I couldn't find him, then Ava certainly can't."

Maybe. We'd see.

When I didn't move, he sighed and said, "Go, it's fine. I'll hang out with my grandkids while I wait."

With a nod, I walked out the back door to find the aforementioned BFF.

7

AVA

Drew and I sat shoulder to shoulder with my laptop in his lap. He had the day off, so we'd set out to do our own little research on the sword and my new witchy ability.

Drew logged onto the hunter's secret database and did a few searches for Vikings and swords, and nothing came up. "Vikings have never been on our list of hunts that I've ever heard of."

Still, he dug as far back as he could into the archives. Nothing. So, we quickly moved on, looking for my electrical powers.

The first few searches didn't result in anything that we didn't already know. The power was tied to earth witches as Brandon and Ben had said, but air witches also were known to have the ability, as well.

Our search did confirm my theory about being the last female witch of my bloodline. We came across a little thing about bloodlines, so I pointed to it. "Click that," I said quietly.

He did, and the information wasn't plentiful, but it said that when a bloodline dwindled to a single female member, that female tended to get all the powers that would normally be shared amongst the family.

Occasionally, males would get a significant amount of power and become powerful warlocks, but this was exceedingly rare. Magic was mostly matriarchal.

"Well, that explains all my power," I muttered. "It would be *exceedingly rare* for Wallie to be extra powerful. Or Owen, or Dad. I wonder what will happen when Winnie and Mom get bodies again. If they get their powers, will that mean there are more women in my bloodline?"

"There's no way to know," Drew mused. "Heck, has this ever happened before?"

I shrugged. "Not a clue. And it's not like we're leaving a record of what we're doing for the next witch who might want to try to do this."

He kept scrolling while I sat back, frustrated. It was cool to know that, but what about my powers?

"Here we go." Drew turned the laptop so I could see it. "The electricity power seems to come from the original witch bloodline."

Drew sat back and looked at me with raised eyebrows. "You're descended from the original witch bloodline?" He whistled low. "That's impressive."

"What does that even mean?" I asked.

After closing the laptop and setting it on the coffee table, he sucked a deep breath through his nose. "The first witch supposedly got her power from the earth in a time before civilization. The magic didn't pass to all of her descendants, which explains why, since the first witch was so many thousands of years ago, her bloodline doesn't cover the entire earth."

"Okay," I said. "So, if I'd had more children, they wouldn't all have gotten powers?"

He nodded. "Potentially. And then, they might've. It's hard to say. Wallie's powers aren't very strong, are they?"

I shook my head. "Nothing like mine."

"Then he might not have children with any powers at all."

I thought about the implications. "Then our bloodline would die out?"

Drew stared at me blankly. "I suppose it could. And then, if Wallie has a daughter, she could inherit every bit of your powers, plus any from her mother's line."

"Geez," I whispered. "It's a lot to worry about."

A noise from the laundry room reminded me that Larry and Zoey were here. Since getting the stones Dad and I took from the chasm, the two of them had gone out into the world to explore. I was thrilled for them that they got a second chance at life. And love. They were nuts for each other.

I'd been worried about them losing their powers somehow and unanimating, but they'd been checking in regularly and seemed to be doing well. And Luci had given the young couple a limitless credit card to use for whatever they wanted. I didn't have to worry about them wanting for anything. I didn't know what terms he'd arranged with them for repayment, but I couldn't have my nose in every detail.

A few minutes later, Larry and Zoey came into the living room and headed to the stairs. Larry stopped and said, "We're going to use the portal in Wallie's closet to stop in to see him and Michelle."

I waved them off. "Have fun. Give them my love."

As soon as they disappeared upstairs, the front door opened, and Olivia entered. She had a sour expression on her face. I laughed and asked, "What's wrong with you?"

"It seems that Carter really is missing. I asked Luci to do a locator spell, and he said Carter is being blocked." Olivia sighed and asked, "Can you try?"

I wasn't sure what I could do differently from Luci. Although I'd never admit it out loud to him, Luci was of course more powerful than me. I could feel it when I was around him. Liv probably did too, now that she had come into her fae powers.

I studied my friend for a second. "You want me to confirm he is alive?"

She nodded but said nothing. Guilt flowed from her. I rose to my feet and went to her, taking her hands in mine. "Don't feel guilty. We both thought he took off on his own. Now, visualize Carter's face, and we'll do this together."

Without letting go of her hand, I let our magic blend while I searched for Carter's soul. Even if he was dead, I wasn't sure I'd find him unless he was in Shipton or close to it. I wasn't sure just how far out I could stretch my necromancer powers. It was something I'd like to test when my to-do list was much, much shorter.

I hadn't done this in a while, but I was stronger now. I stretched my consciousness out over Shipton Harbor. With Olivia thinking of Carter, I was easily able to scan and dismiss anyone in the area. His soul would burn like the sun as long as she thought of him. "Don't stop imagining him. His voice, his looks. Those things about him that anger you, anything that keeps him fresh in your mind, even if it's negative thoughts."

Her power pushed into mine, and I expanded my net. Farther and farther out, miles and miles in all directions. When I hit the ocean, I redirected it south and east.

And then there he was. But his soul was dimmed. It was less like the sun and more like the moon. He was being blocked from magic.

Too bad they couldn't block him in the Inbetween. I was fairly certain that was the realm I searched. That part of us that always resided in that world.

That dim spark of his soul nudged at my powers, but he wasn't dead. "He's alive." If he'd been dead it would've been easy to find him. At least now we knew.

I was sure of it. Olivia's heart rate kicked up a few beats, and I tightened my grip on her hands. I needed her connection to her ex-husband to find his location. All I knew was that it was south and kind of far away. Unfortunately, as soon as I pushed my magic farther, tried to brighten his aura, a wall slammed down and the whole thing backfired.

Olivia and I jerked apart, both of us sparking as we broke our connection. Drew was at my side in half a second. He rubbed my back, and I leaned into him. "Did you feel that?" I gasped.

He nodded. "Yeah. Someone is hiding him."

"I agree." My hands were shaking from the abruptness that we'd been thrown out of the search.

Olivia rubbed her hands down her jean-covered thighs. "At least we know he *is* alive. But who could be hiding him, and why?"

"I don't know," I said, then looked at Drew. "Have you felt anything like that?"

"No."

I knew he hadn't, because I felt his confusion as if it were my own, being as we were, a bonded magical couple.

Olivia hugged her waist. "What am I going to tell Jess and Devan?"

"Tell them that we're working on it. The less they know, the better, for now." We had to figure out if he was being shielded at his own request or if he'd been kidnapped.

"I can have my parents—both sets—to help distract them until we find out more," Olivia said, pulling out her phone. She was on a mission now and setting a plan in place. A mama bear out to protect her children.

I was about to ask her if she wanted to help us dig through the hunter archives with us, but a loud bang came from upstairs. The noise was unexpected and made Olivia and I both jump. Drew wasn't as easily startled.

"Winston?" I whispered.

The house didn't reply. He didn't on most days, but this silent treatment was different. It was odd.

I grabbed Olivia's arm and moved toward the stairs. As quietly as we could, we crept up the stairs, with Drew close behind us. No doubt he would've liked to have been in front of me, but in this case, I was the more powerful one.

When we reached the top of the stairs, Drew nudged me to move so he could go first. Ha. I knew it, but I didn't think so. "I have more firepower than you," I whispered.

"I'm bigger, and I can draw on your power," he argued.

We stared each other down for a few moments. Then he sighed and motioned for me to go.

Yes. I won. It wasn't that I minded being protected. But he had to understand there was a time and a place for his macho stuff. This wasn't it.

Together, we moved down the hall in the direction the noise had come from. I was ready to blast whoever it was with an electrified energy ball. Then Wallie exited his room chomping on an apple, not paying any attention to us. When he saw us coming at him, he screamed like a soprano. The apple went flying, and Winston started shaking.

"Is he laughing?!" I asked.

Winston had set us up. He'd intentionally meant to scare us. The whole house moaned in a rhythm that was definitely laughter. "Winston! You are not funny."

Turning my attention to my son, who was picking his apple off the floor, I smiled while Drew and Olivia died of laughter behind me. "What are you doing here?" I asked.

"I came to grab my favorite sweater I had forgotten." He paused as if needed to catch his breath. "Zoey and Larry are going to hang with us for a while, then they'll be back later tonight. They plan on hitting the road first thing in the morning."

That meant I might not get to see them. Well, that was what I got for giving my ghouls their independence. "Tell them to call me more often. I worry about all of you guys."

Wallie hugged me. "I worry about you in this house. Winston is a prankster, for sure."

Wallie then left through his portal in his closet. Drew, Olivia, and I headed back downstairs. On the way down, I started plotting how to get Winston back for scaring us.

8
OLIVIA

I SLEPT LIKE CRAP, which put me in less of a chipper morning self mood than usual. Why did Carter have to be such a jackwagon? That was one man I would never understand.

Even though he didn't deserve it, I hadn't given up on him. Then again, it wasn't like I was searching for him for his sake. I was doing this for my kids. The ones that he'd kept from me.

I had one more option. It was risky. But I'd do anything for my kids. In for a penny...

Phira entered the kitchen, humming softly. She was just the person I wanted to speak with.

"Morning," I said in a sing-song voice.

She flashed me a beautiful smile. "Good morning, my sweet Olivia."

Here we go. "I was wondering if you could try to find Carter. I'm starting to worry."

Phira frowned a little and took my hands. "I am sorry, darling. I already tried. The kids asked me to do it last night while you were over at Ava's. I hit the same block Loki did."

Loki is what she called Lucifer, aka Luci. When she met Luci, he was going by Loki. The devil had lived many lives and gone by many names throughout his life.

"Could we go to Faery and ask the king to help look for him?" I asked, already knowing what she'd say.

She shook her head, but said, "He'll tell you that a human is not his concern." She mused for a second and cocked her head. "However, it doesn't hurt to ask. Maybe he could offer suggestions on what our other options are."

Just then, someone knocked on the front door. I didn't need to stretch out my senses to know who it was. I'd recognize Ava's energy anywhere. "Come in, Ava," I called.

Ava entered the house and her footsteps moved through the living room to the kitchen. She smiled at Phira as she came through the doorway and then turned to me. "Have you heard anything yet?"

I waved my butter knife at her. "No. But do you want to go to Faery with us to see the king?"

Her eyes lit up. "Heck, yeah. I need to change though. I can't go meet the king looking like this." Ava tugged at her baggy graphic t-shirt. She was wearing floral print yoga pants. She called it her writer's uniform.

She didn't work at the bookstore much anymore. Maybe a few hours a week, but not even every week. The rest of her time she filled with writing since her latest series had taken off. Plus, she'd gotten a pretty decent profit from the sale of her house in Philly.

Phira clapped and said, "Oh, let me." She snapped her fingers, and in a rush of wind, Ava and I were dressed in floor-length gowns.

They weren't as fancy as the ones Luci had conjured when we'd met the king to turn in my crazy uncle, Eodh, because he'd tried to kill Ava in a plot to take over Faery.

These gowns were simple, form-fitting, and as soft as silk. They were the color of the forest, brown and green at the same time somehow. They'd blend into nature almost like camouflage, but *much* more elegant. I lifted the gown's hem and looked at the slippers, similar to the ones from last time. I'd kept that outfit and would absolutely keep this one. "Beautiful," I said with a big grin. I felt like a little girl going to a dress-up tea party.

"Are we ready?" Phira stepped between Ava and me. "Happy with the dresses?" When we nodded, Phira pulled the Luz opal stone out of the pocket of her jeans. She must've kept it on her all the time.

That reminded me. I checked the sides of the dress, and sure enough, it had pockets. Phira could get a job in the fashion industry any time she wanted, and Luci as well, based on how he'd dressed us last time. He'd probably be more of an haute couture designer, though. Those gowns had been hella intricate.

We walked outside, and the inside of the slippers felt like fresh, moist moss. Like taking a walk beside a river, except with no rocks.

Phira opened a portal in the backyard, and a large oval, bigger than all of us, opened. Like before, it looked like an entire galaxy, as I remembered the stone did. There was room to walk through side-by-side, but we went through single file. I didn't want to know what might happen if we touched the sides of that thing.

As before, as soon as I was inside Faery, my fae magic sang. The last time we'd been here, it had been a spring-summer paradise. Now, it was like autumn in the middle of the Appalachian Mountains. Odd, since we were still at the end of summer in our world. Colors of orange, yellow, and browns made me feel like grabbing a pumpkin latte and my favorite hand-crocheted scarf. Yet, as before, everything was richer here. More vivid and healthier. Natural luxury at its finest. Part of me never wanted to leave, but that wasn't an option.

We walked toward the castle under the low-hanging clouds. The metal spires and turrets reached up toward the sky, somehow looking more like gold and bronze this time. Last time, they looked silver. But now, the russet colors went better with the autumn atmosphere. How they'd accomplished it, I had no clue, but it was cool.

We met King Mitah in the great room. When we walked in, he glided toward us and drew me into a hug. It shocked me and at first, I wasn't sure what to do. Sure, he was my uncle. The fact that I had a royal family hadn't fully sunk in yet. I hugged him back, a little belatedly, but still. It was the thought that counted, or something like that.

Mitah pulled back and studied my face. "What troubles you?"

I blurted it right out. "Carter, my ex-husband and the father of my older two children, is missing."

Mitah gave me an inscrutable look, released me, and returned to his seat. Phira ushered us to sit in the plush chairs facing the throne. Mitah gave me a half frown and lowered himself into his seat. "Isn't this the man who wanted nothing to do with his children once he knew they were half-fae? The same man who abandoned his family? Who, before he knew of their supernatural heredity, took his children away from their mother?"

Well, yeah. I didn't answer because I didn't know how to. He wasn't asking the questions because he wanted to know the answer. He already knew. And he was correct on all counts.

Mitah sniffed when I couldn't refute his claims. "Why do you care if this Carter is found?"

I glanced at Ava, then at Phira. "I don't, personally. As you pointed out, he is a terrible man who lacks personality and empathy. But my children love him, and I'm not the type of person to keep my kids from their father." At least not anymore. The old me would have told the kids to suck it up. Their father made his choice and deserved what he gets. I was not that person anymore. I would not *be* that person anymore.

Mitah rose to his feet. "Come. Have lunch with me."

Oh, great. He was going to drag this out. It was no use arguing with the king.

We followed him to the dining hall. When we got there, all kinds of fruits and veggies and meats were laid out. Nothing remotely processed or from a package. Pretty much how I never ate or cooked. I was a modern woman and loved my pre-prepared foods. Even though I cooked dinner regularly for my family, I was not a from-scratch, fifties housewife sort of chef.

"I'm disappointed that you haven't been more active in the Faery circles. I would like to see you attend more royal functions," Mitah said before he took a bite of steak.

I sent a panicked look at Ava and Phira. "I uh, I was told that I wouldn't have to have an active role, especially as I'm so far down the line of succession." It'd be like a mass killing of royal fae before I had to worry about the throne. "And if I'm being honest, I don't know if I'd *want* to come unless Sam was also invited."

Mitah chuckled and said, "Sam is welcome, of course. Though other humans wouldn't be."

Well, okay. That made me feel a bit better, but I still didn't want to give up my life in the human realm. I had family and friends there. I belonged there. Not in Faery. "I might consider coming to a function or two," I said.

Mitah chewed slowly.

I bit into a red and yellow fruit that tasted like a strawberry watermelon and it was abso-freaking-lutely divine. It was all I could do not to moan.

He swallowed and set his fork down. "I might consider sending a delegation of the fae, a *small* delegation, to search for your Carter."

Ah, so it was gonna be like that. "I would appreciate an invitation to the next event that you'd like me to attend," I said, with one eyebrow arched.

A self-satisfied smile spread across his face, and he picked up his fork again. "I'll have my fae delegation drop off an invitation to the royal ball when they go to search for the father of your children."

That was the price I'd pay for his help. Participation in the fae high society.

Super.

We all resumed eating, and each bite was a delight to my senses. I didn't waste time making small talk, I had to try all of these foods. They were similar, yet different. Delicious, each one. *All* of them were a step better than their earthly counterparts.

I could maybe get used to eating here. "Can this food be exported?" I asked. "To Earth?"

Phira giggled. "You're not the first to try. It loses something in the portal."

"Drat," Ava muttered. "I'd had the same thought."

We went on eating, and Ava asked a few minutes later, "I wonder, Your Majesty..."

He inclined his head at her. "Yes, Necromancer?"

"What are the chances that I could have my honeymoon here? I'd love for Drew and I to be able to spend a week or so in this paradise."

Mitah's eyes twinkled. "I appreciate the compliment, but no. We cannot allow you and your betrothed to remain here for that extended period of time, and certainly not without Olivia here to escort you in our realm."

"Ah, well," she said. "We'll go to Maui like everyone else."

Mitah sighed and closed his eyes, as if reliving a fond memory. "Ah, Hawaii. One of the original Fae settlements."

Okie-dokie, then.

9

OLIVIA

Entering Ava's house through the back door that led into the conservatory had become a norm for me since Sam, Sammie, and I temporarily moved in with Luci. Was it possible Winston had warmed up to me? He opened the back door as soon as I reached the patio today. That was new.

"Thank you, Winston." I entered the room full of plants, most tended by anyone *but* Ava, and went straight for the table Ava and Melody had set up.

The setup was a location alarm of sorts. It would, if it worked, whistle if Carter was picked up on the world map laid out on the long table in the middle of the room. I had no doubt it would work if he was findable. Ava was insanely powerful and Melody had helped her.

The process involved setting up his old wedding ring on a string with some pulleys and a bit of magic to keep it circling. Devan had gone to Carter's place to find the ring. It was fascinating, and it seemed to be working, because the ring continued to move, circling the map, though he, unfortunately, wasn't surfacing.

Ava and Owen had both checked the afterlife for Carter's spirit with no luck there either, which meant he was confirmed still alive. Ava said she could sense his soul, but every time she tried to push closer, he disappeared.

With a heavy sigh, I pushed myself to go through the kitchen to the living room. Today was all about wedding planning since there was nothing we could do until we got a lead on where Carter was. My magic was less than useful for this sort of thing.

When I got to the living room, Ava wasn't there. A pile of wedding magazines were stacked on the coffee table as well as the color samples I'd ordered. Everything looked untouched.

"Ava?" I called out.

"Don't yell. I'm right here," she said from down the hall.

I turned as she exited her office carrying a large cup of coffee and a *serious* case of bedhead. I raised a brow at her. "Have you even looked at any of the magazines?"

She shrugged. "No." Her voice was all croaky. No doubt she'd been in her office working all night. She held up a hand before I could say anything else and added, "I don't want anything fancy."

"Why do you care if you aren't planning it? I just need to know the basics. Color scheme, fabric, a theme." I waved her over and sat on the sofa. Then I shuffled through the stack of magazines until I found the one I wanted. "This dress screams you."

"Why?" she asked, eyeing the picture of the A-line gown.

"I mean, look at it. With your hourglass figure, this is going to look like heaven on you. It's ivory, since this isn't your first wedding, and will highlight your long neck. Plus, it doesn't take away from your natural beauty like some complicated gowns do."

When Ava didn't say anything right away, I said, "This dress is simple yet elegant and is perfect for a fall wedding. We could center the wedding theme around it. Simple elegance."

"It *is* beautiful. Do we have a place booked yet?" She blinked owlishly. "The wedding is in two months."

There was a hint of panic in her voice, so I took her hand and squeezed it. "No worries. If there is anything I excel in, it's getting things done. I've got this."

Boy, I hoped I had it.

A knock sounded on the door, and we stilled. We both looked at the front door at the same time. Winston went completely silent, which was weird since the house was always creaking or shifting or something. Or he'd just open the door for people he knew were welcomed. He did it so often that we never paid attention to it until he was silent.

Like now.

Alfred trotted down the stairs and headed to the door. Ava shook her head and said quietly, "Don't get that. Winston went quiet, which tells me this isn't anyone from our inner circle."

I agreed.

Alfred nodded and pivoted, then headed back up to the stairs. "Call me if you need me," he called from the top of the stairs with his high-pitched, mouse-like voice.

Once Alfred was out of sight, Ava answered the door. I stayed by the sofa and pretended I was interested in the magazine and not hanging on to every word and movement.

"Crystal." The slight distress in Ava's tone made me drop the magazine and walk over to stand next to her. Whoever this Crystal was had caused my bestie to be alarmed. I needed to know why.

Ava forced a smile and motioned for Crystal to come in. "What a surprise." She was a necromancer, wearing a low-neck tee that displayed her neck, and witch's mark.

Crystal muttered a thank you and walked into the house, looking around curiously. Ava closed the door and sent me a wide-eyed look. I mouthed, "What?" Crystal seemed a bit mousy. Timid, even.

"Crystal, this is my best friend, Olivia." Ava looked at me. "This is Crystal, Penny and William Combs's daughter."

Oh! Ohhhh, now I understood. "Hello," I said sweetly and reached out to shake her hand. "Nice to meet you."

William and Penny Combs hadn't been good people. At least, we'd assumed William had been a part of Penny and her brother Bevin's underground shifter ring. It was from that ring that Ava had animated our tiger, Zoey. Zoey didn't have family and had begged Ava not to release her. She'd wanted to remain a ghoul.

William was dead, but Penny and Bevin had been taken to Hell by Luci for their heinous crimes. I supposed they were still alive since he'd taken them bodily there. Had that killed them? I made a mental note to ask Luci the next time I saw him.

And now here was the daughter of two of the most evil people I'd ever known, on Ava's doorstep. That couldn't be a good thing.

10

AVA

Now would be one of those times I wished I had telepathy. Then again, I might not have wanted to know what Olivia was thinking.

Heck, I didn't fully know what I was thinking. Standing in my living room was the daughter of the elderly woman I'd put in literal Hell.

I hadn't actually put her there. Luci did after I'd uncovered that the sweet Penny Combs had been running a shifter fighting ring with her murderous brother, Bevan.

"Is there anything I can help you with?" I asked Crystal, not unkindly, but I wanted to get whatever it was over with. I didn't like her presence in my house, however much she may have been innocent of her mother's evils.

Winston didn't want her here, either. Even with him quiet at the moment, he was sending me magical pulses that told me he wanted this woman gone. O-U-T.

That made two of us. Three if we counted Olivia. She'd go along with anything I wanted. Liv was that bestie who would help bury the body with no questions asked. The best kind of friend to have.

A tapping sound at the top of the stairs drew my attention. Crystal snapped her gaze to the stairs, then the ceiling. Of course, she would recognize Alfred's subtle way of getting my attention by tapping on the floor in the hallway. Winston often echoed it, so it carried to me wherever I was in the house.

"It's okay to come down, Alfred." I eyed Crystal as she watched the ghoul who'd belonged to her father walk down the stairs.

Crystal turned to me and said, "I wondered where he went. If he's a bother, then I can take him."

Oh. Heck, no. "Alfred is good right where he is. Your mother gave him to me. Not that he is an object to be passed around."

"Crystal." Alfred's voice was a little higher pitched than normal. I didn't know if that was even possible. "Why are you here?"

Apparently, the ghoul didn't want her here any more than I did. Good.

Then I remembered something. Facing Crystal fully, I locked eyes with her. "You were there the day Penny gave Alfred to me."

Crystal averted her gaze. "I was upset. My father had just been murdered. Thank you for finding out who did it, by the way. I never thanked you."

A spark of sadness reached out to me before I could block the emotion. I knew what it felt like to lose your parents. Crystal had lost both of hers, too.

The difference between us was that she wasn't going to get hers back. Her necromancer powers were slight. Almost feeble, which sort of made sense. Crystal's physical look mimicked the strength of her powers. She looked like she'd blow over in a storm.

I took a bit of pity on the girl and was about to apologize when she said, "I'm sorry. I didn't mean to sound harsh. Alfred had been in our family for a long time. My great-grandfather animated him." Crystal wouldn't look directly at the ghoul.

I let the fact that Alfred was a lot older than I'd thought sink in. How old was that? My brain refused to attempt that kind of math so early in the morning after I'd been up writing most of the night. I'd gotten inspired in the middle of the night and had to get up and get the words down.

A few moments of silence went by, and I tried to be patient, but a nagging feeling kept telling me that Crystal was here for a reason, and it wasn't to be social.

"Luci!" I looked around like I was looking for the cat, Lucy-Fur. In reality, I wanted the oddly reassuring presence of Lucifer but didn't want to be obvious to Crystal.

Usually, when I called the devil, he teleported beside me. Well, not as often since he'd found his lost love, Phira. In this situation, I had to be sneaky about calling him. I didn't want Crystal to know I was summoning Satan.

Technically, I'd summoned him last Christmas when I tried to do a spell to conjure Saint Nicholas. Lucifer used the rift I'd created with that spell to split Hell and take Santa's place. He'd annoyed me every day since. But right now, I needed him.

I also needed my truth stone, which was on my desk in my office.

"Luci," I called out again and moved down the hall toward my office. "Be right back," I said to my guests.

Olivia must have caught on to what I was doing. I heard her ask Crystal, "You didn't see a cat when we opened the door, did you?"

I entered my office and jumped out of my skin. Lucifer was sitting in my chair with his feet propped up on the corner of my desk. He had my truth stone in his hand and was staring at it. Weird.

"What are you doing in here?" I hissed, hurrying into the room and mostly closing the door behind me.

He let out a breath and lowered his feet to the floor, then stood. "Seriously, Ava, I never know if you're calling me or that white furball."

When he stopped in front of me, I snatched the truth stone from his hand. "I never call out to Lucy-Fur, because she never answers." She was hateful like that.

He nodded to me and gave his daughter's large, warm smile. It was creepy. Now that I knew he was Olivia's father, it was *so* obvious. That I hadn't made the connection before seemed ludicrous now.

Olivia slipped in the door. "What are you doing?"

Luci winked at his daughter, then he asked, "How can I help you, Ava?"

With a sigh, I motioned toward the front of the house. "Penny's daughter is here."

Both his brows went up and a wicked smirk replaced the smile. "You think she's here looking for her mother?"

Duh. "Why else would she be here? We weren't friends after we got out of school."

Olivia nodded as if agreeing with me. "Me neither. I think Crystal went to a private school on the mainland. She was only in Shipton on the weekends and during the summer."

That was right. She'd only gone to our school for a little while during freshman year. I'd forgotten that. "Anyway, she has a right to know where Penny and Bevan are." I glanced out the door and saw Alfred hovering. "We're coming."

"I'll fix some tea." He turned to head to the kitchen.

Lucifer jumped up and exited the office next with Olivia and me hot on his heels. There was no way I was going to let him interrogate Crystal on his own. She might faint from fright.

Out in the living room, I asked Crystal if she would like to sit. She shook her head and watched Lucifer. "I went by my mom's house, and she wasn't there. It looks like she hadn't been there in months. I thought I'd stop by to see if you know where she is."

"Why would I know where she is?" I asked, playing along with Crystal a little longer. I was curious to where she was going with this. I couldn't shake the feeling that she knew more than she let on.

"You're the High Witch of the Shipton Coven, right?" Her timid demeanor hardened for a moment as sarcasm slipped into her tone. She was likely one of those people with a huge personality who kept it hidden until she was comfortable with her surroundings.

"Yeah." At least for the time being.

We stared at each other for a long moment before Olivia spoke. "Good grief. Crystal, have a seat. Ava has something to tell you."

I shot my BFF a narrow-eyed, you-will-pay-for-that look. Olivia shrugged at me, and I sighed. "First, tell me how you can go months without knowing your mother was missing."

Crystal's eyes filled with tears, but they didn't spill over. She blinked them back. "Mom and I had a nasty fight when dad died. Right after," Crystal said and sat gingerly on the sofa. "I took off and haven't called her for a while. I figured she would call me when she was ready to talk."

"And when she didn't, you called?" Luci sat in the armchair across from the sofa and crossed his legs, looking suspicious as all get out.

Crystal seemed to shrink under his gaze. "I wanted to mend fences with mom and couldn't get her to answer the phone. I got worried and came to town only to find mom's house was empty and untouched. The electricity is on, but the food is rotten in the cupboards and fridge. Uncle Bevin's house is the same. Like they just walked out."

"The lights are still on?" Olivia asked.

I answered, "If they set the bills to auto-pay each month, then they'd stay on until the money ran out." It was something I hadn't thought of. Then again, sending Penny and Bevan to Hell hadn't been my call. I'd wanted to kill them outright for all the shifter children that died as a result of the fighting ring.

I glanced at Luci, then Olivia. Then Luci's words entered my thoughts, startling me. *"Want to bet that she was in on the fighting ring with her mom?"*

Out loud, I gasped, then coughed to cover it up. Sitting up straighter, I studied Crystal. Not just her physically, but her aura. She was hiding something under that nervous personality. I ran my thumb over the truth stone I still had in my hand and asked, "Did you know your mother and uncle were running a shifter fight ring and over two dozen children died because of it?"

I was so glad Zoey was not here. She was one of the kids who'd died. For some reason, my magic had animated her in the way it had Snoozer and Larry. Only Larry had come to me as a skeleton, who I'd later fleshed out. Zoey had come back to life already fleshed out.

I was fairly sure that the length of time they'd been dead had something to do with how they were as a ghoul. However, when I'd animated all those children, so their families would have bodies to bury, I'd poured a lot of emotion into it. That may have been part of the reason.

I never wanted to do that again.

Crystal started to speak, but no words came out. Then her expression calmed, and she stared straight at me and said, "Yes. I run the operations in Clinton."

Oh, my lord. Clinton was a bit more inland from Shipton Harbor, and farther out than we'd searched when looking for shifters that had been in the shifter ring.

"No," I whispered. "Please tell me you don't have imprisoned shifters there now."

She sniffed. "Not at the moment. All of the ones I had have died. I've been traveling the world looking for shifters. I've been groomed my entire life to take over the shifter ring. I've been out searching for ways to level up the fighting rings. Ways to use exotic shifters, magic users, and trying to imbibe fighters with necromancy powers, even though they're not dead, so they can keep fighting even when grievously injured."

I gaped at her. That was horrible.

"That's barbaric," Olivia whispered. "How could you do something like that?"

Crystal shrugged. "Meh. It's good money."

Even Luci looked perturbed by her callous words. She didn't give a fig about the lives of the shifters and magic users she was so willing to destroy.

Luci stood and held out his hand to Crystal. "Come. I'll take you to your mom."

Crystal looked defeated as she placed her hand in Luci's. She knew she'd blabbed far more than she'd ever meant to. Handy-dandy truth stone, hah.

"Get the details about the deliveries," I told Luci. "We'll have to deal with that."

He nodded and a second later, they dematerialized.

11

OLIVIA

"H<small>I</small>, <small>HON</small>!" I called to Jess as she passed the living room, heading from the portal in the kitchen to her bedroom.

She stopped and entered the living room. "I'm going over to Dad's to grab some things."

The portal Luci has created for all the college kids was popular. They came and went several times a day. But that would no doubt slow down once classes started in a few weeks.

"Okay, drive carefully." I paused, then added, "Do you need me to come with you?"

Jessica's features lit up slightly as if the idea of us taking a road trip to Portland excited her. "Would you?"

"Sure, if you want me to." I didn't want to go to Carter's house, but I did like the idea of spending that time with my girl. Sam was off soon for the day and tomorrow and could handle Sammie. Or one of his many grandparents would no doubt be happy to.

Before she could answer, Luci's doorbell rang. I frowned. No one ever rang the doorbell. Then again, we never had uninvited guests.

Ava and the ghouls didn't count as guests. All the humans in town gave this place a wide berth. It was heavily spelled.

I was the only one home beside Jess. Sam was at work, and Luci hadn't come back from taking Crystal to Hell. He'd sent me a text that he was checking on a lead about Carter after getting her settled.

I wasn't holding my breath that it panned out to be anything significant.

Sammie was off with Carrie and Phira. Yes, you heard that right. Carrie and Phira were becoming good friends. It was a little weird but they made it work. They'd taken Sammie to Faery for a fun-filled day of magical play. I just hoped he didn't come home with wings. Phira had told me any of us could develop them at any time, due to the influence of the atmosphere in Faery.

Or some bull crap like that.

Crossing the room, I opened the door, and my heart fell to the floor. Heck, it fell past the floor. It was probably somewhere in Hell with Luci. It took all my self-control to not slam the door in my ex-in-laws faces. What the freaking frack were they doing here?

"Joan," I choked out. "Chad." Those two words were the only thing that came to me. My mind sounded like a radio that wouldn't find a station. Static. I'd *told* them to stay home. But I should have *known* those two wouldn't stay out of it. And how in magical fairy dust had they known to find me here?

Jess walked up beside me. I turned my head to look at her help-lessly. She smiled widely, but I could tell it was at least a touch forced. "Grandma, Papa. What a surprise." At least she sounded sincere. Hopefully, they wouldn't notice.

"Come in," I said weakly and said a prayer to anyone who would listen that Luci had not come home yet.

Joan and Chad entered the house and looked around. "This is a lovely home. A little outdated by a few centuries, but it's nice." She sniffed and looked around as if a dust bunny were going to attack her ankles.

Always the judgmental b—And now I saw no reason to be overly polite. "How did you know I was here?" I asked, finding a stronger voice.

Joan waved me off like I hadn't been hard to find. "It was obvious you weren't at your house, so we stopped by Ava's. Jess and Devan mentioned you and Ava are close friends now. The cutest girl with little animatronic tiger ears answered the door and said you were over here."

Animatronic tiger ears? Oh, it must've been Zoey. She and Larry must've returned from visiting Wallie and Michelle. Those two were having a ball traveling around, seeing the world. In a way, I envied them. It must've been a hoot.

"Have you found my son yet?" Joan put her hands on her hips and glared at me. Then Chad glared at me as well, both waiting for an answer.

"The police are still looking for him," I said. "Other than that, there's not a lot I can do." As far as they knew, anyway. I couldn't exactly tell them I'd had fairies, the devil, and a witch-necromancer hybrid doing all they could to find him.

"Well. We aren't leaving until our son is found." Joan had a set to her jaw that looked just like Carter's when he was digging his heels in.

Oh, great. This was going to be some drama. Before I could snap back with a reply, Jess touched my arm and said to her grandparents, "I'm going to Dad's house in Portland. I was about to leave here in just a couple of minutes. Do you two want to come with me?"

Bless the child's heart. She was taking one for the team to get them out of my hair. At the very least, I had to warn everyone to be on their best behavior.

And put their ears away.

Joan looked at Jess and back at me, nostrils flaring, but Chad said, "Yes, we'll go."

Joan added, "Of course, sweetheart. But we're coming back here to wait for news on Carter afterward."

The only reason that woman wanted to hang out here until Carter was found was to make my life miserable. She'd never liked me. No doubt wherever Carter was and whatever excuse he gave them for being there, she'd spin it into being my fault, even if he didn't.

Just then, because things weren't tense enough, the front door opened, and Luci strolled in. He glanced around before holding my gaze as if silently asking if everything was okay.

My heart warmed. My father was poised and ready to go to battle for me and looked to me for the cue. It was sweet, but I didn't need him exploding Carter's parents. Sending them to Hell was tempting, but after a second, I rolled my eyes, making him smile. Then I introduced him. "Joan, Chad, this is my friend Luci. He owns this house."

Oh gods, that sounded wrong. Now my horrible ex-in-laws were going to think I was cheating on my current husband. I quickly added, "He's Sam's friend, too." Boy, that sounded lame, but it was the best I could do at the moment.

Luci stepped closer and held out his hand. "It's nice to meet you." He moved his attention to Jess, giving her a direct stare. "You drive safely to Portland." Very grandfatherly. No doubt Jess would have to come up with a reason Luci was so familiar with her.

She kissed her grandpa, the supernatural one, on the cheek. "I will."

Chad gave Luci a confused look, then said, "I'll drive, kiddo."

Once Jess ushered her grandparents out the door, I turned to Luci. "It's a good thing you came in the front door." I sighed and leaned against the wall. "Those two are the worst."

"I sensed that there were humans here." He chuckled and patted me on the shoulder, but didn't move away.

I wasn't even going to ask how he'd sensed that. He probably wouldn't have given me a straight answer anyway.

"Why didn't you tell them I was your father?" So that's what he was waiting to ask. I hoped I hadn't hurt his feelings.

I pulled the scrunchie out of my hair and re-fixed my messy bun. "Because I haven't even told my adopted parents that I have found my birth parents. Joan and Chad know my adopted parents and are total blabbermouths."

He didn't look upset, but he did twist his lips a bit. The man was so hard to read. "Ah. You shouldn't drag these types of things out."

"I know," I said, and turned to leave the room. "But this is intensely personal, especially with the magical aspect. I haven't even totally settled into the fact that you're my *father*. I mean, I've accepted it, but..." I kept walking toward the kitchen. "It's sort of like I'm taking some time to savor it."

He grunted as he followed me. "That makes it sound like you're happy about it. About me."

I shot him a sidelong glance and pulled a couple of glasses out of the cabinet, then pulled the pitcher of water out of the fridge. "I'm not unhappy. Not anymore."

He grinned. "I'll take it."

I slid the glass across the island to my father, and he raised it as if giving me a toast. "The lead panned out."

I froze in mid-toast, then set the glass down, jaw hanging. "Tell me."

"After taking care of Crystal, getting her cozy in her new living arrangements with her mother and uncle, I took a trip to Boone, North Carolina. Sam had gotten a hit on one of Carter's credit cards. It was used at a gas station there. I went to review the station's camera footage. The police have seen it, but I wanted to see for myself." He winked. "Good thing I did. I recognized the man in line behind Carter. He's a hunter." Luci paused as if I needed to process what he was saying.

"And?" I had no idea what that meant for us. Why would the hunters want Carter? He wasn't magical in the least.

"I've dealt with this particular hunter before. *And* I know that the hunters have a base in the mountains not far from the gas station, though I don't know exactly where." Luci lifted both brows.

It clicked. "You think Carter threw in his lot with the hunters?"

"I do." He finally sipped his water while that bombshell sank in. Holy crap. All this time, that little weasel had been with the hunters.

The question now was, did he want to be there?

12

AVA

ALL DAY LONG, I'd been feeling edgy, like I had too much static build-up that was itching to be released. Drew noticed it this morning before he headed out to work and said it'd be a good idea for me to release that energy.

So here I was, in the caves under my house, working on controlling this new electric power. Like most magic, the electricity seemed to be triggered by my emotions. That was not a good thing, though it wasn't exactly a surprise. Heck, I liked being an emotional being. I didn't want to lower my empathy because of a new power.

Owen offered to come help, but I wanted to test things out myself. Plus, I didn't want to hurt anyone by accident. Thus, I was in the caves alone.

Lifting my hands out in front of me, I focused on the magic and tried to pinpoint where inside of me the source of this particular power had come from.

My earth witch magic came from my heart. My necromancer powers seemed to be scattered throughout my mind and heart. It was only tied to my witchy side a little. That was interesting.

Closing my eyes, I focused within. It didn't take me long to find the electric magic. I was surprised to find it cozied up with my witch magic. Like it was an extension of it. That aligned with what Ben and Brandon had said about it being old witch magic.

Even after I found the source of the magic nestled deep inside, I had a hard time coaxing it to come out. I wasn't angry or agitated right now, and the only times I'd used it had been when I was all riled up.

"Okay," I said, speaking to my magic. Weird? Maybe. "I need you to work for me even when I'm cool, calm, and collected. Can you do that?"

Of course, I got no answer. I hadn't expected one. I focused on that energy ball inside me and tried to harness just a little bit of it.

A lightning bolt exploded from my hands and blasted into the rock above me. Distantly, I heard Winston moaning. "I'm sorry!" I yelled. "I didn't mean to!"

I went slower this time, coaxing the magic rather than trying to force it out. Finally, I got the small chaotic lightning bolts to fill my hands. And a few minutes after that, the little arching light came off of my fingertips to obey me. I expanded them, and they danced through the air and bounced off the walls of the cave. Glee rushed through me. It was working. I kept going, doing as much as possible. The more I worked with my powers, the easier it was to control them.

A sound from behind me startled me and I jerked around. A lightning bolt shot out of my hands and hit Olivia. She screamed and tried to jump out of the way, but she was too slow to react to the incredibly fast lightning. It hit her in the shoulder, and her body jerked in all kinds of weird poses before she fell to the floor.

I slammed down the magic, locking it back in its little spot in my mind as I rushed to her. "Oh, Liv. I'm so sorry. Please be okay." My heart froze in terror. What if I'd killed her? I'd never forgive myself. I could bring her back, of course, but would she even want me to?

Those thoughts and a million more rushed through my mind in the seconds it took me to get to her.

Her reply was a groan. At least she was alive. I placed my hand over the wound and pushed in my healing magic. It was easy to control, probably because I was so emotional. Maybe it was adrenaline that helped magic work better. Too bad none of us were scientists. That'd be a cool thing to study.

My mind kept whirring to the most inane subjects, anything except that Olivia might not recover.

It didn't take long before I knew she was going to be okay. After a few seconds, Olivia gasped and sat up straight. "That was not fun."

Pulling her forward, I wrapped my arms around her and tried not to sob. "I'm so sorry. You startled me." I would not be practicing my magic again without being behind a closed door. I'd have to set some ground rules. Maybe buy a bell.

Olivia frowned. "You usually hear me or sense when I'm near."

"I was preoccupied with practicing to control this new power." I helped her to her feet. "It's really hard to control and took all of my focus."

"Where's Drew?" she asked, rubbing the back of her neck.

"He's at work." I dusted her off and ran my hands over her shoulders and upper back. "Are you good? Do you need more healing?"

Olivia started walking back into the cave tunnel that led back to the house. "No, I think I'm okay now. Just a little sore. Drew is important right now. We have to call him and tell him to come home right away."

"Why?" I asked, following her up the narrow tunnel.

Olivia stopped, and I bumped into her. She turned and looked back at me in the flickering illumination from the ball of light I'd conjured earlier. "Luci found Carter."

She then went into a theatrical explanation of what Luci had found out. "All this time, he's been with hunters? Hunters! Do you think he went to them to expose you? Me? Luci? Did the idiot not realize that his kids would be killed right alongside anyone else?"

Oh, boy, now I was mad. From what Sam and Olivia had told me about her ex-husband, the guy was a jerk on his nicest days. Turning his own kids in was a new low. I mean, who did that?

We started walking again while Olivia said, "I don't know if that is what happened. He's always been a good father before the whole fae thing. But he was *so* upset when he left after finding out the kids are magical. And me, of course."

As soon as we got above ground, I pulled my phone out. It didn't get service under the house. "I'm calling Drew home early. He's due to be home in about an hour."

Olivia nodded. "Sam, too. I guess it can wait another hour. It's not like we could do anything right this minute anyway. He's been with them this long. What's another hour?"

We entered the house from the basement and headed to the living room. Alfred was coming down the stairs and smiled at the two of us. "Would you like something?" he asked kindly. "I can make a snack."

"No, I can wait until dinner. Thanks, Alfred." In the beginning, I'd offered over and over to be the one to cook or order dinner. We rarely ate out anymore, because he was always whipping something up in the kitchen. Nowadays, I didn't even bother asking if I could take over for a meal. He'd just say no.

He nodded and disappeared into the kitchen. Olivia and I sat on the sofa and waited for Drew. She looked majorly agitated, so I changed the subject somewhat. "So how are things going with Luci?"

Olivia shrugged. "Okay, I guess. I actually said something nice to him earlier."

I chuckled, but she didn't. She was so mixed up about her feelings for him.

"Don't tell him I said this," I said, "but he's not as bad as we thought, devil or not. He really seems to be trying. Especially since he found out you're his daughter." I'd been so set on sending him back to Hell I hadn't wanted to give him a chance. Now my banter with him had become a game between us.

Olivia sighed and rested her head against the back of the sofa. "He is great with the kids." She sat up. "Oh, get this. Joan and Chad showed up at Luci's house a little while ago." She smacked her hand on her forehead.

"What?" I exclaimed. "How? Why?"

We spent the next hour talking about her ex-in-laws showing up and Jess saving the day by distracting them. We both knew the distraction wouldn't last. "Why don't you let them stay at your house when they return to town?" She, Sam, and little Sammie had been staying indefinitely with Luci and Phira while everyone learned their magical abilities, so their home was empty at the moment.

She raised her eyebrows. "That's not a bad idea, though I need to talk to Jess and see if she told them we're staying with Luci and if so, what she told them about *why*."

I sensed Drew before he entered the house. "Drew's home and Owen's with him."

The men entered the house looking disheveled. No, that wasn't right. They looked annoyed and worried. "What happened?" I asked.

"We sensed necro magic." Drew came over and kissed my forehead, then continued, "I assumed it was you or Owen since you two are the only ones in Shipton."

"Where's Sam?" Olivia asked.

Drew sat beside me on the sofa, which made me have to scoot closer to Olivia. "He had to work a little later. One of the new deputies called out sick." Through our bond, I felt how shaken he was, even though he didn't show it on the outside.

"What happened?" I asked again as Olivia grumbled about Sam working over.

"I was leaving a domestic disturbance call and sensed it in the nearby woods on the other side of town. I went to see who it was, and I was attacked by magic. Death magic from a necromancer. That was when I realized it wasn't either of you." He indicated to me and Owen.

Fury bubbled up inside me. Who the hello fuzzy was invading my turf? "Did they hurt you?"

Because if they had, they'd get a lightning bolt up their—

"No, I'm not hurt. They just sent a blast to knock me down while they took off. I didn't see who it was, but it was definitely necro magic."

Immediately, I closed my eyes and cast a net out for miles in all directions. It took some effort, but I found them. They disappeared moments later as if they knew I had locked onto their magical signature. They knew how to shield themselves, something I'd never learned to do. I'd never thought it was necessary.

Maybe I should add that to the to-do list.

When I opened my eyes, I noted that everyone was staring at me. Owen said, "Your powers are getting stronger. Each time you use them, they grow."

I didn't know what to say to that. I wasn't sure if that was a good thing or a bad thing. Could I get *too* strong? I didn't know. Right now, I had other issues to take care of.

13

AVA

Olivia sent a text to Luci while I filled Drew in on what the devil had found out about Carter. "Isn't your family in North Carolina?" I asked.

Drew bobbed his head as he pulled out his cell. He punched in a number, then brought it to his ear. "Hey, are you able to talk?"

A pause while the person he'd called replied.

"I'm going to put you on speaker." As Drew put the phone on speaker, he said, "Lily, meet Ava, Olivia, and Owen."

"Hi y'all." Lily's high-pitched voice made her sound younger than she was. Drew had told me she was the baby of the family at thirty-eight. "Am I right to assume you need some hunter help?"

While Drew briefed her on Carter, Luci walked in from the kitchen, eating a homemade calzone. He had a plate underneath to catch the crumbly pieces of crust.

Drew used that moment to mention that Luci would be coming along with Olivia.

"Wait, who's Luci?" Lily asked.

Drew frowned and met my gaze, then sighed. "Lucifer."

It took her a second to reply. "As in..."

"Yep," Luci himself said cheerily.

"Wow, Drew, you went from one extreme to another didn't you?." Lily laughed.

Drew smirked and rolled his eyes. "You know me. Anything to piss off Dad."

I should have been offended by that statement, but I knew he was kidding with his sister. Though he did have some major baggage there with his father.

Lily laughed again and said, "Always the rebel. So how can I help you folks?"

Drew glanced at me, then to Olivia. "Will you help Satan and his daughter sneak into the Blue Ridge compound?"

Olivia made a sound and wrinkled her nose at being referred to as Satan's daughter. Even though, heck. It wasn't a lie.

"Oh, that sounds fun. But we don't have to go sneaking in. Mom and Dad are on vacation in Hawaii. Plus, they aren't at that compound much this time of year." Lily paused for a few moments, then added, "I can meet them there tomorrow morning. I'm in Florida at the moment and will need at least eight hours to drive to Boone."

We finalized the details, and when Drew hung up with Lily, I turned to Luci and Olivia. "Drew, Owen, and I have to stay here and deal with the new necromancers in town. I'm curious to find out why they're here." Luci hadn't heard the story, so we filled him in.

This was my town, and I wasn't about to let anyone come in and think they had a right to be here.

Suddenly, dark magic touched my awareness, making me jump to my feet, my powers at the ready. Even the electricity. By the time I reached the door, Drew was with me. Owen, Luci, and Olivia were right behind me. They must have felt the necro magic, too.

I opened the door and walked out onto the porch, Drew at my side. Three male necromancers halted at the edge of the road and assumed a defensive position. Their power wired around them like a protective circle. Like that would protect them from me. Ha.

I folded my arms and glared at them, putting a little magic in my voice to make it carry over to them. "What do you want?"

The one in the middle, an older male with streaks of gray in his black hair, stepped forward. "We've come for the sword! There is no need for us to harm any of you. Hand it over and there will be no bloodshed."

They didn't want to harm us. That was a riot. They obviously didn't know who they were dealing with.

I pushed out my senses and measured each of the necromancer's powers. Although they were fairly powerful, they weren't a threat to me with my myriad of powers. Owen, another necromancer, Drew, a hunter, Olivia, a fae princess, half god hybrid, and Luci, an underworld god. Not to mention my handy dandy new electric magic, which crackled happily across my knuckles.

"What sword?" Playing dumb sometimes worked. Besides, I wanted them to tell me why they wanted the sword. And how they knew it was here. And who the heck they thought they were, to come at me like this?

Today was not their day.

The elder of the little group pursed his lips and narrowed his eyes at me. I simply raised a brow. If he thought he was going to intimidate me, he needed to do a little more homework about my family, especially my father's side of the family. Then again, they might have already. If they did know what we were capable of, could they have had an ace up their sleeves? I didn't want to be *too* cocky.

My powers were still a mystery to those outside my circle of friends and family, mostly. I'd like to keep it that way. Heck, they were still a mystery to those *inside* my circle. And me. Unfortunately. Although, the vampires knew now. That sucked.

The elder waited another few seconds before speaking. "The sword belongs to our family."

"Is that so?" They'd have to give me more than that if they wanted me to believe that. Then I added, "It came to me through a great source of magic. So, I'm not too sure it belongs to you."

It had happened for a reason. I wasn't giving it up until I figured out why. I certainly wasn't handing it over to a group of rando necros.

The necromancers exchanged glances, then huddled together for a second. I leaned into Owen and whispered, "They're too trusting. I could fry them with lightning right now if I wanted to while they're huddled together, defenseless."

Owen gave me the *look*. The one I used to get from my dad before his fake death. The one that said I was being ridiculous. "You'd never do that."

I sighed and shrugged. "Yeah, I wouldn't." Maybe if they were actively attacking us.

The necromancers turned back to us and the elder said, "If the sword came to you, then you must be a descendant of the shaman of our clan."

94

Uhhhh, what? "Now I know you're lying."

They had to be, right? How could I be a descendant of their shaman? It wasn't like I was tall and blonde and Viking-ish-looking. Quite the opposite, actually.

They moved forward a few feet, but I held up my hand. "That's close enough."

The elder glanced at his buddies again before saying, "A member of our clan went bad, very dark. It was over a thousand years ago. He disappeared through what we now know is a ley line, and we followed him here. He took the sword with him. There must be a ley line somewhere nearby, but it's hidden from us. We cannot find it."

Haha. I know where it is, but I'm not telling you.

But their story matched with where we'd found the sword... at a ley line. Luci grunted, but none of us said anything to them.

The elder continued, "It's been our charge to scry once a week for the sword and when we did it this week, we found it here. We arrived in town and sensed your power. We hid in the woods, debating how to approach you. We mean you no harm, but our tribe has searched for that sword for a very long time."

So, they did know I was more than just a necromancer. Again, I said nothing. I still didn't know if they could be trusted. "Give me a few days to corroborate your story. I'm not handing over the sword to just anyone who shows up asking for it."

I could've grabbed the truth stone, but I didn't want to invite three necros to my house. Winston would have had a fit. Plus, the truth stone was freaking cool. Not that many people knew I had it, and I wanted to keep it that way.

The elder frowned. "We cannot leave the sword now that we know where it is. It is our sacred duty to protect it and protect others from it."

That was interesting. What kind of sword needed a protector? Maybe they could teach me more about the sword. But since I've been back to Shipton, I've learned to not trust other magical beings without doing some due diligence first.

The necromancer to the right of the elder said, "If you are descended from the dark shaman, how do we know you're not dark as well?"

These guys were trying to make me mad. I flexed my power out around us and thunder boomed as dark clouds moved in. Lightning streaked across the sky and ricocheted like it was bouncing off of nothing in the space between us and the necros. I controlled the lightning, so it didn't do what it would normally do. No need to electrocute the necros. Yet.

At the same time, I thanked my lucky stars that the lightning did what I wanted it to and didn't fry each and every one of us on either side of the yard.

"You don't have the power to take the sword from me." I sent them a stern look. "I will research and verify your story. Only then will I contact the three of you and discuss what will be done with the sword."

The man that hadn't spoken yet whispered to the elder. I wasn't sure exactly what he said, but I did catch the words, "power of Thor."

Thor? Really? I'd just log that little tidbit away for later when I researched further. Maybe that was their religion. The sword was supposed to be Viking. It might not literally be the power of Thor, but hey, it'd be cool to say I had it.

They still didn't leave.

"Look," I said with a sigh. "I'm far from a dark necromancer. I'm also the High Witch of the local coven." At least until I transferred that position to Melody. "I've helped quite a large number of people and creatures." I didn't mention that the devil was on my side. That might've looked a bit bad. "Give me a few days to look into the story, and I'll get back to you. But you can't stay in town. Too many necromancers in one spot draws too much attention."

At the latter, they flicked their gazes at Drew. The elder said, "What's to say he won't call in hunters to track us down?"

I didn't need to answer that. This was ridiculous. Instead, I said, "I'm being gracious, agreeing to contact you when I've researched. You will leave my town and come back here, to this house, in three days. We'll talk then."

Reluctantly, the elder nodded and they turned and walked down my driveway and up the road. I kept my power at the ready to cast out until I felt them get in a car and speed away.

14

AVA

I woke up the next morning feeling like something was off. After the haze of sleep lifted, I heard and sensed someone pacing outside my bedroom door.

Grumbling, I eased out of bed, not wanting to wake Drew. But he was already awake. "What is it?" he asked sleepily.

It was easy to tell who it was. "Alfred is pacing outside the door. I'm going to see what he wants."

As I made my way to the door, Drew got up and put pants on. I opened the door and Alfred turned to face me. Anxiety and worry rolled off of him. Frowning, I asked, "What's wrong?"

"I need to speak with you." His squeaky voice was softer than normal and a little shaky. He was rattled.

I'd figured he wanted to talk to me by the way he was pacing the hall, but I wasn't going to tell him that. "You know you can talk to me about anything." He nodded, and I reached out and took his hand. It had taken me a while to get used to how it felt. Like old, cool leather. It had been disconcerting, though now I was used to it.

"Go and fix some coffee. Drew and I will be down before it's ready."

With another nod, Alfred left to do as I'd asked. Drew stepped up behind me, slipping his arms around my waist. "What was that all about?"

Whatever it was, it worried me. Alfred had been very tight-lipped about his past. I'd never pressed him to talk about himself, but the unknown freaked me out after all we'd been through. I couldn't help but wonder what we didn't know about him. "I don't know. I sense that it's serious. He's never seemed this nervous."

After I changed out of my PJs and washed my face, I met Drew and Alfred at the kitchen table. Alfred handed me my coffee exactly how I liked it, then sat across from me as I slid into the seat next to Drew. I sipped my coffee whilst waiting for Alfred to gather his thoughts.

He sat there for a long while, tracing the rim of his own coffee. As a ghoul, he didn't need to eat or drink. It was the same for Zoey and Larry and the cats, but they enjoyed food like the rest of us warm-blooded people, so they ate. Alfred ate less than the others. I wondered how the food was processed inside him. I'd never seen him use the bathroom, so it seemed like it'd just rot in there. Ew.

He finally sucked in a shuddering breath and placed his hands firmly on the table, as if steadying himself. "I need to explain who I was when I was alive."

I'd known this day would come. That if I gave him enough space and time, he would come to me and spill his secrets. I had to admit, I was pretty excited to find out. My curiosity had been fierce, if tamped down. "You're worried how I will respond?"

He nodded. "I wasn't a good person, Ava." Pressing his dry lips together, he looked away. "That's an understatement."

I glanced at Drew. He shrugged and motioned for me to give Alfred a nudge. The ghoul was trying to drag it out, whether intentional or not.

"Alfie, just tell me. Whatever it is, we'll work it out. Who you were matters a lot less than who you are now."

He met my stare again and took a breath. "I was a Viking shaman."

Whoa. I'd known he was old, but *holy* crap. A Viking shaman? That was some seriously coincidental timing, considering the sword. Then I remembered how he disliked that sword. Were they connected?

He continued, pulling me out of my thoughts. "I became addicted to dark magic. I fled my homeland, what is now Greenland, and ended up here after traveling the ley lines. The dark magic had clouded my thinking and taken over my morals. Not that Vikings had many to begin with, unless it came to our families."

After a brief pause, he continued. "We did have a certain moral code, but compared with today, it was ruthless. Lawless. Anyway, I became paranoid and trusted nobody. No one but my wife. She was with child when the native shamans found me and killed me."

My heart ached, but at the same time, I understood why he was killed. Dark magic turned people crazy. He'd had to be stopped.

He went on. "The Native shamans entombed me with a spell in the caves not too far from the one you put Phira in. While I was dying, I repented and promised I would change my ways, regretting my darkness. But it was too late."

"How did you become a ghoul?" I knew how and by whom, but I wanted to hear Alfred's side of the story.

"Bill Combs's grandfather found me. Well, raised me from the dead when he was practicing his necromancer powers. He was pretty young. I think he was in his twenties at the time. Anyway, after he raised me, he decided he would keep me." Alfred sipped his coffee and waited for me to speak.

"Is that why you don't want to be fleshed out?" I asked. I'd offered several times to do it, each time he'd refused.

"Living like this is my punishment. I don't deserve to be anything other than undead. I was a monster in life, and I'll look like one in death," he said, as if it was how it was going to be. Like there was no way he could ever be anything else.

I wanted to argue with him about that, but right now wasn't the time. I covered his hand, making him look at me. "Everyone has things in their past that they don't want to let out. Thank you for telling me." For cripes sake, this happened a good thousand years ago.

He covered my hand with his other one. "You needed to know. The child. My son. He is your ancestor."

I sat back in my chair and let *that* news flash set in. Holy cannoli. Mom's side of the family came from the First Witch. And Dad's came from Alfred, AKA some powerful dark shaman. "The necromancers said the sword came to me because I was descended from a shaman. Was that sword yours?"

"Yes." He glanced at the sword that was still in the corner of the living room. We could just see it from the kitchen table. "It is called Skofnung. The blade holds a supernatural sharpness and hardness. Skofnung causes wounds that will never heal. There is only one antidote for Skofnung's wounds. A stone that is matched with the blade. Rubbing it on the wound will heal it automatically. If you kill someone with the sword, their soul becomes bound to the blade."

"We need that stone," I said before taking a long pull on my now cool enough to drink coffee. "Before anyone else gets to it. What if those necromancers go hunting for the cave?"

Alfred pulled in a deep breath. "I can take you to the grave."

Drew and I exchanged a long glance. "Now?" he asked.

I shrugged. "I don't have anything more pressing than figuring out what to do about those necromancers at the moment." I still had the vampire council to contend with, but this was an immediate fire that needed putting out.

We put on hiking boots and followed Alfred out the back door. "Should we drive part of the way?" I asked.

He shook his head. "No. It's through the woods, then halfway to the beach. It's not that far past the chasm cave."

We followed him quietly. For a dried-up old ghoul, he moved pretty dang fast. It was a good thing I'd been keeping up with my work-outs. It was hard to do magic from a worn-out body, so I had to keep on top of things.

Sure enough, we soon came to a hill that had a lot of brush and big boulders. Stone and boulders weren't too unusual around here. What *was* surprising was that I didn't remember seeing this clearing before. I'd hiked all over these woods, especially since coming home. "Why haven't I been here before?" I asked.

Drew sucked in a deep breath. "It's subtle. But there's something repellant about this clearing."

I'd cast spells like that, to keep humans away from a certain area I didn't want them to be in. I didn't think they'd work on me. "I wonder if the Native shamans cast the spell way back when they entombed you?" I asked.

Alfred looked around. "Maybe. It's not strong now, though. The tomb has been found before."

Of course. This was the one Melody had spoken about.

We walked behind some brush, then Alfred led us through a little maze of caves before we walked into a big stone room. "That's where my body was," he said. "And the sword was hidden in a different cave. I hid it there and they never found it. As far as I know, it stayed there until it came to you."

"Where is the stone?" I asked.

He pointed to a spot on the floor. "There, where my body was."

I threw a big ball of light up in the air, illuminating the space better. Sure enough, the dirt was somewhat depressed in the area that must've been where Alfred's body had been dug up.

"See if you can sense it," Drew said.

With a nod, I closed my eyes and cast out a small net, pushing my magic down into the ground, searching for anything that felt like it had magical properties or power.

It didn't take long to find it. It wasn't too far down in the earth. I pointed to the spot and Drew bent down to dig.

"Uh," Alfred said behind us. "Ava?"

I didn't turn as I intently watched Drew dig with his hands. "Yeah?"

"Ava," Alfred said again.

I turned this time to see what he wanted because his voice sounded different. Softer.

"Holy freaking crap," I breathed.

15

OLIVIA

Luci and I went straight to North Carolina, as soon as I worked out where all my kids would be, and that Carter's parents would stay at our place. We spent the night in a motel in Boone, not far from the gas station where Carter had used his credit card. We were both up early, which didn't bother me. I'd always been an early riser. My mom—the one who raised me—said I'd always beat the roosters awake.

"Did you sleep?" I asked Luci when he stepped out of the bathroom. He'd been awake when I fell asleep last night and up before me this morning.

He met my gaze and smiled. "I did not. I don't need as much sleep as you, or most people."

That was interesting. "I'm ready to go." We had adjoining rooms, so I'd gotten ready in mine.

He motioned to the door. "After you."

I opened the door and jumped, letting out a squeak. A woman stood on the other side with her hand raised. She had long, black hair and blue eyes. I looked her over. Thin, but sporty thin. She worked out.

"I'm Lily, Drew's sister. You must be Olivia." Her smile lit up her entire face.

"Yes," I said and held out my hand to her to shake while nodding my head behind me. "This is Luci."

Lily studied the devil for a few seconds, then she cocked her head and pulled out two round metal balls, and held them out. "Take these. They're charmed to hide your magic while we're in the compound."

I went to take one, but Luci pushed my hand away. "What are they made of?"

"Not iron or silver. Since Olivia is half-fae, I didn't want to take any chances of harming her." Lily looked a bit offended at Luci's question.

He rolled his eyes and picked up both balls. "You can't blame me. She's my daughter and I'm a little overprotective of my family."

I wanted to snort in derision. He could be dramatic at times, too. I snatched one of the balls from him and slipped it into my pocket. As soon as I touched it, my magic faded away. Luci didn't really need one, but he likely wasn't going to take the time to explain how his powers worked to a hunter.

Ew. I didn't like the feeling. I'd gotten so used to my powers in the short time since I'd unlocked them that now I felt naked.

As we walked to Lily's car, she outlined the plan. "My parents are in California until next month, so I have free rein of the compound. In fact, I'm the boss while they are away."

"So, does that mean we're going to just walk in?" I asked.

Lily grinned. "Like we own the place."

Sounded like a solid plan to me.

The drive to the compound was pretty. The mountains in August were swelteringly hot but so green. Very close to how it had looked in Faery the first time I went. Flowers everywhere, birds and bugs flying all over the place. It was like stepping into another world, halfway between the human one and the Fae.

Lily took a tiny road, which seemed more like a driveway, but it soon widened out. Likely, the small part was to make humans think it was just someone's old driveway. About a mile nearly straight up a small mountain, a compound appeared in an enormous clearing. After parking in a huge garage, we walked to a large building. "If Carter is here, then he's not a prisoner, because he's human," Lily said. "This building has rooms that many of the hunters use while staying on the property."

Luci and I followed as she went to a receptionist's desk on the ground floor. Lily asked the girl behind the desk, "Do we have a guest by the name of Carter Philips?"

The girl rolled her eyes. "We do, and he is something else, too. He won't leave." Then the girl typed on her computer. "He's in 215."

"Thanks, Donna." Lily moved to the elevators, and we followed.

When we got to Carter's room, Lily knocked.

A gruff voice yelled, "Who is it?" I recognized Carter immediately. The fink.

"Lily Walker. You have visitors."

I wiped my hands on my jeans. I hadn't faced Carter since the night at Ava's when he'd walked out on his kids because they were magical.

Carter yanked his door open, and his gaze instantly fell on me. I lifted my chin and said, "Hi, Carter."

Oh, yeah. He looked panicked. Good. "Why are you here?" he asked, looking from me, to Luci, to Lily and back.

"Your kids are worried. Your parents have turned up on *my* doorstep because they are worried. All because *you* haven't returned their calls. Now your parents are involved, and they want to file a missing person's report with the Portland police."

He curled his lip at me. "I'm not missing. In fact, I'm right where I need to be. I'm here to train to fight the monsters in this world."

Fury bubbled up inside me, and I was glad my magic was contained with the help of the metal balls. Nothing ever worked out well when my emotions ran high. My powers reacted to my mood like Ava's did. However, I didn't want to go home and tell my kids that I blew up their father.

I snarled my lip at him. "You need to be home for your kids." My power was trying to push through the block from the ball. Next to me, Lily fidgeted with the hem of her shirt. Luci placed a hand on my shoulder to calm me. It only worked a little.

Carter glared at me. "I want nothing to do with you or those kids you turned into monsters."

Luci's hand tightened on my shoulder. He was either cautioning me to keep my cool or he was getting just as pissed himself.

"So you're going to become a hunter, and what? Come after your own kids and kill them?" I asked. "Jess? Devan? Seriously?"

He hesitated, and I held my breath. He couldn't be that blinded by his fear that he'd consider killing our children. That was impossible.

I stepped closer, getting right up in his face. Of course, I had to look up, but that didn't matter. "If you ever come near me, *my* kids, or any of my friends, it'll be the last dumb idea you have. I will kill you, Carter. And if I don't, he will." I jerked my head back toward Luci. "Probably happily."

Luci chuckled as the lights in the hallway flickered, then all the bulbs blew. So much for charmed balls. It might've been Luci doing it, but I was so riled up I was pretty sure my magic was overwhelming my ball.

Luci still had his hand on my shoulder. I saw him take his ball and hand it to Lily before reaching into my pocket to retrieve mine. As soon as he handed off the second ball, he teleported us out of the compound and into a bar.

"A bar?" I asked, looking around while still riled up.

He grinned. "You looked like you needed a drink. I know I sure do. I was ready to turn him into a cockroach."

I needed to punch Carter in the face. However, a drink or two might help. Some. "Could you do that?" I asked. "The cockroach thing?" Looking around the bar, I noticed that the signs and pictures weren't in English. "Where are we?"

"Spain. And yes, I could." He grinned, then swiped his hand across his forehead. "Is this not good?"

I laughed and took a seat on a stool at the bar. "No, this is good. Just what we needed after dealing with that cockroach."

He got the bartender's attention and ordered a couple of fruity drinks with straws. We sat in silence while watching the drinks being made. When they arrived, he took them and said, "Come on. We can sit out on the beach."

Oh, nice. Settling into a couple of chairs in the sand, I sipped my fruity cocktail and watched the waves. "How can Carter be a hunter? I thought they had to be born."

"He won't have the same preternatural abilities as a born hunter, but he would be welcomed among their ranks, no doubt," Luci said. "Even if he is annoying everyone."

"But how did he know about the hunters?" I asked, still dumbfounded.

"Google. It's got answers for about anything." He snorted. "If you're willing to believe it."

I kicked off my shoes and dug my toes into the sand. We fell silent for several minutes until Luci said, "I could send Carter somewhere that will really teach him what a *bad* paranormal creature is. All I have to do is snap my fingers."

A laugh burst out of me. That was so tempting. Seriously tempting. "No, I can't do that to him. He hasn't done anything technically illegal or even technically immoral. Not yet. But abandoning his children... that's awful."

Reality hit me in the gut like a boulder. I would have to go home and tell my kids their father wanted nothing to do with them. "What will I say to the kids?" Tears filled my eyes. Even when I'd been at my worst, I'd *always* wanted them. It was bad enough I'd put them through that. Now this? This was too much.

Luci glowered and let out a low noise deep in his throat. "I might have to make sure Carter has no more children."

Why did the devil have to tempt me with his ideas of punishment for the jerk?

Silence fell between us again. It was comfortable and nice. We finished our first drinks and new ones appeared. Not magic, just excellent service. I glanced over to study his profile as I sipped. He looked like he was plotting all the ways to torture Carter. That made me giggle. Well, not that, the alcohol was doing its job—relaxing me.

"Can you conjure something for me?" I asked.

Luci met my stare. "Of course. What do you need?"

"There is a wrapped box on my dresser at your house." This was as good a time as any.

Luci blinked and the box appeared in my lap. Nibbling on my lower lip, I handed the box to him. "It's for you." His eyes brightened, and he did a little dance in his seat. It seemed I wasn't the only one a bit tipsy. How strong were these drinks?

"What is this?" he asked, voice full of glee.

"Open it." Why was I so nervous?

He did, like a kid at Christmas, which made it all the more fun for me. He gasped when he saw the beanie baby. It was the 1996 Bubbles the fish with the error on the tag. He'd seen one at the vampire castle in Milan when we'd broken Ava's dad out of his prison there.

Jumping out of his chair, Luci pulled me into a big hug. "Thank you, thank you. This is the best surprise I've had in centuries."

My heart warmed at how excited he was over a silly little beanie baby. "You're welcome." It felt like something had clicked between us. Slowly, we were building a foundation. A relationship.

After he calmed down, we finished our second drinks—or was this the third?—and stood. He left a wad of cash on the table, held out his hand, and I took it. A moment later, we dematerialized. Time to go home.

111

16

AVA

IT WAS LATE AFTERNOON, the day after we'd returned from the cave with the stone, and I was in the conservatory cooking up the potion for transferring the High Witch power to Melody when Olivia stumbled in through the back door. Her blonde hair was piled on her head in a messy bun. Usually, she wore it down and perfectly styled. The woman got up way too early for my taste.

Not today.

I gave her a raised brow look. "Late night?"

She waved me off and sat on one of the stools that I kept in there. "Luci took me to Spain. We got drunk on the beach."

Surprised, I studied her for a moment. She wasn't kidding. She was still pretty tipsy. Well, no judgment from me. It was five o'clock somewhere. "Bonding with the pops?"

"More like he saved Carter's life." She went into detail about what had happened at the hunter compound. I already knew some of it, because Lily had called Drew as soon as Olivia and Luci vanished, telling us that Olivia's powers broke the enchantment on the power dampeners Lily gave them. It'd caused some questions at the compound, for sure.

"Sounds like Luci was more concerned about you than Carter," I said. "The hunters would surely hunt down a person with that amount of power." I sprinkled rosemary into the mixture of herbs and conjured a tiny cyclone to stir everything together.

Then I turned to her and paused, hearing Alfred's footsteps heading in our direction. Alfred grinned at me as he stood behind Olivia and handed her a cup of coffee. Olivia took the cup and cradled it like it was her lifeline to the world.

"Thanks, Alfred," she said without looking at him. It was all I could do to keep my composure. Then she looked at me and asked, "How was your day yesterday?"

"It was an interesting day." I pointed to Alfred, who was still standing behind her.

Slowly, Olivia turned her head. When she saw Alfred, she gasped and nearly fell off her stool as she jumped to her feet. "What the... Who the heck are you?"

She eyed him up and down. Alfred said, "It's me, Alfred."

"No way."

Momentarily forgetting her half-drunkenness, Olivia circled Alfred. "How?"

"It's a long story," I said. "The short version is I used magic near Alfred, and the effect was that he's been fleshed out."

Her gaze turned from me back to the newly alive-looking Alfred.

His hair hadn't grown, so it was still a neat cut near his head. I'd call it a classic haircut.

That was all that looked similar. His deeply tanned skin looked as healthy as it could be, and it was wrapped around a body any man would've killed for. He was tall, but not *too* tall. Maybe six feet. His broad shoulders held up strong, muscular arms, with a torso that was chiseled from stone. I knew *that* from accidentally seeing him changing shirts last night.

His face, though. That was the real transformation. "Whoa," Olivia said, prodding his jaw with her fingertips. "This is..."

"I know," I said as Alfred chuckled. "It's different."

His nose was on the bigger side, but not so much that it overpowered his face. Mostly because it was a strong face. His jawline was defined, and he had a broad forehead. It all worked together to give him a face that screamed *all man*. Testosterone flowed from the man, at least, it did until he opened his mouth, and his same mousy, high-pitched voice came out.

That part was a hoot.

Once Olivia calmed down, I directed her out of the conservatory through the kitchen. Alfred followed. When we reached the living room, the front door opened, and Sam entered. He stopped short and eyed Alfred. Sam buffed out his chest and grabbed Olivia's hand, pulling her close. "Who..."

"Alfred," I said flatly.

Sam cursed and shook his head. "Drew said you transformed him into who he was before he died, but I had no clue he was a Viking! Hell, Ava, he looks like you pulled him out of the History Channel."

I laughed, noticing Alfred blushing and running off to the kitchen. He had a whole party menu to plan for the coven meeting tonight. His being fleshed out hadn't changed that. I'd offered *again* to do some or all of it myself, "Come sit and I'll tell you all about Alfred and his Viking past."

So I did. At least everything that Alfred told me about himself and the sword and what had happened at the cave where Alfred was buried. He'd allowed me yesterday to tell Olivia and Sam and anyone else who needed to know.

When I finished, a knock sounded on the door. Alfred exited the kitchen and opened it. Sam, Olivia, and I watched to see who it was and to see their reaction to Alfred.

Melody's eyes grew large as she stared at him. Then she looked at me, and back to Alfred. "Wow. Ava warned me, but I'm still speechless."

Alfred did a little bow and motioned her to come in. "Would you like some tea? Or coffee."

"Tea sounds lovely, thanks." Melody watched Alfred turn and head to the kitchen. After a few seconds, she joined us in the living room. "That is a huge and shocking change."

I nodded. "Yeah. I still get startled when I see him because I forget what he looks like."

We laughed. Sam said, "I would be afraid I'd punch him if I saw him in the middle of the night while going to the bathroom."

Olivia snorted. "You almost did that to Luci after we first moved in with him and Phira." No doubt that had been quite the adjustment.

"Ava!" Little Sammie yelled from the kitchen, then ran into the living room. He must've slipped in with Sam. I hadn't realized he was here. He stopped in front of me and glared while putting his hands on his hips. "What did you do to Alfie?"

My immortal cats chose that moment to grace everyone with their presence. Lucy jumped up on the coffee table and swished her long fluffy tail back and forth.

"Ava turned Alfred into a warrior who still likes to cook," Sammie said.

"Really?" She sat and licked one of her front paws. "He looks the same to me."

Ignoring Lucy-Fur, I addressed Melody. "I asked you to come early because I wanted to talk to you about something. I'm stepping down from being the High Witch of the coven. With everything going on and my wedding and the gods only know what else is coming for me, I just don't feel I'm giving the coven or our members enough attention. Since you do most of the work anyway, I would like to nominate you as my successor."

Melody sucked in a breath and smiled. "That is a huge honor. I accept with one condition. You can't leave the coven."

I threw up my hands in mock surrender. "I don't plan on leaving, like ever. I just don't think I'm being a very good leader right now." Truth be told, I'd never wanted the job, but had, at least, grown close to several members. The coven was a great support group for the witches in Shipton.

Melody and I talked about how the power transfer would work. "Are you sure?" she asked. "You'll be giving up the power boost that being leader of the coven gives you."

I chuckled. "I think I've got enough hereditary power that I'll be okay, but if I ever need more, you'll be my first phone call."

One by one, the rest of the coven turned up. This was a mandatory meeting set for this purpose. None of them knew about the power change, because I'd wanted to make sure she'd accept first. Once she did, I wasn't about to waste any time.

"Thanks to everyone for coming," I said brightly. "We've got a surprise for you all."

Melody stepped forward. "Ava is going to pass official leadership of the coven over to me."

Everyone looked pretty pleased with the news, telling me I'd been right in thinking I hadn't been a very good leader to them. I hated that, that was the case. "I think we all agree that Melody is the natural leader of this coven."

"But you're not leaving?" Leena asked. "We've gotten to quite enjoy having you around."

"No, I'm not going anywhere. Neither is Owen nor Olivia, and hopefully, if my parents' mission is successful, we'll be able to add Mom, Dad, and Aunt Winnie to our numbers soon."

We milled about and talked for a few minutes while Alfred handed out drinks. That led to a long discussion about how different he looked when fleshed out. I didn't tell the coven his history, as that wasn't something they needed to know.

When the clock chimed seven, Melody and I both drank from the potion. It was a little bit of superstition, doing it at seven. All I had to do was find that little thread of magic that was the coven, and while the potion coursed through our veins, I took Melody's hand and let it flow from me to her.

I still kept the tiniest thread of the coven, the same thread everyone else had, but the bulk was gone. And though I wouldn't have ever said this to them, in case it sounded too braggy, I barely felt the difference in my power level. I'd been right. My inherent power was far more than I needed.

Not that I'd ever give *that* away.

17

AVA

I snuggled into Drew and pulled the throw blanket a little higher as we cozied up together on the sofa. We stared at the sword. I still wasn't sure I believed I was a descendant of Alfred. I had called Dad, Mom, Wade, and Winnie, who were still staying at Hailey's house in Philly. My old house.

Dad hadn't recalled an Alfred in our family tree but said he would research it and let me know. Not that I expected him to find anything from a thousand years ago, but who knew what kinds of records necromancers kept? Dad also agreed with the other trio of necromancers who showed up a few days ago wanting the sword that it made sense that the sword was drawn to me.

"Before this, I always believed a sword like that was a myth," Drew said, breaking into my thoughts.

"I would like to keep others believing just that." If the sword landed in the wrong hands, there was no telling what kind of chaos would follow. "I can't turn it over to those necromancers."

"I agree," Alfred said.

My to-do list was ever-growing and showed no signs of slowing down. Deal with the necromancers. Deal with the vampire council. Deal with Mom's and Winnie's bodies. Keep learning about my powers. I didn't even know what else. Maybe it was time to keep an *actual* list.

Dark power crawled across my skin, alerting me to the necromancers. A second later they knocked on the door. Winston opened the door before I reached it. Odd that he'd do that. Did he trust them? And if so, how'd he know?

For the hundredth time, I wished Winston could talk to me.

The elder of the three looked like he didn't want to come in. Or maybe he felt Winston's magic. I didn't care either way.

"Come in and have a seat." I glanced up at the top of the stairs and nodded to Owen. He'd gotten home from work at Clint's bookstore about an hour ago and had gone up to shower and read while we waited for the necros. We'd known they'd come sometime today.

The trio took a seat on the sofa and stared at the sword. I took that as my cue to lay down some ground rules. "The sword is safe with me for now. I think I know why it came to me, and what I need to do with it." The oldest opened his mouth to ask, but I cut him off. "No, I'm not sharing that information with you at the moment."

Because I didn't know for sure. It was a theory we had that maybe I could use the sword to force the vampire elders to back off. Again, that was only a theory. We hadn't talked about how or when we would go to Milan to free the necromancers from their prison. It would be soon, that much was for sure.

Another reason for me to hold on to the sword was because it originally belonged to Alfred, which made it a family heirloom. Since Alfred no longer had his magic—once a witch or necromancer or any other magical being died, their power disappeared. It didn't return when they were animated.

The only exception was to find a body that was stuck between life and death and take over their body and hopefully the ability to do magic would return. That was what Mom and Winnie were doing in Philly. They wanted to be witches again. Drew, and I both sensed that we would need the extra firepower in the near future.

The elder moved his gaze from the sword to me. "I am Arne."

"I'm Ava," I said, then introduced Drew and Owen.

He nodded at each of them before returning to me. "You believe what we told you about being a descendent of the shaman the sword belonged to?"

I shrugged. "Let's just say my research confirmed that."

The trio shared a look, then the elder said, "Your power is very strong. That could be why you keep having all these crazy things happening." I stared at him in shock until he continued, "Yes, we also did our own research on you."

I should have expected nothing less.

"It's always been this way when a necromancer's power grows too strong," he continued. "It's both your strength and the fact that you have a necromancer living with you. The necromancer's power breeds chaos. You'll never be able to escape it."

There was a time when I'd wanted to escape it. To have nothing to do with the power, but I'd grown into it and realized that it was who I am. "I don't want to escape it. I'll need all the power I can get, probably very soon."

I met Drew's gaze, and he nodded as if knowing what I was considering. With my mate's encouragement, I said, "It was brought to my attention that the vampire elders are holding necromancers prisoner. I plan to free them."

The lack of surprise on their faces was telling.

"You knew that already."

They nodded and I added, "You also know that you can't use the sword. Only a direct descendent of the shaman's family line can."

And that must've been why they didn't argue with me when I said I was keeping it.

Before I could say anything else, my phone chimed. I pulled it out of my pocket and saw that it was Dana, my ferret shifter friend. I'd helped find her son in the shifter ring, unfortunately not in time to save him. "Excuse me," I said to the necromancers. "I need to take this." Hitting the button on my phone, I answered, "Hello."

"Hi, Ava. I'm sorry to bug you, but I needed to give you a heads up. There is a rumor that some vampires have been coming around recruiting shifters to kill you." Dana's voice was a mix of fury and anxiety.

"Is there now? Thank you for letting me know. Are you well?" I took just a moment to tell her it was nice hearing from her, but soon I hung up and looked at Drew with one eyebrow raised and fury racing through me. "Looks like we'll be going to Milan sooner than we thought."

DON'T MISS Ava and Olivia's next adventure in A Powerful Midlife.

A POWERFUL MIDLIFE

WITCHING AFTER FORTY BOOK 12

For Ashley. We need more girls' nights.

1
LUCY-FUR

—THE CAT, not the devil—

There was nothing ruder than being woken up from an incredible dream. I was about to *finally* catch that darn red light. Like seriously, I was so close to owning that little beam! But noooo, Winston, the house I was cruelly forced to live in with Ava and her clan of ghouls was shaking violently and making awful noises.

Utterly annoyed, I forgot my glorious dream and tried to twitch my ears and figure out what was happening. Something scary had to be going on for the house to react so dramatically. Actually, that wasn't true. He could've been pitching a fit because Olivia came over. Winston really didn't care much for Olivia, though none of us knew why.

Since I was up and wouldn't be going back to sleep anytime soon, I stood and stretched before making my way down the upstairs hallway to the top of the stairs to see what in the ever-loving world was going on. If it was something stupid, I was going to yell at everyone in the vicinity for disturbing my beauty sleep.

Snort. Yeah, right. As if I needed beauty sleep. I was glorious and we all knew it.

The sight on the first floor was not at all what I expected. Chaos was the best way to describe it. Certainly, Winston was right to do his little freakout. Wait let me take that back. Chaos didn't seem to be a strong enough word for what was going on.

Alfred, Ava's house ghoul, had a wooden spatula in one hand and a fishing net in the other, fighting off a rabid bunny and a rat. What in the world did I wake up to? My tail twitched of its own accord, my instincts driving me to go get that rat.

But hang on a sec. Was that a ferret with a knife in his mouth trying to make it up the stairs? Holy crap. My feline instincts were fine with me taking on a ferret, but maybe not one holding a freaking knife!

Thankfully, Winston wasn't having any of it. The stairs moved and rippled to keep the small animal from climbing them. The ferret got smart, or stupid, depending on how you looked at it, and started jumping to every other step. "Don't you dare come up here!" I screamed in my most commanding, forceful voice. "I won't have it."

Lucky for me, Winston turned the steps into a slide. The knife-wielding furball slid down so fast it smacked into the front door, bouncing back enough for Winston to swing open the door and use his magic to shove the vermin outside.

"I'm too sleepy for this foolishness," I yelled at the house in general before turning around and walking to the attic stairs. That would be a suitable spot for me to get quiet to finish my required fourteen-hour afternoon nap.

Olivia

"Finish the last bite, then you can go play." And mommy could get some much needed me time done while no one was home. A rare occurrence around here since I lived with the devil himself. Yep, you heard that right, Lucifer was my father and we lived with him while learning my newfound powers.

It wasn't just Luci and I who lived in his gothic mansion on the property adjacent to Ava's. My biological mom, Phira, my two college age children, Sam, my husband, and our son, Sammie.

Sammie picked up the last piece of his PB&J and shoved it into his mouth. Then he grinned at me, peanut butter and jelly stuck all over his teeth.

The little snot. Trying not to laugh at my almost six-year-old's antics and failing awesomely, I said around my giggles, "Chew with your mouth closed. No one wants to see your chewed-up food."

When he started laughing, I gave him the mom look to stop him before he choked. As I raised my eyebrows for added emphasis, my phone rang. The caller ID read Luci's name, so I answered. He didn't call all that often. My biological father was prone to literally popping in instead. "Hello," I said brightly as I wagged my finger at Sammie.

"Hello, dear." He sounded pleased to talk to me. It'd taken me a lot to come around to my new father, but we were working on our relationship. I no longer hated the thought of him, so that was a big step.

Luci, Phira, my biological mother who'd previously been banished to a specter dimension, and my two older kids, Jess and Devan, were off vacationing around the world. When the kids had mentioned they were going with Luci and Phira, I'd protested, saying they had school. But Luci reminded me that the kids had basically just lost their father. They needed a happy time. And he'd been right.

Carter, my ex-husband and the father of my older two, was worse than a horse's butt. An overabundance of colorful words came to mind when I thought about him.

He was human, and when he'd found out that his kids and I had magic, he'd disowned us. Carter and I had divorced years ago, so I couldn't care less that he wanted nothing to do with me. He'd already made that abundantly clear when he'd kicked me out of our home and took the kids from me. But in my defense, I was a wholly different person back then.

Carter hadn't changed, however. Right now, he was at a hunter camp in North Carolina, training to hunt down paranormal beings. All three of my children were said paranormal beings. As was I. And my best friend, my biological family, and pretty much all of the important people in my life. Everyone but my husband, Sam. My sweet, wonderful man was a hundred percent human.

If Carter thought he would be allowed to come after his own kids, he was in for a very rude awakening. After all, I was half-goddess, half-fae princess, and I was learning how to lay quite the spectacular smackdown.

"What's up? You miss us already?" I teased, earning me a chuckle from the devil.

The goddess half of me came from him since he was Lucifer. Phira was a fae princess and she called Luci, Loki. Say that ten times fast. That was what Luci had been going by when the two of them met and fell in love. He had a bunch of other names, too, but I didn't bother with much other than Luci.

"John called." Ava's father. "He, Beth, Winnie, and Wade are ready to come home, but I can't easily leave. We're on a cruise." Beth and

Winnie, Ava's mom and aunt, were in Philadelphia, shopping for new bodies.

It sounds a lot worse than it is, I promise.

Of course, they wanted to come home now during my down time. "I can portal over and get them." I'd been practicing my magic several times a day, building on my strengths and discovering my weaknesses. My magic was the whole reason why Sam, the kids, and I were still staying at Luci's gothic mansion, which was situated conveniently beside Ava's old Victorian house.

Creating portals was one of my latest achievements, and I was quite proud of myself, thank you very much.

"If it's no trouble, that would be great." Luci paused as Jess's muffled voice in the background made me miss my family. But they deserved this vacation. School or not, they needed the distraction. Plus, Luci and Phira loved the kids and spoiled them all the time. They deserved that as well.

Sucking back a sigh of regret at missing my planned "me day", I brightened my voice. "No trouble. I'll drop Sammie off with Ava and pop over to Philly to pick them up."

"Good, good. I'll talk to you in a few weeks. Ciao!" Luci hung up before I had a chance to reply.

Instead of being offended, I laughed and dialed John's number. Ava had given it to me on the off chance that I would need it. The way our crazy lives had been going over the past several months, it was good to have everyone's contact information.

John answered on the second ring. "Hello."

"Hi, it's Olivia. Luci said you need a pickup?"

"Yes, we're ready. We're not at Hailey's house, though. We're at Wade's."

I thought about it for a few, trying to remember where Wade lived. I'd only been in Philly for a few hours once to pick up Ava. Luci had then sent us on a ghost train that had *conveniently* dropped us into the spectral world where Ava's mom was trapped, along with my mom, and we'd figured out how to free them both. Now Beth was looking for a body and my mom was cruising with my dad.

What was I trying to remember again? Oh, yes. Where Wade lived. I was pretty sure I remembered it correctly. "Got it. I'll see you in a few. I just have to drop Sammie off with Ava. Be there in a bit."

We hung up, and I slipped my phone into the back pocket of my jeans before smiling brightly at Sammie, who'd just drained the rest of his milk. "Mommy needs to go run an errand. Would you like to stay with Ava until I get back?"

"Yay!" Sammie did a little dance in his chair before jumping down. He loved staying with Ava.

Before he made it out of the kitchen, I grabbed him, hurriedly wiped the PB&J off his mouth, then teleported us to Ava's.

Instead of portaling into Ava's living room as I'd been aiming for, Sammie and I landed at the top of the stairs, which was super weird. I was generally good at hitting the intended target. I hadn't messed up like this in a while.

Ava stood at the railing, drinking coffee and looking at something downstairs. I followed her gaze and gasped while covering Sammie's eyes as fast as I could.

A shirtless Viking was in battle with a... "Is that a bunny?" I whispered. "And a rat? What's going on?"

"Shifter assassins," Ava said simply.

I stared at her for a few moments, shocked at her calm demeanor, before I turned my attention back to the chaos unfolding below us.

And boy, was it chaotic. The rabbit and rat were doing everything in their power to get past Alfred—the Viking—and up the stairs.

Something hit the window right behind the melee. I fought back a little squeal and snapped my gaze to it, where a ferret had his face pressed to the glass. He snarled and chirped away, as if cursing at the house, which, to be fair, he probably was. Winston was doing all he could to keep the critter out.

I tore my gaze from the window to Alfred. Once a zombie-looking ghoul, he was now a fleshed-out, seemingly alive hottie. Washboard abs, broad shoulders, and long brown hair with streaks of gold in it. And his long beard with two braids on either side of it was the whipped cream on top of the glorious Viking dessert. The transformation he had gone through was...wow. Chef's kiss. I didn't have words to describe it other than hot.

Don't judge me. I'm just as much in love with my husband as the day I realized I was in love with him six years ago. That doesn't mean I can't enjoy a fine Viking form. And beard.

"Should we help Alfred?" I asked, glancing at Ava again.

Ava shrugged. "I think he's got it." She then turned to face me. "Good morning, by the way."

"Morning." I laughed, then said, "Assassins."

She nodded. "Yep. The vampire council is getting desperate."

"And yet they aren't any smarter."

Sammie squirmed in my arms, and I realized he was looking at the whole scene through my fingers. "Get behind me," I said sharply, and my sweet boy obeyed without hesitation. Probably because it meant he'd be able to watch better by peering around me.

The sound of glass breaking drew our attention back to the battle on the first floor. The ferret jumped through the broken window and locked gazes with Ava. His intended target.

Oh, heck no, he didn't. I twirled a finger, conjuring vines to come up out of the floorboards and cage the little demon. He bit and clawed at the vines, too distracted to notice when Winston opened up the floorboards underneath him. The ferret disappeared. Ha!

"Winston and Alfred make a good team defending the house," I said.

Ava pressed her lips in a thin line. "This is ridiculous. I can't use my magic on them because they're shifters. My magic only works on the undead."

"Well, you have that electricity," I pointed out. "Zap them."

She sucked in a breath through her teeth. "I would, but I'm not super good at it yet. I'd hate to set Winston on fire."

He moaned extra loud at that moment, apparently agreeing.

Just then, Zoey bounced out of the hallway in tiger form and let out a roar that shook the house. It was a good thing our closest neighbors were a good mile away. Sammie squeaked and pressed his face into my thigh. Zoey was one of his favorite people, but it was pretty obvious, even to Sammy, that she was furious.

Alfred darted into the downstairs hallway out of sight while the tiger took over fighting off the bunny and the rat. Movement at the broken window caught my attention. Holy crap. It was a massive wild cat of some sort. Maybe a mountain lion. Ava pointed and yelled, "Cougar!" Same difference. Whatever its technical name was, it was bad news. The big cat had its head and one leg inside the window already.

Not even a second after she yelled, Alfred rushed back in with the Viking sword in hand. The cat was halfway inside the house now, wiggling through the narrow window. Alfred swung and cut the cougar's head. Off. Cut it *off*. I grabbed Sammie again and pressed his face into my stomach while the cat's body dropped to the floor and the head bounced into the living room.

Ava and I said, "Ew," at the same time, drawing out the w sound.

Sammie jerked out of my hold and stuck his head through the wooden bars of the railing. "Cool, Mama. Did you see that?" Of course, he was excited. Of course.

"Um, yeah, buddy. I saw it and wished I hadn't."

Zoey roared again and the smaller shifters froze in place, looking from her to Alfred and then the dead cougar. After a split second debate, they ran flat out toward the front door. Winston opened it and gave them all a little magical push before slamming it shut behind them.

Everything fell silent as Winston stopped moving and groaning. Zoey shifted back to her human form fully dressed thanks to the enchanted clothes Ava'd made her. She took the stairs two at a time and joined us at the top just as Larry exited his bedroom.

He was rocking the bedhead look with one side of his light brown hair sticking straight up in the air. He had red sheet marks on that same side of his face. Rubbing his face and yawning, he stopped next to Zoey and looked down to the first floor with wide, sleepy eyes. "What's going on?"

2
AVA

THE COUGAR shifter's body turned back to its human form just as Larry joined us. Shock still flooded my body that Alfred had actually chopped his head off.

Not looking away from the carnage below, Olivia said in a weak, shocked voice, "Can you watch Sammie for a little while? I need to go get your parents, Winnie, and Wade, in Philly. They're ready to come home."

Before I could reply, Zoey scooped Sammie up, who was recovered from his fright at her roar and said, "I'm on it. Come on Larry, I'll fill you in on what you missed."

Now that Sammie was distracted and out of sight, I motioned for Olivia to follow me downstairs. She scrunched her nose as she glared at the shifter's head on the floor. Chuckling, I crouched down and inspected it. Dead bodies had become par for the course for me. Being a necromancer had that unfortunate side effect.

I was *not* used to all the carnage. Blood was everywhere, soaking into the wood floor and splattered in all directions. It was going to take a lot of bleach to get rid of it. Even after it was cleaned, no doubt it would show up under a black light. Then again, Winston would take care of the mess before I got to it. One of many advantages of having a magical house.

Grabbing a handful of hair, I lifted the head off the ground and animated the dead shifter with little effort. Since the appearance of my newfound electric power, all of my magic seemed to come easily. I didn't have to focus as much. It was amazing and a little scary at times. It also meant I had to work at controlling my emotions and temper, as my magic was prone to react.

I believed my bond with Drew also helped stabilize my power. That was our working theory, anyway. Whatever it was, I'd fully grown into my power finally. It'd only taken me forty-plus years because I suppressed that side of myself.

Dark, slightly unfocused brown eyes locked on me, and the man's lips curled into a snarl. I rolled my eyes. "Why are you here and who sent you?" I didn't have much sympathy for the deceased. He'd been trying to kill me.

A split second after my question, the head began moving as he shouted in Italian. Great. There would be no getting info out of him. Unless... "Does anyone speak Italian?" I asked. Alfred was the one who shook his head, though. "I can only speak English and Old Norse."

All righty then. Alfred had so many layers to him, that I didn't have time to explore them at the moment. But man, he would be a great muse for picking his brain for a book series.

The only other person in the living room was Olivia and although she was great for random facts, I doubted she spoke any other languages. I would've known by now. Maybe I'd get lucky, and she had a hidden affinity for languages I didn't know about.

"Luci would for sure, but he is indisposed at the moment. But I have an app!" Olivia said, pulling out her phone. She brought the app up and held the phone close to the head.

"Why are you here?" I asked again.

He spoke again with a little more aggression in his tone. The translator app said in a robotic voice, "Cat, you must go to kill."

Uh, what?

I glanced at Olivia, laughing. She restarted the app and held it closer to the head. I told him to repeat what he said.

Olivia read the translation, this time with a puzzled look. "It says he's here to walk your cucumber."

I laughed so hard I almost dropped the head. "That app is broken."

"Hold on. Let me try something." Olivia fiddled with the app for a few seconds until a loud ad started, advertising a game where you have to beat levels to win *real cash prizes*. Insert eye roll here.

The ad was so loud that it scared Olivia, and she almost dropped her phone. "Crazy ads!" she growled. "Sorry, it's a free app, so it won't let us do another translation until the ad is done."

After about thirty seconds, which the head spent muttering under his breath—how did he have breath?—in Italian, Olivia put the phone back to the head, who began yelling. When he stopped, Olivia read the new translation. "His umbrella begs for mercy from your stuffed unicorn."

"I don't think that translation app works," I said dryly.

"Freaking free apps." Olivia shut down the app and deleted it. "We'll have to ask Luci to teach us other languages."

That might not be a bad idea. Might even be fun. With a frustrated sigh, I unanimated the head and dropped it on the floor. As I stood,

Alfred rushed forward and picked up the shifter's body and head. "I'll bury them. Then be back to clean up the mess."

Thankful for the millionth time to have him, I nodded and started to walk to my office when the front door opened. It was Owen coming home from his shift at the bookstore, but for a moment, I panicked about someone walking in and seeing the insanity.

Owen froze just inside the door and surveyed the room. "What now?" he asked dryly.

Alfred poked his head out from the kitchen. "Come help me bury the body and I'll explain."

Taking it in stride, Owen shrugged and followed Alfred out.

I couldn't help but laugh. "One thing about living in this house is to expect the unexpected."

"And the strange," Olivia added with a giggle, then looked around the room. "Also, the gross."

"For sure." I couldn't let Alfred clean all this up himself. "Thank you, Winston, for helping with the shifters," I called into the air.

A moment later, the house groaned, then all the blood bubbled up and out of the wood floor, sort of resting on top without soaking in again. It took several minutes before it was all there. Winston let me know he was done with a little creak. "Well, you didn't have to make a *bigger* mess," I teased. If a house could chuckle, that was what Winston did.

I rushed into the kitchen, looking for something to gather the blood in. There was a huge pot sitting on the stove, so I rushed over and grabbed it.

Once in the living room again, I used magic to create a little whirl-wind to gather the blood, then I directed the red cyclone into the pot. Within minutes, the living room and entryway were blood free, so I carried the pot back into the kitchen just as the guys entered from the conservatory.

Alfred glanced at the pot and took it from me with a scowl. "I was going to use that for stew."

Oops. "Sorry. It was the closest thing I had to grab. I didn't want blood all over my yard."

He said, "Why didn't you just magic it down the drain?"

Blinking at him, I tried to think of a reason. There was none. I totally could've done that. "I wasn't thinking. C'mon, don't be mad. I can order dinner and pick up a new pot tomorrow. And now you don't have to scrub blood out of the wood with bleach." I looked into the air again. "Thanks for that, Winston!" I called.

The quirky old house slammed the cabinets open and closed a few times.

He had a grumpy look on his face. After a few moments, he relaxed and said, "Chinese sounds good." Alfred turned to the sink and poured the blood down the drain, then threw the pot in the trash. A nagging of guilt tugged at my heartstrings, but I pushed the feeling away as I reached under the sink for a bottle of bleach. "Can you help me remember to call in the order later?"

Glancing at me, Alfred's features softened, and he took the bottle. "I can do that."

He liked to feel useful, and he *was* more than he realized. When he'd finally told us about his past and who he was, he'd also confessed that being a ghoul was his punishment. It was why he hadn't wanted to be fleshed out. That and he'd been hiding the fact that he was an ancient Viking and one of my long-lost relatives on my father's side.

I touched his shoulder gently. "Thank you, Alfred, for everything you do around here. It's nice to not have to worry about food or cleaning. You make my life easier, but more than that, I enjoy having you with us. Very much." I grinned at him on the heels of that statement. His reply was a grunt, but I didn't miss the slight twist of his lips.

With a sigh, Olivia clasped her hands together. "I have to go, now that things are safe here again. I'll be back in a few." Olivia grinned right before dematerializing. She was really getting a grasp on her powers. I was so proud of her.

I headed to my office to write, which was where I'd been heading when all the shifter assassins stormed my house in the middle of the darn day. Like... who did that? I was betting the vampires had compelled them. Nobody else made sense.

But, oh, no. Did that mean the bloodsuckers were also holding shifters prisoners like they were necromancers?

It was definitely noteworthy. Something to think about. I made a mental note to mention it to Drew as I sat down and got comfortable at my desk.

The ringing of my phone brought me out of my thoughts. Glancing at the caller ID on my cell, I grinned widely. My bonded mate, Drew. "Hello, sexy. I was just thinking about you."

A toe-curling chuckle was his reply before he turned serious. "There's been a murder."

Um, okay. "I'm sorry to hear that. Is it someone I know? Wait, why are you calling me? You're the Sheriff."

"There's something supernatural behind the murder. I feel the residue of magic. It's slight, but it's there." Drew kept his voice low as he spoke, which told me there were humans nearby. After a long pause, Drew added, "Victim's name is Matt Velaski. He's a specialist who deals in gothic revival-style homes pre-1900s. He was staying in the servants' quarters and doing renovations on the Shipton Shores B&B."

Oh no, that was awful. My wedding was supposed to take place at the bed and breakfast in early October. Not that my wedding was more important than the contractor being murdered.

"Can you come and check the body? Maybe do your thing?" Drew asked.

I laughed. "I do lots of things, but I'm on my way."

Jumping up, I rushed out of my office. This was why I never got much writing done. Something was always going on. While I slipped on the shoes that I kept by the front door, I called out to Alfred. "Hey Alfie, I'm going to help Drew with a case. Do you want to come with me?"

He appeared in the archway between the foyer and the kitchen, looking like I asked him to kick a puppy. "Uh, no?"

The single word came out higher pitched and much squeakier than normal. "Come on. It'll be good for you to get out of the house. You're fleshed out and don't look like the walking dead anymore."

He frowned at me for the walking dead thing and shook his head. "No."

I waggled my finger at him and said, "Next time. I won't take no for an answer."

He shook his head and disappeared into the kitchen before I tried to convince him.

Turning toward the stairs, I yelled up, "Back in a bit!"

Sammie came running out of Zoey's room. "Bye, Aunt Ava!"

I blew the little stinker a kiss and took off, marveling at how different my life was from just a few years ago.

3
OLIVIA

I MATERIALIZED on the front porch of Wade's house, remembering the location the first time, thank you very much, and knocked.

A woman I'd never seen before answered. Her golden-brown hair fell just past her shoulder and her light green eyes sparkled with renewed life. She was a witch. I knew that much because her power flowed around her. It wasn't until John stepped up behind the woman and pulled her to him with his arms wrapped around her middle that I realized who she was.

"Beth?" I gasped. Holy crap. She looked great. So different, but amazing. And *so* much younger than Ava and me. I wasn't sure how Ava was going to react to her mom being younger than she was. Okay, so she wasn't actually younger, she just looked it. She even looked younger than she did as a ghoul. It was going to be odd, to say the least.

Beth smiled affectionately and waved me inside. "Yes, it's me." She motioned to another woman. "Meet the new Winnie."

Winnie was sitting on the sofa, reading something on her phone. While Beth had gotten a body that was, while younger, at least similar in looks, Winnie had gone with one that was the complete opposite. Holy crow. She couldn't have looked any more different.

When Winnie was alive, she'd been on the short side and curvy, with short dark hair and gray eyes. Not that she was dumpy, really. She'd rocked her curves. But she hadn't been what one would call svelte.

Now, Winnie's new body was Playboy Bunny gorgeous. She had a slimmer frame with modest curves, long blond hair, and Caribbean blue eyes. "Wow, Winnie." I searched for the right words, but ended up blurting, "You look hot." I stammered. "Not that you weren't before, but..."

She waved me off. "I get it. And thanks. We lucked out." Winnie ran her hand down her body, then rested a hand on top of her breasts, which were considerably bigger than her previous pair.

Beth rolled her eyes. "Win, stop playing with your boobs."

John laughed, then coughed to cover it up. I met Beth's gaze and she sighed. "Her old body didn't have boobs that big, so she keeps feeling them up. It's disturbing."

"It's hilarious," John whispered, then ducked away from Beth's glare.

An unladylike snort escaped me, and I covered my mouth. It was never a dull moment in the Howe family.

Glancing around, I almost asked where Wade was but remembered that it was only late afternoon. As a newbie vampire, Wade would be sleeping. I hadn't thought about that before popping in. "I guess I should have waited until nightfall."

"Don't worry about it. We're eager to get back home and might have called too early. John didn't specify the time for pick up." Beth kissed her husband on the cheek.

"Is it weird that she looks different?" I asked him.

John shook his head. "Not really. I still know it's my Beth. We're a bonded pair, and she still *feels* the same."

Oh, yeah. I'd forgotten that they were. Just like Drew and Ava.

I clapped my hands together, ready to get moving and get back home, but I accidentally made Winnie jump. "Sorry. I was going to ask if you guys need any help packing."

"Sure," Beth said, and directed me to the kitchen. "This is the last room we have to do. Wade is taking some more of his stuff to Ava's, but he called movers to come pick up what he wants. I think they're trusted humans that Jax, the vampire leader of the States, uses. The rest of it will stay in the house. I hadn't decided what I'm doing with the house yet."

Oh, that was good. One less thing to worry about. "Let's get started."

As soon as the sun set, Wade emerged from his room, giving me a sleepy nod as he passed on his way to the kitchen to grab a bag of blood. A few minutes later, he came back with a coffee mug in his hand. "Give me a minute and I'll be ready," he said in a scratchy voice.

My phone chimed, indicating a text was coming in. I checked it and my heart melted. It was a picture of Larry and Sammie lounging against Zoey's tiger while they played video games. The message came from Alfred.

Just thought you wanted an update. All is good here.

I texted back, **Aww. That's cute. We'll be home soon, but Sam might be off work before I get back.**

I had called Zoey earlier to let her know it would be after dark before I returned. Sam was on a second shift today, but with the police department, there was no telling. She'd told me she'd figured and not to worry about Sammie.

Wade downed the contents of his mug and disappeared into the kitchen again. When he returned, he said, "I'm ready now."

We walked to Jax's, which was a few houses down. At least his backyard was. We had to walk around the block to get to his front door. They had the backyard all fenced off with super-high fencing.

Because Wade stood in the front of our group, he knocked. Hailey answered with a warm smile. "Come in, please."

She stepped back to let us enter the room, which was already just about full of other people. I didn't know any of them, but I remembered my mom saying something about fae blood being especially yummy to vampires, so I moved closer to John. He was a necromancer, so I was hoping he'd save me if a vamp or two wanted to make me their dinner. He wasn't as powerful as Ava, but he could hold his own.

We stood kind of awkwardly in the doorway since every piece of furniture was occupied.

"We won't stay," Wade said. "But the body transfer was a success. We wanted to come say goodbye."

"And introduce us," Winnie said. She rushed forward and grabbed Hailey's hand, obviously excited about her new body. "I'm Winnie!"

"And I'm Beth." Beth was equally excited, but she didn't have the same bubbly personality as Winnie. Beth was more serene.

"Geez," Hailey muttered, peering at the women. "Is nothing the same?"

Beth nodded slowly. "We're still us, but no, all sounds, smells, and looks are different."

John smiled at her. "She's definitely still Beth. But yes, it takes some getting used to."

"This is Olivia," Wade said, motioning toward me. "She's come to give us a ride home."

Hailey raised her eyebrows at me as if trying to remember me. "Oh, yes, you were here with Ava, weren't you?"

I nodded and smiled hello to everyone, still a little worried about being around all these vampires. The last time I was here, I was human, and so was Hailey.

Hailey gave me a strange look, then leaned in, and... was she smelling me? What the heck?

A tall, handsome vampire stood and walked over to her. Their auras mingled in a very obvious way, much like Ava and Drew or John and Beth. That must be Hailey's mate, Jax. The leader of the whole United States.

"What is it?" Jax said

"She smells strange," Hailey whispered.

I arched one eyebrow and put my hands on my hips. "Are you going to eat me?" I didn't want to have to use my magic on these people, who were our friends and allies, but I would if provoked. I inched a teensy bit closer to John, just in case.

Hailey shook her head and stepped back. Shock and worry clouded her features. "No, of course not. Why would you say that?"

I pointed to my teeth, trying to indicate that her fangs had elongated. I wasn't sure she realized it.

Hailey's eyes grew large. and she slapped her hand over her mouth, then whirled around to give me her back. I heard a few snickers and chuckles around us.

"I'm so sorry," Hailey mumbled.

"She's fae," Jax explained to the mortified Hailey. "Or at least partly so. Their blood is delicious. It's not surprising you'd react this way."

Hailey pointed to a thin, good-looking man. "Why isn't he freaking out?"

"He's not as close to her as you are. The lady's scent doesn't spread, which is common for the fae. It's a defense mechanism of theirs." He rubbed her arms comfortingly, and their auras flared at the touch. How sweet.

But Jax's statement snapped my attention to him. "Defense mechanism?"

He nodded. "Yes, to help you blend in. As long as you don't get very close to a vampire, they won't sense you as a fae."

I grunted. "Good to know." Then I glanced at Wade. "Why haven't you reacted?"

"I haven't breathed since you got here," he grumbled.

The room erupted with laughter at his tone. Poor guy. I hadn't realized. No wonder he'd been a little brusque at the house and gone straight for the bagged blood.

Jax stepped forward and inhaled, though he managed not to get all glossy-eyed as Hailey had. "You're not full fae?" he asked.

I tossed her hair back. "I'm half god."

Hailey whirled around again and gaped at me. "Excuse me? God with a capital G or god with a lowercase g?"

I chuckled. "Lowercase. My father is Lucifer."

"Luci?" Hailey asked. "Oh, we love him. You're his daughter?"

I nodded and tried not to look too exasperated. "Yeah, that's the old man."

Wade changed the subject, bless him. "I've decided to go home with them. You've been wonderful training me, letting me tag along with Luke's sessions."

The handsome one on the couch waved his hand. Presumably Luke. "It was nice to have *some* of the focus off of me."

"Well, I appreciate all the help. I'm so much better at hunting, compelling, and the like. I just need practice, so I want to go home to my family." Wade held his hand out to Jax and that started a chain reaction of a bunch of handshakes amongst Wade, John, and all the vampire men.

When Beth and Winnie went to shake Hailey's hand, she pulled them into hugs. She opted not to hug me, and I was a-okay with that.

"Come back and visit," Hailey said, seeming to sincerely mean it. "Or invite us to Maine. We'd love to vacation there."

"You got it," Winnie said. "I'd love to introduce you to our crew. You'd fit right in."

"I still want to buy your house," Jax told Wade. "It's close enough that I could use it for visitors."

Wade nodded. "If I ever sell, it'll go to you. In the meantime, you're welcome to use it all you need, as long as any needed repairs come out of your pocket."

Jax laughed and nodded. "Deal."

After a few more handshakes, we managed to make it out.

Once outside, we hurried back to Wade's, where everyone picked up a suitcase or box. Wade had five. Raising my eyebrows, I looked around. "Moving truck?"

Wade shrugged. "This is stuff I didn't want to have to wait on."

With a giggle at how much he was like Ava despite them not being blood, I grabbed John's and Beth's hands. "Everyone grab a hand or touch in some way. I'm new at this and having everyone connected will help."

When everyone did as I said, I portaled us back to Maine and right into Winston's living room.

4

AVA

I PARKED Drew's BMW along the curve in front of the Shipton Shores Bed and Breakfast. The sun was just dipping into the horizon, painting the sky in a beautiful array of colors. The waves crashed against the shore, and the seagulls flew overhead. It was a perfect evening for solving a murder.

Why was I driving Drew's car? Because my older Hyundai had conveniently broken down and was in the shop. The mechanic said it wasn't worth fixing. I couldn't help but wonder if Drew paid him to tell me that since my soon-to-be husband had been threatening to buy me a new car anyway.

He had to be joking, surely. After all, why would he need to buy me a new car when Dia, my cobalt blue Hyundai with the vinyl bench seat and worn carpeting, was still going strong? And I loved her.

Of course, Drew denied having anything to do with my car breaking. Then he'd conveniently said I was in luck because he had an extra car he could loan me: a freaking BMW. When I'd asked him how he could afford a car like that on a sheriff's pay, he'd just flashed that smug grin of his. I knew there was no way he could've bought it with his measly salary. "Hunting was a lucrative business."

He'd gone on to explain that he'd saved up quite a bit of money for retirement and had invested a large sum of his money as well. However, Drew wasn't a man to be content with simply sitting on his laurels. He'd decided to continue working, and gradually increased his investments as well. Over time, he'd become quite wealthy.

You learn a lot about someone when you move in together. For example, you learn that they're constantly leaving their dirty socks on the floor, or that they always turn the toilet paper the wrong way when they replace the roll after it runs out. But at the end of the day, living with Drew had been a completely rewarding experience, faults and all.

One of Shipton's oldest buildings, the B&B is a listed historical structure. The building had been meticulously cared for and it showed. The woodwork gleamed, the spiral staircases threatened to go on forever, and the chandeliers looked like they'd been plucked straight out of a fairytale.

Unfortunately, it had sat empty for the last year or so until the Stamp twins, who were witches and members of my coven, inherited it a few months ago and turned it back into its former glory. It had been their mother's, but it had passed to her sister, and now to the twins.

I wouldn't have called it a B&B based on its size. It was one of the largest I'd ever seen. Almost hotel-sized.

The building had a colonial structure, but with a modern flare. It was cozy and inviting, with a mix of old and new. The main section had been built back in the 1800s, probably around the same time Winston was, really, and had over sixty rooms added on over the years. It was located at the edge of downtown Shipton on about eight acres of coastline.

I got out of the car and made my way up to Sam, waiting outside on the front porch, his features masked by an unreadable expression. His cop look.

It wasn't until I stepped onto the porch that something seemed off about him—not just because he'd found a dead body inside the B&B's lobby.

When I reached him, he offered me a small smile that wasn't quite as happy as usual. "Drew's inside."

"What can you tell me about it?" I watched him closely. I hadn't heard much from Sam in a few months. Drew said he'd been working more hours since he and Olivia moved in with Luci and Phira.

Sam shrugged and glanced over his shoulder to the crime scene inside. "It's weird. The victim was found with a petrified look on his face. Like he was scared to death." Sam thrust his hand through his hair and met my gaze. "He fell backward down the stairs, breaking his neck. Nobody was home at the time, and as you know the B&B is closed for renovations."

"Well, let's go in and check it out." Where were the witchy twins? After all, this was their property. I'd expected to see them flitting around everywhere.

Sam nodded, but before he turned to go inside, I grabbed his hand, forcing him to look at me. "What's wrong?"

"Later." He tried to pull out of my hold, so I tightened my grip. He wasn't getting off that easily.

"Oh, no you don't. We haven't really talked in a few weeks. The dead guy can wait a little longer." I gave him a pointed look that I'd given him our whole lives whenever I wanted something from him. It worked in my favor almost all the time. Almost.

He blew out a breath and sagged in defeat. "Since moving in with Luci and Phira, Olivia and I haven't had much alone time. Jess and Devan hate me. And I'm the only non-magical person in the house. It's better to just stay at work most days."

"Oh, Sam. Have you talked to Olivia about this?" He shrugged, so I punched him in the arm. "Idiot. You've got to talk to her. You and Olivia will be double dating with Drew and me on Friday. Just friends hanging out and having fun. No magic. No craziness."

His lips twitched. "Can you guarantee that?"

"Nope." I grinned at him, making him laugh. "But it'll be fun, or at least interesting."

My lifelong best friend hooked an arm around my shoulders and pulled me into a tight hug before leading me inside the B&B. On the way in the door, I stumbled before catching my balance. Okay, Sam caught it. Whatever. He made sure I was steady before releasing me as we got closer to the body.

Urgh. I was getting used to dead bodies, really, I was. I lived with multiple ghouls, and until recently, had lived with a literal skeleton. Yet a freshly-dead body still gave me goosebumps.

Drew locked eyes with me when Sam and I stopped beside him. There was a question in his depths, and I sent him a thought. *Tell you later.*

Drew nodded, then turned to the officer beside him. "Can you check out the upstairs one more time?"

The officer looked at me, then back to Drew before leaving the three of us alone without so much as a grunt. I was almost sure most of the police force knew I had special abilities, but just like fight club, no one talked about the unexplained.

Once the officer was out of sight, Drew pulled me into a hug and kissed my forehead. He wasn't much on PDA. I wasn't either, but it was okay. Sam didn't count as *public*. He was family.

"What happened?" Drew asked. It figured he'd picked up on my brief panic when the shifters had tried to storm my house. Tried and semi-succeeded.

I smiled at him as if it was no big deal. "Just a little issue with shifter assassins. Winston and Alfred handled it though."

Drew worked his jaw. Uh-oh. He was going into his alpha-male-protector mode. It was so cute, and I loved his protectiveness, but I stopped him right there by placing a finger over his lips. "I was never alone. Winston went into lockdown and Alfred fought off the rabbit and rat. Zoey was there, and I didn't even have to try summoning my lightning. Olivia turned up and could've helped. I was never truly in any danger." I sighed and moved my finger to caress his jaw. "But I get it. This is the last straw for me. Tonight, we'll plan how to break the necromancers out of vampire prison. The council will learn not to mess with Ava Harper and her menagerie. No more."

Turning my attention to the dead guy, Matt Velaski, at our feet, I squatted down beside him. His eyes were wide open, and his mouth was in a perfect oval. Yeesh. It really did look like he'd been scared to death. Animating him might be tricky. Well, not tricky. Dicey? And loud. Screamy, for sure.

Here goes nothing.

I called to my necro magic, feeling it rise from the slumber I kept it in until I wanted to use it. Having death magic running wild wasn't an option for me, especially since I'd developed the weird and insanely strong electrical power.

Releasing the magic to flow over the body, I willed the dead to rise. Not all of the dead. Been there, done that, and got Larry in the process. Back then he was a skeleton and a Valentine's Day surprise I hadn't asked for. Though I wouldn't give Larry back for anything now. He was like another son to me.

Matt's body jerked to sit up straight, and he screamed. No. He didn't just scream. He screeched, like a particularly boisterous owl. Or a teenage girl. Crap. "Shhhh!" I moved, so I was directly in his line of sight. "Matt!" I grabbed his face, so he'd focus on me. "Matt, calm down. You're safe."

He wasn't focusing on me or hearing me over his screaming, so I put a little more magic into him and said, "Stop." Those who I animated had to do as I said whether they wanted to or not.

With an audible snap, he shut his mouth, fear still frozen on his features. I couldn't do anything about that. At least he'd stopped screaming. The cracking of old wood floors told me that the officers upstairs were making their way to see what the screaming was about. I threw up a magical circle and cast out an illusion that everything was nice and normal, and I was not talking to an undead Matt Velaski.

"Matt, can you tell me who killed you?" I kept my magic flowing so that he wouldn't have a choice but to answer me.

At the sound of his name, Matt locked gazes with me. "Ghost," he whimpered. "It was a ghost!" Oh, great. His voice was nearly back to the volume before. I cut him off again.

Dealing with ghosts was such a PITA. But why would a ghost show itself to a human? As I stood there and pondered the possibilities, Matt looked over my shoulder and started screaming again, even more ear-piercing than before.

"Ava, ghost," Sam said, drawing my attention to the entity standing behind us.

With a wave of my hand, I unanimated Matt, letting him fall to the floor with a thud. As I did, I added a little calming magic in the mix

158

so he could rest in peace and hopefully move on. After such a frightful death, I'd hate to have him turn into a ghost himself.

I stood and faced the ghost. To my surprise, the entity standing, well, floating, in front of me was a little girl about Sammie's age, maybe a little older.

"Hello," I said softly. "Who are you?" I took a small step forward and bent a little with the kindest smile I could muster. My movements spooked her—pun intended—and she ran off.

"Wait," I called, but her little white skirt disappeared around the corner down the hall. Darn it. With a big sigh, I gave chase. There was a reason she was here, and I wanted to find out. Had she meant to kill Matt? Or had she been trying to seek out his help?

She ran into the kitchen and then out the back door into the gardens. Barely keeping up with her, I chased her down a stone path, but when I got to the courtyard in the center of the garden, she was gone.

Vanished in thin air. "Biscuits," I said under my breath, trying to go for a non-cussing curse word.

Drew and Sam stopped at my side seconds later. "Where did she go?" Drew asked.

"I don't know." I closed my eyes and searched as far out as my power would stretch. There was nothing there. The only hum of power I felt was Drew's hunter magic. "She's not here anymore." Another reason I couldn't stand ghosts. I couldn't keep up with them.

Sam looked around before meeting my stare. "Do you think she went into the Inbetween?" He shivered as if he could feel her. Oh, Sam. Entirely human Sam.

No more Inbetween. No, thanks. Been there, got the mother. "I hope not, because I'm not going in there after her." At least I *really* didn't want to.

Like... Really.

"We're not going back in there," Drew said with his forehead creased. I wasn't sure if he'd heard my thoughts about not going or if he just felt the same way I did. He continued, "There has to be another way to contact her or draw her out."

I sighed, cursing myself for neglecting the ghostly portion of my powers. I should've been doing more with it, but there were only so many hours in the day. "There is. I have to talk with Ben and Brandon about the history of the B&B." I started walking back toward the main building. "And I'll need to consult with Mom and Winnie about doing a séance."

5

AVA

THE SUN HAD SET in a glorious display of pinks and purples by the time I got home, but that didn't stop me from swinging by the Stamp's house. The twins wouldn't mind, probably, if I dropped in after sunset. However, neither of them was home. Their house-keeper said they'd gone out of town to visit family but should return in the morning. So I left with the plan in mind to call them in the morning to meet at the B&B for the seance.

When I walked in the door of the old Victorian, I froze just inside the foyer and blinked several times at the two complete strangers staring back at me.

If not for the fact that Winston wasn't freaking out and my father, Wade, and Olivia were also there, I might have wrapped the intruders in a bubble of magic and demanded they tell me what the pure heck they were in my house.

It took another second, and I had to stretch out my magic, but I knew exactly who the women were. A slow smile spread across my face as they looked excited for me to figure it out. "Mom? Winnie?" I whispered as I stepped forward.

The brunette smiled brightly at me. "Yes, dear, it's us."

Wow. Even her voice was different. That was to be expected, but it didn't make it any less jarring. She and Winnie did have new bodies, which meant new vocal cords. New everything. And from the feel of it, magic, which was the main objective of their trip to Philly. They'd succeeded then. They had real bodies and real magic.

They were alive again.

Holy crap.

I glanced at Winnie and couldn't help but gape, like jaw on the floor. Mom looked great, and really not *that* different, as far as demographics went. She would still check all the same boxes on any form she had to fill out. Similar height, dark blonde-slash-light brown hair. Even had green eyes.

But Winnie. Holy crap, Winnie. She was a blonde now with a body of a model who'd gotten a primo boob job. And *tall*.

The only curves she had now were her *hips*, and *tits*, and... I walked around to look at their backsides.

Yep. Winnie had an *ass*. "Sheesh, Winnie, did you knock off a porn star?"

Olivia snorted, and everyone laughed at my question. Winnie just flashed me a grin and ran her hand up and down the sides of her new body. "I know, right? I look amazing."

"I mean..." I didn't have words.

Olivia jumped in to help. "You look like the Kardashian's distant blonde cousin, Kunty."

Winnie dragged her hand back up her body and stopped to cup her breast. "Just call me Kandy Kardashian. Maybe now I'll get a hot basketball player boyfriend."

Mom frowned at her, not enjoying the joke as much as the rest of us, who were nearly rolling on the floor laughing. "Winnie, stop feeling your boobs," she said in an exasperated voice as if this was *not* the first time she'd said the same.

"Oh, sorry," Winnie said, lowering her hand. She scanned the living room and drifted toward the door. "Where is Alfred? I can't wait for him to see me." With a little preen, she tossed her hair back before disappearing into the kitchen.

I thought about mentioning that Alfred had gone through his own transformation but decided to let Winnie be surprised. Even looking like she did, she still wanted to see Alfred as a zombified ghoul. She was going to be pleasantly surprised. "I'm not sure where he is," I called, then remembered our dinner. "That reminds me, I was supposed to pick up Chinese food."

I pulled out my phone to text Drew, but at that very moment, he walked through the door, so I slipped my phone back into my pocket. I'd order it for delivery in a minute. My mate and partner crossed the space between us with singular purpose and pulled me into a hug. It didn't matter that we'd just seen each other. I loved his hugs. And kisses. And... other stuff.

After holding me for a good five or ten seconds, he glanced up to greet everyone but then stilled. It took a second or two, but he relaxed while still looking a little confused.

Laughing, I helped him out. "The brunette is Mom. The blonde is Winnie."

He nodded. "That fits, somehow."

Ha! "I know, right?" I moved to the stairs and yelled up to the kids, "Larry, Zoey!"

Both of them came out of Zoey's room. "Alfred said you were picking up dinner?" Larry asked.

"I forgot, could one of you go get it?" I blinked up at them sweetly. "Or order it in?"

Larry pulled out his phone. "I'll order delivery. I'm not missing the big reveal. It's going to be epic."

"Where is Alfred?" I tried to sound nonchalant as I glanced at Winnie briefly. She gave me a narrowed-eye glare, as if suspicious that I was up to something.

If she only knew.

Well, she was about to find out.

"He's playing Mario Cart with Sammie," Zoey said as she descended the stairs. "And he's losing." When she turned into the living room, she smiled broadly. "You two look amazing. Different, but amazing. And so *young*." Yeah, their ages hadn't slipped by me, either. My mother and aunt looked like my kids. Or nieces. And my dad was gonna look like a bit of a perv.

Narrowing her eyes, Zoey cocked her head and one ear popped up on the top of her head, twitching as she studied the women. "Beth?" she asked, smiling at Mom.

"Yep," Mom said.

Winnie preened again, popping out one hip. "Geez, Winnie," Zoey said. "That's... Wow."

I winked at Mom, then looked at my father. He was in his sixties, and while he didn't look that age, he also didn't look twenty-five like Mom now did. "So, Dad, how do you like your new *younger* wife? Now when she calls you Daddy, it will take on a whole new meaning."

Dad chuckled, and Mom grinned while wrapping her arms around his waist. "It totally does," she said. "I enjoy being the younger one now." She practically purred. "Let's keep the nickname, Daddy. We could role play later on."

A spark of desire lit up my father's eyes as he dipped his head and planted a kiss on Mom's new lips. I crinkled my nose and looked away. Blech.

When I was a little girl, Mom would call him Daddy because that was what I called him. Now she was going to call him that because... I clutched my stomach against a heave. "All righty then. Moving on..."

Whirling, I listened to the sound of Sammie laughing out loud from upstairs. Then the two of them descended the stairs. Alfred had Sammie thrown over his shoulder. The kid was cackling in laughter.

The moment the little guy spotted Olivia, he yelled, "Mommy!"

He wiggled until Alfred set him on his feet so he could run to his mom. "You were gone all day," he complained.

Olivia sighed and scooped him up. "I know, I'm sorry. I did check in on you, but you were busy having fun."

Sammie grinned. "I won all the games."

She rolled her eyes at Alfred. "That's great, sweetie." As she hugged Sammie close, she whispered to Alfred "If he wins every game, he'll never learn to lose."

Alfred shrugged sheepishly, but then his attention was taken by Winnie, who stepped into Alfred's space. The two of them stared at each other for a long while, Winnie's new bright blue gaze connecting with Alfred's different-yet-the-same blue eyes. No doubt she was taking in his chiseled jawline while he was inspecting her new rack.

Then Winnie poked Alfred in the chest. A slow, sexy smile curved her lips as she flatted her hand over his t-shirt-covered pecs. "Well, hello, handsome."

Alfred's cheeks tinted pink as Winnie continued to pet his chest and ogle him like he was her main course, and she was starving. It was a little disturbing to watch. I felt sorry for Alfred, so I leaned into Winnie and whispered, "Um, Aunt Win? That's Alfred. Alfred, this is Winnie."

Winnie gasped and snatched her hand away, then turned her wide-eyed gaze to me. But then she laughed and rolled her eyes. "Duh. I lived inside him. I'd know him anywhere." She slowly turned her head back to Alfred, taking him all in. "Wow, Ava, how did you do this to Alfred?"

"Why would you think it was me?" Sure, blame the necromancer for all the weird stuff.

She looked at me with her lips pressed together. "How many ghouls have you raised and fleshed out?"

I rolled my eyes and waved her off, *so* not wanting to answer that question. "Come on. Everyone have a seat. Dinner will be here in a few and while we wait, I have to catch you guys up on some things."

Once everyone took their seats around the living room, I gave them the short version of the shifter attack earlier that afternoon. I left out all the gory details, of course. Big thanks to Winston for getting up all the blood, so nobody had to see it at all. How could I reward a house? Get him a new window or something? I felt like I should get him a present. A nice girl house next door? I had no idea.

The point of filling them in was to start planning how we were going to take on the vampire council. That had to happen soon. This was getting freaking ridiculous.

Mom pursed her lips before asking, "I'm sorry, but why aren't we on our way to Milan? Let's go before they succeed in killing you."

As much as I was on board with that plan, there was no way it would be so easy. "We can't just storm the castle without a plan. I

166

think our focus needs to be on freeing the necromancers they're holding prisoners. I'm betting the vampires are expecting us to retaliate in some way or attack directly. I feel like they'll be expecting that."

Dad shook his head. "I agree, but as far as I know, the other necromancers weren't being held in Milan. I was moved there not long before you found me. They caught me conspiring with the others through a hole I'd managed to poke in the wall to the room next door. They were isolating me by sending me to the palace."

Well, that sure threw a wrench in things. "You didn't mention this sooner. Why?"

Dad rolled his eyes at me. "Because we haven't had the time to sit down and plan our next steps. A lot has happened since you guys freed me." He glanced at Mom. "And I've been spending all my spare time with your mother."

That was true. I'd become too comfortable with the chaos that was my life now. "Sorry. Having assassins at my door for the second time is stressing me out."

"Don't apologize. We're all on edge." Dad draped an arm over Mom's shoulders and pulled her close to him. She cuddled into him. It made my heart happy to see them together, happy, and best of all, alive.

"You don't happen to know where the vamps are keeping the necromancers, do you?" I asked, hopeful.

"No. They drugged me." By the shadows that crept into his eyes, he wasn't happy to admit that.

"We need to figure out where the council is holding them, then go break them out." I paused while everyone nodded and mumbled their agreement with that plan. "Mom, Winnie, Can you work on that?"

Winnie's power surged as she rubbed her hands together. "With extreme pleasure," she purred, though her gaze was still glued to Alfred. I was pretty sure it hadn't left him the whole time we'd been sitting here.

"Great, thanks," I murmured, then snapped my fingers to get my aunt to actually look at me. "I'll need your help tomorrow night. We'll be holding a good old-fashioned séance at the Shipton Shores B&B."

6

AVA

By the time Olivia and I got to the B&B, both twins were there, sitting at a table in the breakfast nook. Brandon poured himself a cup of coffee while Ben wolfed down a piece of bacon.

There was crime scene tape still tied to the banister of the stairs even though Drew had ruled it an accident. He couldn't put that the Matt was pushed by a ghost in the police report.

"Good morning," I said, sliding into the seat across from them. "Brandon, can I get a cup of that coffee?" My energy was waning. The first two cups I'd downed at home hadn't had that much time to kick in. I was just exhausted.

Someone had kept me up all night.

Not that I minded, really. If I *had* to be tired, this was a darn good reason to be.

Brandon handed me the pot, and I poured myself a cup, nurturing it and sipping several times before I turned to Ben and asked, "As I said on the phone, I wanted to come by and talk about your little ghost problem."

The twins looked at each other for a moment before Brandon finally spoke up. "Well, there have been several people who have died on-site over the years," he said. "In a place this old, that's inevitable. But there was only one suspicious death. The rest were natural causes or verifiable accidents."

Ben nodded and said, "It was a little girl. She went missing over thirty years ago and her body was never found."

Olivia and I exchanged a glance. Welp, that wasn't suspicious or anything.

"Do you think she could be the ghost?" Olivia whispered.

"It's extremely likely. But we need to find out more before we can be sure," I replied. "Or before we can begin figuring out how to put her to rest."

Ben picked up the coffee pot and poured himself another cup as Brandon said, "Our mother was the one running the bed and breakfast when the little girl went missing." Ben stood. "She kept journals on every aspect of her life. I'll go grab the ones about the B&B."

While Ben ran off to grab their mother's journals, I helped myself to a Danish from the plate in the center of the table. Olivia had already dug in. She loved her sweets. Somehow, she managed to keep them off of her hips, too.

Ben returned with a box of books and newsletter clippings. "Help yourself. Brandon and I were thinking of displaying some of her notes and writings for guests to read the history of the place. If you see anything good, let us know."

"Oh, that would be cool," Olivia said around a bite of cinnamon roll.

I agreed as I pulled a few books from the box. Opening the first one, I noted how her handwriting was tiny and neat, and always the same.

Ben opened another one and paused, a smile tugging at the corners of his mouth. "Reading her journals is like hearing her voice again."

A lump caught in my throat at his words. I knew what it felt like to lose a mother. Even though mine had come back in ghoul form before finding a new body, I still understood the twins' loss. I just wasn't going to volunteer the news that my mom was alive and well. No one but my inner circle knew, and I planned to keep it that way.

The four of us fell into a companionable silence as we skimmed through the journals for clues. We'd been at it for what seemed like hours, and I was about to give up when I spotted a newspaper clipping on a missing girl taped to a page beside the neat handwriting. My heart skipped a beat as I realized we might be onto something.

"I found it. It says here her name was Sarah. The police searched for her, but they never found a body," I said, reading the twin's mother's notes. "Some people thought she might have run away, but I never believed that. I think something bad happened to her. Sarah had been at the bed and breakfast with her family when she went missing. Her father had been drinking heavily and got into an argument with her mother. Sarah ran off into the woods and her father followed her."

Olivia sighed. "Ugh, that can't be good."

I nodded and continued, "Later that night, her mother reported her missing, and a search party was formed. They found Sarah's father passed out drunk in the woods, but there was no sign of Sarah. They searched for her for weeks, but she was never found. The police suspected that her father had killed her, but they couldn't prove it, and he was never charged with a crime."

Olivia and I looked at each other in horror as we realized what had happened. Sarah's father had probably killed her and hidden her body somewhere in the woods.

"That's why her ghost was still here. She wants someone to find her body so she can move on," Olivia said.

The twins nodded in unison. "That is our guess too," Brandon said and looked me in the eye. "So, you can just call to her, right?"

"No, not without her body. I might deal with the dead, but ghosts are another entity." On the heels of that statement, a thought came to mind. "Although... If her body is on the property still, I might be able to raise it. That might make her ghost come to us."

"That'll work," the twins said at the same time.

I closed my eyes and stretched out my senses, searching as far out as I could for a body of a little girl, or heck, anybody, really. Unlike the first few times I'd done it, I had more control over what and who I animated.

While I found several dead animals buried in various places, I didn't find little Sarah. It wasn't for lack of trying. Opening my eyes and frowning, I said, "I can't sense her. Maybe if I go outside."

Without a word, the twins jumped to their feet. Olivia and I followed them outside the backside of the building. Salt air flowed around us, making me inhale deeply. The ocean was a mix of calm and chaos. And beautiful. It was why I loved my own property. It was great to wake up to the sound of the ocean, to go outside and feel the spray and smell the sand. There was nowhere like Maine in the world.

I walked toward the woods since Mrs. Stamp's notes had mentioned that was where the girl was last seen. Stopping about halfway between the woods and the B&B, I stretched out my senses, pushing my magic as far out as it could go.

Again, no Sarah. "This is odd. I can't sense her or any other bodies."

"Looks like we get to do a séance after all," Olivia said with too much excitement.

Brandon smiled, looking rather excited himself. "Give us about an hour or so and we'll get the lobby set up."

"Sounds good," I said, pulling out my phone to text Mom and Winnie to tell them to meet us at the B&B in an hour.

THE TWINS OUTDID themselves with setting up the circle for the séance. There was salt around the perimeter, candles in each of the four corners, and a crystal ball in the center. Not sure what the crystal ball was for, but it looked cool.

The sound of a door closing made me look up to see Ben descending the stairs. He glanced at Winnie and Mom with a frown. I quickly introduced them as my third cousins on my Mom's side of the family. "This is Winnie and Beth, named after my late mom and aunt. They're my third cousins or something like that." I laughed and waved my hand. "We're never sure whether it's first cousin thrice removed or third cousin." Ben and Brandon laughed as well, their minds hopefully jumping to how cousins are related rather than focusing on the names. "They're thinking of moving to Shipton and will be staying with me. I invited them to join in on the séance."

Ben's features softened a bit, and he relaxed, then pointed to the circle. "Brandon added the crystal ball for *aesthetics*." He air quoted the word, which made me snort out a laugh.

"Why is it black?" Olivia asked.

Mom answered before I could. "It's an obsidian stone. It will aid in absorbing the negative energy."

Brandon entered the room carrying a bundle of sage and rosemary. "Hence why it is there." He sniffed at his brother. "*And* it looks cool." He lit the end of the bundle and let it burn for a few seconds before blowing out the flames.

It did look cool. I loved crystal balls. I had a few around the house for various purposes, not least of which was aesthetics.

Once Brandon finished smudging the room, we sat around the circle, ready to begin. Since I was the one to be asking the ghost questions, I started us off by asking everyone to close their eyes and focus on their breathing.

When we were all calm and centered, I began the incantation. "Spirits of the other side, we call to you now. We seek to communicate with the spirit of a young girl named Sarah who died tragically. Please come forward and join us in this circle."

We all waited with bated breath, but there was no response. Olivia started to get antsy after a few minutes. "Should we try something else?" she whispered.

I was about to suggest using the Ouija board when the crystal ball started to cloud over. Smoke crawled from the outer walls of the ball until the black stone turned almost grey. The surrounding air charged with new energy, making my necro powers tingle with awareness. Holy crap. This was happening.

As much as I was used to magic and freaky things, this whole vibe made my skin crawl.

In the center of the circle, the little girl ghost I'd spotted yesterday appeared. The same one who'd scared Matt and made him fall down the stairs. Drew had ruled it an accident, even though the man's face was frozen in fear.

"Sarah?" I kept my voice low and soothing. I didn't want to spook the poor girl. "My name is Ava, and these are my friends. Can you tell us how you died?"

The sweet girl drifted close to me and studied me for several seconds before replying. "My daddy killed me."

Oh, no. I'd figured that much, and it broke my heart to think about it. "I'm so sorry," I whispered.

She smiled vindictively. "It's okay. I haunted him for a long time."

"How?" I asked. "I thought ghosts had to stay close to their bodies, or the place of their deaths, anyway."

"I learned how to move around." Her image flickered a few times. "I found him. And when he died, he died with my ghost by his side."

The little eyes twinkled, but in a way that made my skin crawl. I couldn't pinpoint why, though. "He died scared, just like I did."

"Sweet girl," Olivia said. "We want to help you. Can you tell us why you scared the man on the stairs?"

Sarah's face fell. She looked sad. "He looked like my daddy. I thought it was him at first, but then I remembered my daddy is dead. He's in Hell."

"How do you know that?" Mom asked.

Uh, yeah. How could she know?

"I watched him go," Sarah said. "If I'm near someone when they die, I can see where they go. Some places are green and blue and feel peaceful. And some places are red and hot and feel angry."

I raised my eyebrows at Olivia, wondering how in the world a little human girl ghost could sense the afterworlds. Nobody was supposed to be able to do that.

"Where are you buried?" Winnie asked. "Let us help you."

"Come on," the girl said. "I'll show you."

She drifted away so quickly I nearly fell over trying to hurry to follow.

As a group, we rushed through the bed and breakfast, out the back door, and into the garden. It was the same path we'd taken before when she'd completely disappeared, but this time when we got to the courtyard, she didn't disappear on us.

"There." She pointed to the center of the courtyard, where a pretty flowery design was etched on the concrete. "I'm under the flower."

I gaped at Ben and Brandon. "How?" Why couldn't I sense her?

Ben shrugged. "The courtyard and this garden were added in..." He glanced at his brother.

"The nineties," Brandon said. "Well after she passed away."

"I don't think they knew I was there," Sarah supplied. "But I was spending most of my time with my daddy then. He was dying then."

"Is there anything we can do to help you move on?" I asked.

Sarah's eyes flashed. "No," she yelled. "I don't want to move on. You can't make me."

She did disappear then, probably into the Inbetween. "Well," I said with a sigh. "We're going to have to dig her up."

Ben and Brandon sighed. "We'd planned on redoing this whole area, anyway. It's on the agenda for next month, but we can move the project up."

"Thanks," I said, patting Ben on the back. "I know this wasn't the remodel you expected, but we have to do something for this poor girl."

"I know a spell," Mom said. "Or, rather, your father does. You'll have to do it, Ava, but I know I've seen John help a spirit move on. When we have the bones, we can do it."

I nodded once and turned back to the group. "That's it, then. When you find the bones, call the police, and Drew will take it from there."

Ben and Brandon exchanged a glance. "We better go call the contractors."

7
OLIVIA

"Come on, Olivia, we're going to be late," Sam called up the stairs.

"Coming," I yelled back as I tugged Sammie's shirt off. The little monster had decided to start finger painting while I was in the shower. His father hadn't been home. Or if he was, he hadn't bothered to come and let me know. Nor had he checked on Sammie. "Just changing Sammie's clothes."

Sensing Sam entering the bedroom behind me, I glanced at him over my shoulder. "Did you see this?"

The paints were still out on the table, and I hadn't yet cleaned Sammie's face. My amazing, supportive husband nodded and smiled. "I thought you knew he had the paints out. Little man isn't supposed to use them without letting us know." Sam fixed his gaze on our son. "And he knows that."

Sammie poked out his bottom lip as he tugged on his clean shirt. "But I asked while Mommy was in the shower. She said yes."

I *so* didn't remember that. Oh, wait. "I thought you asked if you could take your paints with you, not open them here."

179

"Oh." Sammie grinned and gave me his big. Sorry puppy eyes. I sighed. There was no use in staying upset at him when he was so stinking cute. And I couldn't believe he would've intentionally deceived me. This was a mistake.

"It's okay. Go clean your face and be quick about it."

"No playing in the water," Sam added as the little monster darted into the bathroom. Crossing the room, Sam wrapped his arms around my waist and tugged me close. "He's just going to Ava's. Zoey and Larry and the rest of them won't care if he's a little messy. That's his normal state anyhow."

Wasn't that the truth? Our son managed to get into *every*thing. It seemed the messier he was, the happier he was. Thinking back to when Devan was little, he'd also loved to be dirty. The nanny had to constantly clean up after him and the boy himself.

"It must be a guy thing," I teased Sam and fisted his shirt to bring him in for a kiss.

He sighed and deepened the kiss. I melted into him, loving how he seemed to center me in every way. I couldn't remember the last time we'd been alone. Well, I could remember, but it'd been a while. Before we'd moved in with Luci and Phira. *Weeks.*

"I've missed you," Sam muttered against my lips.

"I'm sorry." I hugged him tightly, resting my head against his chest. "Things have changed so fast, and I haven't been dealing with it well."

Of course, I'd been training in all things magical and reuniting with my older children. In the process, I'd neglected my husband and our marriage.

Sam pulled back and framed my face. "And I've been dealing with things by working longer hours and giving you space."

"I don't want space," I said. "I want you here with me, doing these things alongside me."

He smiled wryly. "I can't do magic."

Bumping him with my forehead, I grinned. "Of course not. But I want you here. I always want to spend time with you."

Sam pressed a sweet kiss to my forehead. "Okay. Long hours won't happen anymore. I'll be here for you and the kids."

"And I'll start making Jess and Devan spend time with you. They don't get to snub you just because their stupid father hates me and filled their head with garbage." I was still bitter at Carter for that. His recent actions only made me want to curse him with a nasty rash or something even more uncomfortable.

I couldn't believe the once-loving father turned his back on his kids just because they had magical powers. Carter then took it a step further when he'd run off to hide out at a hunter's training facility. He was training to be a hunter.

Yeah, Carter deserved something far worse than a rash.

"Is the water still running?" Sam asked.

Frowning, I said, "Yep."

"Samuel Wallace Jr.!" Sam called out with his deep, stern Dad voice.

The water shut off and Sammie ran out of the bathroom. He was clean and his hair was even brushed. The little stinker lifted his hands and said, "Look what I can do."

Water droplets flowed off his fingertips, and he used his magic to float them in the air, adding more droplets as he went. "Isn't that cool?"

Sam and I shared a look. "He's an elemental." Among other things. I wasn't sure what that meant, all the powers he would have.

181

"He is part fae, so I guess that makes sense," Sam said, then turned to Sammie. "That is so cool, bud. But we have to go. We're late. You can show Zoey and your friends when we get there, okay?"

I searched for my phone to text Luci and Phira about Sammie's newfound magic. The phone was on the table beside Sammie's paints. As I picked it up, I used my magic to clean up his mess and pack up his paints to take to Ava's.

Staring at my phone, I decided not to call my biological parents. At least not tonight. Tonight was mine and Sam's night. I wouldn't bring the rest of the family into it. Sammie's new powers weren't a critical crisis. We could deal with it later.

When we reached Ava's house, we found my BFF and her future hubby standing outside Drew's SUV with the passenger door open.

"You can't come with us. We're going on a date," Ava said to someone inside the vehicle.

My curiosity got the better of me, so I peeked my head over Ava's shoulder to see who she was talking to. To my utter amusement, Lucy and Snoozer were sitting in the back seat of the SUV.

Lucy scowled at Ava and said, "We want to double date with you guys. Olivia and Sam get to go, why can't we?"

Ava glared at Lucy. "Because Olivia and Sam were invited. Not to mention, dating is for humans."

"Well, it's a good thing you aren't humans, then." Lucy stared at Ava.

Snoozer let out a meow that sounded very close to *please*.

I tried to keep from laughing as I said, "Let them go. We could go to the drive-in instead of the theater. I haven't been there in eons."

Sam grinned at me. "We had our first date at the drive-in." My heart warmed at the memory. We'd been all nervous and excited. Ahh, new love.

"Fine, you can go. But Lucy, you can't talk around the humans," Ava said, then turned to face me.

I laughed softly. "It's cute they want to come. Let me take Sammie inside. I'll be back out in a jiffy."

Sam opened the back door and held it open for me. "I'll take him inside." He kissed me quickly, then took our son inside the house to let Zoey know he was there. A few minutes later, we were off and on our way to the drive-in.

We'd been planning to go to the Mexican restaurant in town, but since we'd changed our plans, we picked up some burgers and fries on the way. And yes, we got Lucy and Snoozer something too.

Lucy insisted on milkshakes, too.

Everything was going pretty smoothly. We were about forty-five minutes into the movie when things started to get a little loud. Up to that point, having the cats with us had been kinda fun. People would walk by and comment on how cute it was that the cats were lying there as if watching the movie.

Of course, Ava had to warn Lucy several times to keep her mouth shut. For the most part, Lucy waited until the humans were out of earshot before she'd make a snarky comment.

Neither Ava nor I had any idea Lucy's behavior would take a turn. But boy did it. And honestly, what had we been thinking would happen? It was Lucy! Of course, she was going to be a wild card.

The nutty cat started yelling at Snoozer at the *top* of her lungs. Something about looking at the cat on the screen way too long. Her words.

"That's it," Ava said and stood. "Back in the car. I told you to keep your trap shut."

Lucy didn't want to, but we managed to wrangle the cats into the car before heading home.

When we pulled into Ava's driveway, she said, "I'm sorry the date went all wrong. These two won't be going with us again."

Lucy grumbled something about not wanting to go with Ava because she sucked all the fun out of everything. Then the cats got out of the car and trotted off into the woods.

I laughed. "Don't be sorry. It was fun. Did you see the faces on the couple closest to us when Lucy started yelling?"

That had been the highlight of the evening.

Sam and I went in to collect our son and found him asleep, snuggled up to Zoey on the living room couch. They were watching a movie. Larry was on the other side of Zoey, snoring. I gathered my sleeping baby boy up in my arms, then opened a portal to Sammie's bedroom at Luci's house.

After we tucked our son in, Sam and I went to our room and closed the door. Sam stalked toward me with a sexy smirk on his face and desire in his eyes. I started to strip, which only deepened his desire for me, sparking to light my own.

Crossing the room, he took me into his arms and kissed me. Gods, I'd missed him.

8

AVA

T<small>HE</small> <small>CLACK</small> of my fingers on my keyboard had long since faded into the background. Normally I'd have loud music, but it had turned off for some reason. I was far too focused to stop to turn it back on. I was sitting at my desk, totally engrossed in the story, completely absorbed in the world of my characters. I'd started writing around eight, but that felt like ages ago. My fingers flew across the keyboard, laying out the perfect murder with a splash of sexy romance. All that glorious brain work came to an abrupt stop when I heard voices behind me.

No, they weren't the voices of my fictional characters. I wish. The voices weren't even coming from my head. Nor were they coming from my office, as I'd initially thought. Maybe out in the hall?

Rolling my office chair back, I stood and followed the voices, craning my neck to stick my ear out and listen. Pausing in the hall, I looked around and figured out what direction to go. Toward the living room. The closer I got, the softer the voices whispered, as if they knew I was coming. *Or this whole thing could be my imagination running wild*. But in my world, it wasn't likely to be my imagination. My life was *far* too crazy to brush anything off as imaginary.

As soon as I stepped foot into the living room, I knew exactly where the voices were coming from. Holy Viking sword, Batman. The voices were coming from it. From... inside it.

Alfred had hung it on the wall over the fireplace after he'd carefully cleaned the blood from the lopped-off head of that shifter. I shuddered at the memory. Thank goodness he'd been here. I probably would've burned the house down using my lightning.

Studying the sword with narrowed eyes, I cocked my head and listened to the voices, trying to discern one from another. There were too many to tell what they were actually saying, each one overlapping the other, vying for my attention and maybe my understanding? As I began filtering out one voice from another, I realized few of them spoke English, so I didn't know what the heck they were saying.

I stepped closer and whispered, "Hello?"

The voices grew a little louder, apparently hearing me. Oh, wow. Were they responding to my presence or my magic? Most likely both. After all, the sword had belonged to Alfred when he was alive and a Viking shaman. Oh, and we were related on my father's side of the family. I was still processing *that* little morsel of information. This having been Alfred's sword, and me being his distant progeny, maybe it liked my magic, too.

As I opened my mouth to try to talk to the voices in the sword again, footsteps behind me distracted me, so I turned to see Luci, aka Lucifer. Yes, literally the devil, have you not been keeping up? Anyway, he was entering the living room from the kitchen. It'd been just a few short months ago I'd been dead set on finding a way to send him straight back to Hell. Things changed considerably, and the devil had proven that he was kinda helpful to have around. Then there was the minuscule tidbit about him being my BFF's biological father.

Olivia, not Sam.

Now I didn't even blink when he came strolling into my house unannounced, eating... was that one of my banana popsicles? Sure, whatever.

He met my stare and grinned. "I hope you don't mind." Waving the popsicle in the air, he said, "We're out."

That made it okay to steal mine. No, but really, I didn't mind. I did like teasing him about it, though. "Wait, what are you doing here, anyway? I thought you were on vacation with Phira, Jess, and Devan." He and Phira had taken Olivia's older two kids for a stress-relieving vacation more than a week ago.

He gave me a playful wink and crooked smile. Darn, he really was hard not to like. "We just got back."

Like him or not, he was still the devil and had to be treated with a certain level of wariness. "Come to think of it," I said as I walked toward him, "How are the kids not in school? College classes started a few weeks ago."

Luci tapped his nose and said, "Sometimes being the devil pays off. You don't worry your pretty little head about the kids' educations."

I rolled my eyes as I remembered why he was sometimes super infuriating. "Again, why are you here?"

"We have to go deal with Crystal's little side gig." He grimaced. "I don't want to either, but it's got to be done."

Crystal's side gig? It took a few more seconds before I caught onto what he meant. I gasped. "I'd totally forgotten about it."

So much had happened since Crystal showed up at my door and confessed that she'd been in on her mother and uncle's little shifter fighting ring. Crystal had been in the process of setting up another operation in Bucksport, Maine. Luci had sent her down to Hell with her mother and uncle, but we'd had information about shifters she'd recruited. No, recruited wasn't the right word. Trafficked was more like it. I had *no* doubts these shifters weren't going to be here of their own free will.

As I ran off to get my shoes from my office, Luci said, "Grab that handy little truth stone of yours."

Oh, good idea. I grabbed it and slid it into my pocket, then snatched up my phone and sent Drew a text explaining where I was going. He replied a few seconds later. **Be safe.**

I sent him a kiss emoji, then pocketed my phone, putting it in the opposite pocket from the stone. When I got back to the living room, Luci was peering at the sword, one hand on his chin, as if he was deep in study. Without turning to look at me, he said, "Those souls are so tortured."

He turned then and grinned at me, making me frown at him. "I'm not sure all of them deserved to be trapped in a hell dimension." Well, he sure looked way too happy about it as he wagged a finger at me. I'd been about to open my mouth and suggest freeing them, but he spoke before I could. "It's too late to set them free, so don't get that idea into your pretty little head. I know how you are. You'll be on another saving mission in no time. They've spent centuries in there, slowly going mad. They're beyond repair." He drifted to stand next to me, then he held his hand out. "Now, shall we go set free those who can be saved?"

He was probably right. The souls in the sword were as evil as, if not more than, Phira had been lost to evil before Olivia's blood freed her. I knew that, while at the same time feeling and torture for the ones that might have been innocent. I wasn't entirely sure why, but probably it was the souls calling out to me that made the feelings surface.

"Let's," I said and placed my hand in Luci's. He slid his hand out of mine so that only the tips of our fingers touched. I studied his profile, noting that all the flirtiness was gone. Of course, it was. The only woman he wanted was Phira, and no other would do. He couldn't help but speak in a teasing and coy tone, but when dollars came to donuts, he had no desire to flirt with anyone else.

It was precisely how I felt about Drew. It was different from what I had with Clay. Of course, while I was with Clay, he was the only one for me. Don't get me wrong, Clay and I had a great relationship and life together. We'd been as close as Drew and I were, but what Drew and I had was a magical connection that only intensified our passion for one another all the more.

It didn't do to compare the relationships. They were each unique and fantastic in their own ways.

The sensation of being pulled through a portal yanked me from my thoughts. Before I could blink, Luci and I materialized beside a warehouse-looking building in a marina. Several yachts and smaller boats floated nearby. "Are we in the right place?" I asked.

I would have thought that Crystal's shipment of shifters would come on an industrial ship or something. Then again, what did I know about ordering exotic shifters for the use of illegal fighting rings? Nothing.

Crystal obviously knew some things though, and that was why she was locked up in Hell with her mother, Penny, and uncle Bevan.

"I'm fairly sure we are, perhaps, on the wrong side of the docks." Luci motioned to our left. "Let's go that way."

I shrugged and started to walk. He fell in step with me. It wasn't long before we were in the smaller area where the fishing boats docked. There were more warehouses along this section of the docks. And fewer lights.

And a much higher creep factor. Ugh. This place was like a mafia movie set.

As we rounded the next building, Luci grabbed my arm and pulled me back to squat down behind a shipping container. I went on high alert. I didn't need to ask why he did that, because a large fishing boat was coming into the closest slip to us.

Quietly, we watched the boat dock. "How many people do you think are on board?" I whispered.

"Maybe two crew members, but I sense several shifters on board." We waited a few more seconds before we stood and walked to the boat.

I wasn't sure what Luci was waiting for, but *I* was waiting for him to take the lead. He was immortal. I was not. Although I couldn't teleport out of here on my own, I had a phone-a-friend who could. Olivia.

When we reached the boat, a man appeared at the top of the ramp and looked at us suspiciously. "Who are you?" he asked.

Luci held the man's stare as he walked up the ramp. "Crystal sent us." Act as though you belong and people believe it.

I palmed the truth stone in my pocket to activate it, hoping it would work from its hiding place. I was about to find out.

"What's your name?" I asked when Luci and I reached the top and stepped on board, forcing the man to take a few steps back.

"Lee." He then motioned to the back of the ship where the containers were. "We have several exotics on board. I'm a low-level wizard and my magical gift is concealment. I'm able to move from port to port without being detected, and thus I'm great at smuggling."

I shared a pleased look with Luci. It seemed the truth stone did indeed work from my pocket. That was good to know. "So, Lee, how large is your crew?"

"Oh, it's only me and my nephew on board. The fewer people on the crew, the fewer ways to split the payment." At the mention of money, Lee gave us a pointed look, expecting to get paid.

Luci said, "Let's get unloaded first. See what we have."

Lee and his nephew, a scrawny guy who looked *intensely* like he was on meth, got to work unloading the crates. These were crates big enough to hold a person or large animal. My emotions quickly turned over to the dark side at the thought, and my new lightning power tingled across my hands. No person or animal should be caged up and sold for the entertainment of others. Ever. For any reason.

Luci turned to Lee and his nephew. "Good. Now follow me, and we'll discuss your payment."

The three of them disappeared behind the closest warehouse, and I stared at the crates nervously, the moonlight shining down on them. What were we going to do with them? I nearly jumped out of my dang skin when one of the crates growled and rattled. Sorry, no, the crate didn't growl. Whatever was inside it did, and it sounded big.

And super pissed.

Inching a step closer, I tried to peek inside to see what type of animal was in there. It radiated the power that was usually associated with shifters, so it wasn't a literal wild animal. It was as human as I was, which... wait, was I a human? I had no idea, and this wasn't the time. Different emotions, rage, desperation, and worry flowed from the crate, pulling at my heartstrings. But I wasn't crazy enough to believe that the animal-half of these shifters would welcome us. We had to get them calmed down before opening up the crates or they might seriously maim us—or try to—in their frenzy.

"What are you doing?"

The sound of a deep voice made me jump and scream as I twisted around to see Luci, just behind me, laughing. I slapped him on the chest, which only made him laugh out loud. "Don't sneak up on people. I could have zapped your butt."

Not that it would've killed him, but it would have hurt.

He held up his hands. "I did *not* do it on purpose. To be fair, though, I didn't make an effort to make any noise either."

"Laugh it up, Satan." My tone was light and even if I wouldn't have admitted it out loud, I was growing to like Luci. There was never a dull moment with him around.

About ten minutes later, and with a little magical help, we managed to get all the crates inside the closest warehouse. I was glad to see that the building was empty inside and appeared abandoned.

Luci snapped his fingers and opened the first crate to reveal a metal cage. Inside that prison was a gorilla wearing a thick metal collar. The large beast growled as soon as it saw us. Tears pooled in my eyes. I couldn't blame the gorilla for being furious. Who knew what it had gone through up to this point?

Luci held his hands up and said, "We are not affiliated with those who imprisoned you. We're here to save you."

9

AVA

THE GORILLA SQUINTED its eyes at us, taking several minutes to process Luci's words, then nodded and scooted toward the bars. Luci reached in and unclasped the collar. As soon as it was off, the enormous gorilla shifted and a tiny woman with purple and brown hair appeared.

Seriously, she was little. It was difficult not to laugh.

Not because any of this was funny, but the stark difference between the woman to her shifted animal was startling. She was naked, of course, from the shift, and hunched over, hiding her private areas. I'd bet she weighed no more than a hundred pounds. *Maybe* a buck-ten. Her features didn't resemble a gorilla at all. If I'd met the woman in another situation or another time, I would have guessed she would be a mouse or a squirrel or something tiny. Not a *massive* gorilla.

Luci waved his hand out in front of the woman, and, in a flash, she was clothed. With a sigh of relief, she stood as Luci opened the cage. When she stepped out of the cage, I realized that she *was* only a child, younger than Zoey, and even smaller than I'd realized.

The poor thing. I made shushing sounds and walked slowly forward. "You're safe now. Do you know where your family is? Is there anyone we can call for you?" I really shouldn't have been surprised that she was a kid because the people from the fighting ring Penny had been running had been children as well.

The girl replied, but her English wasn't clear. Luci switched to speaking in what I recognized as French. I listened to them talk softly. For the second time in the last few days, I wished I spoke other languages.

Luci turned to me and translated what she said. "Her family is probably very worried about her. She was kidnapped while at a market. They had nothing to do with it, so I'll take her to them. Be back in a few blinks."

He smiled sweetly at the girl. Funny, I kept him at arm's length, but when push came to shove, I didn't have a single qualm about letting the girl go off with Luci. I trusted him at my core. It was all my preconceived notions about him holding me back.

I nodded at my discovery and found a crowbar nearby. While he took the girl home, I worked on getting the next crate opened. After trying a few different spots, I stood back and sighed in frustration. The crate wasn't opening as easily as the first one. That was when I felt the pull of magic.

Someone, most likely Lee, sealed the crate shut with a spell. Then I remembered Luci had opened the first with a finger snap. Magic.

I tried to use my witchy side to counter the spell while still using the crowbar to pry open the side. It wasn't working, so I called my new electric power. I just needed it to give the spell a little zing so it would disintegrate, but too little, too late, I realized that I put far too much magic behind it. The wood crate exploded in all directions as I squealed and ducked, covering my face with my hands.

Luci materialized beside me as the pieces of crate clattered in all directions and gave me a flat look before turning his attention to the metal cage that was inside the crate.

Inside was… well, I wasn't at all sure what it was. It was fairly small and looked even smaller in the large crate. The little creature was reminiscent of maybe a weasel or ferret, but its body was chunkier. The little face reminded me of a ferret, though.

I had a ferret flip me off once. That wasn't a face you forget. Hm. Maybe a ferret who mated with a large rat? Could be.

"A Tasmanian devil," Luci breathed. "Haven't seen one of these in ages."

Or that.

Impressive. It was small but looked fierce. Luci again explained to the little creature that we were there to help. The creature stilled and turned its head so Luci could reach in and snap off the collar.

I turned to the third crate and used my magic, but less explosively that time. I focused on zapping the spell around the crate and let out a tiny spark of lightning. The spell fell away, making it easy for me to break it open with the crowbar.

By the time I got the wood off of the third cage, the little devil had turned into a man, distracting me from seeing what was there in the third cage. A tall, muscular, blond man who looked *seriously* like a movie star stepped out of the second cage. Slap a cape on him and he could play Thor. He spoke in an Australian accent as he and Luci discussed how he was grabbed. He was a part of a small shifter population in New South Wales, Australia. Luci offered to get him straight back home, and he eagerly agreed. I waved as they dematerialized.

I turned to see what was in the third cage.

Crammed into the cage with barely any room to move was a baby elephant. "Oh, no," I moaned. "Oh, I'm so sorry." I reached through the bars to take off the collar since the elephant couldn't move around to stop me or attack me. The poor thing couldn't move at all. Once the collar was off, the elephant immediately turned into a svelte woman. Okay, so she wasn't a baby.

She didn't bother hiding her private places. Instead, she stood and tossed her hair over her shoulders in a regal sort of way.

It took a healthy dose of confidence to appear regal while naked inside a cage.

Luci appeared just as I said, "I thought you'd be a child."

The woman laughed and spoke in a heavy Italian accent. "No, I am one of the famous miniature Sicilian elephants."

I'd never heard of them, but I would definitely look them up the first chance I got.

The lady then said, "I need to get home to my children if you please."

Luci waved a hand between us to conjure clothes on her body, then offered her his hand. When she took it, they vanished. She hadn't even stopped long enough to explain how she'd been captured. It occurred to me none of the people had told Luci precisely where to take them. How'd he know?

That was a question for another time. I had one more person to free. I moved on to the last crate.

I raised a hand to zap away the spell on the wood, but I paused. A strange sound was coming from this crate. Was it... water?

Cautiously, I zapped the wood. I could only hope if there *was* water inside the thing, my electrical power wouldn't blast inside and shock the creature. Wincing, I did my thing and to my relief, nobody got electrocuted, because, unlike the other cages, this one was made of glass.

I stood there, shocked at what I saw.

A mermaid.

A freaking mermaid.

Luci appeared beside me and whistled through his teeth. "Wow, I thought they were extinct."

I looked at Luci in shock and said, "What? I never knew they were real at all." This long into my supernatural journey and I was still learning about the paranormal world.

The mermaid glared at us and drifted closer to the glass, watching us through narrowed eyes. Luci looked around and found a chair to climb onto, then leaned over the top of the glass enclosure to unclasp the collar.

"Why couldn't she just unclasp it herself?" I asked. She was more able to remove it than the others.

Luci jumped down from the chair and said, "The nature of the magic on the collars is that someone else has to take them off."

Of course, it was. Why wouldn't we have collars that kept a creature shifted and couldn't be removed?

Now free from the collar, the woman didn't even give Luci time to clothe her. She vaulted out of the tank and took off running. We chased after her out into the night, but then we lost her when she jumped into the ocean and immediately disappeared.

Alrighty then.

I turned to Luci and said, "Our work is done here?"

He nodded. "Great job." Instead of waiting to take my hand, he touched my shoulder. Moments later, we were back in my living room.

And that was one task off of my to-do list.

10

AVA

As soon as Luci left, I headed upstairs to get some sleep. The sun was rising, with pink and gold on the horizon in a beautiful display, but I couldn't enjoy it. By gosh, I was tired. About halfway up the stairs, Mom and Winnie came running into the room from the conservatory, stopping at the bottom of the stairs. "Wait! The locator spell worked. We have a location."

Turning, I stared at them, trying to remember why we were doing a locating spell. My fuzzy brain didn't want to catch up with what they were telling me. Then it finally hit me. The necromancers being held prisoner by the vampire elders.

Welp. Okay, then. It looked like I wasn't going to bed anytime soon.

Not that I minded, really. It was worth it to be sleepy if it meant I could free a bunch of necromancers who'd been held captive. No way I wanted anyone imprisoned a minute longer if I could help it.

I called out to Luci, summoning him back to my house, then I sent a text out to Olivia just as Drew exited our bedroom looking sleepy. "We have a location," I said when he reached me. "For the necromancers."

A magical shift in the air alerted me to Luci, teleporting into my foyer. Turning, I met his gaze. His expression went from inquisitive to morphing into a scowl, but I somehow knew it wasn't aimed at me.

"What's wrong?" I asked.

He shook his head and swatted around his face as if some large fly or wasp were buzzing there. I was close enough to him to be pretty sure no such bug was bothering him. "Not sure." Swat, swat. "Something downstairs. I'm going to have to bow out of this adventure." Wave, swat. "I'm needed in Hell. Something is going on that I need to deal with."

"Okay," was all I had time to get out before he dematerialized. I didn't think I'd ever seen him so serious and determined at the same time. Hm. Could it have something to do with the occupants of Hell that we'd just finished dealing with? Crystal, Bevan, and Penny?

Surely not. He would've said.

"Ava," Drew prompted.

I nodded and moved down the stairs. "Right." When we reached the bottom, Olivia appeared. "Luci said you needed a ride."

"Yes," I said, then glanced at my mom. "Where are we going?"

"Marstrand, Sweden." The words came from my father. He hurried into the foyer behind Mom and Winnie with Alfred, who had the sword strapped to his back.

Alfred shrugged. "Never know if we might need it."

That squeaky voice was comical coming out of his handsome mouth, though, really.

Winnie stepped forward and put her hand on his arm. "You take care of us so well," she whispered.

I really didn't want to hear her next words, so I focused on Mom. She offered Olivia the map with the magical X marking the location.

Olivia studied the map, then pulled out her phone. "Everyone get comfortable," she said. "I've never been there, so I want to do this right."

She, Mom, and Winnie sat at the kitchen table and hovered over Olivia's phone, working to figure out precisely where we needed to appear.

"Okay, I'm ready." Olivia finally said, sounding decidedly *not* ready.

Still, she was my best friend, and I trusted her implicitly. Without hesitation, I put my hand in hers and braced myself for the portaling.

A split second later, we appeared on a dirt lane. Everyone was intact and uninjured, and by the smell of the sea in the air and bright, mid-afternoon sunshine, we were somewhere island-like a good five or six hours ahead of us.

"Seems good so far," I said.

The road was lined with massive homes on small plots of land. I could just see a beach between two of the homes.

A flare of magic came from one of the houses. "Weird," I whispered, looking up at the white home. "If I hadn't just felt the surge in magical energy, I would've thought the residual magic in the air was old."

"There?" Drew asked.

I nodded. "Yeah, but something is blocking the magic. It makes it feel like... Old, I don't know any other way to describe it. I would've said we were too late, but someone is actively doing magic inside that home." Good timing on our part.

We hurried up the lane, and I stopped and studied the gate. It was hi-tech, which meant I could fry it. Ha. I zapped it, and sure enough, the lock disengaged.

Unfortunately, as soon as it did, an ear-splitting alarm filled the air. I covered my ears, then thought the better of the action, instead using my hands to fry the speaker on the side of the gate. The alarm silenced.

"Well, they know we're here now," Olivia said wryly. "Let's hurry."

We surged forward, Drew and Alfred in the lead. Alfred pulled out a little way ahead of Drew, walking quickly, nearly a jog.

Without warning, Alfred went flying back, high in the air, over our heads.

"Stooooop!" he screamed as he flew through the air.

Luckily for him, he was a ghoul. The impact didn't even knock his wind out. He jumped to his feet and ran forward. "There's a ward," he called as he joined us again.

It had all happened so fast, all the rest of us had done was stand there and gape at him like a group of... well, shocked witches pretty much summed it up. Drew wasn't a witch, and who knew really *what* Olivia was, but shocked. Yeah.

"Can we touch it?" I whispered.

"I'll test it," Alfred said. "I'm the only one it won't hurt at all."

He was right about that. I had abso-freaking-lutely no desire to go flying through the air.

This time, Alfred moved far more cautiously toward the house. I didn't know if he could tell, but I had no idea exactly where the ward was that had thrown him back.

Reaching out a single hand and stretching forward a single finger, Alfred moved forward cautiously. In a moment or two, which felt like a year, he must've touched whatever it was, because his arm flew back as if someone had grabbed it and shoved it as hard as they could. He ended up on the ground, on his butt.

"Whoa," he muttered.

"Okay," I said. "Let me try something."

My electrical power was getting easier and easier to control, and it came quickly when I called to it. I hit the general area where Alfred's finger had been thrown back.

"Oh," I murmured as a gigantic ward lit up. It was over the entire house, and the electricity added to it, which made it light up like a lightning storm, slowly moving across the ward to give us the true span of the thing. I kept hitting it with the power, hoping to over-load it and kill it.

Now I got to test my powers. I'd been working hard to control it since I had discovered I'd had it. Instead, I let it go wild. More and more power erupted from my fingertips. As I stood there, energy rushed through me, filling me with a high, unlike anything I'd ever felt.

"Oh, this is amazing." I laughed and let the lightning keep going wild, the power building and building.

"Ava," Olivia called, but her voice was hollow, as though she was far away. "Ava, stop!"

With great effort, I slowed the flow of power, but as I did, I realized I wasn't standing on solid ground anymore. I was floating a good six feet off the ground.

With a yank, I pulled the power back and heard Drew for the first time. He was in my head, screaming for me to stop.

I fell to the ground, where Dad waited to keep me from falling on my butt as Alfred had. Whirling around, I looked for Drew to find him down on one knee, an expression of strain on his face. As I rushed toward him, he climbed to his feet and held out his hands. "I'm okay."

"What happened?" I exclaimed.

"I think I know," Dad said. He prodded the ward. "It's weak now." Nodding toward Mom, he said, "Carefully. I think it's a rebound ward."

Her eyes widened. "Oh."

She threw a ball of energy, then ducked, but nothing came at her. Dad spread his hands out in front of him and walked farther than any of us had been able to go yet. "That did it," he said.

"What is a rebound ward?" I asked.

"I can imagine," Drew said wryly, rubbing his forehead. "If I'm guessing correctly, it takes whatever you throw at it and throws it back at you?"

Dad nodded as I let a little healing magic filter through our connection into Drew just to help him along. "Judging from how hard Alfred was thrown back, it probably multiplies the impact of whatever magic or impact hits it. Maybe tenfold."

I gasped. "That electricity was flowing through you?"

Clutching his arm, I looked him all over. "Are you sure you're okay?"

With a chuckle, Drew pulled me into his arms. "I'm fine. I'm a hunter, remember? That much electricity would've killed anyone else here."

"Not me," Alfred said, breaking our tension.

"Thank goodness for you, Alfie," Winnie cooed. Somehow her hands were all over him, and yep, there he went.

And now they were kissing. I wasn't surprised, really. They had shared a body. And that sounded a lot weirder than it was.

"Okay," I said, drawing away from Drew. I didn't want to throw out the PDA like that. As happy as I was for both Winnie and Alfred... Gross.

Cautiously, I shuffled forward. If I was going to hit this ward, I wanted to make sure I barely touched it, so the rebound would be minimal.

No such rebound came. "Oh, thank goodness." I started forward, but a hand on my shoulder stopped me.

"Me first," Alfred said. "Who knows what other boundaries they've set."

He moved forward, taking a slow and steady pace, alert for any danger. We made it to the front door before anything else happened.

"Should I knock?" Alfred whispered.

I shrugged and exchanged a glance with Drew.

"Just go in," Drew suggested. "We're here to save them, not calling for tea."

Alfred threw open the door and a blast of air hit us with the force of a tornado. At least, that's how it felt as we went flying.

Can we take a moment to appreciate how fast I thought? As I blew off of the stairs and to the cobblestone sidewalk in front of the house, I conjured a bunch of mattresses.

When we landed in a heap, at least we landed on mattresses. Every bed in Winston was now missing a mattress, but we weren't injured, and I didn't have to heal anyone.

Slightly bedraggled, we climbed to our feet and followed Alfred in the front door.

As soon as we were inside, I sensed the magic like a blast. Mom, Dad, Winnie, Drew, and Olivia did, too, because we all surged forward together.

"Someone's got a portal open," Olivia said. "We have to hurry!"

Alfred sprinted ahead of us and up the beautiful, velvet-lined staircase. "We want to save them, but be smart," he called over his shoulder.

We skidded around the corner at the top of the stairs just in time for Alfred to take an arrow to the chest from a hidden alcove.

Olivia waved her hand and the door on the hidden spot closed. Alfred snapped the arrow off and threw open the first door we came to.

A man stood inside the room, on this side of a big portal. A few people stood on the other side of the portal with panicked looks on their faces.

Not the man in front of them. If anything, he looked smug. Maybe even flat-out happy. "Close it," he barked.

I sent a blast of lightning through the portal before it closed but had no way of knowing if it connected or had any impact at all.

With a sigh, I slumped against Drew. "I really hope he was one of the vampire elders behind all this crap, cause if not, I just blasted an innocent person."

Dad patted me on the shoulder. "That was Soran. The worst of the bunch. I hope you lit him on fire."

"Me, too," I muttered.

"Now what?" Olivia asked.

"Let's see what we can find out," Drew, the cop, said. "Look for clues."

Bless him.

We spent the next several minutes searching around, careful about booby traps, of which we found a few. One set of staircases leveled out the way Winston had done in defense of me, but this was an elaborate mechanical setup, not a magical house. One piece of floor gave way. A trap door. Alfred went plummeting but caught himself on the lip and, between Drew and me, we were close enough to haul him back up. I conjured a board for us to walk across. That led us to a room that made my father go silent. "This is it," he whispered. "This is where I was imprisoned all those years."

My mom put her arms around his waist, and I squeezed his arm. My heart ached at the thought of him here all that time. "Is there any magic that exists that would let me go back in time?" I whispered.

Mom shook her head against Dad's shoulder. "I wish."

We didn't stay there long. Dad shut the door with a snap. "No use dwelling on the past. What's done is done."

By the time we triggered fireballs, we stopped and froze, silent, because someone was calling from the front door. We were deep into the massive house at this point, in what used to be a library. It was empty now.

"Hello?" the voice called. "I know there are multiple someones here. I can sense you."

We exchanged a glance, but nobody moved to volunteer our location.

Not that we needed to. A few seconds later, four intimidating men appeared in front of us.

"Ohhh, heck no," I said, holding up one arm. Nobody moved that fast except for vampires. "Freeze," I commanded, yanking my necromancer magic to the forefront and commanding them to do as I said.

The large men stopped moving. "Who are you?" I demanded.

But they didn't answer, because another vampire, this one with bright red hair, appeared, moving as fast, if not faster, than the others. "My enforcers," he said as he stopped a respectable distance away unlike his enforcers, who were far too close for comfort. These guys had to be related somehow. They were all precisely the same height. They had brown hair and brown eyes, and each of them had what curiously seemed to be the same jawline.

"Brothers?" I asked, easily expanding my power to include this new vampire. He wasn't exactly under my control, but all I had to do was *think* about what I wanted him to do, and he'd do it.

"Cousins. Can I ask what you're doing in my home?"

Dad stepped forward. "This isn't your home. It's Soran's."

The ginger vampire stepped forward and bowed his head. "Respectfully, Soran hasn't lived here in many hundreds of years. As a matter of fact, we closed this home up long ago." He looked around. "I'm quite impressed you managed to get in."

Slipping one hand into my pocket, I thumbed the still-there truth stone while my father spoke. "Soran has been holding necromancers here for at least thirty years."

"Who are you?" I asked, following up on my father's sentence before the vampire could respond.

"My name is Zeke," he said. "And Soran, my father, hasn't set foot on my lands since I kicked him off nearly two hundred years ago."

He was telling the truth.

"Zeke," I said, stepping forward. "My name is Ava. And I'm the most powerful necromancer in the world."

If a vampire could pale, Zeke did. His gaze jerked from me to his enforcers. He was just now realizing they were completely stoved up. "How?"

I let a little bit of my magic trickle over him and forced the proud vampire to walk over to a chair and sit down. He fought me tooth and nail, but it was laughably easy to control him. "How old are you?" I asked.

He had to tell me the truth, but his voice went stiff. This man did *not* appreciate being controlled. "I am over four thousand years old, ma'am. And I do not appreciate being controlled when I have done nothing to indicate I mean you any harm."

He was right. His enforcers had startled me, but they hadn't harmed us. I released him. "Now you know what I can do. And that didn't even begin to strain my magic."

Rolling his shoulders around, he grimaced at me. "Your claims about my father cannot be true."

"When was the last time *you* were over here?" I asked.

Zeke blinked. "I couldn't say. My father lived here for many hundreds of years. We don't have a good relationship, so I avoid this place, though I stay on the island that was once my home."

"What about you guys?" Dad asked.

"Oh, let me," I murmured. Releasing them from my magic, I held up one hand. "If you come an inch closer, I'll freeze you up again."

"Step back, please," Zeke said.

They did as he said, then I asked, "Did any of you know necromancers were being kept here?"

Okay, were these guys one brain and four bodies? They nodded in unison, then each, at the same time, opened their mouths and intoned, "Yes."

"What?" Zeke asked in a hushed, deadly tone. "You knew?"

One of the enforcers stepped forward. When he did, the other three scooted closer to one another with military-like precision. "Your father swore us to secrecy," he said. "And everyone else in the household. Since he is your sire, and leader of the council, we could not break that command."

Zeke pursed his lips and turned back to me. "I am sorry. I had no idea. I wouldn't have condoned the keeping of necromancers here."

"Do you feel necromancers should be controlled, imprisoned, or killed?" I asked as I thumbed the truth stone.

Shaking his head, Zeke backed away a step. "Only in situations of war. As long as your kind leaves my kind alone, I'm content to do the same. We go our separate ways."

I could accept that answer. "Fine. We will leave now."

Without taking my eyes off of the vampires, I reached behind me, trusting Olivia would grab me and we'd disappear.

Sure enough, half a second later, we arrived in my living room.

"Oh, thank goodness," I breathed. "I could've gone on controlling them forever, but it's nice to be home."

Drew pulled me into his arms and buried his face in my neck. "That was impressive," he said.

After indulging in the comfort of a Drew hug, I turned to the rest of my family, who'd taken seats around the living room. "What are you all doing?" I asked.

Mom furrowed her brow at me. "What do you mean?"

"I mean, the necromancers are being held somewhere. Probably that vampire palace they have. Let's go."

Dad held up one hand. "Hang on, honey. That was a pretty harrowing journey, and we were just going through a house that had been booby-trapped and abandoned."

"Yeah, but," I threw up my hands. "I controlled those vampires with complete ease. And one of them was over *four* thousand years old. Who knows how old the four-in-one goons were?"

"Ava," Drew said gently. "Your father is right. If you want to take on their palace, fine. We probably need to. But we need every ally we have before we go."

"Speaking of allies," I said. "I should call Hailey. I bet they'll want to help."

"Or at least they'll want to know about it," Olivia said. "Plus, I'm going to the fae ball this weekend. I can ask my uncle if he'll consider sending any warriors."

As much as I wanted to argue with her and storm the castle, so to speak, she was right. "Okay," I finally relented. "Let's wait and see what the fae king says."

11

AVA

The sound of little Sammie's voice echoed down the hall to my office, making me smile. I loved that he spent so much time at my house. It was nice having a little one running around. Not quite a grandchild. I was far too young for that. But like a nephew.

And if Sammie was here, so were his parents and probably siblings, ready to go to the ball. I hurried out of my office and to the front of the house. Olivia, Sam, Jess, and Devan stood in the foyer talking with Zoey and Larry about watching Sammie.

They looked amazing. Like royalty. "Oh my goodness, you guys look great." I couldn't stop my eyes from misting.

Olivia wore a hunter-green A-line style gown with ivy embroidered up one side of the dress in a light green thread. The gown brushed the floor and had a small train in the back that Olivia had clipped to her bracelet.

Jess wore a light blue mermaid-style gown. The bottom of the dress looked like it had peacock feathers on it. Both of them wore shoes similar to the ones I'd worn when I went there. Easier for walking on the moss and grass of the Fae realm without having heels sinking into the ground.

The guys both wore black tuxes. Their jackets had tails. And each of them had a single white rose in their breast pockets. So elegant.

Sam scrunched up his nose and fidgeted with his jacket. "Thanks, I guess."

Olivia laughed at him as she adjusted his tie and smoothed down the front of the jacket. "I have a feeling that we'll have to get used to dressing up for my family functions."

I agreed. From what I'd gathered, the fae loved their lavish parties and celebrations. But I wouldn't be doing my job as Sam's lifelong BFF if I didn't pick on him. "I wasn't talking to you, Sam. I was talking to Jess and Devan."

The kids chuckled softly, picking up that I was teasing Sam. Jess added, a bit begrudgingly, "He does clean up pretty good."

Sam stilled for a breath for a moment, as if he hadn't expected a compliment from her. I was a little surprised myself.

It'd been hard for Jess to accept Sam as her stepfather. Olivia and I suspected Carter had filled the kids with a bunch of crap that turned them against their mother, so they instantly hadn't trusted Sam. I was happy to see that they were starting to come around and accept their step-dad. He desperately wanted to bond with them.

Olivia stepped forward. "Have you heard from Hailey?"

I shook my head. "Not since she told me to wait on her and Jax to be ready so they can help us in Milan."

"You guys have fun. Don't worry about Sammie. He can stay the night." I pulled Olivia and Sam into a group hug. Then, I ushered them out the door and waved as they walked through a portal Olivia created into the fae world.

Zoey and Larry took Sammie up to Zoey's room to watch a movie, and I went back to my office to finish the next few chapters of my next bestseller. Hopefully, a bestseller.

A few hours later, a scream echoed through the house. "Sammie, no! Don't! Ava!"

The fear in Zoey's voice propelled me to my feet and down the hall as fast as my legs would carry me. Zoey stood in the middle of the foyer, looking up at the ceiling. I followed her line of sight and gasped, my heart almost lurching out of my chest. "How did he get up there?" I whispered, waving my arms completely ineffectually.

"He just... floated," Zoey said. "Like he's full of helium or something."

Larry appeared at the upstairs railing. He tried to reach for Sammie, who was now up higher, floating inches from the ceiling. The little imp was laughing like he was living his best life. And he kind of was. It was dangerous as all get out, but it did look fun.

"Sammie Thompson, come down here right this minute." I gave him my best mom tone, hoping that would be enough for him to reverse whatever magic had gotten him up there.

He stared down at me, floating flat now as if he were lying on a table. I didn't budge, and soon his little bottom lip poked out and he began the slow, scary process of floating back down until his feet touched the floor.

I knelt to be at eye level with him and took his little hands. "You scared the mess out of us. Your magic isn't always as strong as you think it is. And your powers are still growing and changing. That means that accidents can and will happen. You have to be careful."

Sammy's little face was the picture of contrition as his eyes welled with tears. "I'm sorry, Aunt Ava. I didn't mean to scare you, but it was so cool to fly!"

My mouth twitched, but I had to hold it together and not encourage him to be reckless. "As cool as it might be, there is always a risk of falling. You should talk to your mom and grandparents when you have new abilities so they can help teach you to control them."

He nodded and grinned at me. "You have powers. You can teach me."

Shaking my head emphatically, I tried to discourage that course of thought quickly. "I can't fly. My magic is different from yours and your mom's." I wasn't sure if he understood all I was saying. Magic was difficult to explain and understand, especially for a five-year-old with as much power as Sammie had.

I stood and faced Zoey. "Take him to your room and keep the door closed. I might be able to heal him, but I'd prefer that his parents not come home to find out their son was turned into a ghoul."

Olivia would never forgive me. Hell, I'd never forgive myself. Sam'd probably kill me. And Dad would have to animate me, and it would be a vicious cycle.

Zoey ruffled Sammie's hair, then led him up to her room. When I turned to go back to my office, I jumped at the sight of Luci standing a few feet from me. He looked rough, like he'd gotten into a fight or something.

"Are you okay?" I asked, appalled at his appearance. I'd never seen him looking anything but debonair.

He waved me off with a crooked smile that seemed more like a grimace. "I'm fine. Never better."

With a moan, Luci took a step forward and stumbled. I rushed forward, catching him before he faceplanted on my floor. First Olivia's son and now her father. Geez. With my hand flattened on his chest, I pushed so he'd stand straighter. "You are not fine," I mumbled while moving so my shoulder tucked under his arm. Together, we made our way to the sofa.

I sat down, Luci's weight pulling me off balance, and we landed in an awkward position. Quickly righting myself, I put a little space between us while he got in a comfortable spot. "What happened?"

He started to shake his head, then sighed. "I had some trouble with a few baddies in lockup. Got a little roughed up, but I have people handling it."

He was being cryptic, as usual. I thought about prying for more information. Mostly, I was wondering if the trouble he was referring to had anything to do with Crystal, Penny, and Bevan. However, I trusted that he wouldn't let them escape. Instead of asking, I said, "Let me heal you. And don't argue, because I can feel how badly you're injured."

As the latter words left my mouth, Phira materialized beside us. She was dressed in a gown similar to Olivia's, only Phira's was a deep purple. "What has happened?" she demanded in a tone of voice that would allow no delays or arguments.

"It was just a scuffle, my dear, I assure you, I am fine." Luci winced as I placed my hand on his chest and pushed healing magic into him.

After a few seconds, he took a deep breath and relaxed against the sofa. Phira sat beside him, holding his hand. "We will talk about this later." Ohh, I wouldn't want to be Luci later. Phira was not happy about Luci's injury. She locked eyes with me and said, "Thank you for healing him."

I shrugged and was about to say it wasn't necessary to be thanked, but Luci took my hand and gently squeezed it. "Accept the gratitude. You have a gift, many of them, and you always use them for good. Don't ever change."

By the time I blinked, Luci was standing and dressed in a tux like Sam and Devan had been dressed in. They were going to the fae ball as well. That was probably a given since Phira was the niece of the fae king.

I stood and stretched, thankful that was one grand occasion I did not have to endure. "You have fun at the ball."

They waved and disappeared, and I went back to work.

12
OLIVIA

THE PALACE BALLROOM had been beautifully decorated with multiple types of plants and flowers. Magic flowed in the air heavier than the natural power of the Faery realm. Pixies danced in small groups around the room, flying from flower to flower. Their tiny voices tickled my ears as they flew past me, too fast for me to make out any specific words.

"This is so cool," Jess said as she looped her arm with mine. My heart filled to have her so close and to be finally able to mend what Carter had done to our relationship.

HER WORDS REMINDED me that she and Devan hadn't been to Faery before. "It really is. We have to come back and explore." A long vacation here was just what we needed to explore our heritage and connect with one another.

JESS NODDED. "Definitely.

"I am so pleased you came and brought your beautiful family." I turned at the sound of the elegant male voice behind us. The corners of my lips lifted into a smile. Then I curtsied. Jess did the same and smacked her brother on the leg, making him bow. The king waved his hands. "Please. We are family and family aren't so formal with each other." He paused and raised one finger. "Unless we are in court."

Ah, that was good to know. The whole fae royalty thing was so new to me. "Thank you for extending the invitation to all of us."

"As I said before, your husband and children are welcome here any time." King Mitah paused and scanned the room before asking, "Where are your mother and father?"

It took me a few seconds to realize that he was talking about Luci and Phira. Duh. "Luci had something to deal with in He—" I cut myself off. Maybe not say Hell to the king. "In his realm, but he told Phira that he'd be back in time to come. She said she'd wait for him, and they'd come together."

Mitah held my gaze for a few moments longer. He wasn't happy that his niece was late, but he didn't comment on it. When a slow song started playing, his features softened, and he turned to Jess. "This is the father-daughter dance. Why don't you dance with your stepfather?" He indicated toward Sam, the first he'd really spoken to him.

I held my breath and waited for my daughter, who was too much like me, to speak her mind about her feelings toward her stupid, good-for-nothing father, how she felt about her stepfather, Sam, and how life was so unfair. But she didn't say anything as she faced Sam and offered her hand to him.

Sam glanced at me briefly with heavy emotions in his blue eyes' depths, then he took Jess's hand and wrapped it around his arm. They stepped out onto the dance floor.

I watched with tears in my eyes as they started to slow dance. Their bodies were stiff, and they put a good distance between them, but progress was progress. "I was expecting her to throw a fit and storm out," I confided in my uncle.

To my surprise, Mitah chuckled. "Children always find ways to surprise us." He offered his arm to me. "Care to dance?"

"I would love to." I looped my arm with his and met Devan's stare, then hesitated, not wanting to leave him out here standing alone. Devan must have sensed my emotions because he smiled and said, "Go. I'll be fine."

Just then a beautiful young fae girl about his age appeared at his side. "Would you like to dance?" She giggled and ducked her head as if embarrassed that she'd even asked.

He stared at her for a long moment before gulping, then nodding and leading the girl out onto the dance floor.

"Who is she?" My mama bear instincts were on the rise.

Mitah walked me to the dance floor, stopping close to Jess and Sam. "That is Gemma. She is the daughter of my head of security. She is a good girl. Feisty and headstrong, she is also smart and isn't afraid to go for what she wants. Much like her father."

"Ah, so she would keep Devan on his toes."

Mitah laughed. "Yes, he will have his hands full with that one." Then he tapped his ear and pointed at Sam and Jess.

I fell into a soft rhythm with Mitah and listened to my husband and daughter talk softly as they danced.

"You really love mom." Jess's words were free of resentment that she'd carried when she first came to live with us a few months ago.

Sam's face lit up at the question. It usually did when he first saw me after work or other times we spent time away from each other. "I do, with every fiber of my being."

"I can tell," Jess said, relaxing a little. "Dad never looked at her like you do."

Sam worked his jaw but forced a smile. He knew about my relationship with Carter and that it hadn't been the dream marriage that it should've been. The marriage had been doomed from the start but both of us had been too stubborn to admit it.

Sure, I had my issues and faults, but Carter's faults had amplified mine. We were too alike, yet different enough that we'd grown to hate one another.

I'd been stupid enough to believe that he wouldn't take the kids from me. And I'd been very, very wrong.

Jess went on. "Dad wasn't very nice to mom. I realize that now. I see it when I watch the two of you. She's changed because of your love." Jess glanced around the dance floor and met my gaze. She gave me a warm, knowing smile. Aw, my girl was too smart. And she had a kind heart to go along with her personality.

Sam glanced at me, winked, and then directed Jess a little further away.

"Looks like I've been caught eavesdropping," I whispered.

Mitah chuckled. "It does appear so."

Studying my uncle, great-uncle, actually, I wondered if it was inappropriate to ask him about helping with freeing the necromancers. Maybe if I just asked to schedule a time to discuss it, then I wouldn't look selfish?

"Speak what is on your mind. I can sense your mind whirling with thoughts. Something troubles you?" Mitah asked.

"It has to do with Ava and the...*vampires*," I whispered the word vampire because I didn't want too many people around us to over-hear. But they probably did anyway. "The vampires sent shifters to assassinate her. Well, not all the vamps, but part of the council. And they're holding necromancers prisoner."

"Just ask me what you wish." At least he sounded kind.

I took a breath before asking, "Could you provide us with a couple of warriors to go to Milan to free the necromancers?"

He studied me for a long while. I thought he would deny the request, but then he said, "My warriors are out on a recon mission at the moment. I will send them to your friend's house as soon as they return. Be prepared to go when they arrive. They will not wait."

"Thank you," I whispered. "It is greatly appreciated."

He nodded just as Luci appeared behind him. Luci winked at me but directed his question to Mitah. "May I cut in?"

The king stepped back and nodded to him and then winked at me before leaving us alone.

Luci took my hand and bowed. So formal. When he straightened, he put one hand on my waist and linked fingers with the other.

"You're late," I said as we settled into a slow dance.

"There was a mishap with a prisoner, but all is being handled now." He flashed me a smile, but it was forced. Whatever mishap there was had clearly upset him. At the very least worried him.

"Did you need help? Ava and I are here if you need it."

His smile was genuine now. "Thank you, but I have it under control."

Even though his words were spoken softly, there was an edge to his voice that said he was done talking about it. So, I changed the subject. "How was the vacation?"

We hadn't had a chance to talk much since he'd been back.

"It was great. We toured Europe, hitting all of my favorite spots. Jess and Devan are such bright young people." He grinned like a happy grandpa gushing over his grandbabies. "You and the Sams will have to come on our next trip."

I snorted at the *Sams* reference. Luci referred to Sam and Sammie as the Sams most of the time. It was cute.

"Yes, we'll have to take a family vacation once things settle down."

If things ever settled down.

13

AVA

Mid-morning the next day, I stood in front of the sword, staring at the thing. The souls were being chatty, and I was trying to figure out what the crap they were saying. All I got for my efforts was a bunch of gibberish and a few screams. And a whole lot of aggression.

I knew I should pull away and go back to working on my next best-seller, but I was entranced by the unknown. And for once, nobody was home. I didn't know where anybody was, except for Owen. He had a shift at the bookstore. He'd been working there a lot lately, saving up his money.

The magic that flowed in and around the blade was dark, which was to be expected since it was death magic. There was also something much stronger mixed with it. Possibly it was the power from the hell dimension where the souls were. I couldn't pinpoint it.

The blade was the door to the dimension, like a portal that sucked me in, begging me to solve the problem.

Lifting my hand, I slowly reached out to touch the blade when a larger hand gripped my wrist, scaring the crap out of me. "Dad!" I exclaimed as I looked up at him.

"What are you doing?" His features were full of worry and fear.

I blinked and glanced back at the sword. "I'm not sure." What had I been doing? The souls had called to me. They wanted me to set them free, or they wanted me trapped in there with them.

The latter thought made me put some distance between myself and the sword.

"You stopped breathing. Drew was trying to call you. When he couldn't get ahold of you, he called me." Dad brushed some stray hairs from my forehead, and I was transported back to when I was an upset little girl.

Smiling at the memory, I relaxed and hugged my dad. "I was too focused on the souls and let them pull me in. Sorry. It won't happen again."

I pulled out my phone and sure enough, there were ten missed calls from Drew and twice as many texts. I called him back as soon as Dad released me. When he answered on the first ring, I said in a rush, "I'm okay." Then I told him about what happened with the sword. "I made a mistake."

"It happens with unknown objects. You're naturally a curious person. But don't do that again. I felt it the instant you stopped breathing. Then your heart started to slow." He blew out a breath and I felt his fear drifting down our bond. "That was terrifying. I'm almost home. I've been driving with the lights and sirens on until I felt you come back to me."

I didn't tease him about being an overprotective alpha male because his fear was real and justified. I had a vampire council that wanted me dead. For all he knew, they could've gotten to me. "I'll talk with Alfred and have him teach me to use it correctly."

"That is a great idea. In fact, I was going to suggest it." His happiness radiated through the bond.

"I'll talk to you tonight and I promise no more communicating with the souls in the sword. Love you." I tried to push a big wave of love back at him.

I heard the smile in his voice as he said, "Love you too."

We hung up just as Olivia walked through the front door. "How was the ball?" I asked.

"It was *amazing*. Sam and Jess are making progress with at least talking to each other. I think my oldest son has a girlfriend." Olivia frowned at her last statement. "She's fae and the daughter of the king's head of security. They danced all night. Devan said she plans to start training to be a warrior in the fall."

She was leaving something out, but she'd tell me eventually. Olivia wasn't great at keeping things to herself.

"I think it's great he has a girlfriend, especially with everything going on with Carter. It'll be good for Devan and Jess to make new friends." I walked to the kitchen on the hunt for Alfred.

Since the ghouls had gotten their own power sources that kept them animated, they weren't tied to me so I couldn't always tell where they were anymore.

"He said he wanted to start training too," Olivia said in a forlorn voice.

And there it was. The source of the sadness I felt coming from her. I turned to face her. "Is that a bad thing?"

"Yes!" She frowned and shook her head. "No. It's a great opportunity. Plus, Mitah said that eventually me and my kids will be required to go through the training anyway since we didn't grow up within the fae family."

And still, Olivia wasn't ready to let her kids go. Not that I blamed her, especially as she hadn't seen them for so long. I sure did understand that feeling.

I closed the distance between us and took her hands. "Then do the training with him. And Jess. They can put their human educations on hold while the three of you train and learn all about your heritage. It will be a good bonding experience for the three of you." College was important, sure, but these kids were *fae*. That trumped most things.

Olivia's face brightened. "It will be. And it will bring us closer together. That's a good idea. Phira has already started training Sammie. Since Jess and Devan have been in school, they don't get as much time to work on their magic and fighting skills."

"Jess and Devan could take a couple of semesters off of school." I watched as she processed everything. After a few seconds, I asked, "Did you talk with your uncle about sending warriors?"

"Yes," Olivia said, all business. "He didn't give me a date. He just said he would send them when they got back from some kind of mission he had them on. And we need to be ready as soon as they get here."

Well, it was better than nothing. The best thing would've been if he'd promised us an army, but we'd take anything we could get at this point. "That's good news, I guess. I just hate waiting, but that'll give me time to do a little training of my own." I laughed as she raised her brow. "I'm going to ask Alfred if he could teach me to use the sword."

"Oh, I'm so watching this," Olivia said with way too much enthusiasm.

I rolled my eyes, not sure I wanted an audience, but whatever. When I entered the kitchen, I froze, which made Olivia run right into my back. I stumbled forward a little but couldn't take my eyes off the two people in my kitchen, making out.

"Winnie! Alfred!" Olivia squealed over my shoulder.

The two of them split apart faster than a couple of teens caught necking by their parents. Winnie smoothed down her hair, then adjusted her top. "Ava. Don't you knock?"

Oh, geez. She really was hot for ol' Alfie. "You're in the kitchen. This is a public room."

Olivia snickered beside me. "I had to set a rule at Luci's that there is no sex in shared rooms."

"Looks like I have to implement the same rule here." I sighed, then shuddered and quickly changed the subject. "Alfred, I was wondering if you could teach me to use the sword."

"Sure," he said in his normal mouse-like voice, although it was softer than usual. "When would you like to start?"

"Now if you can tear yourself away from Winnie long enough," I teased.

His cheeks tinted, and he averted his gaze. "We can start now. I'll go get the sword."

"I'll wait for you in the backyard," I called and went through the conservatory to the backyard.

It was a good thing I was already in a pair of yoga pants and a t-shirt. I'd need the flexibility for training until my muscles started to remember the movements I'd need to wield a sword. I conjured a scrunchy to put my hair up in so it wouldn't stick to my neck when I inevitably got hot.

Olivia conjured a lounge chair and some popcorn. I snorted at her and asked, "Are you comfy?"

She flashed me a playful smirk. "Oh yeah. This is going to be fun."

For her, maybe. I wasn't betting on myself having too much fun. My body would scream at me later. I pulled my phone out of my pocket and handed it to Olivia. "If Drew calls, take it so he doesn't think assassins are kicking my butt."

Even though I'd told him I would ask Alfred to train me, I hadn't said it would be right away. After the episode inside, Drew would be in panic mode for sure.

Alfred exited the back door moments later, holding the sword. He'd changed into a pair of grey track pants and a white tank top. Winnie followed behind him and when she reached Olivia, she conjured her own chair and sat.

Seconds later, Snoozer and Lucy-Fur came outside and lay in the grass in front of Olivia and Winnie.

Oh great, I had an audience. This should be fun.

Alfred handed me the sword. "Do *not* pay any attention to the souls. They will try to convince you to release them. Trust me, you don't want that to happen."

No, I didn't have time to chase down evil spirits. Not this week. "It's hard to focus with all their chatter. Can't you hear them?"

He nodded. "I learned when I was alive to block them. But you may be able to tell them to shut up. They might listen."

Really? "Why would they listen to me?"

"Because the sword came to you, it is yours to command. Why do you think the soul of the shifter I killed didn't go into the sword?"

I hadn't thought about it. "I didn't pay attention to where his soul went. I can animate bodies without their souls."

"The magic in the blade only works for the one it calls to." He paused as if to think, then added, "And it only works on the living, so you don't have to worry about stabbing me with it."

What?

"I don't plan on stabbing you at all." I just wanted him to show me some moves, and I wanted to get used to holding it, swinging it, and so on.

He gave me a flat look. "You can't kill me, Ava, I'm already dead."

Well, yeah, but still.

He pointed to the sword. "Can you conjure a duplicate sword? One without magic but the same weight for me to use?"

I possibly could. Usually, when I conjure things, it was items I already possessed and when possible, were already nearby. It wasn't the same as creating an object out of thin air. But that didn't stop me from trying.

Closing my eyes, I visualized the sword and every detail about it, minus the magic and the souls. I held out my hand and directed my magic to my palm while focusing on creating an exact copy of the sword. When something appeared in my hand, I opened my eyes and frowned. It was a leg bone of some kind, and I had no idea where it'd come from.

"Apparently I cannot conjure items that don't exist." I glanced at Olivia and asked, "Can you?"

She shrugged and gave it a try. Moments later she squealed with glee as a perfect replica of the sword materialized in her hand. "Ha. That is cool."

Alfred walked over to her and took the fake sword from her, then dipped his head in a bow. "Thank you."

He moved back to stand in front of me. "This first exercise is to take you through the moves and get you used to the sword's weight. Mimic my movements."

I nodded and held the sword in my right hand. He gripped his with both hands, his right over the left. Studying the way he stood, I mirrored him. He walked me through the steps the first couple of times, but it didn't take me long to pick up the movements.

An hour later, my muscles burned, but I was a lot more confident with the sword than I had been. I was also sweaty and in need of a shower, because I wasn't spending my cuddle time with Drew smelling like I'd been working out all day.

"Thanks, Alfred," I said. "I owe you one."

At least now I didn't feel like I was going to stab myself in the foot if I tried to use the darn thing.

14

AVA

MY BODY ACHED from all the extra exercise I'd been doing. It hadn't even been pleasurable activity either. Who knew sword fighting could be such a workout?

I'd surprised myself by getting up earlier than usual this morning. There was something in the air about today. It felt like our impending battle with the vampires was growing closer. It might not be today, but it was soon. I felt it in my bones.

As I entered the kitchen to grab a cup of coffee, my phone rang. I answered, expecting Hailey or Jax. It wasn't either of them. The name that flashed on my screen was Drew.

"Hi, hon." I chirped.

"The twins have excavated the concrete. Sarah's body is there. Did you want to come and see it before it's taken to the morgue?" he asked.

"Yes, I'll be right there." In my excitement at seeing the body and trying to figure out why I couldn't sense her with my necro magic,

I'd forgotten to tell Drew I loved him. I called him back and he answered instantly. "I love you," I said.

He chuckled. "Love you, too. See you in a few."

We hung up again, and I turned back to the stairs, then called up them. "Dad, did you finish the potion?"

He appeared at the top of the stairs. "It's in the conservatory with the chant for the spell. Just pour the potion over the bones and speak the words. Her soul will be free from this plane, and she'll move on."

"Thanks, Dad." After waving at Owen, who was getting ready for another shift, I darted off to collect the spell, then hopped in Drew's BMW and headed over to the B&B.

It was a beautiful ten-minute drive down the coastline from my house to Shipton Shores B&B. By the look of things, every cop from the Shipton PD was there. I was thankful that the media hadn't started rolling in. But they would soon, which meant that I needed to get the spell done as quickly as possible.

I parked the Beemer and made my way to the courtyard where they'd found her body, right where Sarah had said it would be.

Drew turned and locked eyes with me as I stepped onto the pathway that led to the courtyard. A ghost of a smile formed, then he dropped his gaze to my hand, noting the potion. When we first met and started dating, magic had made him uncomfortable to the point he couldn't be in a room with more than a couple of witches. Drew had said it felt like his skin crawled.

Now that we were bonded, it was more than that. His hunter magic was similar to witch magic, except... not. It was different. It was hard to explain so I didn't try to analyze it for too long. He didn't know how to explain it either. He just always said there were so many myths about how hunters had come to be, that he didn't know what to believe.

I had worried that he wouldn't want to move in with me because of the levels of magic inside Winston and the fact that everyone who lived there was magical in some way. Drew had chased those worries away when he moved his stuff in and put his house up for sale. He had a buyer now and was just waiting on the closing.

And we were getting married in less than a month. If we survived our encounter with the vamps, that was.

I stopped next to Drew and nodded to the twins, Brandon and Ben, who stood on the other side of the hole in the earth. "Afternoon."

"Afternoon," Ben said, tipping his hat at me.

Brandon added, "We'll put up an illusion barrier while you perform the spell. Just let us know when you're ready."

"Thanks. I'm going to try to call Sarah's ghost to us. She might already be here since she wanted her body found." I knelt and hovered my hand over the bones. Even after all this time, I felt the girl's magical signature. Holy crap. She'd been a witch! Maybe that had something to do with me not being able to sense her bones out here before. Or the age... I still wasn't totally sure. This was a type of magic I didn't recognize. It felt familiar like I'd sensed it once or twice before. For the life of me, I couldn't place where I recognized it from.

Closing my eyes, I magically scanned the area around me. It didn't take long for me to find Sarah's ghost. She waited on the far side of the courtyard, a good distance from us. I opened my eyes and she appeared in her ghostly form, so I sent her a finger wave and she waved back.

The twins turned to see who was there. They drew their brows together, and I guessed they couldn't see her. "She's here," I whispered. "Do your illusion spell. I want to get this done before the media gets here."

"Good point," the twins said at the same time. Then the barrier went up, pushing me into motion.

I opened the amber-colored jar and poured the potion on top of the bones, making sure that each one was covered. Then I pulled the parchment with the spell on it out of my pocket and began to chant. Light blue swirls of magic drifted up from the bones as Sarah's spirit drifted closer until she hovered over her body.

She met my stare and smiled. "Thank you." Then, rather anticlimactically, she was gone.

Happiness and peacefulness seeped into my heart, telling me little Sarah was finally at rest. Standing, I wiped a tear from my cheek and said, "It's done." It hadn't been flashy or eventful, but I'd helped a soul find peace. That meant the world to me.

Drew circled my shoulders and pulled me closer. I melted into him, letting his love for me flow from the bond. He was concerned as he always was when I used magic. Before releasing me, he kissed my forehead.

Just then my phone chimed indicating a text coming in. It was from Hailey. **Going to Milan at 3.30pm eastern tomorrow the 14th. Come if you can, bring anyone who will help. Tell Luci to meet at the courtyard outside the palace. He knows the place.**

I showed the text to Drew, not wanting to alert the twins about what we had planned. This didn't involve the coven, and I wanted to keep them out of it and safe.

I sent Olivia a quick text after telling Hailey we'd be there. **Can you call your uncle to see if help can be here tomorrow?**

She replied with: **Yes, I'll do that now. At least, I'll try.**

Hopefully, the fae would show in time. But either way, we had to go while we had the advantage.

15
AVA

"IT'S ALMOST TIME," Owen said. He couldn't seem to stop pacing and that was driving me crazy.

With a sigh, I lumbered off of the sofa, feeling like the weight of the world rested on my shoulders. It didn't. Not the whole world. Just mine. "I know."

I'd hoped the fae would show, but it wasn't looking good.

"The fae aren't coming," Olivia said, disappointment heavy in her tone. "I'm so sorry. I really thought Uncle Mitah would come through."

I stopped in front of my friend, who was leaning against the cold fireplace mantel. "It's not your fault. Without you, we wouldn't have stood a chance of even *asking* the fae king for help."

She waved me off and started pacing behind Owen.

"Are we ready?" A tingle of nervousness shot through my gut, though I couldn't pinpoint why. I was the most powerful necromancer in the world. If I wanted, I could go to Milan and take on all those vampires all by myself.

Instead of going alone, though, we'd have every ally we could come up with, plus all of Jax's friends and supporters. *If* there was to be a bloodbath, it wouldn't be on our side.

"We are here."

I jumped and whirled in shock. Three fae stood in my foyer. "Thanks for warning me, Winston."

He groaned in response, and the front fae, who I recognized as one of Olivia's aunts, either Octavia or Evie, I couldn't remember, spoke with a bit of a laugh in her tone. "The magic from the chasm doesn't work on us."

Well, that was new information. Winston had no defenses against fae? Was that why he was so testy with Olivia? "He certainly can fight against Olivia," I said, remembering how he'd done her when she tried to set up a birthday party without me here.

Octavia-Evia inclined her head. "She is not pure fae."

"So, you're coming with us to Milan, Aunt Octavia?" Olivia asked excitedly as Phira strode forward. Now I knew which sister it was. I didn't recognize the two men behind her at all.

"Sister," Phira said gravely. "These are troubling times."

"They are always troubling times," Octavia said. "But I have great faith in the abilities of our warriors."

Phira added, "And you."

There was real amusement in her tone this time as Octavia replied, "Of course. I am the best warrior in our army."

Well, she wasn't modest, that was for sure. But then, it could've been pointed out that I wasn't very modest, either. I was the strongest necromancer in like a thousand years or some such. And I knew it. Not because everyone kept telling me I was either. I felt it, and my powers were growing.

"We thank you." Drew stepped forward and inclined his head in a show of respect.

Octavia assessed him coolly. "Ah, the reformed hunter. You will be an asset in the fight."

He'd better keep his butt safe in the fight was what he'd better do.

Stop it.

Oops. He'd heard that particular thought. I must've felt the need to keep him safe so strongly it crept through our bond.

I can't help it. You can't be hurt in all this.

We'll both come home, you'll see.

Hmph. Like he had a magic ball to see the future.

Maybe I do. You don't know.

Octavia had said something to me, and thanks to Drew in my head I hadn't heard it. "I'm sorry?"

"I said, is this everyone?"

I looked around the room and my heart squeezed. Everyone I loved stood in my living room and foyer, pretty much. "Not all here are going, but yes, this is everyone." Oh, wait. It wasn't. I signaled Owen, who was going to go try to rouse Wade. We weren't sure if we'd be able to.

Turning my wrist over, I saw the time. Three-twenty-five. "Five-minute warning," I said as I pulled out my phone and fired off a text to Hailey and Jax.

The fae showed up. We're ready.

The reply came quickly, from Hailey. **Yay! Four minutes, then meet us there.**

"Let's gather," Drew said. We had moved the living room furniture against the walls and put the coffee table in the kitchen for the time being. There was a large space to gather in.

I closed my eyes and breathed deeply to control my nerves, but Olivia's voice made me jerk my gaze to her. "Oh, hell, no," she said. "You are not going."

Sam glared at her. "This isn't the time for this argument," he said through clenched teeth.

Um, I was with Olivia on this. Sam wasn't going.

"We talked about this," Olivia said angrily. Oh, yeah, she was hot. All I could do was nod from behind her. "You are human. I know you're highly trained, but guns and normal muscles don't work on vampires, Sam. You can't go."

My poor childhood friend, Sam. His face turned bright red as he backed away from the group, moving to stand in the foyer with the rest of the crew staying behind, which was only Olivia's kids and mine. Devan, Jess, and Wallie looked terrified. I hated leaving them like this, but at least they weren't going into this danger with us.

"Wallie?" I asked softly.

My son turned to look at me with an expression on his face that said he already knew what I was going to say. "No, Mom. These people have been trying to kill you. I'm not staying behind."

"Me, either," Michelle said. His girlfriend was fierce. I hoped they stuck it out for the long haul.

"Fine." I tried not to sound mad. I wasn't angry, just worried and tense. "But you stay *very* close to me."

Wallie nodded his head in acquiescence. "That I'll gladly agree to."

Olivia and Sam continued to argue, across the room so I couldn't really hear it. Plus, it was mostly in whispers. I checked my watch again. "One minute, guys. This is it."

Luci stepped forward. "If everyone will please touch someone else. We just all have to be connected."

At the last second, Owen burst out of the basement door, into the foyer beside the kitchen door. "I can't get Wade awake."

"That's okay, he can keep an eye on the kids when he wakes up," I said. "Just grab hold of someone."

I looked around at my friends and loved ones, all the people who'd come together to support me and help me handle a true threat. As we disappeared from my living room, tears filled my eyes. Whatever happened in Milan, I had to keep them safe.

1 6

AVA

"Damn it, Sam," Olivia exclaimed. Her voice echoed across a great stone chamber. I looked around and discovered we were standing beside what looked like a subway track. In front of us, though, the stone entrance of the underground vampire palace seemed to melt into the walls of the subway. The style of the door and the building that could be seen this far underground was kind of gothic. Black veins of what looked like onyx were etched through the gray stone.

Luci rushed forward and shushed her. "I know we're not in the palace proper, but I encourage you not to shriek, daughter."

She waved her hands at her husband, who must've grabbed hold of someone at the last second. "He came!"

"Sam," I said softly. "I don't think we have time for Luci to take you back. Just stick very close to me, okay?"

He walked over, glaring at Olivia over his shoulder as he came. "Fine. I'll stay close to you with Wallie."

The expression on his face said he didn't appreciate being put at the kiddie table, but I was with Olivia on this one. I wanted to throttle him.

Olivia glared at us, but then her attention was taken by something behind us, near the ground. "Um, Ava?"

I whirled to find none other than Mr. Snoozerton and Lucy-Fur staring up at me. Lucy grinned her cheeky, kitty grin. "We want to help."

"Absolutely not," I said in my lowest, angriest voice. "The last thing I need to worry about is two freaking felines running around. Luci, can you?"

Luci snorted, then put one hand over his mouth to curb the sound of his laughter as he waved one hand. The cats disappeared, thankfully.

"Those two, I swear." I started to ask if he could wave Sam away too but a slight whooshing sound drew my attention away from the freaking felines and my stubborn human BFF.

On the other side of the chamber, luckily not in the *exact* spot we were standing, a whole bunch of people appeared. My heart leaped and I started to go on the defensive. The fae certainly did. Long swords appeared in their hands, and they moved into a defensive posture.

"No," I said quietly, rushing forward. "They're our allies." I recognized Hailey and Jax.

The fae stepped back, their swords disappearing somewhere as I hurried forward to greet Jax, Hailey, and the dozens of people they'd brought with them. A large, handsome vampire I'd seen before had another male vamp in his arms. He was sleeping, but he woke as we hurried forward. Probably a young one who couldn't rouse until we got here, in the darkness. I could've had someone carry Wade, but I was just happy he wasn't here.

"Wow," I said as I pulled Hailey into a hug. "You weren't kidding about allies, but hopefully we won't need all this fuss."

Jax shook Drew's hand and gave me a wry smile. "You don't know this council as we do."

Hopefully, he was underestimating my power, too. I'd love to go in there and prove him wrong. And make all the vampires in the world understand that I wasn't someone to be trifled with at the same time. That would be *awesome*.

Jax took the lead, snapping his finger so everyone gave him their attention. "We are not surprising anyone today. There is no possible way they don't know we're here. We must proceed carefully and cautiously. They may react diplomatically, but more likely there will be violence. Support one another."

Octavia stepped forward. "This mission is to kill the council, yes?"

"No," Jax exclaimed and waved his hands. "No. Two members of the council are corrupt. We are here to persuade them to step down. We will only move to violence if they force our hands."

With a small bow of her head, Octavia stepped back. "As you wish."

"The chances of them not turning to violence are slim," I said, then reminded everyone that the council had sent assassins after me on a few occasions.

Jax nodded. "Agreed. That's why we need you to hang back with me and Hailey. It's imperative we make it to the council chambers, and we will likely face fights along the way."

"Why don't we just portal straight in?" Olivia asked.

Luci answered for her. "We can't. I've tried."

The witch friend of Hailey's stepped forward. Kendra said, "I also have tried, and my method of portaling is different from yours."

Luci's face lit up. "Kendra! I didn't see you before." He clasped his hands together and looked around at the crowd. "Yay, all my friends are here."

"This isn't a party, Dad," Olivia said as she tugged on the back of his shirt. "Calm down."

Luci whirled around and stared at her. "Olivia," he said in a hushed voice. The whole room quieted to listen to the exchange as if we weren't standing outside the vampire palace about to pull off a coup. "You called me Dad."

Shrugging and looking around the room, Olivia stepped closer. "Can we talk about this later?" she whispered.

Luci cleared his throat and turned back toward Jax and me. "Of course. Shall we?"

A man, a vampire, walked forward from the crowd. "Come on," he said. "Meredith and I will see you to the chambers safely."

I didn't know who he was, nor all the vampires who followed him. One of the women wore a business suit—an expensive one, by the looks of it—and heels. I leaned in to Hailey. "I really want to see her fight in those Louboutin's."

Hailey snorted and the woman froze. She looked over her shoulder at me. "It's a sight to behold, my dear."

I sent her a genuinely amused smile and saluted. "I'll look forward to it." There was no animosity between us. Just camaraderie. That was nice.

The fae went next, all but Phira. Octavia and her male shadows strode up the stairs after the dozens of vampires.

Wallie started forward, but I grabbed his arm. "You wait." Turning toward Sam, I glared at him. "I know this is going to be a big argument between you and Olivia when you get home, so I'll only say this. Stay in the back. If something happens to you, I won't hesitate to reanimate you as a ghoul." I leaned in and poked him in the chest. "Death is not an option for you, Samuel Wallace Thompson."

Wallie was named after him, of course. Have I ever mentioned that? No? Sorry. But yeah, Wallie was named after Sam and his dad–Wallace Clayton Harper.

Sam's face softened and he grabbed my hand, the one which had just been poking him. "I'll be right by your side so you can protect me. As usual."

Olivia snorted. "Oh, but me you're mad at?"

That wasn't going to be fun, the argument those two were going to have. They'd figure it out, though. If anyone was meant for the other, it was them. That was a realization I'd come to over the last year, watching the two of them together.

I grabbed Drew's hand in time to see Hailey grab the arm of a handsome vampire with dewy skin and perfectly coiffed blonde hair. I hadn't met him, but presumably, he was her brother, Luke. Who else would she be so protective over?

"Stay with me," she hissed at the handsome man. I stifled a giggle. It was either a brother or son, and he looked too old to be her kid.

We moved into a natural progression as we followed the rest of Jax's crew through the doors. For a moment, Hailey's friend Kendra was close to me. I startled, looking at her in shock. I could feel her magic, ready and waiting on her to use it, just under the surface. I sidled close to her as we neared the stairs. "What kind of witch are you again?" I asked.

She smiled at me and said, "I actually only found out recently. I was gifted my powers at birth by a goddess, though I don't know which."

A goddess. Kendra's power exactly matched the power I'd felt off of the bones of Sarah, the little girl buried at the B&B. No wonder she'd felt familiar. I just hadn't connected the two of them. "I'd love to pick your brain about that sometime," I said. Kendra hurried forward as a tall, black female vampire motioned for her. I'd seen the woman before at Jax's but hadn't been introduced.

Wallie went right in front of me, with his grandparents, Aunt Winnie, and Alfred in front of him.

"This is it," I said, slipping my hand into Drew's. "It's time to show them what we're made of."

Drew pressed a kiss to my forehead. "What you're made of."

Geez, I loved that man.

17

AVA

By the time I made it through the doors, the entirety of our party had spread out in the foyer of this massive underground palace.

And it was quiet as a tomb inside. It felt incredibly ominous. The floors in here were some sort of marble that was no doubt incredibly expensive. My footsteps echoed on the floors, something all of the vampires managed not to do, even the gorgeous one toward the front of the crowd. The one in the heels. How'd she walk on marble floors without heel clacks? It was unnatural.

Nobody spoke, but Jax, Drew, and the Louboutin woman made some hand signals at one another. *What was that?* I asked Drew in our special way.

It's a military thing. I didn't know they knew it until just now.

And I hadn't known Drew knew. He surprised me all the time.

The crowd moved forward, up a short set of stairs. I couldn't see where they went next. There were too many of us following quietly through an empty space.

And it was totally empty, which bugged me. Where was our welcoming committee? Where were the vampires I'd have to control? This was wrong. Something wasn't right.

As I opened my mouth to express my concern, I was one of the last people to set foot on the staircase. Most of our group was going right down a hallway.

"Oomph," Ransom said as he bounced off what seemed to be an invisible wall. Then he gasped. "No." The sound of horror in his tone made my blood run cold. "Luke!" he yelled.

Pushing forward, I got beside him and looked down the hallway, but it was empty. Ransom began banging on... well, it was midair, but his fist was definitely hitting something solid.

"Stand back." It was another ward of some sort. I'd managed to weaken the one in Sweden. "Let me see."

I wasn't too panicked that I couldn't take a ward down. Wallie was right beside me, so I turned to tell him and Drew to hang back in case this ward did that rebound thing, but he wasn't beside me anymore.

Turning in a circle, my panic found me. "Wallie," I cried. "Where is he?"

"They were beside Phira," Sam said. "Still very close to you, but not close enough."

"Move," I thundered. "Let me kill this ward."

I blasted it with a jolt of electricity, then looked back at Drew. "Did that hurt?"

He shook his head and grinned. "No rebounding. Kill it."

With a probably maniacal grin, I opened my powers and let them fly, waiting for the same build-up I'd felt in Marstrand.

It didn't come. What the heck?

As electricity flowed from my fingertips toward the ward, which was lighting up in spectacular colors, I tried to force it to build, but it wouldn't. It was still a steady, strong flow. Definitely would electrocute any human, for sure.

But it wouldn't increase. "Something is wrong."

"Maybe they've dampened you somehow," Hailey suggested. "Let me try something."

I stopped the flow of power, upset at feeling weak for the first time since I'd embraced my powers, and looked around while Hailey pulled out a potion from her bag. It hit the invisible wall, but nothing happened except it looked like slime sliding down air.

"Darn," Hailey said. "That one was labeled *wall melter*."

Ninety percent of our allies and friends were gone. Drew was still with me, as well as Sam and Olivia. Owen stood off to the side with Jax and Hailey. The beautiful blonde was gone, and the big guy, Ransom, was distraught.

Everyone else was gone. My Mom and Dad and Aunt Winnie. Luci, Phira, Hailey's friend Kendra. Gone. Where did they go, though? I could see down the hallway behind the ward and it was just empty. It was like they just vanished.

A vampire approached from behind, fast. As soon as I sensed him, I turned as fast as I could, whipping out my power and yelling, "Stop!"

But I was a split second too late. Sam had been behind me, safe. Not safe. Not safe at all.

I'd stopped the vamp, but not before he'd reached out a clawed hand and ripped a huge gash in Sam's throat. No!

Huge. Like, most of his throat was just gone. I rushed forward as Sam slowly crumpled to the ground, making gurgling sounds and clutching his throat as it poured blood. "I'll heal you," I said desperately. Olivia hadn't even registered what was happening in front of her, I didn't think.

"Jax," I cried. "Deal with the vampire."

I saw him nod his head out of the corner of my eyes, and the big vampire, Ransom, jumped on the attacker and the next thing I knew, his head was gone. But that barely registered as I dropped to my knees beside my best friend. "Sam." I tried not to sob as Olivia fell beside me, too shocked to even speak. "Hold on, Sam."

I put my hands on his chest and focused all of my energy on my best friend. "Oh my God," I whispered as I grabbed my healing magic and shoved it into Sam.

The corners of his neck began to knit together but the blood kept gushing. He'd already dropped into unconsciousness. But after the corners healed, it stopped. "No," I said through sobs. "No!"

With everything I had, I pushed and pushed my magic, but it just wouldn't budge. "How is this happening?"

"I can change him," Jax said. "His life force is still there, but it's fading."

Olivia and I looked at one another, but we were at a loss. "Would he rather be a vampire or a ghoul?" she asked.

I had no idea. We'd never talked about it. I'd told him I'd animate him if he died, but I never really expected him to get injured like this, nor could I ever have predicted my power would be dampened here.

The helplessness rushing through me was one of the worst things I'd ever felt, and that included all the grief at losing all the people who'd died in my life.

Switching gears, I grabbed my necromancer magic and animated Sam before it was too late.

"What's going on?" he asked groggily.

"Sam, I can't heal you." I grabbed his face and forced him to focus on me. "You must decide now. Would you rather be a ghoul, like Alfred and Zoey, or a vampire?"

He blinked hazily and sucked in a breath that made the gash in his throat, still pouring blood, gurgle harder. "If I were a ghoul, could you put me in a real body like your mom?"

Shaking my head and trying not to sob, I held him tighter. No doubt Olivia wanted to talk to him, but I had to know and know now before he died. "No, that only works with witches."

"Vampire then," he whispered, and my magic ran out. He sighed and closed his eyes, slipping into unconsciousness again.

Jax rushed forward as Olivia scream-sobbed, throwing herself across Sam's blood-stained torso. "The blood is slowing," he said. "Let me work."

I pulled Olivia back. "He's going to save him, Liv. He'll be the same man, don't worry."

"I know," she said through her sobs. "I just can't live without him."

My stomach churned as Jax drank blood from Sam's gaping wounds. Then he used his teeth to gash open his wrists and let the blood drip directly onto Sam's injuries.

And they began to heal. "Oh," Olivia said. "It's working."

My tunnel vision began to clear, getting better and better as Sam's throat slowly closed up with every drip of Jax's blood. Jax drank more from the remainder of the wounds before they closed, then kept dripping blood onto Sam's neck.

Soon, the wounds were gone. Sam looked pale as a ghost, literally, but he was breathing. "Now what?" I asked.

"Take him home. Keep him safe. He'll sleep for three days, but watch over him," Jax said. "I'll be in touch after this is all over."

Olivia sat on the ground in the puddle of blood and pulled Sam into her lap. She looked at me, her face full of hope. "Be safe," she whispered before disappearing.

"You, too," I said to the empty air.

Jumping to my feet, I wiped the blood off of my hands on my jeans as best I could. My knees were soaked with it, but my attention was quickly taken by the ward around us. Several vampires surrounded the ward. "Who did this?" There was a dome over us made from a gorgeous blue fire.

"Kendra," Hailey said. "But once we break it, I don't have another one. It was a potion and she said it was really hard to make." She indicated her purse. "I have a few more, but they do different things."

"Pity," I muttered.

Owen stepped forward. "Before you break it... Ava, you animated Sam."

I raised my eyebrows at him. "Yeah?"

He shook his head and stared at me like I'd grown two more ears. "Ava. You animated Sam before he died."

I blinked at him and processed his words. "Well, okay. That's not supposed to be possible."

How had I done that? Especially amid my powers being weakened. Was this a new power? Could I do more when my powers were at their normal level? I'd never tried to use my death magic on someone not dead! Holy crap.

"Now what?" Drew asked. "I count a dozen vampires."

They were all standing outside the ward, not trying to break through. Just waiting.

"Let me try," I said. I summoned my necromancer magic and looked at the waiting blood-suckers. "Leave," I commanded.

Two of them turned and walked away. They didn't come back, so I tried again. This time only one went. The third time I tried, nobody left.

Owen took my hand. "Here," he whispered. "Use me."

His magic rushed into me, feeling like a warm breeze on a chilly day. I commanded the last of the vampires to leave, and three more left.

Three. With Owen's power, I'd commanded three. With mine, only two, then one more. Not three at once.

Six remained. What the heck was going on with my magic?

"We will not harm you," one of the vampires said in a loud voice. "We are here to escort you to the council chambers."

Ransom rushed forward. "Where is my mate?" he roared. "Where is Luke?"

The vampire smiled cheekily. "They have been transported far away. They're safe, but who knows how long it will take them to find their way home?"

What the vampires didn't know was that Kendra had disappeared with the crowd. She could create portals, so hopefully, they'd return to us. Sooner rather than later.

"It's about to die," Hailey said, but I'd realized it. The color on the ward was fading.

I tried my darndest to command the six vampires to freeze, but they strode forward.

"Do we fight?" I asked.

Jax shook his head. "Not yet. We need to get to the council. It all depends on who is with us and who is against us. If Tobias sides with us, we may not have to spill any more blood at all."

I didn't know who Tobias was, but not spilling any more blood was a darn good idea to me.

18

AVA

WE FOLLOWED THE VAMPIRES, half of them at least. The other half brought up our rear, which made my skin crawl, but Jax was the one who knew the way of things here, and I trusted him as much as anyone could trust their former vampire neighbor.

It took a few minutes to make our way to the chambers. I took advantage of the delay to speak to Drew. *I love you.* If we were going to our deaths, with my powers zonked, I wanted him to know that.

I love you more. We'll get through this.

Suddenly, I was glad most of our family had been sent away. If they didn't make it back that would be fine. At least they'd be safe. As would Olivia and Sam.

We walked into another hallway. At the end were two massive doors, flanked by vampires on either side. We filed toward the doors, and two of the waiting vampires opened the doors. Jax and I went in first, followed by Drew and Hailey. We formed up that way without a second thought from any of us. Jax and I had the most to deal with this council, and hopefully, my powers would cooperate, and I'd be able to handle this quickly and easily.

Owen came behind with Ransom. And that was all we had, us six against five of the most powerful, oldest vampires in the world. They stood as we approached. Jax held out his hand, speaking politely as if this were just a fun walk in the park rather than about to be the fight of our lives. Vampire politics is so weird.

The sound of the door shutting behind us made me turn to see we were alone. The other vampires hadn't come in.

The council must've thought a lot of themselves.

"Ava," Jax said formally. "May I present the elders. Soran." The man in the middle, the one I'd seen before, glared at me. Black hair swept against his shoulders as he stared at us with dark, beady eyes over sharp cheekbones.

He also looked surprised to see me. "What are you doing here?"

My lips curved into a slow smile. "Surprise."

He snarled, but Jax continued to introduce the council, dismissing Soran altogether.

"Gretchen." This one was the other that we knew was treacherous. She'd been a part of the attempts on my life. She didn't nod so much as her expression went from disgusted to absolutely disgusted. Her red hair and green eyes looked more like Zeke, who was Soran's heir.

Oh, I bet there was a story there.

"Amaya," Jax said, and this woman smiled. Not pleasantly, not really. But then, she didn't look like she smiled often. She was supposedly one of our allies. I nodded at her, taking in her striking brown eyes. They looked like they had red in them. Not creepy at all for a vampire.

"Tobias." Tobias was our wildcard. If he sided with us, we were in for a much easier time. I couldn't get a read on him at all as he stood there with his arms crossed and a blank expression on his face.

"And my sire, Dominic."

Dominic, in contrast with the other vampires, smiled broadly. "Good to see you, Jax."

"I wish I could say the same," Jax replied. "We are here to charge Gretchen and Soran with treason."

"As well as imprisoning or killing necromancers," I added. "Including my father."

Soran glared at me. "If any necromancers were imprisoned, it was at the behest of this council."

I smiled and put my hand in my pocket. Soran didn't miss the move. "You never imprisoned a necromancer without the approval of this council?" I asked as I palmed the truth stone in my pocket.

Oh, yeah. I'd remembered that little bad boy.

"I did," he said, then his eyes widened in horror.

"Please explain," I said, stepping forward. "Tell us how you've been plotting to take over the council."

"This council is weak," Soran spat. His expression hardened and he glared at me, catching on that I had something to do with his newfound honesty.

His peers turned and stared at him in shock. "What?" Amaya asked, but I could tell she wasn't as shocked as she pretended to be. "What are you talking about?"

"I'm talking about taking over," he yelled. Oh, yeah, he was off the deep end. Gretchen stayed quiet, but she wasn't getting out of this. "You fools cannot expect to run an entire vampire empire with your soft logic and bleeding hearts."

"Soran," Tobias said. "This is a private matter. Why are you saying these things?"

I let go of the truth stone, but it was working. "I cast a spell," I said, not bound to be totally truthful, though everyone else in the room would be compelled to tell the truth for any question I asked. "You all must speak the truth."

Looking at Gretchen, I smiled. "Where do you stand?"

She tossed her red hair. "With Soran. Always."

Tobias's jaw dropped. "I had no idea." Which had to be true.

"Amaya?" I asked. "Do you stand with us?"

She walked around the table to take her place beside Jax. "I do. Gretchen and Soran have been unchecked for too long."

Scraping his chair back further, Dominic joined us as well. "Of course, I stand with Jax." He smiled around his progeny at me. "And Ava."

As a group, everyone looked at Tobias, even Gretchen, and Soran. "And you?" I asked. "Where do you stand?"

"I stand with the council," Tobias said. "I don't condone Soran working to undermine this body of government, but this should be dealt with internally. Not by an upstart and necromancer." He waved at the people behind us. "Nor their little rabble of support."

So, he wouldn't help us.

"Gretchen and Soran," I said in a firm tone, shoving as much of my necromancer power as I could into my words. "I command you to stand down."

A slow, evil smile spread across Soran's face. "Or what, little necromancer? I can feel your power, and it's not that impressive. Perhaps I should've dealt with you a long time ago myself. It shouldn't be difficult."

Sit, I thought, focusing on him so he had to do as I said.

He sat. Thank goodness.

But that seemed to set something off. "Kill her," Soran screamed. He did *not* like me commanding him. Whoops.

Gretchen and Tobias vaulted across the table, moving fast, as vampires do. I split my attention between them, trying to force them to stop, which was no easy task. I succeeded in getting Gretchen immobile, but as I did, Soran was then able to move. I was starting to think that there was more going on than a dampening spell. My magic just hadn't shown up.

Sensing that I was magically struggling, Drew stepped in front of me, and someone put their hand on my shoulder. Owen's magic flowed into me, which helped, but not tremendously.

If I could just get Gretchen and Soran to stop fighting! Every time I split my focus, the other was able to break free. I felt like a brand new witch trying her powers for the first time.

The doors burst open behind us, and vampires flowed into the room. All of the enforcers who'd been waiting outside the council chambers. I hadn't realized there were that many of them before.

We were screwed.

"You've got this," Drew whispered, then he was gone from my side. Our bond threatened to distract me from my part of the fight, but I had to tuck it into the corner of my mind and trust that Drew could take care of himself.

Owen and I soon found ourselves fighting Tobias, Gretchen, and Soran on our own. I didn't know where everyone else had gotten off to, but from the sounds behind me, it was the battle for their lives.

I'd managed to split my magic, bolstered by Owen's, so that Tobias, Gretchen, and Soran were moving slowly. No matter how hard I tried, I couldn't draw enough magic to completely stop them, but at least we could keep them from advancing to the point of touching us. We backed away, looking over our shoulders to make sure we didn't run into the fight.

As I looked back, I watched Drew fighting a large female vampire, his fists and feet flying nearly as quickly as hers. Holy crap. He'd been holding back on us. I'd never witnessed a hunter fight before. Then again Drew was the only one I'd met.

In our attempt to avoid the three vamps, we'd moved perilously close to the fighting.

"Ava!" Owen yelled. Snapping my gaze forward, I lurched to the side in time to avoid a slow-for-a-vampire slash of Soran's claws. "Ha!" I said, glaring at him and backing away again.

A blast from somewhere behind me stole my attention away from the fight. I whirled around to see Hailey smirking as she watched a vampire consumed by flames. How in the world did she do that? As soon as the question formed in my mind, I saw Hailey reach into her bag of potions and pull out another magical bomb. She threw it at another vamp, and he started melting.

Hailey met my gaze and said, "I think that was supposed to be saved to melt a wall in case we needed to escape. Oops."

Before I had the chance to reply to her comment, pain cut across my neck. I ducked and twisted while thrusting a leg out, making contact with Gretchen's knees. The kick knocked her off balance.

"Hailey," Jax yelled seconds later. I didn't turn and look this time since the trio in front of me and Owen were advancing on us again and it took all I had to keep them from reaching as we did circles on the opposite side of the room from the fighting. A body hit the ground, making a thud and I could only pray it was one of theirs, not ours.

Things were bad. Really bad. The blood on my neck only served to excite the vampires in front of me. They'd drawn first. They knew we couldn't keep this up for much longer.

"Give up," Soran said in a low, threatening voice. "Give up now and your deaths will be swift and relatively painless. We can even make you drift off to a serene sleep."

"Never," I snarled.

"We're here!"

Phira's voice came to me like sunshine breaking through a cloud. We were saved.

19
AVA

I RUSHED BACK, away from the part of the council who wanted my throat lying on the floor like Sam's earlier and looked over to see the rest of our party streaming in through the council doors.

"Necromancers," my dad yelled. "To me!"

I couldn't help a little giggle from bubbling up my throat as my father rushed forward with what was presumably the group of previously-imprisoned necromancers.

"Lend my daughter your power," he yelled over the din of the fighting vampires, fae, and witches.

Hands slapped me on the back, touching and gripping anywhere they could reach, and power flowed into me, a river of cleansing water, eager to do my bidding. It fused with my own and built like a pressure cooker. When I released it, the vampires would not know what hit them.

And just in freaking time, too! Soran was nearly on top of me. He lunged forward, but it was too late. He'd lost. I raised one finger. "Stop," I said in a low, severe voice.

Every vampire in the room froze. The good and bad. Even Jax and Hailey stared at me askance, frozen in their battle with other vamps.

"Stop touching one another. Let's keep our hands to ourselves for a moment." I stepped back and watched happily as all of the vampires righted themselves. "Hands by your sides."

If Gretchen could've killed me with the glare coming from her eyes, she absolutely would've.

"Ava," Dad whispered. "You've also frozen Alfred."

I looked around to find Alfred giving me a little half-grin, which looked silly plastered to his face like that. It took me a second, but I was able to discern Alfred from the rest of the dead things in the room and release him. He strode forward and handed me the sword. "It will only work for you."

Oh. He was right. That meant I had to do the dirty work this time. I certainly didn't relish the thought.

I took a moment and freed Jax and Hailey as well. The rest of the vampires would have to wait.

"Ava." Luci stepped forward, still holding Phira's hand. I doubted he'd be letting go of her anytime soon. "I can take care of them for you." He put a gentle hand on my shoulder. "You don't have to do this."

But I did. At this moment, I knew, beyond reason, that this was the reason the sword had come to me. These vampires were the worst of the worst. Living—sort of. Breathing—kind of. Evil—definitely. I was meant to do this myself. "Thank you," I said, sending Luci a sincere smile. "I can't tell you how I appreciate the offer, but this is for me to do."

In a way, it was like the moment of my destiny I needed to fulfill.

Next, Jax stepped forward. "I'm happy to dispatch them myself as well. I understand if you feel the need, as they've tried to kill you many times. But I'm here if you need it."

Also giving him a genuine grin, I shook my head. "Thank you. But the magic in the blade will only work with me."

I reached into my pocket and rubbed the truth stone, activating it. "Soran, whatever-your-last-name-is, do you deny hiring multiple people and creatures to attempt to kill me?"

"No. And I'd do it again and again until you're dead," he spat.

The smile I gave him wasn't so genuine. I turned to Gretchen while the rest of the frozen vampires watched on. "And you? Do you deny attempting to have me killed?"

A slow, rather terrifying smile spread across her face. "Like Soran, I'd do it over and over."

"Then I condemn you to the sword," I whispered.

"It won't take much," Alfred said. "Just a cut."

Focusing on both vampires, I mentally prodded them to hold out their hands.

"Wait," Jax said. I pulled up the sword just before I'd been about to slice it against both hands at once.

"What?" I turned to him, not eager to delay this thing.

"We need their testimony first," he said. "If I ask questions, will the truth stone work?"

I nodded. "It should, yeah."

We split apart then, and, necromancer entourage in tow, I stood near enough that Jax could question them on one side of the room while I checked on my people. Now that I had a good grip on their powers, they didn't have to touch me.

"All of you, good and evil, go stand quietly over there and listen to your elders explain how evil you let them get without doing anything about it." I waved the vampires to one side of the room. I didn't need to know all the details of their vampire business. I was exhausted by it at this point.

"What happened?" I asked Luci. "How did we fare in this fight?"

He sighed. "Some of the vampires died in the desert."

"So, it's true," Drew said. "You went to the Sahara?" He was holding his arm a little funny, so I reached over and tried to trickle a bit of healing magic, but none would come. Like... none at all. What the heck was going on? Dampening magic shouldn't completely block parts of my power.

Phira nodded. "The little witch, Kendra, was wonderful, but she couldn't move fast enough to create a portal to bring us back."

I looked over at Luci. "Why couldn't you do it?"

He shrugged. "Haven't the foggiest. I tried and tried, but my magic wouldn't work. It must've been something to do with the ward that transported us to the desert. Your mom and aunt couldn't either. Kendra's wasn't working either. She drew a portal and tried it, but nothing."

"How'd you get back then?" I asked. "You certainly didn't walk."

"It wore off, we presume," Luci said. "We probably weren't that far behind you, but Meredith insisted we go find her mate."

I looked over at the vampire delegation. "Where are they?"

Mom blanched. "We found him, all right. Dead. His heart had been ripped out. It looked like it was done days ago."

Almost like she knew we were talking about her, Meredith stormed into the room, slamming the doors open. I didn't try to stop her with my necro power. She was on a mission.

"I'm going to tear you limb from limb," she shrieked.

"Stop her," I yelled. "She can't kill them."

Jax and Hailey worked to calm Meredith down, and I focused on the vampires I knew were on our side, releasing them from the bond so they could help, then went back to finding out what happened. "So, you got here, found her mate, found the necromancers, obviously, and came *just* in time to save the day."

Dad grinned. "Yeah, we were a big white knight, weren't we?"

I couldn't stop myself from throwing my arms around his neck.

"Ava," Jax said quietly a few moments later. "We're ready."

My heart sank. This was my job, my duty. Fate, destiny, whatever I called it, I had to imprison these evil creatures. Stalking toward them, I realized they both still had their hands out, palm up, as I'd left them.

A giggle almost escaped me at how ridiculous they looked, but I bit it back. This wasn't the time to be funny. I was consigning two souls to what was essentially a hell dimension. No time for giggles.

"Now, again, Soran and Gretchen, you are being sentenced to spend eternity in, well, basically in Hell." I didn't give myself time to think about what that meant for them or the other souls in the sword. I just sliced.

And poof. Quietly, without fuss or pomp or circumstance or any other frivolity, the two evilest souls I'd ever met disappeared.

The rest of the day passed quickly, thankfully. The necromancers helped me long enough to question every vampire in the room. Nobody got out of it. We found out a few embarrassing secrets—Dominic had a *massive* crush on Amaya. He let that one slip but seeing the look on Amaya's face was priceless. It was like she was looking at him for the first time.

Tobias was the biggest surprise. He'd supported Gretchen and Soran, sure, but he'd *said* it was only because the council should've handled its own problems.

Turned out he was behind some massive plot to take over the *whole freaking world*, which included using a witch to turn day into night so vampires could enslave the human masses.

"Talk about a silver-freaking-lining. We saved the world tonight," Kendra said. "We should be getting medals."

Jax snorted. "That'll never happen."

The rest of the vampires were sorted into bad, not-so-bad, and good groups. Jax assured me they'd be dealt with, and we helped him get the bad vampires into cells, then finally we could go home.

Luci took most of our group home to watch over Sam and brought back Olivia. Olivia, Luci, and Kendra worked to get all the necromancers home. Drew kept trying to get me to come home and let them do that work, but I couldn't leave until each and every one of them was home.

Finally, the last one left, and I took Olivia's hand. "Let's go home," I whispered.

20

AVA

I stood in the chasm cave, glaring at the sword lying on the flat stone table my dad and Alfred had built for rituals. I'd tried every destruction spell I could think of to destroy the sword, but nothing had worked. I'd tried to melt it down with my electrical powers with several failed attempts. Not even my death magic seemed to penetrate the sword's defensive shield. Maybe if I could've gotten my powers to work, I could've done it, but they were still totally wonky.

It hadn't been a dampening spell. Something was *wrong* with me.

The longer I stood in the cave with the sword, the more the voices of the souls called to me. The shields that I'd created to block the voices were wavering. It was difficult to resist the thought of helping the poor souls in the sword.

I didn't have to tell the others, because they'd seen the change during the battle. My family was concerned about what that meant, even though no one had offered any suggestions on what it could mean. Were my powers possibly changing again? Would I gain a new ability? I hoped not. I didn't want to be more powerful. At this point, I just wanted to learn all of my current abilities, including that I could potentially animate someone *almost* dead.

Shaking the worrisome thoughts out of my mind, I focused on the sword. There had to be a way to destroy it. But how?

The large crystal, which held an incredible amount of power and linked the ley lines together, flashed. I turned and watched it, not sure if it was trying to tell me something or just a coincidence. I'd already tried to use the chasm a few times to try to destroy the sword, but it hadn't worked.

Help us. Their begging was heart-wrenching.

That voice was the clearest I'd ever heard come from the blade. There were innocents trapped in there and they wanted me to free them. I leaned closer to the sword, trying to figure out if I could free the innocents without letting the evil ones out.

I reached out to grab the hilt when Luci materialized beside me. "Oh, no you don't," he said, snatching the sword off the table. I didn't even have time to react as he twisted and slammed the blade straight into the chasm.

Magic exploded outward, throwing both of us out of the cave and onto the sand. That was a long way for magic to pick us up and move us. Holy crow. Had the chasm done that to keep us safe? What in the world?

My skin tingled with power from the blast. I stood and brushed the sand off of my clothes while scowling at Luci. "What did you do that for?"

Holding up a finger, he cocked his head and breathed slowly, as if trying to sense something or maybe smell something. "Huh," he murmured. "The innocent souls are now at peace. They moved on." Then he turned to me with a wicked gleam in his dark depths.

"The rest are mine," he said, throwing his head back and doing his best villain laugh.

I shoved his shoulder. "Stop being so creepy."

He laughed sincerely this time and threw an arm around my shoulders. "Come on, let's go tell the others that the sword is no more."

When we walked into the house, everyone was gathered in the living room. All eyes were on me as I took a seat beside Drew. "The sword has been destroyed," I told them about how Luci had just driven it into the chasm. Also, how much lighter I felt now that it was gone. It'd been weighing me down in a way I hadn't recognized.

Luci pulled Phira into a hug. "My theory was that Ava wouldn't be able to destroy it anyway."

"I'm strong enough. I could've done it," I said, a little offended at his words.

He pursed his lips at me before saying, "I mean that the sword called to you and wouldn't let you destroy it."

Oh. That made a little sense. Or it could have been the fact that Luci was a god, and I was not.

"Why do you think I'm as powerful as I am? Well, before my magic decided to go wonky." I stared at Dad. "On your side. I know why on Mom's."

"My family line is very old and is one of the strongest necromancer lines," Dad answered as if that made perfect sense and explained everything. Which it didn't.

Then Alfred said, "Once every century or so there is a necromancer born to our line with great power. You are that necromancer, Ava. Being the last and only female witch in your mother's line adds to that power. It all adds up to a lot."

Wow. That was...crazy. I'd known about being the last female on my mom's side, of course, and that the combo of necromancer and witch had made me powerful. But the bit about the great power every century was news to me. "And you're just now telling me?"

Alfred shrugged. "I thought you knew."

Uh, no, I hadn't. Then a thought occurred to me, and I directed my next question to Mom. "Do you think that my powers are being weird because you and Winnie are alive again?" That could've explained it.

Mom shook her head. "No. We took new bodies to be alive again and our biological makeup is different and as a result, so is our magic."

In other words, their magic had already passed to me when they died. "So you just inserted yourselves into another witch's bloodline?"

"Yeah, basically," Winnie answered. "Or perhaps it's more correct that we created new bloodlines."

"Maybe my magic is evolving again." It was a thought that everyone was thinking, and I just spoke it out loud. Really, I was just shooting out ideas and possibilities.

"We'll have to move your wedding date to the first week in October. Since the B&B construction was delayed, we need to find a new location," Olivia said, changing the subject. She'd been unusually quiet since we got back from Milan. She had also been getting Sam settled into his new life as a vampire. I still couldn't believe he'd died on us.

Wade had been a huge help with Sam. I had a suspicion my uncle liked that he had another vampire around.

Alfred rushed off to finish dinner and the rest of us sat around chatting about the wedding and other random life choices.

Then Mom looked at me and said, "You know, come to think of it, my powers went wonky when I was pregnant with you, Ava."

The room got eerily quiet. Even Winston was silent, the house still and shocked. I looked up to see everyone's eyes on me. There was no way I was pregnant. I couldn't be, or could I?

No way.

A WEDDED MIDLIFE

to Katrina Hamlet

May your ghouls always mind you and may your cats have clean vocabularies.

1
AVA

"Negative."

Why was I sad? I wasn't sure, to be honest. I was *so* beyond my baby-making days. Then again, the thought of having a little bundle of joy and a little piece of Drew growing inside me wasn't such a bad thing.

I'd only had about an hour for the idea to fester. Once Larry and Zoey had gotten back from the closest drug store with the home pregnancy test, Drew and I had rushed to my bathroom. Then I'd peed on the stick.

Three minutes later. No baby.

Drew slipped his arm around my shoulders and pulled me close as we balanced on the edge of the tub and looked at the pregnancy test. "Have you had any other symptoms besides your powers being off kilter?"

Shaking my head against his shoulder, I sighed and breathed in his clean, citrusy scent. The new body wash I'd ordered smelled divine on him. "No. I don't know why I thought this would say positive.

It's the least likely option, really." I was on birth control to help regulate my crazy midlife hormones. *And* getting to the age where a pregnancy would be dangerous for both the baby and me. It wasn't ideal, me being knocked up.

Could someone tell my heart, please?

Lifting my mood wasn't going to be easy, but nothing had changed. "I still have to figure out why my powers still aren't working right. And try to fix it. If something happens to us, I'm not going to be much help."

"Listen." Drew took my hands and caught my gaze. "The only thing that's going to happen is we're going to get married and then leave for one heck of a spectacular honeymoon. Everything will be great."

How dare he? Pulling back, I glared at my soon-to-be husband. "After all we've been through, you're going to put something like that out into the universe?"

"What?" He had that look on his face like he thought I was crazy but was going to placate me. "Put what out there?"

"Now that you've said that everything is going to go well, something will go wrong, absolutely." I jumped up, then pulled him to his feet. "Turn around in a circle three times or spit over your fingers or something." There had to be a way to break the curse he'd just set on us. "Salt! I need salt."

Rushing out of the bathroom, I bustled down the stairs and ignored the startled gazes of pretty much everyone I knew and loved as I rushed toward the kitchen.

Was I acting a little bit insane?

Yeap. But what else was new? Insane was my life.

Was this behavior keeping me from crying about a baby I was never pregnant with?

Also yeap.

I grabbed the saltshaker and hurled salt over my shoulder to dispel whatever bad omen Drew had birthed into the world.

Ugh, birthed was a bad word choice.

"Ow!" Olivia squalled behind me. "What'd you do that for?"

Whirling around, I found my best friend dancing around the kitchen with her hands covering her eyes. "Oh, it burns."

Sam hurried from the room and returned with my bottle of contact solution a moment later. Of course, he knew I kept some in my office. He knew me so well, even though we hadn't been as close since I'd moved away from Shipton all those years ago. Even after moving back, I was now closer to Olivia than Sam.

It was weird how life worked sometimes.

We helped her rinse her eyes out, and then I had to explain my antics while everyone crowded in the doorway to watch. "Drew said something about everything between now and the wedding going smoothly. I was trying to compensate by doing every ward-off-evil thing I could think of."

"Ava." Olivia glared at me with blazing red eyes. "Forget Drew's faux pas. What did the *test* say?"

Oh. That. "It was negative."

Their shoulders slumped, sort of as one unit. It was a little bit comical. If I wasn't so disappointed still, I would've laughed at them. Everyone rushed forward, and soon I was enveloped in hugs from my mom, dad, aunt, and the best friends I could've ever asked for.

"Come on," Alfred said. "I've got a cup of tea ready." He guided me through the sea of bodies and to the kitchen table where everyone continued to fuss over me.

"I'm okay," I said after taking a swallow of tea to get Alfie off my back. "I'm a little disappointed, but honestly, it's nice that I won't have to get up at all hours of the night."

"You do that anyway," Zoey said. "There's always something going on."

"Haven't you ever heard of declaring your intentions?" Drew asked, finally joining the rest of us in the kitchen.

Larry nodded, his head ever-so-slightly wobbly, even now, with him fully fleshed out. It never did want to reconnect correctly. "I have. You speak out what you will to happen in your life, and it will manifest."

I tried to cover up my snort with another swig of tea, but it was hot, so I ended up gasping instead. "No, that's not how that works, my love. If you declare something like that, the universe does every-thing in its power to prove you wrong."

That set off an argument amongst my friends, each trying to explain why their side of the debate was more reasonable.

Olivia used the cacophony to start pushing people out of the kitchen. "Go," she urged. "Argue elsewhere."

Eventually, it was just us in the room. Sam and Drew had wandered out onto the back porch with Uncle Wade and Owen. Sam hadn't been a vampire long and being in the crowd was prob-ably a lot for him.

"I'm sorry." Olivia scooted her chair close and put her head on my shoulder. "I really wanted you to have another baby. I was gearing up to convince Sam we needed one, too, so we could be pregnant together."

Aw, that would've been fun, but... "With the way our lives have been going?"

Olivia snorted, and we both dissolved into giggles. "Can't you just see Luci babysitting?" she asked.

I looked over at her, and my giggles quieted. "Yes, actually. He probably would've *loved* it. Every minute of it."

Well, crap. Now I was sad again.

Distraction in the form of a firm rap on the door saved me from settling into melancholy. I stood to answer, but Alfred was closer. Except, before he got close enough, it opened on its own.

Winston must've known—and liked—whoever was on the other side of the door. He didn't welcome very many people with open doors.

An older woman, tall with short silver hair, glided through the door. Someone was on the porch behind her, but I couldn't see since the outside light wasn't on.

If Winston was being so helpful, he could've turned it on. The porch glared into light as if he'd heard me, illuminating a large man holding several suitcases. He was thinner but not overly thin. More lean muscles like he worked out. His hair was dark brown, and he looked super grumpy.

I opened my mouth to welcome this person and ask who they were, but Lucy-Fur appeared from somewhere in the living room, beating me to it. She stopped short; her wide blue eyes surprised against her pristine white fur. "Who the hell are you?"

Everyone dissolved into quiet giggles at her question, but I wanted to throttle the sassy feline. "Lucy!" I exclaimed. "Don't be rude."

If a cat could shrug, it sure looked like she did as she sort of lifted her shoulder into one. "What? I've never seen her in my life, and she's just waltzing into my house."

Hurrying forward, I glared at Mr. Snoozerton's girlfriend. "It's *my* house, and you hush." Looking at the older woman in my entryway,

I held out my hands. "I'm so sorry. She's got a mouth on her and no sense of decorum."

Rather than replying, the woman sniffed and looked around. "I expected as much."

I fisted my hands and was about to inform this broad who she was talking to when Drew walked in from the back porch with Wade and Sam. "Grandmother? What are you doing here?"

Holy freaking crap. She was Drew's grandmother. I recognized them now from a family portrait hanging in Drew's living room. Dang it. The silver hair should've tipped me off.

Pearl Walker had an intimidating reputation. She was the matriarch of the hunters and as cold as ice. Drew loved her to pieces, but at the same time, he knew who she was. Not someone to mess with.

Hell, she was everything he'd walked away from.

She wasn't the baking cookies and knitting kind of grandma. She was the kind of grandma who gave crossbows and flamethrowers as Christmas gifts.

Standing in the foyer, Pearl looked up at Drew, and the woman's expression didn't crack one whit. No gladness to see her grandson. No emotion whatsoever.

Freaking ice.

"Isn't there a wedding coming? Shouldn't I be here?"

"Of course, you're always welcome," I said while Drew moved around his grandmother to take some of the suitcases from the man waiting patiently behind her. "Please come in."

"Nice of you to finally ask me," she grumbled and moved toward the living room as Drew greeted the man behind.

A while back, Drew and I had the conversation about inviting her and, he hadn't wanted to because there would be no way she'd ever accept me for who I was—a witch-necromancer hybrid.

"Ian," he said, sounding genuinely pleased. "Get in here, little brother." Ah, so this was Ian. I greeted him with a warm smile.

Ian gave Drew an awkward hug while I looked him over. They had similar features, but Ian's nose was flatter and his eyes brown rather than Drew's vivid blue. He wore an enormous knife strapped to his hip, too. Bit of overkill around here, but okay. His expression was... less than pleased.

Turning to follow his gaze, I understood. Pearl stood at the entry to the living room, utterly silent as an absolute mob of people stared back at her.

And Zoey's tiger ears were out. Welcome to our normal house, hunter family. "Uh, Zo?" I whispered.

Her ears twitched as she heard me. I pointed to the top of my head, and a few seconds later, she grunted, and the ears disappeared.

I swept my gaze across the rest of the assembled crowd to see if anyone else was looking less-than-human. They all looked normal, except for Winnie. She was half-naked again, wearing what looked like a party dress that probably had to be taped over her boobs, so it didn't expose her nipples. Thank the gods for small favors?

She'd been doing that a lot lately. Ever since she got a younger Playboy body, at least.

Pearl sighed and turned around to walk into the mostly empty kitchen. "I'm here to see if I need to put a stop to this wedding."

2

OLIVIA

"MAN, I feel so bad for Ava."

I smiled up at my husband. Sam really was the most considerate man. In the middle of all he was dealing with—Hello! Being turned into a vampire—and he was worried about our bestie, Ava.

We were back at home. Once Drew's grandmother had announced that she was there to see if the wedding needed to be stopped, I'd rushed Sam out the back door and headed home to Luci's place.

"You're sweet. But yeah, I'm a little worried about her too. She's usually the bounce-back type, so I'm sure she'll be fine, but oof. That's not fun." I was talking about both the pregnancy disappointment and Grandma Pearl.

"It's not like she *lost* a baby," he said. "She only suspected she might be pregnant for what, a couple of hours?"

I pursed my lips at him. "No. Finding out you're not pregnant when there's a part of you that thinks you could be and a part that hopes you are? It's nothing like losing an actual baby, no. But it hurts, for sure."

It'd happened to me more than once over the years. We'd had a miraculously easy time conceiving Sammie. He'd been our happy little surprise. After that, nada. Zip, zilch, until we'd decided we were happy with our family dynamic as it was, and I'd gone back on birth control.

"Do you still *not* want more?" Sam asked.

Shrugging, I rubbed moisturizer into my face. "I wouldn't be upset if it happened. But no, I think we're done." Ava was right. Our lives were far too insane. "Besides, could we even now?" Now that he was a vampire, it probably wasn't possible. There was so much we still didn't know. We thought of new questions every day.

"How about that grandmother?" Sam said after a few minutes of looking upset at the thought that he couldn't have more children. "I really feel bad for them for that."

"Yeah, she was something else." A few minutes after she'd settled herself into the kitchen chair and rapped her cane for a cup of tea, almost everyone at the large gathering had beaten tracks. Owen had mumbled something about helping Wade with something in the basement.

Zoey and Larry had taken off up the stairs, giving an excuse about promising they'd go spend some time with Wallie and Michelle, who'd been at their dorms for a few weeks now. I never did see where John, Alfred, the scantily clad Winnie, and Beth had gotten off to, but they'd disappeared as well.

Carrie had come by not long after Pearl and Ian showed. We'd planned a big dinner to celebrate the distraction of the sword, but it had all gone to the wayside with everything that happened tonight. Carrie had whispered a quick goodbye to Ava and me, but not before mentioning how attractive she found Drew's brother, Ian.

Yep. I was logging that little bit of info away for a rainy day.

In the end, Sam and I said our goodbyes to Drew and Ava. She'd barely heard us as she'd tried to convince Lucy to go away so they could talk to Grandmother Pearl.

Granny P had given us the stink eye all the way out the door. No doubt she could sense that my husband was a vampire. I was willing to bet she couldn't figure me out, though.

Good. Let her wonder.

After slipping my PJs on, I opened our bedroom door, so we'd hear Sammie if he woke. Luci and Phira had stayed home with him so we could be at dinner with Ava. He had lessons with Carrie in the morning, and we hadn't wanted him up late.

Ava'd been right about that, too. Luci would've been *thrilled* for either of us to be pregnant. He'd taken on the role of the proud grandfather of Sammie, Jess, and Devan with gusto. He would've made a great middle-of-the-night rocker, too.

Oh, dang, so would Sam. Maybe being a vamp had perks, after all.

Thinking of the devil—literally—and he walked past our bedroom door. "Hey," I called.

He almost didn't turn around. When he did, he looked bewildered to see me standing there. "Oh, hello, Olivia. How are you this evening?"

I exchanged glances with Sam, who'd spread out on the bed to wait for me to join him. Dawn was still several hours away, but I liked to fall asleep with him beside me. He'd wait until I was conked, then would go off and do whatever he needed to do until time to crash back into bed. It usually involved going out with Wade to learn to feed. I hadn't mustered up the nerve to ask for details.

Most mornings, I tried to get up early to have a few minutes with him before he slept, but that wasn't likely to happen tomorrow, not with how late it was now.

"Good. Tired."

When he didn't respond, I stepped forward. "You okay?"

With a head shake, he smiled. "Of course. I'm dealing with some stuff in Hell that's distracting me. I've been walking the mansion, trying to think of a solution."

"Can we help?" Sam asked. He and Luci had been getting along well, especially now that Sam was a vampire.

Creatures of the night and all that.

"No, it's nothing for you to worry about. You've both got quite enough to be getting on with." An idea seemed to pop into his head. "Oh, how was Ava? Any buns in any ovens?"

I shook my head. "No, unfortunately not."

Aw, how sweet. He did look a bit disappointed. "Well, that's too bad." He stood there for a second, looking adrift, then his gaze focused on me. "You need more sleep."

"I know, I know. But we're getting used to this new dynamic. It'll come with time." He wasn't wrong. I never knew how hard it would be to change my sleep schedule. I'd always been a morning person, waking up as soon as the sun peeked over the horizon. Of course, that was the exact moment my husband fell asleep. Jax, the vampire leader of the US, had said it would be like that for a while.

Until then, I tried to stay up as long as I could so that Sam and I spent quality time together. I wasn't sure what else I could do.

"Have you gotten a full night's sleep since Sam was turned?" Luci asked. "I know you didn't sleep for the entire two days he was out cold."

After Jax had turned Sam to save his life at the Milan fight, Sam had slept right through the transformation. That had been the worst two days of my life. Not knowing if the turn would take or not had almost killed me.

Not literally, but emotionally it had.

"I'm fine. It's only been a week. Give us time to figure it out."

Luci looked over at Sam, who hadn't gotten up off of the bed. "How about you? How are you?"

Sam just shrugged. "Olivia is helping keep me stay sane."

Hmph. Easy for him to say. He was driving me freaking crazy. He had to be near me pretty much all of the time he wasn't with Wade hunting and learning how to navigate this world as a vampire.

Another big change was Sam's work schedule. He wasn't sure he'd be able to fulfill his duties as Drew's right hand anymore. Sam would have to work nights. Daylight was no longer his friend. At the moment, he was on a medical leave of absence. The humans believed he'd been injured in a rock-climbing adventure that none of the rest of us had gone on.

"Listen." I pointed at my biological father and the king of the underworld, changing the subject. "If you miss Ava's wedding because of some nonsense in Hell…"

He held up both hands. "I'll be there. Come Hell or high water." He chuckled at his joke as he backed out of our bedroom. "Promise!"

When I pushed the door slightly more closed and looked over at my husband, my heart dropped. "What is it?"

Poor Sam looked like he was about to cry.

He shrugged again.

"Stop." I climbed up on the bed beside him and took his hand. "This isn't your fault."

He squeezed my hand and a little bead of a tear appeared in the corner of his eye. "If I'd listened to you guys and stayed home, I'd be fine now."

"Oh, Sam. No." Leaning over, I grabbed his face and made him look at me. "You were *human*. Whatever the dynamics of our relationships, the responsible thing for Ava and me to have done would've been either to have forced you to stay home or to actually have protected you. We failed you. It's my fault, and Ava's, and Jax's. And everyone else who was there who had the ability to protect you and failed."

I'd never forgive myself for it, either. It wouldn't have been right to leave him home against his will, not really. It might've damaged our relationship irreparably. But we all should've done more. Done better. Not left him alone, vulnerable at our backs.

"I don't like feeling like I need to be protected," he said in a low voice. "I'm a cop, for crying out loud. I risk my life every day."

That was true. He could've been shot on duty or stabbed. Hell, he could be run over by a car walking across the street. We never knew when our number was up. Well, Luci might, but it wasn't like he'd tell us. He didn't like tempting Fate.

"Well, bright side." I gave Sam my sunniest smile. "Now, you don't need to be protected. No more than any of the rest of us need to watch each other's backs, anyway."

Pulling on my arm, Sam wrapped me up in a big hug. "That's true. We'll figure this out."

"We will. And all this weirdness isn't your fault. I didn't blame myself when I started having Fae powers and we had to move into my biological devil father's mansion. Did you blame me?"

Sam stilled. "Maybe a little."

Rearing up with one hand on his chest, I looked at him in outrage. Then I caught the hint of a smile tugging at his lip. I should've known he was teasing me.

I poked him in the chest. "Not funny, fang boy."

"It's like that, is it?" He flipped me onto my back faster than I could track. My whole body flushed and responded to him like it always had, from the first time he kissed me several springs ago.

Tracing a finger down his cheek, I said, "Now I can create a portal for us to go anywhere we want. Just say the word, and we'll be on our own little vacation. Of course, we'd have to bring Sammie with us."

I couldn't be without my little man for long. Nor could I be apart from my two adult children, Jess and Devan, not now that I had them back in my life.

"Sleep," he said after a brief pause as he rolled off of me and pulled me close once more. "Luci is right about you not getting enough rest."

I settled against him, then raised my wrist. "Have a nip. You'll need it."

And he did. I could sense that he didn't feed as often as he needed to. It worried me that he wasn't taking the whole being a vampire thing well.

"Promise you're taking your vitamins?" he asked, but his eyes were on the vein in my wrist. His nostrils flared slightly, and a hint of fang poked out from his upper lip.

"Every morning. I'm being good. And I'll get into a schedule with you. It's no worse than when you take night shift rounds at the station."

Before he became a vampire, he and Drew would rotate their schedules, and each took a couple of night shifts per month so the other officers would have more flexible schedules.

"Maybe you should start napping during the day."

Oh, I'd thought of that. "With Sammie homeschooling and having classes with Carrie, maybe I can." Luci, Phira, Carrie, Sam, and I had divided up Sammie's schooling so that he'd learn how to be a fae, how to be the devil's grandson, and how to read and write and all the other academic credits he'd need to pass to the next grade. We were lucky that we'd found an online private school that worked with his needs and interests.

Little Sammie was gonna be the complete package someday.

Sam gripped my wrist and kissed it. He inhaled as he did so, and I braced myself for the bite. But it never came. Turning in his arms to face him, I studied his features. But he said, "I have a few blood bags in the fridge. Plus, Wade and I will go out later."

I didn't argue because I knew the reason he was hesitant to drink my blood. Fae blood was addicting to vampires. He was afraid that if he drank from me, he wouldn't be able to stop. So instead of saying anything, I wrapped my arms around his neck and kissed him.

"Have a good sleep," he said after breaking the kiss.

No doubt I would. I was too tired not to.

3
AVA

My phone jangling on the kitchen table next to my laptop yanked me from the world I was building into a story bible. I was about to start a new series about witches, pulling from my own life experiences because come on, you can't make this stuff up.

Like...seriously.

I was going with write what you know. And who would believe it was real, anyway? Just people who already knew. Hopefully, they'd get a kick out of it, and I'd make a bunch of money.

Picking up my phone, I frowned. It was a local number, but I didn't recognize it. Usually, I'd ignore numbers I didn't have in my contact list, but I was planning a wedding, and that meant people I don't talk to often would be calling. So, I had to answer the phone and risk speaking to the person who kept trying to convince me my auto warranty had expired. I knew it was. Because I'd bought my Hyundai as is. There was no warranty. Plus, there was the fact that Drew had killed my car because he'd thought I needed a newer model.

I just hoped he didn't get any ideas when *I* got really old.

"Hello?" I tried to sound bright-eyed and professional. I wasn't sure if the word sounded the way it did in my head.

"Hello, may I speak to Ms. Ava Harper?"

"Speaking." It was hard to stifle a yawn, but I managed it. I hadn't been getting very many of my afternoon naps lately.

"Ms. Harper, this is Cecily from Rosestone Manor. I have some bad news."

I sat back in the kitchen chair and tried not to cry as Cecily explained that the venue where we'd been planning our nuptials had caught on fire that morning, and there was no way they'd be able to get it up and running before our wedding.

"Is there any way at all to make it work?" *Please say yes.*

"I'm afraid not. Even though the fire was isolated to the kitchen, the smoke damage to the ballroom was extensive. I'm sorry, Ms. Harper, but it is not safe to have guests right now." Cecily sounded sincere in her apology.

I grilled the poor woman a few more minutes about other alternatives, but she was adamant. It was either to find somewhere else to have our wedding or move the date. I didn't want to move the date, not again.

The moment I hung up, I called Olivia. She had her enchanted phone on her, so she got service in Faerie. She and Sammie had gone for lunch with her fae relations.

The phone rang and rang, but she never picked up. Eventually, her cheery voicemail ended, and it beeped. "Hey, friend." I tried not to sound to panicked. "I just got a call from the venue. There was a fire and now we need a new place to have the wedding. *Please* call me back."

After pressing *end* a bit harder than was strictly necessary, I threw my phone down on the kitchen table and bit back a small scream of frustration. We'd already been through all the venues in town. They were either too public—not great for a wedding full of ghouls, witches, and the like—or too small, or booked.

"Maybe it's a sign."

I'd heard the creak of the floorboard as if someone was heading in my direction, so Pearl entering the kitchen didn't startle me, but it did make me grind my teeth. I *so* didn't need to put up with granny hunter. Not in the mood I was in.

She'd been a *peach* the last few days, to say the least. Insert a load of sarcasm into that thought.

Biting my tongue, I turned and looked toward the archway that separated the kitchen from the rest of the ground floor, where Drew's beloved grandmother stood with her cane, which I wasn't entirely sure she needed, not with how she glided around. She continued in her superior tone, "Perhaps the wedding should be canceled."

If I bit my tongue any harder, I'd draw blood. *Why* couldn't Drew have been off today?

I knew why. He was working pretty much every day leading up to the wedding so we could enjoy our honeymoon guilt-free. Luci had already given us our wedding gift: an elaborate honeymoon. Drew and I were going to spend an entire month in the Scottish Highlands, and I *so* wanted to leave right now.

Back to reality. Where could we host a night wedding? As Pearl headed toward the chair across from me at the kitchen table, I began searching the internet for the answer.

Before she could reach out and adjust the chair to be able to sit, it slid back *seemingly* of its own accord. I squinted up at the ceiling and muttered under my breath, "What are you up to?"

Of course, Winston didn't answer. He never did. Pearl opened her mouth to probably tell me what a horrible person I was, again, but Mom and Winnie walked in. "What's wrong?" Mom asked the moment she saw my face.

"The venue burned down. Or burned some, but it's not available for my wedding." Tears pooled in my eyes as my emotions threatened to overcome me. I didn't want to cry, especially not in front of Pearl.

"I'm telling you, it's fate. At least consider putting the wedding off a bit. How long have you two really known each other, anyway? Isn't this a bit of a rush?" Pearl was in fine form today. She said what she thought, and nuts to anyone who didn't like it.

"Hey," Winnie said sharply. She turned and pointed her finger in Pearl's face. "You may be old enough to remember the coronation of Elizabeth the First, and you may be Drew's grandma, but if you don't watch your mouth, you're gonna be out of here. I mean it, lady. You've been nothing but venomous since you arrived."

My heart swelled in appreciation for my aunt, but it didn't do any good to fuss at Pearl. She never rose to the bait. Drew had warned me that was one of her more frustrating qualities. She'd make him mad; he'd end up snapping at her, then she'd ignore it like he hadn't said anything. He'd said it was worse than if she'd slapped him.

Pearl slowly turned her head to look at Winnie. "Put some clothes on." Her voice was low, even, and without emotion. "You look like a stripper."

"Not that there's anything wrong with strippers..." I tried to sound placating. "...But why *are* you wearing a bikini in the middle of September? It's kind of chilly outside."

Winnie tossed her blonde hair over her shoulder and flounced with one hand on her hip, sticking her perfect breasts out. "I never had a body like this. Not even close, not even in high school, not even on my best day. Now that I do, heck. If everyone wouldn't yell at me, I'd be naked twenty-four-seven."

That was understandable. It wasn't likely I'd be walking around in a bikini unless it was on the beach, but I'd definitely be sporting some tighter, more revealing clothing if I looked like Winnie did now. "I get it, Win. But please. Go put some shorts on at least. Don't sit down at the kitchen table in a thong."

She turned to look at her butt, opening her mouth as if to protest, but the back door opened. Ian walked in, then stopped short when the four of us looked up at him. Owen walked down the stairs and into the kitchen at about the same time. "Hello, all," he said. "Just off to a shift at the bookstore. Does anyone need anything from town?"

Pearl glared at Owen, and under her ire, he seemed to shrink. Gone was the tall, lanky man, replaced with a little boy whose jet-black hair needed a trim and a good scrubbing.

Owen's hair never quite looked clean, even right after he showered. I'd long since given up on it.

"Okay, then." Owen winked at me, then beat tracks out the front door like his behind was on fire. I wished I could go with him, but I had to find a new venue. Ugh.

"So," Mom said brightly, looking at Ian. "What have you been up to?"

His eyebrows lowered and he looked a bit defensive. "Nothing."

Pearl turned in her seat to look straight up at her tall grandson. "Nothing?"

"I've just been out, okay? Is that a problem?" He walked around the table toward the refrigerator, but when he opened it, it was nearly empty. Having this many people in the house was murder on our grocery bill. "What gives?"

"Alfred is at the grocery store now," Winnie explained helpfully. "He did a huge order on the app and is picking it up. I'm sure he'll appreciate some help unloading it if you're free."

Ian slammed the refrigerator door shut. "Whatever."

"So, just out? Do you need a guide around town?" Mom asked. "John and I would be happy to show you around."

Ian fidgeted from foot to foot. "Do I grill you about where you were? I was at a party. I met some people and we hung out."

"Oh, I figured you'd be with Drew," I said. Ian had been a police officer in North Carolina before finally joining the family business, hunting full time. "Where was the party?" I held up my hands. "Not that I'm questioning you. Just trying to make conversation."

The front door opened, and Alfred walked in with an armload of groceries, sparing us from Ian's reply. "I've got the car full. Does anybody want to help?" Ian took a look around and then hurried toward Alfred, disappearing out the front door, hopefully to actually help with groceries.

Well, okay. That wasn't super weird at all.

4

AVA

"WHERE'S LUCI BEEN?" Beth asked as she flipped through one of the many wedding magazines on the coffee table. "Seems like he and Phira have been gone a lot lately."

The wedding was exactly twelve days away, closer to eleven since today was almost over, and Mom was right. Luci hadn't been here, helping out with his unique method of problem-solving, which was generally ridiculous but in the end, effective. It wasn't like him.

I opened my mouth to explain that Olivia had told me Luci was dealing with a bunch of crap in Hell and Phira was spending a lot of time in Faerie, but someone knocked on the front door. With a sigh, I stood to answer it, but Winston opened the door again.

"Hello?" A woman's voice came from the other side of the open door.

I walked around until I could see and found Drew's sister standing there looking bewildered. "What, do you like hunters or something?" I said under my breath to Winston.

Her long black hair was pulled up in a high ponytail. Lily had a thin athletic build and was absolutely gorgeous. I'd seen multiple pictures of her, plus I'd mistaken her for Drew's date once last year. Otherwise, I might've been wondering who was on my front porch on this nice September day.

"Lily," I said with true happiness. I'd been wanting to meet her. "Please, come in."

Alfred appeared out of nowhere and took her suitcase as I ushered her inside. "Drew should be home any minute," I said. "He'll be so happy to see you."

"Not likely," Lily muttered. Heck, she might've been right. The last time they'd talked, it had been to argue about Lily telling secrets that weren't hers to tell. I wasn't sure how Drew would react. Ultimately, though, she was his sister and he loved her. He was closer to her than anyone in his family.

Speak of the, well, not devil. Speak of the fiancée. He pulled into the driveway as I began to shut the door. "How'd you get here?" I asked. There was no car in my driveway that I didn't expect to see.

"Cab," Lily said simply. "I figured Ian would have his car here, plus from the way Drew talks, you guys have a used car lot outside when you add up all the cars of all the people who live here."

I snorted and walked into the living room. "True." Looking around, I smiled. "Guys, this is Lily. I guess you've come a bit early for the wedding too?"

She nodded and waved at my mom and dad, Winnie, who, thankfully, was wearing a modest, if tight, dress, and Zoey, who had her ears tucked safely away. Olivia and Sam would likely be over after dark, but at least we had a smallish crowd now to meet Lily for the first time.

"Nice to meet you," she said and sat on the couch. "Yes, I figured you guys could use some help with Grandmother, so I picked up an earlier flight from Florida."

The front door opened—by Drew. Winston wasn't polite enough to open it for him—and as soon as Drew's gaze landed on his sister, his face lit up like a Christmas tree. "Lil!"

She ran to him, and I couldn't help but feel the warm fuzzies when he pulled her into a big bear hug. "I'm so glad to see you." But then his face darkened as he pulled back and grasped her by the shoulders. "Though I am still mad at you."

"Oh, come on, Drew. I had to do what I had to do. You know how it is." She pulled out of his hug and looked around the room as if she didn't want the whole family to know what she'd done.

"We have some work to do in the conservatory," Mom said, pulling Dad to his feet. "Come on, you two."

Winnie and Zoey followed, perhaps reluctantly, but at least they went.

"You didn't have to tell the hunters that vampires aren't extinct," Drew said, cutting directly to the point. "They'd managed to slide under the radar for so long."

Lily plopped down on the couch and stared at her brother with an expression on her face I recognized. I'd given it to Sam more than a few times. He wasn't technically my brother, but he might as well have been.

"Andrew Walker, you should turn this around on yourself. How could you live with yourself knowing vampires were out there and *not* telling Grandmother or anyone else? They're incredibly dangerous."

I held up one hand. "Hold up. If they're so dangerous, how'd they go years, decades, really, without anyone on your team knowing they weren't extinct?"

"They started self-governing," Drew said. "They took care of their own rogues and set up their operations under the radar so that humans are harmed the least amount possible."

"And well compensated," I added.

"That is true. And that's a huge reason we haven't attacked. They're organized now. Competent." She sighed and slumped back onto the couch. "Truthfully? We're embarrassed. We've been having meeting after meeting, virtual and in person. The families are all in a tizzy."

The hunter families could've called themselves factions or clans, or crews, anything normal, but no. They'd gone with families. Like they were the dang mafia or something. Can someone say God complex?

"Good," Drew said. "They should be embarrassed. But they need to consider the fact that the vampires have been disciplining their own. They aren't the deranged, mindless killers we once believed them to be. They're human, but with heightened emotions and a different dietary need."

Lily scoffed. "Come on, Drew. Don't be naïve. They lose something in the transition. They're not completely human."

"That's true." Uncle Wade's voice surprised me. A first. He was undead and I should have sensed him the moment he woke. Then I realized it'd gotten later than I thought. "We aren't exactly the same. I have less empathy than I used to."

Lily jumped to her feet and froze with one hand in her pocket.

"Leave it, Lil. He won't hurt us." Drew's voice was deadly calm as he gripped her wrist.

Lily snatched her arm from his grasp and took a step back, fear flashing in her eyes but only for a second. "He's a vampire."

"He is also Ava's uncle." Drew threaded his fingers through his hair, and I felt his frustration through our bond. That made me wonder if his family knew about it.

I was going with no, and I wasn't going to be the one to tell them.

Lily stared at Drew for a long while before asking, "What happened to you?"

Drew jerked his head back. "What do you mean?"

Lily motioned around the living room with her arms. "All of this. You're marrying a witch. And not just a witch, she's a *necromancer*."

"A necromancer who can control the undead. What's to stop her from raising an army against us?" At the sound of Ian's voice, I sent him a glare. He didn't like me, and I didn't care. But that didn't give any of them the right to talk about me like I wasn't there.

I wanted to say something but stopped when Drew met my gaze in a silent plea to stay out of it. Hmph. I'd stay out of it for as long as I could stand to. "Fine," I said out loud then marched to the kitchen where I found Alfred making food.

Moving to the fridge, I pulled out items to bake cookies. Alfred tried to take over, but I pushed him back toward the stove. "I need something to do while I listen to what they say."

He chuckled, which kind of sounded like a mouse squeaking. "Okay, you can help."

Like I needed his permission, but I humored him as I grabbed the dry ingredients from the pantry.

Just then I heard Pearl coming down the stairs. I knew it was her because her cane clicked against the wood flooring on every other step on the way down. I swore she did that on purpose.

"If you would bother to get to know my wife then you would understand why that doesn't make any sense. The only army Ava is raising is a family that protects one another against people like you," Drew said with his voice louder than I'd ever heard him.

He was a pretty mellow-go-with-the-flow kind of guy. I'd never heard him yell at someone before. Apparently, his family knew all the right buttons to push. Alfred and I stared at each other with wide eyes as the Walkers continued to argue.

"We hunt paranormal creatures, Drew. It's our duty to rid the world of as many of them as we can." Lily broke my heart with her words. I'd thought she would be on Drew's side.

"Now Lily, you're just being defensive. We only go after the bad ones. As long as they are following human laws and not hurting humans, we leave them be." That voice was Pearl, which surprised the heck out of me.

There was a few moments of silence before Ian said, "They all go bad eventually."

Drew exploded. "That. Right there! That was why I got out. You're no better than Dad."

That opened the floodgates for all kinds of family drama and arguing. Alfred and I kept them in food, but I tried to stay out of it. They weren't going to fully listen to any good points I made, given I was a witch and necromancer. And I was destined to "go bad eventually."

Finally, I gave up and went to bed. Drew wasn't too far behind me, as he had to work the second shift the next day.

Despite the fact that Drew wasn't down there now, they continued to argue, making getting a good night's sleep impossible.

5
AVA

HUNTERS WERE A HUNGRY BUNCH, at least the Walkers were. We'd all been taking turns in the kitchen, despite Alfred's protestations.

As I set a plate of sandwiches on the table, someone knocked on the door. I glared down at my houseguests, far past the pretense of false politeness. Especially after last night, when they'd expressed their true feelings about me and my kind. "If this is another unannounced Walker, I'm kicking you all out to live in the devil's house next door."

We hadn't yet broached the subject of Luci. That was sure to cause another whole night's worth of arguing.

Without giving them time to ask me what I'd meant about the devil living next door, I hurried to the foyer. Winston hadn't opened the door himself, so it wasn't likely to be Drew's family.

I pulled the door open and gaped at my caterer. "Oh, my gosh, Janice, I'm so sorry. I completely forgot you were coming today." Not only had I forgotten, but I thought when she'd said she'd be bringing samples of the menu for me to make the final selection, that she'd meant *small* samples. She had a good fifteen bags all around her on my porch, each emblazoned with her company's logo for The Sea Kettle.

"Just leave those," I said. "Let me grab a tip."

I rushed to my office to get a five out of my purse, but when I came back, Janice was already through the door with a bunch of the bags. "No, really," I said, rushing forward. "You don't have to bring them in."

It wasn't like I was embarrassed about the state of the house. Even as full as it was, between Alfred and Winston, the place was spotless. Winston couldn't *stand* a speck of dust, so he kept things crystal clean. Alfred kept them decluttered, though those of us who lived here weren't exactly a messy bunch.

I was terrified someone would do something or say something decidedly *un*human, and Janice was one hundred percent normal. Not a magical bone in her body. She didn't know about the magical world, either.

Lunging out onto the porch, I scooped up far too many bags and nearly had to drag them all in. "Thanks again."

Janice reached for one of the bags I'd grabbed, but I set them down by the stairs and thrust the five-dollar-bill into her hand. "Really, above and beyond. I'll let you know tonight which of the meals we decided on." We were paying her out the nose for her food, including paying for the samples, which was fair. I wouldn't expect her to eat the cost, and while I appreciated the delivery service, I had to get her out of my crazy house.

Drew's family still sat at the table, still as statues, staring at my awkward attempts to dissuade Janice from going back into the kitchen.

"You don't mind if I set up the plates do you?" Janice pulled more bags into her hands. "That way you get the full impact of the port in the sauce. It doesn't hit right without the port."

One of the bags clanked. Presumably the bottles of liquor. "No, I, um—"

Suddenly, Drew's family jumped into action, clearing the table. "Please," Lily said as she scooped up the plate of sandwiches I'd just set down. "Go ahead."

I glared at Drew's sister and motioned for her to go away behind Janice's back.

Everything was going fine. Even Pearl was being polite, which maybe she was usually polite to humans. It was just us weirdos she didn't care for. Janice was just spooning sauce over what, admittedly, looked like a delicious piece of beef, when the door to the back porch opened. Larry walked in with a very worried-looking Zoey behind him.

I should say, Larry's skeletal feet clanked on the kitchen tile as he walked in because he was completely defleshed and carrying his head in his hands.

Would the Universe just swallow me whole now?

Janice turned around and froze, gasping while Ian and Pearl moved into a defensive position. I hadn't seen the old bat move so quickly the entire time she'd been here.

"His stone broke," Zoey said in a shrill voice.

Ian managed to catch Janice before she hit the ground. She'd fainted dead away. The poor thing.

"What in the world?" I exclaimed. "How did you break your stone?"

It was magical for crying out loud.

"We were climbing on the cliffs," Zoey said. "We love to do that. We've done it several times. Well, Larry's jewel came loose from his necklace and fell really far. It hit a rock a couple of times and he went zip! Back to his bones."

"Nearly lost my balance, too."

Lily gasped this time, staring at the talking skull in the hands of the skeleton. "It talks."

"Yeah, don't try to figure out the magic," I said. "It'll make your head hurt."

Larry the skeleton could do all sorts of things he physically shouldn't have been able to. Everything except keep his dang head on.

"I found the stone." Zoey held it out. "It's not completely broken, which is why he's still animated, I'm guessing. But there's a big crack in it."

"I don't have time for this," I muttered. Walking over to the stairway, I looked up and sucked in a deep breath to yell, "Dad!" Footsteps told me he'd heard me and was on his way.

"Keep an eye on her." I motioned toward the still-asleep caterer on my kitchen floor.

Ian nodded.

When Dad jogged down, I told him what happened. "Can you please take Larry and Zoey to the chasm and see if you can repair the stone? I've got to deal with this."

He winced at Janice. "Oof. Bad luck. What was she doing here?"

"Don't ask," I said darkly. "Just get Larry out of here before she wakes up."

Once they were safely gone, I turned back to the caterer. "Let's get her up."

Ian lifted Janice with ease, propping her up against him as she began to stir.

"What happened?" she mumbled. "Why am I being held?" She smiled up at Ian, seemingly not too upset at the attention.

"You passed out." I patted her on the arm. "Leave the food with us. We'll make a decision and let you know, but really I think you might want to go check your blood sugar. Do you have problems with it?"

She shook her head, but then said, "No, but you know, my mother did. Maybe I will have it checked. Couldn't hurt." I felt kind of bad about her possibly going to an unnecessary doctor's appointment but if her mother had diabetes, maybe it wouldn't hurt for her to be checked. At least, that's what I told myself to stop the guilt.

We managed to get her on her way. I shut the front door behind her, turned back to the kitchen, and stopped to see Pearl standing in the doorway with a disgusted look on her face. She tutted once, then clomped past us, her cane making a thump with every other step.

The front door opened for her, thanks so much to Winston, and then slammed behind her.

Wow.

"Hey, let's try this food," Lily called. "It looks amazing."

I followed them back to the table. The chairs slid out for everyone, even me, which was something Winston never did. "Why aren't you this nice all the time?" I called.

Maybe he was trying to be super polite so the family would like him. "Thank you," I said in a sincerely sweet voice.

Ian and Lily looked at me like I'd grown a second head.

Whatever. "Winston, the house, is magical. But you probably guessed that by now."

No one else commented as we dug into the food samples. Everything was so good it was hard to pick. Winnie and Mom joined us to help vote on our favorites. Once the selections were made, I went to my office to shoot Janice an email with my choices. I had said I'd call her, but after the Larry the Skeleton incident, I was sure Janice was still trying to make sense of it all. I debated on sending Luci over there to do his compulsion. Or Wade.

Once the email was sent, I opened my current WIP—work in progress—and got lost in the new story.

A few hours later, I started to feel queasy. What the heck? I got up and started to go to the kitchen for some medicine. When I passed the living room, I saw Ian watching TV. He looked fine. Lily exited the bathroom off the hallway looking a little green. "You okay?" I asked.

She paused, shook her head, then ran back to the bathroom.

Oh no, if she was sick and I felt ill, that meant food poisoning. Or a stomach bug. I didn't need to be sick. I didn't have time for it.

But sure enough, a minute later I was rushing to the bathroom to pray to the porcelain gods, but Mom was already in my bathroom. Winnie walked out of her bedroom wiping her face with a wet washcloth. "Sick?" she asked.

Moaning, I rushed past her and headed toward the new bedrooms, and vomited in one of the pristine, never before used toilets.

Welcome to the house, new bathroom.

6

AVA

"Thank you." Drew pulled Lily into a hug and squeezed her until she grunted.

She was taking *dear* Grandma Pearl out for the day to get her out of our hair. I could've kissed her myself. Anything to get the old bat away while we moved the furniture.

I still felt blah from the food poisoning the day before. One thing good about being magical, I was able to get over it faster than a human would. Apparently, that was the case for the Walkers as well. We weren't a hundred percent but at least we weren't fighting over who gets to spend time with the toilet.

The fact that Ian hadn't gotten sick, and he'd eaten more than any of us, didn't go unnoticed. I didn't bring it up, but something besides the food was rotten here.

"I'm here." Olivia sailed into the room with her arms spread wide. "Allow me to start directing traff—oh, hey." She deflated when she spotted Grandmother Pearl coming slowly down the stairs.

Pearl had been staying in Wallie's room. Wallie had been warned not to use the portal in his closet unless he checked with us first. And we'd locked that door so Pearl wouldn't accidentally wander into Wallie's college dorm room.

Pearl walked past Olivia without acknowledging her existence.

"Oookay," Olivia said sarcastically, crossing her eyes at the woman's back. "Have a nice day, Old Lady Hunter."

Not even a moment's hesitation from the ice-cold Pearl. She was a tough one.

Shaking her head, Olivia shut the door behind Lily and Pearl and looked up at Drew. "Dude. Your family is worse than mine. How is that possible?"

He stuck his nose in the air and walked past Olivia, mimicking his grandmother as he ignored her. There was a slight twitch of his lips as if he was holding in his amusement.

I snorted and pulled on her hand. "Come on, I need to talk to Winston."

Everyone was here to help unload the truck with all of Drew's things. He was officially moving in today. Well, everyone was here but Sam and Wade. And Luci was who-knew-where presumably dealing with Hellish issues. "Phira still in Faery?" I asked as Olivia accepted a mug of coffee from Alfred.

"Yeah, she's not happy Luci has been so busy. I heard them fighting the other night, but then they both left again."

Uh-oh. Trouble in paradise. Phira had spent three decades locked away in a prison realm. It made sense she wouldn't want to lose any more time with the man she loved.

"Winston?" I called. "Are you listening?"

The wood around the kitchen groaned in response.

"Thanks." I wiggled my eyebrows at Olivia and Alfred. Drew wandered into the kitchen with a puzzled look on his face. "Hey, Winston, I was thinking. With Drew's furniture coming, and us having all these houseguests, I thought it would be nice if we added a wing to the house. Maybe upstairs and downstairs. We could have a den downstairs, over there, on the other side of the kitchen. The door for it could be around by my office, opposite the staircase. And upstairs, two new bedrooms and a bathroom?

The house only had two full bathrooms, which was a bit sparse with all these people. "Also, if there's a way, and you have the energy, expand the basement and add a bathroom down there for Wade?"

Winston's wood groaned again, and if I wasn't mistaken, he sounded excited.

"I think he wants to do it," I muttered.

The whole house began to shimmy and shake. Unlike the last time, he'd expanded, this time I sensed power all around me. "Whoa," I muttered. "This is cool."

A loud popping sound was followed by banging and clanking, and then about a minute later, it all stopped. I rushed out of the kitchen, to the right past the stairway, and into the hall where my office and the half bath were. On the other side of the half-bath doorway was a new door. "Oh, cool, Winston, thank you!"

"What was that?" Zoey and Larry rushed down the stairs. "What's happening?"

"Winston expanded." Drew pointed toward the new doorway. "Den."

"There are four new bedrooms upstairs," Larry said. "And the attic door, at the end, is way farther down the hall now."

Four, awesome. I'd only asked for two. I opened the new door to find a room made of red brick. It had a beautiful hardwood floor and a bunch of windows. "Oh, I can't wait to decorate." The room was absolutely huge and would be a wonderful place for the guys to play video games. Or the girls, for that matter. Jess and Zoey got vicious playing a game of Mario Kart.

"You guys start bringing the living room furniture in here," I said. "And we'll go check out the new bedrooms."

The original plan had been to donate most of Drew's furniture, saving some pieces we liked better than mine. But before they'd started loading yesterday, I had this idea and told them to load *everything* onto the truck. His place was now empty, and the key had been turned back over to the landlord. The truck out in the driveway was completely full. We couldn't have squeezed in another polo shirt.

"Um, Ava?" Drew stood in the doorway to the new den, staring at me expectantly.

"Yes?"

"Don't think I don't understand that this was a careful manipulation to get my recliner out of the main living room and hidden back here in the new den." He gave me a crook smirk and a raised eyebrow.

Oh, crap. He'd seen right through me. "We really did need a couple of guest rooms. We're full to the brim right now."

Nodding, Drew held up one hand. "I understand that. The den was a happy bonus." His expression flattened. "For you."

"Maybe it was," I admitted. "But that doesn't change the fact that your chair is the ugliest thing I've ever seen in my life." Grabbing Olivia's hand, I squeezed under Drew's arm and darted down the hall before he could try to convince me to put the plaid monstrosity in my mid-century-mod living room. "Come on, hurry. Let's go see the bedrooms."

They were perfect. "Gosh, I might move Drew and me into this one." It was enormous. Winston had put a bathroom in each room, and big ceiling fans with wide blades. Sunshine sparkled through the windows, making the hardwood shine. And each of the four rooms was a different color. Jewel-tone accent walls with complementary pastel shades on the other walls.

"This is perfect, Winston, thank you so much," I called.

He didn't answer.

There wouldn't be enough furniture from Drew's to fill all the rooms. "We get to go shopping," I told Olivia excitedly as we walked down the stairs. "Maybe after the honeymoon."

Alfred was coming in with the first piece of furniture, so Olivia and I began to direct traffic, sending everyone all over the house.

It was nice to be in charge and not the muscle. "Hey, Ava," Drew called. "A little help?"

He and Larry had a large armoire. It looked heavy.

"Allow me," Olivia said. She wiggled her finger, and the armoire lifted into the air, just a few inches off the ground, and slowly floated into the house. "Where to?"

"I think the teal bedroom," I said. "If you don't mind."

She shrugged. "This actually isn't so difficult. I have to focus so it doesn't slip down and ding the floors, but it's not too bad."

While she floated that big thing upstairs, Drew and Larry went back for more stuff.

Soon, Drew was moved in, and one of the spare bedrooms was full of boxes for him to unpack at his leisure. "I don't mind helping to unpack," I offered. "If you don't mind me going through your stuff."

He put his arm around me. "You can help me unpack if we can put my recliner in the living room."

Pushing his arm off, I snorted. "No deal. You're on your own, buster."

His laughter followed me into the house.

Smiling, my heart full of the knowledge that my almost-husband now officially lived with me, I jogged up the stairs. When I got to the top, I spotted Snoozer sitting in the hallway peering into the new rooms. Lucy sat next to him. When she saw me, she walked closer. "He's not happy with all these people and the changes going on."

"Snoozer, it'll calm down after the wedding." I moved closer to him, but he glanced once at me twitched his tail and ears, and then walked off.

A moment later, he disappeared up the attic stairs.

Great, now I had an emotional ghou-cat to worry about.

7
OLIVIA

"We should send them a bill for how long we're having to wait." It was an old joke, but a good one. And it was freaking true. They told us to come in fifteen minutes early only to be late getting us in to see the doctor.

Ava nodded absently as she drummed her fingers on the waiting room's pleather seat. "Seriously. It's been an hour past my appointment time." She sighed so deeply it sounded like the air came from her toes. "But they did fit me in, so we won't complain... too much."

Ugh. I'd already played Candy Cane Crash until I ran out of lives, and the generic games that tried to imitate it just weren't as fun. The magazines in the OB/GYN waiting room weren't holding my interest.

Antsy as all heck and not liking the silence of the waiting room, I said the first thing that popped into my mind. "Male giraffes will headbutt females in the bladder until they pee. They then drink the urine, tasting it to determine whether or not the female is ovulating."

Ava slowly turned her head away from the crossword puzzle on her phone until she was staring into my eyes. "Why?"

I repeated my random fact. "Why do I know that, or why do they do it?"

The snort she let out as she dissolved into giggles had every other eye in the busy waiting room pointed toward us. "Why do you know that?" she whispered between her barely contained laughter.

With a shrug, I bumped my shoulder into hers. "I know lots of random stuff." I was about to list off that the Appalachian Mountains used to be connected to the Highlands in Scotland before the plates split, so they're technically all one big mountain range, but a nurse opened the door. "Ava Harper?"

She jumped up, and I hesitated, not sure if she wanted me to follow her or wait here. But then she paused a few feet away and turned back at me with wide eyes and raised eyebrows. Oops. That meant I was supposed to follow. I scrambled to my feet, grabbed my purse, and hurried behind my bestie.

The slight thumping of my heart reminded me how lucky I was to have Ava as my best friend. I'd been kind of horrible as a young person, and as a result, hadn't had anyone but Sam to call a true blue. Until Ava came back. I'd decided to do anything I could to make up for the fact that I'd been a total b-witch to her, and most everyone else, in high school, and she'd forgiven me and welcomed me into her crazy life with open arms.

Now I couldn't imagine it any other way. Rushing, I caught up to her and whispered in her ear, "Want me to help you be lighter on the scale?"

She grinned but shook her head. "No, best to be honest with the medical peeps." I held her purse and phone while she was weighed, then we stopped by a room where a lady in a white coat took several vials of blood. Finally, we were put in a room and left alone, so I shared my facts about the Appalachian Mountains.

Ava shook her head slowly. "What would I do without all the things you know?"

"Boredom." I held up both hands. "Insanity. Probably you'd all be dead by now without me."

She squeezed my hand and smiled. "Probably."

It didn't take long after that. The doctor came in and asked a few questions, told Ava he'd let her know when the results came back, and we left.

"That was anti-climactic," I said as we walked out of the office. "I expected them to tell us something now."

"No, they send it off." Ava unlocked the car, and I slid into the passenger seat. "I should know something, hopefully tomorrow."

"You're not pregnant." I stared at her as she focused on driving. "We'd *know*. We're all magical. Wouldn't we sense it?"

She pursed her lips and spared a glance at me. "I have no idea. I mean I didn't know for months with Wallie. I wasn't using my magic back then, so I didn't notice the signs."

"Do you *feel* pregnant? I knew the moment little Sammie was conceived." I'd just known and had never questioned it. Now, knowing everything I did about my heritage, I knew it was most likely the magic inside me that had informed me.

Stopped at a red light, Ava stared at me for another moment before replying. "I...no, I don't feel pregnant. But I still need to know for sure because if I'm not, then there is something else going on with my powers. I'm not sure which scares me more."

I understood where she was coming from. Having a baby at our age was risky, even for magical beings. But I'd take a baby over unpredictable powers any day.

By the time we stopped at the grocery store, and the bookstore, and swung by to pay the rental on Drew's tux, it was nearly six. It would be dark any minute, meaning Sam would be up and all in my biz.

Heavens knew I loved the man, but if he didn't find a hobby soon, I was going to finish the job the vampire had started back in Milan. Oh, crap. That was mean of me. I wasn't going to do any such thing, but he really was driving me bonkers.

I didn't know why he'd been clinging to me like I was his security blanket and his life depended on it, but I was going to have to think of something to help him.

Sure enough, as I walked into the house, he appeared from upstairs in a flash. Literally. There was a blur trail from where he'd stood a second ago to where he now stopped in front of me. "There you are." At least his voice was cheery. He wasn't as down today. That was nice. "What have you been up to?"

I took his hand and closed the door. "Help me get Sammie ready for bed?"

Sam nodded and wrapped an arm around me as we walked to our son's room. It was a little awkward, but I didn't say anything.

As we bathed Sammie and got him ready for bed, I told him about our day, Ava's pregnancy test, and everything else I could think of. "You know," I said after we tucked Sammie in, "If you're not busy, I'm sure Ava would love a visit tonight. She could use a distraction." I stifled a yawn. I could use an early night's sleep.

Sam smiled and seemed to perk up a bit. "I'll go say hi."

He kissed me and left, but as I looked down at our bed, I knew he'd be home soon and though he wouldn't mean to, he'd end up waking me up.

Was it mean of me? Probably. But I got out my phone anyway and texted Phira. **Are you here or at Faery?**

She replied quickly that she was down the hall in her bedroom.

Great, thanks. Can you keep an ear out for Sammie tonight? I'm going to hide and get a good night's sleep.

I nearly heard her laughter from down the hall or at least imagined I did. She replied she'd be happy to. Then, I scribbled a quick note on the back of a receipt. *My love, I'm running away for the night to catch up on some sleep. See you tomorrow night and love you so much! – O*

My next text came as I headed downstairs. This part would be tricky, but I'd recently learned a spell to make me sneaky. Not really invisible, but... unnoticeable. I put the glamour over myself as I texted Ava. **I'm hiding out in your new guest room. The teal room. Don't tell S.**

Ava didn't reply until I was already sneaking up her staircase. Sam's voice rose from the living room as he laughed along with Wade. I loved hearing him happy. Almost like I'd gotten him a babysitter for the night.

I swiped a pair of Ava's PJs out of her bureau and then settled into the bed in the guest room. A good twenty minutes later, as I was just about asleep, the door opened, but nobody came in. Sitting up, I looked around in the shadowy room, lit by the hallway lights. "Who's there?"

"Just me." Lucy jumped up on the foot of the bed. "You should latch that door better."

I squinted down at the sassy white cat. "Indeed. Wouldn't you be more comfortable somewhere with Snoozer?"

Lifting one leg, she delicately licked behind it in a feat that would've paralyzed me if I'd tried it. "No. He's mad that Ava had Winston extend and that she got new furniture. He's hiding in the attic, where he says nothing ever changes."

I snorted, but then cocked my head when someone yelled something downstairs. "What's that?"

"Oh..." She paused to lick a few times. "Drew got hurt at work. A human stabbed him with a big knife."

"What?" I screeched and sat straight upright, prepared to run downstairs.

"Don't get your panties in a twist. Ava already healed him."

Grabbing my phone, I shot off a quick text to Ava. **Need me? Lucy told me what happened.**

She replied within seconds. **No. He's fine. Sam's keeping him company now. Go to sleep and enjoy it.**

Well, if she insisted.

8

AVA

AFTER SAYING goodbye to the nurse, I set down the phone and tried not to feel disappointed again. I'd already known I wasn't pregnant. The blood test had simply confirmed it. But I had no time to cry over spilled pregnancy tests.

Drew stared at me with his eyebrows raised. I just shook my head. He probably figured out it was negative from my emotions through the bond. "Why are we disappointed?" I asked. "We had zero plans to have a baby."

Were we going to try to get pregnant? No. We'd talked about it, and a late-in-life baby wasn't what we truly wanted.

Stop being sad. Right now.

And I wasn't going to think about the possibility that something else was happening to my powers, something far more nefarious. I needed to get through this wedding so Drew and I could escape to the Highlands for a month.

"Come on," I said, pulling the covers off of him. "You have to make yourself scarce so I can do my final dress fitting."

Pulling the blankets back up to his chest, he winked at me and smiled. "You don't really believe in that superstition, do you?"

"Should I get the salt again?" I arched one eyebrow, and though I was somewhat joking, I really didn't want him to see my dress. Not for superstition, but because I wanted the first glance to be a total surprise. I wanted to watch his face when he saw me for the first time.

"No, no." He held up his hands and rolled over in bed. "I'll stay up here and nap before my shift tonight. I'm beat."

"As long as you don't come down before I text you." I gave him a warning look. "Promise?"

With a fake snore, he closed his eyes. "Promise. I'm already asleep."

After a fast shower, I went downstairs wearing the corset and petti-coat I'd bought just for underneath the dress and over that, my big, fluffy robe. Of course, most of Drew's family was assembled in the kitchen.

"Hey," I said nervously. "The lady making my dress is a witch, so you don't have to be on guard or anything, just..." I looked at Ian and Pearl nervously. "Try not to seem too threatening, please."

On cue, someone knocked on the door, then it opened. "Yoo-hoo." Olivia stuck her head in. "I'm here, and I've got Alissa with me. Can we come in?"

"Yes, come in, please." I hurried over and pulled the door wider. "Drew's in bed for a while so we're good."

"Alissa, this is my soon-to-be brother-sister- and grandmother-in-law. Ian, Lily, and Pearl." I nodded at the family. "This is Alissa, a friend of mine and the maker of my gorgeous dress."

Alissa held up the poufy garment bag as if for proof. "Hi-ya!"

Lily rushed forward and smiled warmly as she greeted Alissa, but Ian and Pearl hung back like a couple of disapproving statues. Great.

"I'll just go get changed into this." I took the garment bag from Alissa.

"Oh, I'll help." Olivia hurried behind me and we went into my office to change so we'd have enough room.

I paused and scanned the faces of the Walkers and thought about inviting Alissa to come on in with us and just doing the fitting in there. However, the kitchen had the best lighting according to Alissa. I'd just have to hope the hunters would be on their best behavior.

Once Olivia got me into the dress, I sighed and looked down at myself, then at the full-length mirror we'd conjured to keep in my office when we'd done the first fitting here at the house. "This dress is amazing."

It looked even better in person. It was white with a floral design embroidered in pale green, representing my earth witch heritage. The gown was form-fitting and flared at the hips. The long sleeves were made of lace, and the train was at least four feet long. Everything about the dress was perfect.

"Come on. Let's let her do her thing, then we can go get some breakfast." Olivia grinned at me. "Ready?"

Feeling like the world's oldest princess, I pranced out of the office and headed into the kitchen. Alissa liked doing the fittings in there because the lighting was better than in the living room.

Perhaps, if I'd been a smart woman, I would've conjured extra lamps in the living room.

I'd never called myself particularly smart. And I certainly didn't have the gift of premonition.

I stepped up onto a little step stool and stood with my arms out while Alissa tugged on the material and measured one side, then the other.

My future in-laws had scattered, but as I turned around to let Alissa do her thing in the front, Ian walked back in. "Don't mind me." He covered his eyes and walked toward the fridge. "Just grabbing a drink."

I eyed him as he pulled a huge, iced coffee out and took a drink. Too late to react, I noticed one of Alissa's feet sticking out at the same time Ian, who was supposed to be a hunter, which meant athletic, suave, competent, tripped over said foot.

He yelled, and I watched the cup of iced coffee go end over end, and a mortifying arc of brown liquid arched out of it—straight for my dress.

Everything happened in slow motion. Olivia, Alissa, and I yelled as one, "Noooooooo." I even threw up my hands and blasted magic at the coffee, but it did no good.

The iced coffee wasn't dead. And I didn't have any particular affinity to liquids. Michelle did, but she was a portal away, sitting in some early morning class, completely unaware that her boyfriend's mom desperately needed her to stop a spray of iced coffee from hitting her wedding dress exactly nine days before her wedding.

Then, time righted itself, and I stared down at my half-white-half-brown dress. "Oh, no."

"Don't freak out." Olivia walked around and grabbed my face, so I had to look directly at her while Ian stared at us over her shoulder with a shocked expression on his face. Olivia ignored him and said, "We can fix it. We're magical. We can pull the liquid out."

"Michelle," I said weakly.

"That's right. She's a water witch." Alissa bounded to her feet. "We'll call her. Let's get you out of this and we'll call Michelle."

Ian stared at me as I stepped off of the stool, then a loud bark of laughter erupted from his mouth. He clapped his hand over his lips and stared at me with wide eyes as I considered all the different ways I could hurt him without lifting a finger. To really show him why hunters and vampires feared necromancers.

Was it worth it? Drew did love his brother. Maybe I could do it quickly and make it look like an accident. "Did you just laugh?" I said in my lowest, full-of-warning voice.

He giggled, high-pitched and odd sounding coming from him. He usually had a deep voice. "I didn't mean to. I have a nervous laugh."

I could forgive a nervous laugh. Just not right now. I stalked away rather than turning him into a toad.

After getting me out of the dress, Alissa promised she'd get the stain out with magic, even if it meant calling Michelle. I texted her Wallie's girlfriend's number, and as I walked out of the office holding the dress, back in its bag, Drew peeked over the railing. "Is it safe to come out?"

"Yeah, I'm dressed," I said. I was back in my robe, but it was fine. "You missed the drama." I explained what happened as he came down the stairs.

He clenched his jaw at me, then marched into the kitchen. I followed, as did Olivia and Alissa, then I set the dress on the kitchen table as Drew lit into his brother like nothing I'd ever heard from him before.

"What are you trying to do to us?" he roared.

Ian pushed back with one hand on Drew's chest. "I'm not doing anything. It was an accident."

"Are you trying to sabotage the wedding?" Drew asked. "So far, the venue caught on fire, then we all got sick on the caterer's food, so we had to find another one, then I got *stabbed*, and that one better not have been you. Now this?"

"Hold on a minute." Pearl's quiet, calm voice made everyone whirl around. I had no idea where she'd come from. "It's one thing to accuse Ian of spilling on the dress on purpose. It's quite another to accuse him of arson and stabbing."

Drew looked a bit contrite, and if I was honest, surely I didn't believe Ian would be behind something so vile as stabbing his own brother.

The stabbing had happened two nights ago when Drew was on his way home from work. He was a block away from the house when he'd stopped to help a lady with a flat tire. After he changed the tire and sent the woman on her way, a knife came out of nowhere as if someone had thrown it from a distance.

They'd been a good shot too, and if Drew hadn't moved, the blade would have hit his heart. I would've been forced to marry a ghoul.

Lily walked in and was just about to put in her two cents while Alissa, Olivia, and I looked on, but a huge crashing sound from outside pulled all of our attention to the front yard. I got to the door first, flung it open, and found a car smashed into one of the large trees in the front yard.

"Holy crap, come help!" I yelled. Everyone was right on my heels as I sprinted as fast as I could toward the vehicle. A man in the driver's seat was conscious but looked completely confused. He was about my age, with a little gray in his beard. "Are you hurt?" I asked through the open driver's window.

He looked up at me, blinking rapidly. "I don't think so. Where am I?"

"You're in my yard. Bridewater Street, Shipton Harbor. Any of that ring a bell?"

"Frank?" Drew nudged me aside. "What happened?" Drew glanced back as Frank squinted at Drew. "Frank runs the local barber shop." He gave his attention back to the clearly confused Frank.

I stepped back to let Drew do his thing. He was already on the phone, calling emergency services, and Ian was in there, helping him get Frank out of the car.

If I didn't know better, I would've thought Frank was under the influence of something. But something told me it wasn't an illicit substance causing this.

As Alissa, Lily, Pearl, Olivia, and I stood there and watched, unable to help—it occurred to me I had the ability to heal. "Drew," I said quietly. "Let me touch his skin."

A feeling of surprise came through the bond and Drew nodded. He stepped back, and I touched Frank's arm, giving him just a bit of healing magic. His eyes cleared, and he looked around as if noticing us for the first time. "What in blazes is going on?"

Drew started talking to him, and Frank didn't remember anything happening over the past few hours. I whispered to Drew while Frank was on the phone calling his daughter. "Hey, he wasn't under the influence. I think I cleared a weak spell from his mind."

Again, with surprise from Drew. "I don't think Frank is magical in any way," he whispered. "That's insane."

"Someone spelled him to crash." I was sure of it. The more I thought about it the more it made sense.

I didn't have time to puzzle it out because a massive crashing sound from inside the house told me something was going on in there. But the sound didn't stop as I turned and looked at Winston. I held up one hand. "Stay. I'll go see."

Leaving Drew and Ian to deal with Frank and wait on the ambulance to make sure Frank really was okay, Olivia, Alissa, and I rushed back inside. Lily and Pearl were right behind us.

It was Winston making all the noise. Every door in the house was opening and closing and all of our belongings had been knocked off of shelves and out of cabinets onto the floor. When we reached the kitchen, I stopped midstep, then did a circle as I searched for my dress.

It was gone. "The dress is gone." And the door to the deck stood wide open.

My heart sank to my feet, and I dropped into the nearest kitchen chair. This wasn't happening.

Lily and Pearl took off out the back door, saying something about tracking down a magical trail. I hadn't sensed any. Then again, my magic had been wonky, and I wasn't a hunter.

I looked up at Olivia and tried not to cry. "What am I going to do now?"

9
AVA

"This is never going to work," I moaned, not at all feeling like dress shopping. "She won't have the right dress."

I had the perfect one until it was ruined and then stolen. We still didn't know who took it.

"Yes, she will." Olivia patted my hand as she navigated the shopping center parking lot in town to Porcelain Threads, the upscale dress shop Alissa owned. The shop was open by appointment only, and she was normally closed on Saturdays, but given what had just happened yesterday at the house, she was opening up for us.

And by us I meant... everyone. They'd all wanted to come. Olivia had me, Beth, and Winnie in her car. Michelle and Wallie had come through last night to stay in Wallie's bedroom so she could come with us today. Thankfully, Pearl had been somewhat gracious about moving to one of the new guest rooms.

Well. She had only sniffed a few times, and hadn't said anything scathing, so I counted that as a win.

Lily drove Pearl in Drew's truck behind us. He was resting for another second shift tonight. Pearl, apparently, had an eye for fashion, whatever that meant.

Bringing up the rear of our trio was Michelle driving Zoey in my car.

"That's who she reminds me of," I exclaimed as Olivia parked. "Miranda Priestly from 'The Devil Wears Prada'."

Olivia gaped at me and the duo in the back seat dissolved into giggles. "That's so accurate. We just watched that movie the other night," Mom exclaimed. "Winnie is making me watch a movie every other day or so to catch up on all the cinema I missed while I was in the Inbetween."

My mom died when I was ten. I'd recently found out that she'd been killed by a curse which had also made her stuck in the Inbetween.

"Smart," I said around my giggles. "But it's true, right? If you take out the fashion stuff and sub it with hunter stuff, she's totally the editor-in-chief of the Walker Family."

We had to curb our laughter before Lily or Pearl herself asked us what had us so giggly, but I'd have to tell Zoey and Michelle at the first chance I got.

Carrie was already inside with Alissa. "Come in, come in," Alissa cried. She held a tray full of champagne flutes, which about half of us took. Pearl, of course, passed by with a sniff.

"None for you," Alissa said to Zoey and Michelle. "Are either of you twenty-one?"

"I am," Michelle said. "But I'm driving, so I'll pass."

Olivia looked at her, surprised. "I thought you were Wallie's age."

"No," I teased. "Wallie got himself an older woman. She's a *junior*." Wallie was just starting his sophomore year and was nineteen now. I didn't mind that small age gap, especially considering what a peach Michelle was. She truly was. I loved her to pieces.

I took a flute of champagne. "Sure that's a good idea?" Olivia asked.

Rolling my eyes, I gulped down half the glass. "Other than it being before noon on a Saturday, it's a great idea." I lowered my voice to make sure Pearl didn't hear. "The blood test was clear."

"Okay, Ava. I've got five gowns selected that put me in mind of the one that disappeared." Her gaze shifted just briefly toward Pearl and Lily.

We were all thinking it. Somehow, Ian had gotten the dress or put someone up to it. But it did no good to mention it now. I surged forward and into the dressing room. "Let's do this!"

Olivia helped me in and out of each gown. The first two were too tight, and the way they fit, I didn't feel like a bigger size would help. I was all boobs and hips, and these flowed in all the wrong places. Alissa's cheeks pinked up when she realized she'd picked the wrong style and when she came back, it was with a structured gown that was almost mermaid style, but not quite that severe. I was pretty sure I wouldn't like it but put it on anyway.

When I walked out to show the crowd, they ooh-ed and aah-ed, but Michelle winked. "You don't have that look on your face."

"What look?" I asked though I was pretty sure I knew what she meant.

"You know. The look that says you're sure this is *the* gown." She looked around. "She's gotta have the look, right?"

After saying that, she furrowed her brows and put a hand to her lips. "Oh, my. Could I have some water?"

I rushed over and sat beside her, but she waved me off. "I'm fine. Don't bring the dress over here, though, just in case."

Alissa squeaked and rushed forward with a small white trash can she'd pulled out of nowhere. "Are you going to vomit?"

"No." Michelle was looking a little green. Maybe we did all have a stomach bug the other night and it hadn't been food poisoning. "I'm not going to vomit. I've had a particularly heavy course load this semester, and I haven't been getting enough sleep. I think it's catching up to me."

Pearl harrumphed. "If you don't take care of your body, girly, it'll force you to."

With that sage wisdom, I stood. Pearl turned her sharp glare to me. "That gown is wrong. Try the next."

Oh, boy. She was wonderful.

It wasn't until the seventh gown that we knew. Olivia met my gaze, and tears welled up in my eyes. The gown was completely different from the stolen one.

This was cream-colored and sleeveless. It had a deep vee in the front, a wide strip of fabric going horizontal across my upper abdomen, and a long, flowing skirt. "It's almost a maxi dress," I said.

"But way fancier," Olivia added. "It's perfect. You can wear your hair down."

"Now I'm sad it'll be too chilly to have it outside," I said. "This is the perfect beach gown."

"True." She winked at me in the mirror. "It's the perfect gown, period."

We stepped out of the dressing room, and everyone gasped. Their oohs and aahs were sincere this time. "Now you have the look," Lily pointed out.

Carrie clasped her hands together and sighed. "Oh, I'm so happy for you. Not at all jealous."

Olivia chuckled. "Maybe a little jealous." She stepped back and she and Alissa fluffed out the skirt. "Makes me wish I could do it again."

"Hello," Zoey said. "Vow renewal!"

Everyone but Pearl laughed as Olivia waved them off. "Not until we've been married longer. Maybe for twenty years."

"Or a hundred," Carrie suggested.

Olivia looked puzzled. "A hundred?"

Oh, Carrie was right. I hadn't thought much about it before now. "Olivia, Sam's immortal now."

Olivia's face morphed from confused to shocked, to thrilled. "And so am I. Oh, my gosh. We haven't even *discussed* this aspect of him being a vampire. We'll be together forever!" She pulled out her phone, halfway to dialing when she remembered. "Crap. He's asleep."

10

OLIVIA

"Have a little bite before you go to sleep," I said, holding out my wrist to my vampire hubby. "Just a sip."

Sam shrugged as if uninterested, then unlaced his boots. "I'm not really hungry."

I pushed away feelings of being rejected. Because he hadn't rejected me. Just my blood. There was no reason for me to take it personally. Sam loved me. I knew that without a doubt.

He was just down and depressed and I feared that he was regretting his choice to be brought back as a vampire.

Climbing onto the bed, I rubbed his shoulders and tried to think of a way to cheer him up. He'd been so down lately since his change. There had to be a way for this to be spun positively for him. "Hey, you know, we're both immortal now. We've been thinking about the short term for a while, but we haven't really stopped to think long term."

He turned on the bed to face me, then blinked, twice. "That's true. Though, we aren't sure how long you'll live, are we?"

Shrugging, I took his hand and stroked his knuckles with my thumb. "No, but my mother is fae and my father is... well, we don't know, but he's been alive pretty much forever."

"Speaking of that, haven't you wondered if he has other children?" Sam looked up at me with a twinkle in his eyes. I liked seeing that.

"Every day. Good lord, he's so old *you and I* could be related."

We both froze and looked at each other with totally icked-out expressions on our faces, then shuddered. "Changing the subject," I said and stuck my wrist in his face. "Eat."

"Drink, technically," he mumbled, then with a sigh, he opened his mouth. I looked away, not the biggest fan of watching the initial piercing of his teeth into my skin. Normally, his fangs came out, and he bit. Then he'd drink, lick my wrist, heal me up, and that was that. There wasn't anything particularly erotic about the blood exchange, but it was rather intimate. I didn't like the idea of him biting another human, much less another woman, but I also understood he had to survive. So, I didn't ask. Trust was earned, and he'd more than earned mine.

A few seconds ticked by, and no pinch of pain on my wrist. I looked at Sam to find him sitting there with his brow furrowed, mouth open, and no fangs.

"What's wrong?" I asked.

"I don't know." He closed his mouth, swallowed a few times, ran his tongue around his teeth, and then opened his mouth again.

This time, I watched. His fangs never came down. "What the hell?" He pursed his lips, and the corners of his eyes squinched together like he was hyper-focusing.

It really wasn't funny. So why was a giggle trying to force its way up my throat? "What's wrong, honey? Do you have Efangdile Dysfunction?"

I burst out laughing and rolled around on the bed while Sam stared at me. "Har, har." He didn't find it amusing. Although I did see the hint of a smile twitching on the corner of his lips.

Sobering up, I climbed onto his lap, straddling him. "What is it?"

"I don't know. Sometimes I worry I might lose control. You're fae, and that's supposed to mean I'll lose control with you." He looked sheepish. "I worry about that."

"Is that why you haven't wanted to eat?" I pushed at his shoulder. "I'm only part fae, hon, remember? I'm part minor god as well. So, if you go too far, I'll blast you with magic."

Sam got a mischievous look on his face, and his fangs slid down. He knew I'd do it, too. "Deal."

An hour later, he was satiated in more than one way, and I started my day with a long shower. Then coffee, cause I'd gotten up way early to spend some time with my Sam, then I got Sammie up and off to his private lessons with Carrie.

With Sammie being homeschooled, I could start moving his bedtime as well as mine. I would when Ava's wedding was over. There was still a lot to do, and all of those things had to be done in the daylight hours.

With a sigh, I closed the door behind Carrie and Sammie and turned toward the kitchen, eager for another cup of coffee. When I entered the kitchen, I jumped a mile, squeaked, and had to stop myself from blasting my Aunt Evie with magic. "What are you doing here?"

I gasped and had to really focus to dial down my magic. Evie was one of my mom's sisters. She was Mom's opposite in appearance, except for the blue eyes that the whole family seemed to have. Evie's dark brown hair was pulled back into a thick braid with flowers woven in it. Her naturally sun kissed skin glowed slightly.

All of my fae relations had that perfect glowy skin. Mine only glowed when I performed high levels of magic.

"I didn't mean to startle you. I was hoping to see your father," she said, tossing her braid over her shoulder. "Your mother is in Faery and she's down. She doesn't like that he's spending so much time away."

"I know," I said, heading for the coffee pot. "But he's got some drama or other going on down there and he's having to spend a lot of time dealing with it."

And my mom wanted no part of it. She didn't like Hell much. Then again, I hadn't met anyone who did, besides Luci.

"Well, see if you can talk some sense into him. I won't have your mother upset." Those words were spoken like the true royal she was.

I saluted her, then added cream to my coffee. "Yes, ma'am." When I looked up, she was gone. "Okay, then."

Not in any hurry to have to spend my day tracking down my father, I leisurely finished my coffee, left a note on the off-chance Sam woke up, then tried portaling to Hell. I'd never been there, nor had I ever had a desire to go, but that was the more likely location to find Luci.

I appeared in a room that was just... "Wow," I muttered as I drank in the throne room. The flooring was the color of black ice, and the walls were light gray stone like a castle's walls, at least where I could see them. Massive portraits and tapestries covered most of the walls. The portraits were framed in gold. No doubt it was real gold, not that cheap leaf crap.

Luci sat on a massive gold throne, looking dejected with his head in his hands, but he looked up when he heard my voice. "Olivia," he exclaimed. "You're here."

Turning in a slow circle, I took in the enormity that was my father's throne room. "This is…"

"Yeah." He stood and walked down the steps of the dais. "I need to redecorate. I haven't had it done since Henry VIII did it in the sixteen hundreds."

"King Henry VIII is in Hell? No, don't answer that question." I held up one hand. "It makes perfect sense."

Luci burst out laughing as he advanced toward me. "Oh, yeah he's *totally* here. He's currently spending most of his time as a member of one of my top female demon's harems. As I understand, she's quite dominant with him."

"That's… TMI, but also somehow fitting." I looked around at the medieval-looking throne room and sighed. "So, Mom's kind of pouting that you've been gone so much. Where have you been?"

Rubbing his face, he moaned deep in his chest, then shot me an apologetic look. "I'm sorry. I've had this thing going on and I'm not any closer to resolving it. I promise I'll check in with your mom soon, okay?"

"Deal." I took one final look around, shook my head again, and went home for my coffee.

11

AVA

I SPREAD my hands and leaned forward. "So, there we were, on a *ghost train* of all things, and Sam says, 'Hey, at least it's not a ghost *plain.*'" Everyone at the table—except for Grandma Pearl, shocker though it may be—burst out laughing.

Olivia laughed so hard she had to wipe tears from her eyes. "I love that joke."

Sam sipped on a mug of blood and smiled to himself, too modest to laugh too hard, but I knew him well enough to know he appreciated the laughter. Who wouldn't?

Drew's phone rang as Olivia started describing some of the ghosts we'd met on the train. He got up to excuse himself to answer. I ignored him, for the most part, until anger and upset came through our bond. "Excuse me," I muttered and rushed from the table and out the door into the conservatory.

The conservatory was where I grew my herbs and indoor plants used for spell work. My other half was an earth witch, so I used the conservatory for spell casting. Tucked into one corner was a small antique wood-burning stove. One side of it was my workstation.

Drew stood in the center of the room with his brows pinched together, and his lips pursed.

"What is it?" I mouthed, moving to stand in his line of sight.

"It shouldn't have been declined," he said into the phone. "Did you run it twice?" He put the phone on speaker. "The caterer," he whispered. "Card is being declined."

Geez. Now what? "Come with me." I rushed to my office with Drew behind me. As I passed the kitchen, everyone stared. Olivia looked like she was about to jump up and come help. She had to put her two cents in.

I didn't mind, though. I liked her two cents.

Once in the office, I got my emergency credit card out of my purse. Drew rattled off the info to the caterer, then hung up.

Spreading my hands, I shook my head. "Why are they calling at nine o'clock on a Monday night?"

He put his wallet back in his pocket. "They were putting in the final food order with their suppliers and the card was declined."

We headed back out to the kitchen, where everyone was enjoying a cake Alfred had made. "Check the website for your card company and see if there's a reason. Otherwise, we'll have to call in the morning."

Drew grunted and pulled out his phone to look it up while I told the rest of the people at the table why we'd run off.

Olivia and Sam took up the story of the ghost train again, but once again, the bond clued me in that Drew was extremely unhappy. This time, it was hot rage. I looked at him in surprise.

Through clenched teeth, he said, "Someone got my credit card number and ran up about eight thousand dollars of online gambling charges."

Almost every head at the table turned to Ian. Sam and Olivia had no real reason to assume it was him, but when they saw everyone else looking at him, they did as well.

"No," Ian said loudly. "I'm clean. I've been clean for six years. I haven't so much as scratched a lottery ticket."

Ian was a recovering gambler. Drew had told me that little tidbit a few days ago. This really did seem like something he would've done years ago, according to what Drew had told me. "I've been so proud of you, man," Drew said. "Now this? You do this right before my wedding?"

Jumping up, Ian threw his napkin over the cake and stomped for the front door. "Enough of this," he said just loud enough for us to hear. "I'm out of here." Flinging the front door open, he disappeared into the night.

Drew slung the kitchen chair back to follow his brother, and duh, the rest of us followed. This was gearing up to be a doozy, and I wasn't about to miss it. I didn't have siblings to fight with.

Pfft. Like anybody else would, either. As we passed the stairs, I even saw Zoey and Larry peeking over the landing, curious about the yelling.

"Stop!" Drew yelled. "You don't get to ruin everything then just leave!"

"Drew, the boy says it wasn't him," Pearl said, stomping her cane once on the porch steps. "Why won't you consider it could be someone else?"

"Because everything points to him." Drew moved closer to Ian and for a second I thought he was going to throw a punch. "First, the venue burned down, and don't think we didn't notice that you came in and wouldn't tell anyone where you'd been right after that."

LIA DAVIS & L.A. BORUFF

Ian glared at me. Of course, I'd told Drew what had happened. Who wouldn't share that sort of thing with their fiancée?

"Then," Drew continued, "Everyone who ate the caterer's samples gets food poisoning, *except* for *you*." Drew jabbed his finger in Ian's face and Ian slapped it away.

Everyone sort of gasped or clutched their pearls, so to speak. "Oh, stop it," I said. "It's not Jerry Springer." Moving forward, I put a comforting hand on Drew's arm because his anger had spiked when Ian smacked his hand. "Ian, it really does add up to looking like you did these things."

"Nobody ever figured out who stabbed me, either," Drew said menacingly. "Where were you that night?"

"I was here." Ian's demeanor changed, then. He went from furious to looking betrayed. "Drew, man, come on. I can see how you'd think I'd do stuff like mess with the food or gamble. I get it, I don't have the most trustworthy past. But do you really think I'd stab you?" He backed away a few steps. "That's hurtful."

"Drew," I said quietly. "Maybe it's time for the truth stone." We'd already talked about using it but had been afraid even suggesting the idea of it would make his family mad enough to leave. We wanted to make peace with them, not make things worse.

"You have a truth stone?" Ian gaped at me. "Get it. Now. I want to use it. Then you'll all eat crow."

Drew nodded once, so I conjured it out of my office drawer. Holding it out, I asked, "Where were you when the venue burned down?"

"I met a couple of people in town and went to a party," Ian answered without hesitation.

I didn't give him time to think, moving straight into my next question. "Did you mean to ruin my dress?"

He shook his head. "You know that was an accident."

Nodding, I said, "Yeah, just checking. Who stabbed Drew?"

Ian folded his arms over his chest. "I don't know. I wasn't there."

"Did you have *anything* to do with any of the wedding mishaps?"

He let out a dramatic sigh. "No. I'm a hunter, and it's in my blood to dislike the paranormal, but I can clearly see my brother is happy with you and your crazy life. I would never do anything to hurt him."

Every word he spoke was the truth. That's how the stone worked. While in its presence he couldn't lie.

"Now do you see?" Ian pressed his lips together, clearly emotional. We'd hurt him. "I'd never stab you, Drew. No matter who you marry." He turned back toward the house, and everyone parted to let him walk inside. Winston opened and closed the door for him, too.

My chest tightened and a heavy weight of guilt settled over me. But in my defense, it had appeared as though he had done those things.

If it wasn't Ian, then who would want to stop my and Drew's wedding?

As I sniffled and squeezed Drew's arm, something stung me on the back of my leg. "Ow," I squealed.

The yard was bright with moonlight, but it wasn't enough to see what had gotten me. "Something stung me." I danced around for a second, but then Drew hollered, too.

"What the hell?" he roared. "That hurt!"

We all started running around, slapping, as we kept getting stung. "Go inside," Olivia screamed.

A ball of light appeared above us as my mother leaned out of her bedroom window. "What's going on out there?"

I didn't take the time to explain. "Shut the window!" I screeched as I followed everyone in the house. Pearl was the last to come in, but she walked, took her time, and didn't react when I clearly saw a small flying thing sting her cheek.

Slamming the door shut behind her, I picked one of the insects off of Drew's shirt and threw it to the ground, then stomped on it. Bending over, I squinted to see. "It's a bee," I said. "Just a bee."

"I've never heard of honeybees being that aggressive," Drew said.

Me neither except in those creature feature movies I'd watched as a kid.

Just then, the bees outside started slamming into the windows. Winston was having a fit. His floorboards and walls shook. "Winston, you are not helping."

He stopped, and I breathed out, "thank you," as I glanced down at the floor where that dead bee was. It was gone. "Um, did anyone pick up the dead bee?"

Everyone shook their heads. Weird. I stretched out my necromancer senses. As soon as my magical awareness touched the bees outside and inside, I knew without a doubt that they were undead. "The bees are dead!" I exclaimed. "Someone animated a nest of dead bees. Who would do that?"

Dad and Owen rushed down the stairs with Mom and Winnie behind them. Zoey and Larry entered the living room from the kitchen. Larry said, "All the windows and doors are shut."

The bee I'd stepped on moments ago flew past me. It only had one working wing and its body was squished. I wasn't sure how it was still able to fly around.

"This is crazy even for me." I stretched my magic out once again and tried to inanimate the bees. But nothing happened. "My stupid magic isn't working on them."

Owen stepped up next to me. "I got it."

A few moments later the sad, squashed bee, still trying to sting us without his stinger, dropped dead on the floor. The sound of them hitting the windows stopped soon after, so I went to the closest window and peered out. It took a little bit for my eyes to adjust to the moonlit lawn. When they did I saw a bunch of dead bees.

"What the heck was that?" I turned from the window to see everyone looking at me. "What?"

Drew eased forward. "Your powers have been wonky lately."

"You think I did this? No way. Where did the bees come from?"

Alfred came in with a broom, dustpan, and a trash bag. "There was a bee's nest inside the old tree out front. I moved them earlier today. Any time you move bees, a bunch are likely to die, but I didn't want Sammie stung."

Well, that explained that. "I must have done it when Drew and Ian were arguing. Emotions were high."

Mostly Drew's emotion rushing through our magical bond, but I wasn't going to say that out loud. I wasn't sure his family knew about that.

"Those weren't bees."

I and everyone else turned to look at Larry when he spoke. I said, "Yeah...they were bees."

He shook his head and said, "Nope. They were zombees. Get it?" A smile spread across his face. "Zombees. Zom-BEES."

A real knee slapper.

1 2

AVA

"WHERE IS MR. SNOOZERTON?" I asked Lucy at breakfast the next morning. "I haven't seen him in days."

Before you ask, yes, Lady Lucy-Fur sits at the table with us, but only when she wishes to grace us with her presence. I had a feeling she wanted to say something.

She finished her bite of scrambled egg and sighed. "I told you, he's hiding in the attic."

Where was I? That cat was losing her mind. "You didn't tell me. I didn't know that."

With another mouthful of egg, she did her little shrug thing again. "Maybe I told Olivia. All you humans look alike to me."

Taking a bite of my own eggs, I gave her a second before asking again. "So, where is he?"

"He's hiding in the attic." She gnawed on the end of her sausage link. "And won't come out."

"Why?" My poor Snoozy. "Should I go talk to him?"

"No, don't bother. I've talked until my fur fell out. He's mad because there are new rooms and furniture in the house." She lapped at the cream that Alfred had set beside her plate. "It won't do any good. You'll just have to wait for him to come around." Another first for me: she rolled her blue eyes. I'd never seen a cat do that, not even her. "You know how cats are."

With a hiccup to hide the giggle, I nodded. "I do know how cats are."

Seconds later, Drew walked in with his uniform on, ready to go in for his mid-shift. He had his cell in his hand. "Can you repeat what you just told me?" he said into the phone.

As the person on the other end of the line spoke, Ian, Lily, and my mom walked into the kitchen. I recognized the voice. It was Janice, the caterer. "I said, something happened with my ordering system. Your part of my food order was dropped, though I *know* it was there last night when I hit submit. The company that fulfills my food orders swears they didn't get it, and they've already picked my order in the night. It's too late to get another order that will be here in time."

"Can't you just go to the grocery store?" I asked. This didn't seem like that big of a deal to me.

"No, I'm so sorry. I can't. There's no time to figure out what I'd substitute, and in what quantities, and I don't have the staff to spare to go do the shopping. I'm so sorry, Ava. I can't do your wedding."

Drew walked away to say goodbye, and I sat at the table with tears in my eyes.

Lucy finished up her breakfast. "This seems like a human kind of moment. I'll leave you all to your blubbering."

Ian took a mug of coffee from Alfred. "Thanks." Then he looked at me with a hard expression. "Don't even think about accusing me. I can barely turn on a computer."

"That's true," Lily said. "He's hopeless with technology. That's part of the reason I believed it wasn't him doing online gambling so quickly."

"Yeah, I didn't even think about using that as a defense." Ian shrugged. "I really wouldn't know how to do online bets."

"I'm sorry," I said miserably. "I'll apologize a million times if that's what it takes. I truly hate that we suspected you."

The truth was I'd been a mess since everyone started to arrive. With my powers on the fritz and not knowing why I'm surprised I hadn't exploded.

He sighed and sat beside me at the table. "I can understand why you'd think some of it was me. I'm not really happy about my big brother marrying a witch-necromancer, and I'm not afraid to say it."

"Maybe we're not happy our daughter is marrying a hunter," Mom said defensively, though I knew she was blowing smoke. She loved Drew.

"Stop." I didn't have the energy to raise my voice. Another thing going wrong with the wedding was taking it all out of me. "We still don't have a venue, and now we don't have food. What are we going to do?"

"Ava, if you'd let me, I'd love to make the food for your wedding."

I turned to look at Alfred and hope soared in my heart. "Do you think you could? Here in this kitchen?"

He twisted his lips. "Winston, do you think you could make a temporary kitchen for us on the wedding day? Something bigger?"

Winston clapped the cabinets open and shut in quick succession. "I'll take that as a yes!" I jumped up and threw my arms around Alfred's neck. "You're the best."

"You still need a location."

Great. The peanut gallery had arrived. I let go of Alfred to glare at Pearl. She'd just walked in. "We'll figure it out. If we have to do it out in the woods, we'll get it sorted."

"I'll start now," Alfred said. "Zoey and Larry can help me, and we'll do it buffet style, so we don't need servers."

He grabbed a notebook and disappeared upstairs.

Drew pulled me into his arms and pressed a kiss to my lips. "Don't forget I have to go to that ceremony this afternoon for Sam and me. I'm accepting a commendation for us solving the murder that *you* actually solved."

They'd had to put something on paper for why that little girl's body had been found. They'd made up some mess about finding an old stain and it leading them to investigate further until they'd found the body in the garden and the knife buried with it. "Are you sure you don't want me to go with you?" I asked.

With a chuckle, he shook his head. "No. We didn't really solve that murder. I feel bad accepting an award for it, but if we refuse it, we'll look fishy. I have to go."

After breakfast, I spent the day researching locations, but everyone I called, each one increasingly more desperate, was booked. I finally hung up with the local arcade and banged my head down on the desk. It was nearly closing time for all of these places.

My phone rang a few seconds later, and my heart soared. Drew was feeling really good, and it was his ringtone. Maybe he had some news that would cheer me up. "Tell me something good," I said as a way of greeting.

"This ceremony is being held at the bed and breakfast on the far side of town."

"The one Ben and Brandon don't like because it's their biggest competitor?" I asked. It was too bad they hadn't been able to get their B&B ready in time. That would've been the perfect location.

"That's the one. They had a cancellation. I stopped by the desk on the way out and asked, on a whim, if they were open the day of our wedding, and it had *just* happened. I booked it."

"You did?" I put my hand on my chest and sent him all the loving feelings I could muster. "Have I told you lately that I love you?"

"Tell me again."

"I love you."

We hung up and I jumped to my feet. Who to tell first? I texted Olivia. **New location. Claireborne B&B. Can you tell your parents?** They were doing the flowers. Her human parents, not Luci, who was still MIA.

What next? The food. Hurrying up the stairs, I ran straight to Alfred's room. He'd gone up to work on his menu a few hours ago. I was so excited I flung his door open without knocking and froze for a second. When my brain finally registered what I was seeing, I screamed and covered my eyes.

Then Alfred screamed. His was a lot shriller than mine.

I slammed the door shut. After a beat to give myself time to breathe again, I yelled through the door to tell my aunt Winnie and Alfred, who had been doing naked, ahem, *yoga,* the good news through the door.

"Now I have to go bleach my eyeballs," I muttered as I headed downstairs to tell everybody else.

13

OLIVIA

HAVING a leisurely coffee wasn't in the cards for me this week. I'd just gotten Sam to bed and Sammie off to his lessons with Carrie when my phone rang. It was Ava's signature ringtone, from the *FRIENDS* TV show theme song. "What's up?"

I knew my coffee break was over when her voice came out all shrill and upset. "The bed and breakfast called. All of their electrical panels were destroyed last night. It was sabotage, clearly, someone did it to them."

"No," I drew out the vowel, shocked that something else had happened to disrupt Ava's wedding. "Who could've done it?"

"Well, don't even think of Ian. I still feel terrible accusing him."

"Ava, I know she's older, but she's pretty spry, or so it seems. What are the chances it was Granny Pearlie?"

"I don't think so." She sighed and I could picture her throwing herself back onto her pillows. No way she was up yet. Ava hated mornings. "I can't see her hurting Drew or burning down a venue.

She seems fond of humans, and this was some major damage. They say it's going to be weeks before it's repaired."

"What now? Are there any other places?"

"Nothing." Poor Ava. She sounded like she was crying now. "I joked about having it in the woods, but it's too cold."

We sat in silence for a moment, thinking. "Where's Luci?" she asked. "He's usually good with this sort of crap. Maybe he can do something to figure out who is trying to stop the wedding. Or portal us all to Paris."

I'd told her about finding him in Hell in a room that had looked like the medieval version of Buckingham Palace had vomited into it. "I'll go see if he's still in his throne room, pouting. If I can, I'll get him to come help."

"Thanks, Liv. I appreciate it." She hiccupped as she hung up.

Yep. I had to try to help my friend. Without any idea who could've been doing this or no knowledge of how to figure it out, I needed help. If Luci wouldn't or couldn't leave Hell, I'd go find Phira and see if she or any of the aunts and uncles could help. The Fae were pretty magical. They might know how to find the culprit.

Popping into the throne room, I found Luci there, all right, but he'd redecorated. "Holy guacamole."

Man-with-cigar chic. Wow. "I... Love what you've done with the place?" The walls had been paneled in a dark wood, and there was an actual antler chandelier. It looked like a hunting lodge had thrown up this time. I turned around to find a stag's head mounted on the wall, beside a— "What the *hell* is that?" Pun intended.

Luci walked over proudly and reached up to pat the dead creature on the snout. "This was Killer. My first hellhound. He was the best pup I've ever had. When he died, I couldn't let him go, so I had his head mounted. It's been in storage for years."

"And you thought mounting it... Okay, yeah whatever, listen..." I tried to gather my thoughts as I stared up at the horrible creature. He was a mix of brown and black fur with wild-looking eyes and half his face looked like it was exposed bone. "Um." His teeth were huge and stained red. *Ew.* "Ava needs us."

"Olivia." Luci's sharp tone got my attention. "Careful. The hellhounds have the ability to enchant. Even dead this long, you have a hard time looking away from him, yes?"

"Whoa, that's wild. Yes." I whirled around and kept the vile creature to my back. "Ava's wedding is being sabotaged. Someone keeps messing with stuff, so she's worried the wedding won't even go off. Fires at the venues, canceling the caterer's order, stuff like that. Drew got stabbed, too, but we're not sure if that was related."

Luci hung his head. "Come on. We better head to Ava's. I think I know what's going on."

He disappeared before I could ask what he meant, so I hurried and portaled myself to Ava's front porch. Walking in, I found Alfred pushing coffee into Luci's hand and Ava hurrying down the stairs.

"Thank you," she whispered and squeezed my arm. "Did you tell him?"

"I did, and he said he might know what's going on."

We hurried into the living room, where Drew's family and Ava's family sat with only a *lot* of tension in the air. "Who is this?" Granny Pearl asked.

Oh, this was going to be fun. I smiled brightly and made the introductions. "Pearl, head of the Walker Family of hunters, meet Luci." I pushed my father forward. "Lucifer, head of Hell."

Lily, Pearl, and Ian jumped to their feet, and then there was *real* tension in the room. "Relax," Ava said. "He's a friend."

"Literally?" Lily asked, her gaze on Luci, but the words directed at me. "He's literally Lucifer?"

"Yep. And my father." I added with my grin still in place because it kept me from laughing.

Pearl looked truly shocked for the first time that I'd been around her. She shifted her attention to me with wide eyes. "He's your father?"

"Yep." I slapped him on the back. "Ol' Dad."

Luci rolled his eyes but looked at me with amusement.

Ava bustled around us. "Sit, sit. He's harmless."

With a sniff, Luci gave Ava an affronted look.

"Well," she amended. "He's harmless to *us*."

"As long as they don't pull out those weapons," he said dryly. "I'm harmless to everyone here."

I stared hard at Drew's family but couldn't see anywhere they had weapons on them. "Whatever you say. Tell us what you were going to."

He sat in one of her armchairs and cleared his throat. "I have a confession to make." What the heck was wrong with him? I'd never seen him look so guilty. "So, you know I took Crystal to Hell a while back and imprisoned her with her mother and uncle?"

Ava's eyes narrowed. "Yes. What of it?"

Before he could answer, drawing out the moment, Phira walked into the living room. "There you are," she said, chastising him. "Where have you been?"

"Later, Phira." I waved her over to me. "He's just about to tell us why he's been gone so much."

He gave my mother an apologetic look. "Crystal sort of escaped. And so did Bevan and Penny. We think that Crystal got herself caught on purpose. Her cell and theirs were melted by some sort of a potion. We don't know where she had it hidden."

Ugh. "I don't want to know." After a shudder, I looked at Luci. "Crystal, Bevan, and Penny have been loose in Hell all this time and you didn't tell us?"

It was a betrayal, is what it was. He hadn't trusted us enough to confide in. Standing, I told him exactly that. "We're supposed to be a team," I said, throwing my arms around. "That wasn't team-like."

"I know. I'm so sorry. I should've told you and your mother when it first happened. But we thought we had it confined to Hell, and I'm not used to dealing with problems as a family." He jumped up, grabbed my shoulders, and looked me in the eyes. "I really am sorry. When you turned up today I was thinking about how I was going to break it to you and apologize."

"Apologize?" Phira said. "You owe me a big one for ignoring me so much.

Luci let go of me and turned to pull her into a hug. "I did apologize. In your room in Faerie." A big smile spread across his face. "Three times."

"Oh, gross. Stop." Ew, ew, ew.

"Wait a second." Ava jumped to her feet. "What do you mean you *thought* you *had* it confined to Hell?"

Luci let Phira go and faced the wrath of Ava. "We now think they're here. Not in Hell."

"So, all this sabotage?" she asked.

"Probably Crystal."

Ava sighed. "Honestly, I'm relieved. I can handle Crystal, as long as we can find her. And we can start scrying right away." She looked at her mom. "You and Winnie get on it?"

Beth jumped to her feet and ran out the door, calling behind her, "I'll find Win and get to it!"

"I still have nowhere for the wedding." Ava moaned and rubbed her hands on her face.

Luci wandered into the kitchen for a few seconds, then came back. "Ava? What about this?" He motioned toward the kitchen.

Once in there, he pointed out the back door. I followed Ava over to look outside when she gasped.

Out the windows was an enormous spread. Tents, heat lamps, and chairs stretched out from Ava's deck all the way to the cliffs.

We hurried out onto the deck and looked to the right. There was a huge dance floor surrounded by heat lamps in the field between Ava's house and Luci's. And the lawn had been perfectly manicured.

"Give me a few minutes and tell me what décor you like, and I'll do more." Luci ducked his head. "It's the least I can do since I should've told you all about Crystal."

"Oh, Luci," Ava breathed. "It's perfect." She stepped slowly off of the deck with tears in her eyes. "I couldn't have done all this myself."

I put my arm around Luci's waist and squeezed. "Good one."

After Ava took a few moments to be emotional, she whirled around and pinned her gaze on Larry. "You and Zoey call all the guests and give them the updated location."

With a groan, he saluted halfheartedly. "Again."

Ava clapped her hands. "Let's kick Crystal's butt and have ourselves a wedding!"

14

AVA

"Well, that was easy." Mom walked down the attic stairs as I came out of my bedroom. "She's at her mom's house."

"Penny's?" I asked in surprise. "That seems a little on the nose. Why would she hide out in such an obvious place?"

Mom shrugged. "No idea, but she's there now."

Hmm, that was convenient. I was betting it was a trap. Or Crystal wasn't very smart.

"Well, come on." I hurried downstairs and looked at my crowd. "Okay, who needs to stay here to do wedding stuff, and who wants to come to help me with Crystal?"

"I have a shift," Drew said. He leaned over and pressed a kiss to my cheek. "Kick all the butt, honey."

My heart warmed at his absolute faith in me.

Of course, it didn't hurt that his brother and sister were going with me. They both looked eager. A little too eager.

Pearl sniffed and sat in the living room. "I'll sit this one out."

Good.

I looked at Alfred. "I think it might be best if nobody who has been animated goes."

One, Crystal was half necromancer. I didn't think she was especially powerful. She wasn't as powerful as me, that was for sure. I wouldn't be taking any chances with my ghouls.

"No, that's fine." He waved his hands at me. "I have too much to do to prep for Saturday."

"We're still on the phone," Zoey called from upstairs. Which was a good thing because Larry and Zoey were also ghouls.

Vampires wouldn't be any help, either. Wade and Sam sat together at the kitchen table, sipping on the blood we all regularly donated to Wade. He'd gotten pretty good at hunting, so he had enough bagged blood to share with Sam. Plus, I'd heard them talking at some point about a blood bank, and I just didn't want to know.

Plausible deniability was a thing.

Owen was on his way back from the bookstore and would be disappointed we left before he got home, but we knew where she was, so we needed to move.

"I'm in," Luci said, and Phira waved at me, acknowledging her participation.

Olivia grinned and bounced on her toes. "Me, too. I'm ready to flex my magic."

Shaking my head, I looked over at Lily and Ian. "We might be a bit of overkill."

Mom and Winnie volunteered to stay behind and help Alfred, as did Dad. He pressed a kiss to my forehead. "Have fun, honey."

Have fun. On my way to capture or possibly kill a rogue necromancer he says have fun. "I'd have a lot more fun if my powers were working and I could just take care of all of this on my own."

Mom tutted with sympathy. "I know sweetie. We'll figure it out eventually."

She better believe we would. Right after I get hitched and get back from my honeymoon.

"Well, let's go." Luci spread his arms out and a portal opened. He put one finger over his lips, so we'd be quiet going through.

We stepped into what I recognized as Crystal's father's office. The last time I'd been here was when Olivia and I had broken into the house and taken Bill's journal. That was where we got the spell to place Mom's and Winnie's souls into new bodies.

Looking back, I froze and stared at Pearl, then shrugged, as if to say, *What gives?*

She didn't bother lowering her voice at all. "I wanted to make sure you lot do your jobs right." With some side eye to Luci, she pushed her way to the front of the crowd, right behind Ian.

Sneaking out of the office, we stopped and listened. Ian took the lead, using finger signals I didn't recognize to lead us down the stairs and into the kitchen, where Crystal stood at a stove with headphones on, making what looked and smelled like stir-fry.

I stepped forward while Lily and Ian guarded my flank and pulled the headphones off of Crystal's ears. "Hello."

She shrieked and flailed her arms, hitting the skillet handle. Stir fry flew everywhere. A blob landed on my arm, burning me a little.

"Hey," I yelled. "Stop that."

But she'd used the flying stir fry to her advantage. She flung a knife none of us had noticed at Ian, and it wedged itself squarely in his shoulder. I started toward her, but Lily, trained from infancy to be a fighter, beat me to it. Olivia used magic to bind Crystal, and Lily whapped her a good one right in the eye. Since they clearly had Crystal under control, I turned to Ian, praying to all the deities who would listen to give me enough power to heal him. The knife was awfully low in his shoulder. I worried about it nicking a major artery.

"Hold still," I whispered. Putting my hands over the knife, I didn't remove it in case this didn't work.

The wonder of wonders, my powers worked. As he healed, the knife slowly worked its way out of his shoulder and finally clattered onto the floor. "Thank goodness," I breathed and sat back.

Pearl thumped the ground with her cane. "You'll do." Then, she glanced at Luci and the others, who had Crystal trussed up like a Christmas goose. "Home, please."

Luci bowed his head. "Ma'am." With the snap of his finger, a portal opened into my living room. "Olivia can close that."

"Aw, I didn't even get to use my magic much at all." She shot Crystal a glare. "You could've been a little more difficult."

Crystal's eyes flashed, but someone had slapped a gag in her mouth, so all she could do was grunt.

Luci and Crystal disappeared, and we went home.

"That felt way too easy," I muttered.

"Easy!" Ian exclaimed. "Pfft. Not for me."

"Next time, don't get stabbed," Olivia said and walked past him, then closed the portal.

Ian looked at her with... could that have been a touch of respect in his eyes?

Possibly. But I wasn't holding my breath.

"We have company," Mom called from the kitchen. I hurried through in time to see Lily and Ian rush forward to embrace an older couple who had just risen from the table.

"Mom," Lily said and hugged her. Then she turned to the man. "Dad."

Pearl stood beside me as they turned to me. Drew's mother, Aisling–pronounced Ashling–seemed friendly enough as she smiled at me. "You must be Ava."

His dad, however, looked pretty hateful. "The witch," he spat.

With one resounding bang on the floor, Pearl slammed her cane down. "I like her."

She turned and walked up the stairs, leaving the rest of us gaping after her.

Lily giggled and looped her arm through mine. "I do, too. And so will you, Dad, when you give her a chance."

"We'll see," he said as he eyed me as if trying to figure out why his mother liked me.

"Come on." Lily grabbed one of the suitcases in the foyer. "Ava, the teal room?"

I nodded and watched them follow her upstairs. "Four more days," I muttered to myself. "Four more days, and they'll all go home." They were flying out the day after the wedding.

Everyone had difficulties with their in-laws... right?

15

AVA

"You look beautiful." Mom and Olivia stepped back with their hands over their hearts and Winnie clasped hers together.

I couldn't get ready with one or two women. Oh, no. But, really, did I want any of them to *not* be there?

No. I didn't. These were my favorite three women in the world. Well, who were living.

Mom had curled my hair into an elegant bun with thin ringlets that framed my face. Olivia'd done a great job on my makeup. I hardly recognized myself.

"Ready?" I asked, smoothing down the skirt of my dress—a simple but elegant blue maxi-style gown. My rehearsal dinner dress complemented my wedding dress. Same style, slightly less fancy. Olivia had insisted I needed a special dress for tonight as well as a third dress for the reception.

Together, we headed downstairs. I was nervous because things had been going so well. The only problem thus far was that Luci and Snoozer were MIA. Luci'd been gone since he took Crystal to Hell.

He'd popped in once on Olivia and let her know he was looking for Bevan and Penny. They'd done something to block themselves from being scryed. Mom and Winnie had a spell going pretty much constantly up in the attic, set to emit a loud shriek if it found them.

We had nothing to do right now but enjoy the rehearsal dinner. Somehow, that felt wrong. I kept waiting on the other shoe to drop.

We stepped out of the back door, and then I saw Drew, and everything fell into place. All my worries melted away as I looked at him, dressed in casual black slacks and a white button-down with the sleeves rolled halfway up his forearms. Why was that a sexy look for men? Winnie'd just given his salt-and-pepper hair a trim earlier today.

When he smiled at me, sending love through our bond, I turned into a puddle on the ground.

Even if the other shoe dropped, we'd handle it. That was what we did. And together, we did it *so* well.

This was just a rehearsal for tomorrow, and already I felt like I was going to bawl.

"Okay," Olivia said. She was my official but unofficial wedding planner. "Let's do this."

Melody, my dear friend, and the new High Witch of the Shipton Coven, stood at the end of the aisle talking to Drew. Melody was also a notary for the state of Maine and was marrying us.

Drew's mom and dad were behind him, with Ian and Lily. He'd had a really hard time choosing the best man between his brother and sister and Sam. But in the end, it was Sam who'd been there for him and who was so connected to us. Ian and Lily had understood.

There'd been no hesitation on my part, in choosing Olivia as my Matron of Honor. I loved Mom and Winnie, but Olivia was my ride-or-die girl. If it hadn't been her, it would've been Sam.

It worked out so Sam walked Olivia down the aisle, Ian walked Lily, and Drew had asked Alfred to be a groomsman.

The sweet, ancient man had cried. And also squeaked a little.

Olivia got us all organized, signaled to Melody, who helped get Drew in his proper spot, then we waited patiently for the music to start. Owen started the song we'd picked: *I Get to Love You* by Ruelle. I headed down the aisle on my father's arm.

I'd never dreamed this day would come. My heart swelled with love, which was compounded by the love I felt coming through the bond.

And a roar in the distance shattered the tranquility of the moment. "What in the world?" I turned toward the sound to find Luci running as fast as he could around the side of the house and toward the ocean. I'd never seen him run before, and it was comical. Like that pirate in that movie, all arms, elbows, and knees.

"Run!" he screamed as he flew by with impressive speed. "It got out!"

"What got out?" I asked faintly, now sure that the other shoe had fallen.

I was proven right a few seconds later when the ground shook and another roar filled the air. This time, the sound was much closer, and so loud it hurt my ears.

A gigantic monster slithered around the side of the house, roared again, and kept going toward the cliffs where Luci had disappeared.

Holy crap. It was as tall as the house, maybe taller, and had skin like a... I didn't even know. Maybe an octopus?

It also had tentacles, but many more than an octopus had. Probably ten or fifteen, all flailing in the air as it stopped and roared again.

It disappeared over the cliff a few moments later.

I turned to look at my wedding party, but they'd already jumped into action. Drew and Lily now held crossbows, and Ian reached into the pocket of his slacks and pulled one out.

Um. What? Either the weapons were magically enchanted to fit in their pockets, or the pockets were, cause *no way* they had those crossbows a few seconds ago.

"Now this is a party!" Ian yelled and took off running toward the cliffs.

"Sorry, hon." Drew shot me an apologetic look and went after him.

No need to apologize to me. I was still processing what was going on. Zombies and ghouls and vampires I could handle, but gigantic, roaring tentacled monsters? That was out of my league.

"This is what we do," Lily said as she kicked off her heels and sprinted after her brothers. Their parents were right behind them, magical weapons in hand.

"Don't think you're leaving me behind!" Pearl's cane was suddenly a *shotgun,* and she ran after them as well, not as fast as the others, but a darn sight faster than I would've thought she could go. She kicked off her shoes, sending them flying in different directions as she went.

"I better go see if I can help." Melody looked a little too eager as she took off, conjuring a ball of fire as she went, and Mom and Winnie hiked up their skirts and followed.

Dad patted my hand. "I don't know what help I can be since that thing's alive, but I'll try."

Alfred ran to the side of the deck and rummaged around underneath it, coming out with an ax. He sprinted after them as well, with Zoey in her tiger form by his side. Larry ambled after them, probably going more to watch than actually help. His head would probably fall off if he tried.

Sam and Wade glanced at each other. "Am I the only one who really wants to see what that thing's blood tastes like?" Sam asked.

"Yes," Olivia and I said at the same time, but as we did, Wade said, "No, I'm kind of curious."

Sam pecked Olivia's cheek and took off. "Back in a bit!"

"Well, I'm not staying behind." Wallie kissed Michelle's cheek and took off, too.

Soon it was me, Michelle, Owen, Olivia, and Sammie. Everyone else was down on the beach, presumably battling a gigantic monster. We heard a few roars, and Olivia practically danced on her feet.

"Go," I said. "I'll watch Sammie."

"Eep!" She hunkered down and looked her son in the face. "Stay with your aunt Ava."

"Okay, Mommy. You show that monster who is the boss." He went back to his puzzle, completely ignoring the rest of us, and not at all perturbed by the fact that his grandfather had been chased by something out of a kid's nightmares.

As Olivia portaled away, Owen walked over with a bottle of wine and three glasses. "Thirsty?"

"Boy, am I."

Michelle declined a glass of wine, saying that she had an early morning. I was about to tell her that one glass wouldn't hurt, but I didn't. Something nagged at the back of my mind, but I pushed it away.

We sat in the front row and sipped on rosé while the ground periodically shook, roars filled the air, and blasts of magic and fire alternated in the air.

About half an hour later, a timer went off in the house, so we went in, and Sammie 'helped' us get the last of the casseroles out of the oven. Alfred had gone for comfort food for the night's dinner.

The four of us had just finished placing the food on a large dining table outside when Drew and Ian came up the walking path over the cliffs dragging the creature.

Dang, it was huge.

Luci came next over the hill pushing Grandma in a wheelchair. They stopped and he grabbed her shoes along the way. Pearl was a hard person to figure out. I shook my head as I watched her laugh and joke with the devil.

Drew's mom and dad appeared next with Lily following, carrying the weapons. Everybody was smiling and laughing.

Drew and Ian dropped the creature a few yards from the house. Then Ian ran straight for me. Before I could fend him off, he pulled me into a huge bear hug, picking my feet off the ground, swinging me around, and covering me with disgusting, slimy monster goop. "Welcome to the family!"

1 6

AVA

"Oh, my dear. You do look lovely." Yaya smiled at me through the mirror, held by my mom. We'd finagled a steady stream of magic from one of the stones into the mirror. It was a subject we'd broached before, but the problem was, when we weren't actively holding the mirror, what were we to do with it? Leave it on a table, or hang it on the wall? I didn't like the idea of leaving her hanging there doing nothing.

Yaya herself made the final decision. She'd said charging up the mirror for special occasions was quite enough for her.

I didn't blame her. I wouldn't want to hang out in a mirror for the rest of eternity either.

Now that I was fully dressed, I had to agree with my semi-mostly-dead grandmother. This dress had been a perfect choice, almost making me glad the first had been stolen.

It hadn't been at the house where we'd found Crystal. No telling what she'd done with it. Probably burned it and danced on its remains.

"Whoa," Olivia said. She'd just walked in from getting ready in the only spare room we had left.

She looked beautiful in her floor-length baby blue A-line gown. Her blonde hair was perfectly coiffed and suited her expertly applied makeup. Her eyes shone as she looked me over. "Oh, Ava."

I hugged her as gently as I could, trying not to squish our dresses together, or smudge our makeup, or get a hair out of place.

"Everyone's here," Olivia said. "Are you ready?"

"I'm beyond ready. I can't wait to be married to Drew. I mean we're already—" I cut myself off. I'd almost said we're already bonded, but Drew's family didn't know. I looked around and remembered Lily and Pearl weren't in there. It was safe to speak freely. "—bonded. But somehow the wedding thing seems more... Something."

"The bonding ceremony was quick and small, and recent." Mom shrugged. "But marriage is a concept ingrained in you from childhood. You must've planned your wedding sixteen times before you were ten."

That was true. I'd had the big, blowout church wedding with Clay. Church wasn't something I was brought up with, but I'd gone with Clay and his family. The wedding and the marriage had been wonderful.

This was still going to be a blowout, but I wasn't sure we wouldn't all burst into flames if we stepped into a church. Especially Luci.

"Let's go." I pushed those thoughts away and headed out of the room.

Everyone followed me out, and I walked very carefully down the stairs. I wasn't a particularly clumsy person, but I was wearing heels, which I didn't often do, and a floor-length dress. No way I was ruining this day by tumbling down the stairs.

"Luci?" I asked, remembering that Olivia had said everyone was there as I carefully descended. "Did he make it?"

Who would've thought a year ago I'd be upset at the thought that Luci wouldn't be at my wedding?

A few moments later, I peeked through the sheer white curtains covering the windows in the kitchen. Hailey, Jax, and Kendra were just about to sit down under the tent full of our friends and family. "It looks like they're the last to sit," I whispered.

Jax and Hailey turned around and looked toward the house. They'd probably heard me. "Hey, guys," I said, unable to keep the excitement out of my voice.

Hailey waved and bounced in her seat a little.

"Oh, there's Rick and Dana Johnson. How nice they came." They were the ferret shifter couple I met when I'd discovered the shifter fighting ring Bevan and Penny had run.

I peered out to see who else had gotten here. Everyone had RSVP'd, but that didn't mean they'd actually show. I spotted Melody and the rest of the coven: Ben, Brandon, Mai, Alissa, and Leena.

The music changed and Olivia slipped out the back door. When she came back, a curtain had been drawn at the back of the tent, so the guests, and Drew, couldn't see me approaching.

"This is it," she said with a hint of squeal in her voice. "Come on."

I let out a nervous laugh as we assembled on the deck, getting in order. "Hold on," I said quietly, knowing all the vampires could hear me. "Where's Snoozer? I can't get married without him."

"You are so dramatic." Lucy strolled out from behind one of the deck chairs. "Way to ruin it." She turned her white head and looked behind her. "Come on out."

Mr. Snoozerton, my sweet fluffy cat, came out from behind the same chair.

"Oh, my goodness." I nearly squealed. He looked so cute. Someone had gotten him a little kitty-cat tuxedo.

Lucy rubbed her head against him. "The little bags on either side of his belly are full of flower petals."

Olivia leaned over and pointed at the little bags. "When he starts down the aisle, we pull those, and the flower petals fall out on their own."

"You guys." I had to blink rapidly and look up to keep the tears from forming. "Thank you."

I turned and looked around for my father. He stepped forward and held out one arm. "Let's go, Dad."

Mom kissed my cheek and then slipped around the curtains and went to her seat.

Snoozer and Lucy stepped up to the curtain and waited for the music to start. When nothing happened, the little white nag looked at a small booth tucked in the corner of the deck where Owen stood, ready to man the DJ booth.

"Owen!" Lucy snapped. "Start the damn music, you greasy snake-man."

Owen glared at her, but a few seconds later, the beginning notes of the song came on. Olivia waved her hand, and the curtains rose in the middle. I hadn't realized it, but there was a second set a few feet in front. Olivia opened the bags on Snoozer's side, and he and Lucy walked through.

Sammie went next, holding the rings. Then Ian and Lily, followed by Winnie and Alfred, and Wallie and Michelle. Finally, it was Sam and Olivia's turn, and she waved her hand behind her. The curtain opened one more time. Dad and I stepped through, the music changed, and the second curtain in front of us opened as everyone stood.

My heart froze in my chest. This was it. My gaze lowered, so I saw the flower petals that had floated down from the bags on Snoozer's sides... along with a big clump of black cat hair. Shaking my head, I looked up at the wedding. *My* wedding.

And then I saw him. Nothing else mattered. Not the people in the chairs on either side of us. Not the flowers or the venue or the food. Nothing but Drew. The music barely registered. I trusted my father to keep my feet moving because as I got closer to my husband-to-be, it seemed more like I was floating along rather than walking.

And float, I did.

Melody did her introduction. "Thank you all for coming today to witness the marriage of Andrew Marcus Walker and Ava Calliope Harper. I am pleased they asked me to perform their ceremony."

The crowd clapped and cheered. When they settled down, Melody asked, "Who gives Ava away?"

Dad stepped forward with me clinging to his arm still. "Her mother and I do." He loosened my grip on him and squeezed my hands before he kissed my forehead and placed my hands into Drew's.

Melody and I had already discussed not asking the crowd if anyone had any objections. It was far too late for anyone to object anyway since Drew and I were bound for life. Plus, I didn't want his family to step up and say anything. Not that it would've mattered.

It was best not to go there in the first place.

"The happy couple has written their own vows." Melody waved for Sammie to come forward with the rings.

Drew took my band, and I picked up his. He held my hand and slipped the ring on. "I knew from the moment I saw you in the grocery store a year ago that you were trouble."

I snorted and several people laughed. Most likely people who knew me well.

Drew's lips twitched as he continued. "I fell for you instantly and haven't regretted one moment I've spent with you. I love you, Ava Harper, and will always be at your side and have your back."

My eyes filled, blurring my vision. It was my turn, so I slipped his ring on his finger. "There definitely was a spark when we first met. I fell before I realized what I was signing up for."

I winked at him. "Our first year together has been a wild ride, and I look forward to many more adventures with you. I love you and will forever be your partner in life and love."

Drew pulled me into his arms and kissed me. My heart soared as our lips touched, as it did with every kiss.

Melody laughed and said, "You may kiss the bride."

17

AVA

WHILE EVERYONE MOVED over to the reception tent and dance floor, Drew, the rest of the wedding party, and I hung back for photos.

Our young photographer took tons of pictures in various poses. Zoey had taken up photography as a hobby, originally by using her phone. When she'd started posting pictures of her and Larry's adventures, her social following went viral. Between her accounts and Alfred's, we were a regular influencer family.

The kid had a talent for photography. So, Drew and I had hired her to do the wedding. That gave her a chance to give her brand new fancy camera a good workout and let her add a wedding to her portfolio. And we got a nice discount off of a great photographer.

By the time we got over to the reception, the party was hopping. Music played and the kids took to the dance floor. Some of the shifter kids were in their animal form and I looked around to find Zoey. Sure enough when she saw them running around she immediately shifted. I'd figured she would. Her tiger loved playing with kids.

Drew and I were the last two to leave the photographs, then I'd gone up to change into my third dress, very similar to the rehearsal dinner dress except for pale green and knee length where it had been long.

Olivia headed over and stopped us at the entrance of the tent. Then she clapped her hands to get everyone's attention. The music stopped and all eyes landed on us.

"I present to you, Mr. and Mrs. Walker." Olivia did her best impression of Vanna White as we entered the area.

Everyone clapped while we waved, then they went back to enjoying themselves, some eating, some dancing. "Time to party," I whispered, and squeezed Drew's hand. He chuckled and kissed me on the lips before breaking away to grab a beer with his family. I started my rounds, greeting everyone.

I stopped by to say hi to the Johnsons first. "Dana, Rick, it's so good to see you. Thank you for coming."

"It was a beautiful wedding," Dana said with a bright smile.

We chatted a little longer about how things were going. They were expecting twins. The couple was overjoyed, and I was for them. The twins wouldn't replace the child they'd lost, but it was a new beginning. Plus, their seven-year-old son, Zane, whom we'd rescued with a group of kids from the shifter fighting ring, was going to be a big brother.

I didn't have the heart to tell them Bevan and Penny were on the run.

The day we'd saved Zane and the other kids, the ones we'd found alive anyway, was also the day that Zoey came to me. She'd been dead and didn't want to pass on to the afterlife. So, she'd come home with us. And it had been the perfect fit into our ever-growing family.

A little ferret ran by chirping as he went. Snoozer and Lucy and a gold-colored kitten were on their heels. Where did that one come from?

"Goldie, stay close," Hailey called to the escaping shifted children as she stopped beside me. I turned and pulled her into a hug. "You and Drew look gorgeous. I think I cried tears of joy the whole time."

"She did," Jax added, wrapping his mate into a hug.

I pointed to the gold kitty as she streaked by. "Goldie?"

Hailey's features brightened like a proud mama. "We found her squatting in the house of the woman who shot Luke. Goldie had lived in her cat form for so long she's more comfortable in it."

Dana nodded. "That happens a lot with kids, especially if they've suffered a tragic event."

Hailey frowned. "She's been through something, but she won't talk about it. We just shower her with love and don't pressure her to talk about it."

"Oh, Hailey, I'm so glad she found you guys," I said, squeezing her hand.

"Luke and Ransom are just as involved, if not more than we are." Jax chuckled. "Luke especially took to her." He nodded off to the side. Luke and Ransom stood in a spot where they could keep an eye on the little kitten. I hadn't realized they were here.

Hailey smiled sadly. "As much as we'd like to just keep her, we need to find out her history."

"Meaning you have to start investigating where her family is," I added. When Hailey nodded that I was right, I motioned to a nearby table. "Let's have a seat."

Dana turned to Hailey and held out her hand. "I'm Dana and this is my mate, Rick. We're ferret shifters, so if you have any questions about raising a shifter baby, we'll be glad to help in any way."

Just then Hailey's brother, Luke appeared beside her. "Did I hear someone say shifters? I have so many questions. I'm Luke, Goldie's official guardian."

Then Luke looked at his sister and waved at the two of us. "Go visit with Ava. I'll talk with the Johnsons and fill you in later."

Hailey rolled her eyes at her brother but looped her arm with mine and directed us to a table next to the one the Johnsons and Luke sat at. "I've noticed Sam is always in Olivia's personal space. I know they're married and all, but that seems a little..."

"Obsessive? Yeah, it is. He'd been like that since he turned." I frowned and glanced over at my two BFFs. Sam met my gaze. No doubt he'd heard our words. He surely knew I'd never speak ill of him. I waved him and Olivia over to our table.

Once Sam and Olivia joined us, Jax spoke. "Hailey asked me about the way Sam has been clinging to Olivia." He locked gazes with Sam and asked, "Have you fed from her?"

Sam sat up straighter, and at first, I didn't think he wanted to answer. Finally, he did. "Yes, a little. I'm afraid of taking too much because she's part fae."

Jax smiled and watched the couple a little closer. "I'm sure now that Olivia is your true mate. I wasn't certain from a distance but being closer to you two, I can sense it. Congratulations on finding your one true mate."

Olivia stared wide-eyed at Jax, then Hailey, and then me before turning her attention to Sam. "Is that why he can feed from me?"

"Yes. The Fates aren't cruel enough to give us a mate we can't give love bites to." Jax leaned into Hailey and nibbled her neck.

I was about to leave this conversion because it was getting a little TMI for me, but Wade set a tray on the table, picked up a glass of wine and handed it to me, then passed out three large mugs to Sam, Hailey, and Jax before taking the last one for himself.

The mugs had blood in them. Jax and Hailey thanked him and sipped from theirs. Hailey pulled her cup away and glanced at Jax. "Why does this taste different?" she asked. "It's delicious."

I answered. "That could be ghoul blood. It's the same as human but with the magic that animates them. No ghouls were harmed in the bleeding process."

Hailey and Olivia snorted at my bad joke, making everyone at the table laugh.

After a few more minutes of blood and vampire jokes, Sam said, "I really don't know what I'm going to do. I can't work days anymore. I thought about working the night shifts, but I think I just want a change altogether."

Drew came over, picked me up from my chair, and sat in it while placing me on his lap. I snuggled into my husband; my heart full of love for the man I'd be spending the rest of my life with. I'd gotten unbelievably lucky with this man.

Hailey looked at Jax and said, "You know what they need here? I know there are only two vampires living in Shipton, but it would be cool if they had a place like Catch and Release."

Oh, that would be great. Jax owned a nightclub that was geared toward making sure all the local vampires had access to blood. "I bet Wade and Sam could run it."

Sam had never been to the vampire nightclub, but I had told him about it. Plus, Wade had probably mentioned it to him a few times.

"How would we fund it?" Sam asked. "I've never worked at a bar."

Luci materialized in the empty seat at the table. "I'm in." His appearance surprised nobody, and we carried on the conversation as smoothly as if he'd been there the whole time.

"How will it work with the blood?" I asked, curious about how two vampires could pull this off.

Olivia suggested that they could buy blood from the supernaturals in the area. "There are a lot of us. We could also do blood drives if we need to, but with the two of them it really wouldn't be too much of an issue."

She was right. As long as the seaside nightclub didn't draw the attention of other vampires. However, I'd let the guys figure that out. And Luci was all in on being a third owner of the place. They were in good hands.

The night was going wonderfully when everyone went quiet. The vampires jumped up first, probably hearing our new visitors before everyone else.

Drew and I, followed by his family and pretty much everyone, moved to the far side of the dancing tent to watch two men walk across the vast yard. They'd come out of the forest.

"Can anyone tell what they are?" I asked quietly.

Jax shook his head and Luci squinted their way. "I'm very mixed, but I think they're necromancers."

When they got close enough to make out their features, Alfred sighed.

Well, he squeaked, but I knew him well enough to know it was a sigh. "They're here for me. I don't think they pose us any danger." Stepping forward, he walked toward them.

Winnie and I exchanged an eyebrow-raised glance before rushing to follow.

"They're freaking hot," Winnie whispered as we hurried to catch up with Alfred. I glanced around and realized pretty much the entire wedding party was behind me.

"Stop," I hissed. "At least stay here"

They gave us about twenty feet of space. Except for Drew. He grabbed my hand. "Come on."

"Gandr." They bowed their heads at Alfred. "We're here to ask if you've reconsidered our offer."

Alfred turned back to me and shrugged one shoulder before looking back at them. "What offer?"

The two men, both tall and broad, one with jet-black hair and the other so blond it looked bottled—but likely wasn't—exchanged a glance. "We sent you the sword," Blondie said.

"Bad luck, friends. That thing is gone." Who were these guys?

The dark-headed man scowled at me. "When we were here before, your power was almost overwhelming. Now it is not. Are you ill?"

Now it was my turn to exchange a glance with Drew. "Why are you here? And what do you mean you were here before?" I flat out was not answering that question since I still didn't know.

"We've come to offer rebirth to Alfred. You may not recognize us, but I am Arne. We visited before."

These were two of the three necromancers who'd visited us before. They'd looked like decrepit old men before, and now they were as fit as Alfred. "What happened? Where's your third?" Alfred asked.

"We found the spells," Arne said. "We achieved the impossible."

Alfred's shoulders fell. "The spring of life."

A slow, almost evil smile spread across Arne's face. "Indeed." He looked at me, then. "You could do it as well, should you find your power again."

His brow furrowed and he looked out at the crowd. "It is here but muted."

I looked back at my family and friends. Was he saying someone had my powers? Like, intentionally?

Before I could question him, Alfred spoke. "The spring is a dark, evil magic. I won't be a part of that again."

Arne inclined his head once. "That is your choice. We will give you one week to think about our proposition. Then, we will return. Please make the right choice." They turned to walk back into the woods, but Arne stopped and turned back. "Your rightful place is with us."

18

AVA

The following morning, well mid-morning. I slept in. Finally, I was up and not really ready to take on the day, because I had a *little* too much to drink the night before. Hey, don't judge. I was allowed; it was my wedding.

Drew and I were in the middle of making our last-minute preparations for our month-long honeymoon in the Highlands of Scotland. I was a little too excited about the trip because I'd never been before.

But there was still one more thing I had to do before I left. Find the source of my wonky powers. Someone in my family was pregnant, and I was going to find out who.

It wasn't me; I was sure of it. Mom and Winnie were possibilities now they had new bodies with all working organs. Alive, working organs. Just being alive should've been enough for them to disrupt my powers. We'd figured when they'd come back in new bodies, that meant their power was new now. But maybe they were pregnant.

Magic was weird.

I made my way downstairs and to the kitchen where Alfred had a cup of coffee waiting for me. "Thank you."

I sipped the warm go-go juice and stepped into the conservatory where the women in my family were all waiting. Olivia and Wallie were also there. It was too early for me to figure out why they needed to be there, so I sat on my stool next to my workbench and motioned to Mom. "Will you perform the spell? I'm still waking up."

Plus, I wanted someone who wasn't having magical issues to do it.

Mom smiled and went around gathering the herbs she needed. Winnie grabbed pink, blue, and white candles from the drawer. They worked together to clean the workspace and set up the spell.

"Ready?" Mom met my stare. When I nodded, she mixed the herbs while chanting a few words of Latin.

Mom was so old school about magic. I just spoke the spells in English most of the time.

She added the last sprinkle of herbs in the bowl and a bloom of pink smoke puffed into the air, then the pink and white candles lit on their own.

Someone was having a baby girl.

I leaned forward and said, "Show us who."

The cloud of pink smoke floated in the air to each person in the room, slowing down at each female and bypassing Wallie. I eyed it as it floated in front of me. I held my breath until it moved on. Shew. Even after a pee test and a blood test it made me nervous.

Then it stopped in front of Michelle. She eyed it too, but I could tell she wasn't surprised when the pink magic cloud leaped at her, coloring her purple shirt with pink.

I snorted because it looked like a ghost covered in pink powder went right through her.

Then the reality of it all sank in. Michelle had been a bit ill lately, but not sick with a cold. She'd said it was stress from school. Now we knew the truth.

"I'm going to be a grandma!" I squealed.

I jumped off my stool, spilling coffee on my sleep shirt, and rushed to my soon-to-be daughter-in-law and to yank her into my arms. "You knew?"

She nodded as I pulled back. "Wallie?"

He ducked his head. "We were waiting for the right time. Everyone has been so busy with the wedding."

"We didn't want to steal your thunder," Michelle added and grabbed Wallie's hand.

"We talked about it, and we want to stay in school. We just need to figure out how to make it work." Wallie reached over and placed his hand on Michelle's belly.

I felt a squeal coming on. A grandma. Sure, it was a little sooner than I envisioned, but Wallie and Michelle were in love. The kind of love that Clay and I had shared at their age. And to be honest, I wasn't much older than Michelle when I got pregnant with Wallie. And Clay had been in college. It was tough, but we'd made it and we didn't have half the people these two kids had to help. They had a village to help raise this baby.

"You two will live here. Use the portal in Wallie's closet to attend classes. The house is full of babysitters." I was wide awake now.

Mom pulled Wallie and Michelle into her arms next. "Oh, I can't wait to babysit for you."

Olivia rushed to my side. "We need to shop for baby girl clothes."

I added, "And tiny shoes!"

I walked out of the conservatory with my notepad and pen floating in the air beside me, making lists of things we needed to do to prepare for the baby.

"And a nursery!" I turned and almost ran into Wallie. "Has Michelle seen a healer or doctor?"

Some witches preferred magical healers to human doctors.

Michelle pushed Wallie out of the doorway. "I've seen my coven's midwife; she is also a doctor. I'm about six weeks along, so I'm due in June."

When we entered the living room, Drew was there with his family. They looked at us like we were up to no good. I rushed over to Drew and hugged him. "We're going to be grandparents! Wallie and Michelle are expecting."

Drew smiled wide. "That's wonderful news."

It was amazing news.

The front door opened, and Owen walked in. He was dressed, and I got the feeling something big was about to happen. "What's going on?"

Owen crossed the room to me and took both my hands. "I've been offered a job working with the hunters. The Walkers are going to start using paranormal beings to hunt down evil paranormals. I'm moving to the Asheville headquarters so I can take classes and train."

Oh, wow. "That's good." My voice wavered. "Isn't it?" I thought... hoped it would be a good move for him.

He squeezed my hands. "It is. I'll be in a place where I feel I'm making a difference in the world."

He would definitely be doing that. "I'll miss you."

Drew looked at his parents and his mom shrugged. "We all must change with the times. This trip, meeting Ava and her unusually dysfunctional family showed us that not all supernatural creatures are bad."

Ian nodded. "If the devil himself can be good-ish, then there is hope for others."

We all laughed at that. It was true. Luci was nice to people he liked. But he was the devil, after all.

Pearl stomped her cane on the floor once. "Yes, we are opening up to options and accepting that they aren't all bad. Except for the vampires. They haven't proved anything to me yet."

It was a good thing that my two vamps were sleeping at the moment. But when I met Pearl's gaze, she winked at me.

The old woman was more accepting than she seemed.

I looked around at my family, full of hope and excitement for the next generation to come, and happy that even though I was losing Owen, it was to progress. I could go on my honeymoon free of worry.

Well, except for what Alfred would do about the ancient necro-mancers. And that something bad might happen to the baby. And what might happen to my powers once the baby was born if they were this wonky thanks to a new *unborn* female in my bloodline?

But mostly... free of worry.

A NEWLY-WEBS MIDLIFE

For Wayne and Tony. How they'd hate being married to a necromancer. They're lucky they have us. <3

CHAPTER ONE

"I ALMOST DON'T WANT to leave." I slid my arm around Drew's waist as we walked the footpath back to the castle that had been converted into an inn. There were several cottages near the main castle, all dating back to the mid-seventeenth century.

The castle cat, who I'd been calling Nix, peered out of a window high in the turret. I could just see her little black face peering down. She'd been a constant companion over the last few weeks. Drew and I had spent the most wonderful time here, relaxing, eating far too much, and taking advantage of the castle's many amenities. I'd never had so many massages in my life.

The Andarsan was gorgeous inside and out. It was nestled in the Highlands and sat on a loch. We'd spent a significant amount of time doing indoor activities to work off the delicious food. We'd also spent time on the loch in kayaks or paddle boarding.

This was a picture-perfect location for a honeymoon...if it hadn't been for the ghosts. That part had been a surprise.

The castle was *very* haunted. It tracked that a castle *that* old, even a small one like this, would have seen its fair share of death.

If I were human, I wouldn't have noticed the wandering spirits. I would've spent three weeks basking in my new husband's love and soaking up every possible amenity.

But I wasn't human, was I? I was half witch, half necromancer. Heavy on the necro power. In fact, my ex-roomie and mentor, Owen, had told me on several occasions that I was the most powerful necromancer he'd ever heard of. According to him, my father's side of the family—where my dead death powers came from—was one of the oldest bloodlines.

Everything I'd learned about my family since Owen had first told me that tracked. I'd found out that our necromancer lineage dated as far back as the freaking Vikings.

In fact, I'd recently learned that Alfred and I were related. I was still digesting that one. Alfred, the ghoul I'd inherited from another necromancer. We'd since given Alfred his old body back, in a manner of speaking. He looked like his old self, anyway. And his old self was gorgeous.

My mother and Aunt had done a ritual that had basically put them in new bodies, and ever since, Alfred and my Aunt Winnie were, to be frank, disgustingly in love. Like teenagers who couldn't keep their hands off of each other. It was nice to not have to see that for three weeks, but time was starting to run short. We would have to go back to reality sooner or later.

"I won't miss all the ghosts, but yeah, it'll be hard to go back to work." Drew gave me a little squeeze as we made our way to the onsite restaurant, and the source of all the good food we'd eaten. Except for a few excursions into the village, we'd mostly let the castle chef make our culinary dreams come true.

It would be hard getting back to our lives when we returned home, but we had to eventually. This honeymoon had been like someone had pressed pause on all the chaos in our world. No doubt when we returned home the pandemonium would slap us in the face.

The slow pace since we arrived had been nice. Although I did miss my family and friends at home. Mmm, not enough to leave yet, however. We had a couple more nights.

My phone chimed as we entered the restaurant through its enormous oak doors. They were at least ten feet tall and opened into a great hall of a dining room, decorated in a lot of wood and gilding. It put me in mind of how it must've looked in its heyday when lords and ladies dined before hosting great balls.

Along the front windows were intimate tables for couples to sit and enjoy the view of the loch. There was a great table for the communal dinners they frequently had, and all around that were tables for smaller parties who might not want to join in the middle. It was a great setup. Drew and I had taken our meals at the various locations, sometimes socializing, sometimes sitting together intimately.

I glanced at the message and smiled while Drew talked with the hostess. It was from Wallie and Michelle and had an audio message attached.

Once we were seated at our table, one of the cozy ones by the window, I played the audio. Of course, it started out loud, drawing the attention of others around us. I ducked my head, whispered, "Sorry," and turned down the volume so only Drew and I could hear.

The rapid sound of a heartbeat flowed out of my phone as I grinned like an idiot at Drew. "That's the sound of our grandbaby." I almost squealed but caught myself before I yelled out. I did let a tiny whisper of a sound come out. I couldn't help myself. My heart was beating almost as fast as the sound coming through the phone's speaker. My granddaughter. Oh, my.

Drew's smile grew into amazement as he listened, then replayed it again and again. "It's so fast."

"That's normal," I said after he handed my phone back to me. I reopened my messaging app to text the kids back. "Especially since the baby is a girl. Their heartbeats tend to be faster." Wallie and Michelle weren't kids technically, but they would always be my babies. And yes, I was claiming Michelle as one of mine. She was having my first grandbaby, after all.

Wow. Such a strong heartbeat. It sounds magical. Name?

Wallie texted back quickly. **Yes, she definitely is magical. No name yet, but we have time to figure that out.**

My grin was probably sappy and huge, but I didn't care a bit. **She'll be here before you know it. We're at dinner, so I'll talk to you two later. Hugs!**

I set my phone on the table between Drew and me as a tingle crawled up my spine. I glanced around the dining room trying to pinpoint the source of my ghostly spidey senses. There were no ghosts in the restaurant, or at least there shouldn't have been any. I'd warded the place after the first time we'd eaten here. The last thing I needed was ghosts staring at me while I enjoyed my dinner. It made for difficult digestion.

The ward only worked while I was actually in the dining room. The rest of the time, the haints could do their worst with the other, oblivious diners. They couldn't really hurt them.

Unfortunately, even when I *was* here in the dining area, some ghosts figured out how they could ignore the magical warning to stay out. Inevitably, one or two made their way in. Maybe they were the stronger ones? I didn't know enough about ghosts to be sure. Probably something I should study, eventually.

My gaze landed on a man sitting alone. There was a half-eaten meal in front of him, and he seemed sad. More than that. He was grieving. The emotions flowed off him, reaching out to my overly sensitive empathy. Maybe his intense sadness was making my ghost radar go off.

I'd been in his shoes before, so full of grief and regret I couldn't see past it. When my Clay died, I'd thought I was drowning.

Drew covered my fingers, drawing my attention to him. He lifted my hand and kissed my knuckles. Warmth flowed through me as I leaned in to press my lips to his.

My husband.

I was still getting used to being married to Sheriff Drew Walker.

Our relationship had been a bit of a whirlwind. It had only been a little over a year since we'd met. What an incredible year it had been. I'd reconnected with my necromancer powers, become close to my now best friend Olivia, adopted Zoey and Larry and Alfred and Michelle and Lucy-Fur and Lucifer and my Uncle Wade. Plus my Mom, Aunt Winnie, and Dad were essentially back from the dead.

It'd been an absolutely insane year. And through it all, Drew had been there. My constant. My rock. The handsomest, kindest, every-thingest man I'd known since my dear late husband Clay died six years ago. I couldn't help but stare into his vivid blue eyes and thank my lucky stars I'd come home to Shipton Harbor when I did... before some other woman snapped him up.

After we finished eating, we made our way to our room, which had a waterfront view. It was also, *most* unfortunately the ghost's favorite place to hang out, which made sexy time for hubby and me a little bit interesting. These ghosts didn't seem to care much about my wards. Sure, I could've forced them to leave. But they usually came back ten minutes later, and sometimes when they came back, they were aggravated and loud.

Once inside our room, Drew backed me up to the door and kissed me. I threaded my fingers in his hair and pulled him closer. When he ended the kiss, I smirked at him. "Hurry get under the blankets before the ghosts show up."

He wiggled his eyebrows, then pulled me behind him to do exactly as I'd said.

I JERKED awake but wasn't sure why at first. The first few days we'd woken up here, I'd been super disoriented, but it hadn't taken long to acclimate.

Tonight was a different story. I was befuddled until I saw a dead woman standing over me. We stared at each other for a long few moments. What in the world did this one want? Most of the specters here had just been bent on disruption and irritation. Or they only wanted to live out their afterlives alone, in relative peace.

This ghost was different. It was like she was actually looking at me. She had her black hair put up in a neat bun and wore an elaborate floor-length ballgown. I didn't know much about ballgowns, but it sure looked like expensive material to me. It had a tight bodice and a long, flowing skirt. In one hand she carried a mask that looked like it came from a masquerade ball.

As impressive as she looked, I was far too sleepy to fool with the crazy lady. "Go away. I'm sleeping." I tried to roll over, planning on ignoring the ghost, but she placed a hand on my arm. Uuuugh. It was cold and so icky when they touched me.

I sat up with a sigh, causing Drew to wake. He rolled over and then flopped back on the bed. "Not now. Why can't they ever come to visit while we're awake?"

"They do. But most of them don't actually try to interact."

The woman just stared at me, so I gave her a magical boost so we could talk. She obviously wanted something, and I didn't feel like trying to sleep with her standing over me or maybe touching me again. "What do you want?"

One rule about dealing with ghosts was don't be nice to them or you'd get a tagalong. For life and beyond. They liked to linger.

"Follow me," the woman said, then floated through the door to our room.

"This one's used to people doing what she says," Drew muttered. "Figures."

After a quick glance at each other, we pulled on our robes and headed out of the room. Drew leaned in and whispered, "This isn't a lady in white thing, is it?"

"The urban legend?" I asked. He nodded and I replied, "Gods, I hope not."

The ghost woman reappeared at the end of the hallway, waiting for us. Drew and I rushed to her as quietly as possible since it was the middle of the night. The castle was old and a bit creaky. The hardwood floors had been beautifully restored, but some things couldn't be restored in a building this ancient.

We tracked her to what seemed to be the unused portion of the castle. We'd explored here before, but it had felt like it was a section that the guests weren't meant to be in. Some of the rooms we passed looked like they were used for storage while others looked to be under construction or being remodeled.

We turned a corner and followed the ghost down yet another long hallway. Geez, how big was this place?

At the end of this one, the ghost stopped at a set of stairs, looking down them with a mix of anger and sadness. "Here," she said in an ethereal voice. The moment Drew and I reached the stairs, the ghost disappeared. It didn't take long to see why.

At the bottom of the stairs was the man from dinner, the one who had been so sad. He was crying over a woman's body. From the awkward position of the body, I had to guess she had fallen down the stairs.

Moonlight shone through a nearby window, illuminating the poor dead woman. She wore a white nightgown and had blond hair really close to the color of Olivia's hair. From this angle, it was almost a little unnerving. It could've been my bestie, except I knew she was home safe in Maine with her newly-turned-vampire husband Sam and her mother and father, *the* devil and his fae lady.

Moving my gaze from the woman, I studied the man. "That's the guy from dinner," I whispered to Drew.

Drew made a soft grunt noise. "Yeah, but I didn't see her with him."

"Neither did I." I descended the stairs with Drew close behind, walking on my tiptoes to be as quiet as possible. When we reached the bottom, the man didn't even glance over at us. He just stared at the woman's body with tears rolling down his cheeks. I wondered if she was his wife or girlfriend. Daughter, maybe? It was kind of hard to tell ages when she was dead.

I moved closer until I was almost touching them. Still, he didn't look up. Nothing I did seemed to bring him out of his shock. Or was it grief that had frozen him into place?

"Sir," I prompted without a reaction. "Excuse me, sir?" He still didn't look over. This dude was seriously upset.

"Careful," Drew said. "Maybe he was sad at dinner because he knew he was going to have to kill her tonight."

A chilling thought. I bent down and touched the woman, pushing my magic into her. Maybe the deceased could tell me what happened to her.

She opened her eyes and sat straight, locking gazes with me. "You didn't save her. You couldn't save her."

What the freaking frack? Before I could ask her what she meant, she fell back against the floor, dead once more. I tried to animate her again and had the same result with the same cryptic message. She wouldn't respond otherwise.

Who were we supposed to have saved? Not her, surely, or she would've said *me*.

Drew tapped me on the shoulder. "Don't touch anything else. We have to report this."

Nodding, I stood and used my magic to erase all evidence that I'd touched the body. While Drew called the police, I moved to the man. He'd moved away from the woman but still sat nearby, staring at her.

"Hello. Did you know her?" It seemed like a silly question, but I really wasn't sure if he'd known her or was just sad that she died. He could've been the first to find her and it shocked him into this stupor.

He didn't answer so Drew tried. "What's your name?"

Nothing. Drew and I shared a look. Drew motioned with his head for me to follow, and we moved to stand a few feet away. "This whole thing is weird," I said.

"And that is seriously saying something considering what we deal with on a daily basis."

"True," Drew agreed with a chuckle. "I feel like something isn't quite right with this."

"Yeah, and I'm not talking about the dead body."

When I looked back to try to talk to the man again, I gasped. He was gone.

Oh, yeah. That wasn't suspicious at all.

CHAPTER TWO

IT WAS late morning before I crawled my sleepy self out of bed and stumbled to the shower. But sleeping late wasn't unusual for me, especially since we'd been on our honeymoon. I just wished I'd gotten more sleep actually *during* the night. I was frikkin' exhausted, even after sleeping late.

But at least I felt more human. Well, as human as I ever was, now that I had some coffee in me. Drew had gotten up before me, no surprise there. He was such an overachiever. I loved him in spite of it. He'd gotten me a gigantic cup of coffee. I sucked down another long drink and sighed. The man was definitely a keeper. He needed a gift. Maybe I could swing a solo trip into town before it was time to go home. He had said something about a few rounds of golf. If I got him busy with that I'd go see about a just-because-I-love-you present.

I had just pulled my jeans over my hips when the ghost woman from last night appeared in front of me again. "Fu—" I cut myself off with a growl. Just like in the middle of last night, she still wore her floor-length gown. It had jewels all over it. Now in the daylight, I could actually see a floral design down one side, too. It was stunning. The formal gown's design didn't help me try to pinpoint when she'd died. If she'd been in normal clothes, it might've been easy. But expensive ball gowns didn't seem to change too much over the years. Not to my inexperienced eyes, anyway. Fashionista I was not.

She stared at me while I zipped up and buttoned my jeans. I raised a brow at her. "Morning."

"You must save them," she said. "You're the only one who can help."

It had probably been difficult for her to say that much. I reached out to give her some power in hopes that it would clear her mind enough to explain what she wanted, but she disappeared before I could ask any questions.

Well, then. Okie dokie. How the heck were we supposed to help when we didn't know what the problem was? And why me? Why was I the only one?

Cause it was always me, that's why. Ugh.

Probably she was coming to me because I was the first necromancer to stay at the resort. That made the most sense. Lucky me.

Drew stepped out of the bathroom, and I drank him in, momentarily forgetting how to breathe, much less what the bejeweled party lady wanted. He'd emerged with a white towel wrapped around his waist and his short brown hair was wet and going all over the place.

Have I mentioned that he was ripped? The man worked out daily. Dollars to donuts, that man had been in the resort gym this morning while I snoozed the day away and dreamed about a French toast breakfast.

The term silver fox had been created for men like him. I needed to send his photo to Webster's to go beside the term in the dictionary.

Drew smirked at me as he slowly removed his towel, rubbing it along his chest with the towel hanging down to obscure the part I wanted to see. He twisted around, still hiding all the pieces I wanted, to hang it on the bathroom door. *Finally*, he turned, giving me the money shot. Oh, yeah.

"Ava?" He snapped his fingers. "My eyes are up here. Who were you talking to?"

"Ghost lady." I sipped my coffee and watched him dress with disappointment. He wasn't in the mood, apparently. I could've changed his mind, but I still needed a good shower, too. Maybe later. "She said something to the effect of only me being able to save them." We spent a couple minutes going over who them could've been. "I think I'll call home and check on things. Maybe Mom has some ideas on how to get the ghost to talk." She'd lived for years on the ghostly plane, which we called the Inbetween. She knew stuff.

"Good idea. I'll go and call the authorities to see if they have any other information about the dead woman." He leaned in and kissed me on the lips, letting it linger a bit.

"Do you think the ghost lady and the couple from last night are connected? Other than the ghost led us to the crime scene."

"Surely they are." He shrugged. "Why else would a ghost tell you, of all people, about a dead woman?"

"Yeah, I guess that was a stupid question."

Drew stopped short, turned to me, and put one finger under my chin to lift my gaze. "It was not. We shouldn't discount the fact that it could in theory be unrelated. With us, we can never tell." He dropped a soft kiss onto my forehead. I watched him grab his phone and head out into the hallway. Then I called home to tell everyone about the craziness of the ghost. Alfred, my beloved Viking ghoul, answered.

"Alfred, I think this honeymoon is cursed," I said as a greeting. "We're being haunted by a ghost."

"That does sound like quite a problem," Alfred said. "I'm sure you can handle it." His squeaky voice had all the confidence in the world.

I appreciated his certainty of my abilities, even if I didn't always feel the same way. "Is my mom around?"

"She's in the kitchen. I'll get her for you." He set the phone down, and I listened for background noise. Everything seemed to be quiet.

A few moments later, my mom was on the phone. "Hi, honey," she said. "What's going on?"

I quickly related the story of the ghost woman and what she'd said. My mom had been a ghost before I'd animated her and magically placed her spirit into another body. So, she'd know more about ghost behavior than me.

"It sounds like she wants you to help her solve a problem," my mom said. "I'm not sure what you can do to get her to talk more. Especially if she is avoiding your magic as you explained. You might have to solve this mystery the old-fashioned way."

I'd been afraid of that. It was the only explanation for why she kept moving away or disappearing when I tried to use magic.

At least I had a sheriff to help me with the detective work. Maybe someone here knew the woman who died last night. If we knew more about her, then we might be able to figure out how the ghost lady was connected. "Great. Thanks," I said in a flat, teasing tone. "How is everything there?"

"It's good. Don't worry about us. Enjoy your new husband and your alone time with him."

I was for sure doing that. Now we had a mystery to solve. We'd at least do it together. "Okay, if you say so. I'll talk to you later. Love you, Mom."

"Love you, too, sweetie."

I hung up and turned around. Shrieking, I dropped my phone as my heart jumped out of my chest. Luci was lounging on the bed, eating popcorn like he'd been here the whole time and belonged nowhere else. He wore black skinny jeans and a white t-shirt with a black leather jacket thrown over it. His hair was bleached blond and styled in its signature coif. "What's shakin'?" he asked around a mouthful of popcorn.

I eyed him and asked, "What are you wearing? You look like you just left the set of Grease if Grease was starring David Bowie."

He winked at me. "I was at a punk concert last night. It was killer." He threw up the devil's horns with his fingers. "It was like they were saluting me all night!"

I rolled my eyes and said, "Of course, you had to dress the part. You're lucky I don't have time to deal with you right now."

He jumped up and looked around, spotting the very large, full-length mirror on the wall. It was old as crap, and I was pretty sure the frame was at least gold leaf if not somehow real gold. If that was even possible. Whatever it was, it looked expensive. "This will do," he mumbled and waved his hand over the front of it. A shimmering portal appeared in it. The glass had been slightly warped with little black dots on it. I could still see them faintly behind the portal. At least he hadn't damaged the antique.

Probably hadn't. *Probably* hadn't damaged it.

Peering over his shoulder, I furrowed my brow when I recognized the room. "Is that a view from the big mirror in my bathroom?" I asked. "What did you do?" And why did he do it?

He ignored me as he shivered and scanned the hotel room. "Yeesh. This place is way too haunted for me. Laters, baby." And with that, he stepped through the portal he'd created in the big mirror on the wall of the ancient castle and disappeared.

Typical Luci.

I stared at the mirror portal like I expected a creature to come out of it. Heck, it connected to my house. There was every possibility a creature of varying deadness could come out.

Rolling my eyes, I went to the desk by the large picture window and sat down to check my email while I waited for Drew to come back.

"Did someone say ghosts?" I didn't have to turn around to know it was my bestie.

I burst out laughing and whirled around in the desk chair. Of *course*, Olivia would be interested in this. Heck, I was glad she was here. I'd missed her cheery personality and how she loved to spout random facts. "Welcome to the honeymoon. A ghost visited us last night and again this morning."

"What did it want?" she asked, her blue eyes wide with excitement.

"I don't know," I said, chuckling as she caught sight of the room. As she oohed and ahhed over the four-poster bed and giant tapestry, I gave her the play-by-play of the events in the last twelve hours.

When I finished, she jumped off the bed. She'd been testing the mattress. "Wow. I'm so glad I came to help solve a mystery," she exclaimed. "Let's go interview the staff."

CHAPTER THREE

"WHERE IS SAMMIE?" I asked Olivia, amusement lighting up my insides at Olivia's excitement. She had that effect on me. I'd felt burdened before. Now I wanted to go gung-ho with her to figure it out. Olivia was good for me.

"He's with Phira in Faery for a few days for some camping thing they're doing." She smiled and added, "Besides, I had some free time and needed a break from clingy Sam, love his heart."

Poor Sam. My best friend since we were in diapers had been turned into a vampire when we'd gone to Milan to free the necromancers the vampire council had imprisoned.

Our friend Jax, who was the vampire leader of the United States, turned him after he'd almost died during the fight with the bad vampires.

Since being turned, Sam had been stuck up Olivia's behind. She had been used to him working long hours as a police officer, but now he was home all the time since he couldn't work during the day. Baby vamps sleep during the hours of sunlight. They had no control over that. As soon as the sun came up, they conked out like flipping off their light switch.

We'd found out when Jax and Hailey came to our wedding that Olivia was Sam's fated mate, which was a vampire and shifter thing. His need to bond with her, despite already being married to her, was strong. He'd never felt it before being turned, and if he hadn't been made into a bloodsucker, he never would've felt it. He was overprotective—far more so than usual—and didn't like to be separated from her for very long.

Olivia was still adjusting to all the attention, which she normally loved, but she'd also been trying to focus on being a good mom. That was something she felt like she'd failed with her first two kids, Jess and Devan.

I had faith in my two besties that they will find their balance again. "How did you escape Sam?"

Olivia grinned and peered into the small bathroom. "Wade distracted him with finding the perfect location for the new vamp bar."

"Good for them. I'm so happy they're going to be working together like this."

My deceased husband's uncle, Wade, whom I claimed as my own uncle long ago, had been turned into a vampire back in March when I'd gone to Philly to sell my house. He'd been turned by a rouge vamp. I'd helped Jax catch the rogue, which had actually been a lot of fun. I'd figured out then that necromancers could control vampires, since bloodsuckers were dead. Or more technically, undead.

"I'm glad you could come and help us out," I said. "This place is a little bit haunted."

"No kidding," Olivia said as she looked around the room, pulling the tapestry back from the wall. "Darn. No hidden passage. So, what do we know so far?"

"Well, not much, actually," I admitted. "I guess we need to find out who the dead woman is. Drew went on a walk to call the local cops to see what he can find out."

"And how she died," Olivia said. "Although, I have a feeling the fall down the stairs might've had some contribution to it."

I nodded and snorted. "Yeah, me too. Let's go talk to the manager and see if we can get some more information."

When I finally pulled Olivia away from knocking on the walls, we went downstairs and found the manager.

He was a middle-aged man with graying hair. "Hello, Niko, how are you?"

He smiled warmly at me. "Mrs. Walker. What can I do for you this morning?" He'd been the kindest since we'd arrived.

"This is my good friend Olivia Thompson."

Niko's face lit up. "Mrs. Thompson. Will you be staying with us?"

She shook her head as she took Niko's hand. "No, I'm just here for a visit."

I leaned forward conspiratorially. "We came down to ask you about the woman who died last night."

His face fell. "Terrible business, that. Simply terrible. She was staying here." He dry-washed his hands and bit his lip. "Am I a terrible person for being worried about what it's going to do to our bookings if this gets out?"

"No," Olivia and I said at the same time.

We chuckled and Olivia said, "Not at all. You can have empathy for the woman's family and friends while also being concerned about your own livelihood."

He gave her a grateful smile. "Her name was Annette. She'd been staying here at the resort on a writing retreat."

Oh, a writing retreat. That sounded like exactly what I needed to do to get my next book off the ground. I'd had a hard time getting into it.

"Did you know her?" I asked. "Were you familiar with her work?"

The manager shook his head. "I'm afraid not," he said. "She kept to herself mostly. I only spoke to her a few times, though she was kind during those conversations."

"Do you know if she was having any problems with anyone?" Olivia asked. "Any conflicts or anything?"

Again, the manager shook his head. "I'm sorry, but I don't know," he said. "Like I said, she kept to herself."

"What about the man we saw with her?" I asked, then described the man. "Did you see him? Do you know who he is?"

The manager's eyebrows furrowed in confusion. "What man?" he asked. "I didn't see anyone matching that description." He tapped on the computer keyboard behind the counter, then shook his head again. "We have a lot of guests right now, but I don't think any of them match that description."

Olivia and I exchanged a glance. This was getting strange. Why would the manager say he hadn't seen the man when we saw him ourselves? Unless...

"We should go," Olivia said suddenly. She must've had the same thought I had. "I think we're done here."

I nodded and we thanked the manager before walking toward the front doors. Once we were outside, Olivia turned to me. "That was weird," she said. "Why would he lie about seeing the man?"

"I don't know," I said. "But I have a feeling we're not going to get any more information from him." It seemed too unlikely that Niko had never seen one of his own customers.

"So, what now?" Olivia asked.

"I guess we need to find out more about Annette," I said. "See if we can figure out why she was really here."

Olivia's eyes sparked with her fae magic, and she gave me a slow, mischievous smile. "We should break into her room and nose around."

I laughed. "I was just going to suggest that." Great minds.

She threaded an arm around mine and led me back inside and down the hall to the elevators. "If we're gonna share a brain, we might want to try to get one that works."

CHAPTER FOUR

Olivia used her magic to get Annette's room number, a nifty little trick her biological father, Lucifer, had shown her. It involved astral projection and a bit of possession, so I wasn't sure it was something I wanted to learn, even if I could. Probably, I wasn't even capable anyway.

On our way to the floor Annette's room was on, I texted Drew to meet us there. Hopefully, after this long, he'd be done talking to the police, but I knew my Drew. He could go on and on about a case for hours. He and Sam sometimes got on a roll. When that happened, Olivia and I generally snuck out to do our own thing.

My hunky hubby was waiting on us when we arrived. Grabbing his hand, I beamed up at him. "How did you get here so fast?" I wanted to touch him all the time. I'd wanted to do that before we were married, too, but here in the romantic castle, it was stronger.

He held out a key, looking a little too triumphant. "I'm helping with the investigation. I spent most of the morning having my credentials sent over so I could be given privileges with the local DCI.

That's what they call their detective force." His grin widened." Hunters aren't without our own tricks."

Boy, did I know that. After having the Walker family stay with us for the wedding, I could write a book on hunters and their tricks. When they'd taken on the tentacle monster that had escaped from Hell during the rehearsal dinner, the hunters had seemed to conjure weapons left and right. Their skills were limitless. As was their ability to be grumpy, but that was another story.

I waved a hand toward the door and said, "Shall we go in?"

He handed Olivia and me gloves to put on, then opened the room. "We might as well do this right." Inside was clean even though the maid hadn't been in, since it was a crime scene.

"Forensics has already been in, but still don't move anything," Drew said as he put his own gloves on.

He started with a quick scan of the room, using his hunter's instincts while Olivia and I looked around with our own flares of magic and investigative eyes.

Olivia headed over to the closet while I sat down at the desk and opened the laptop that had been left sitting there. It fired to life instantly, indicating she hadn't turned it off when she'd last used it. It was only in sleep mode. In this day and age, computers were a great source of info about a person. At the least, I'd be able to find out if she was emailing anyone. Or maybe if she'd had any inkling that something bad was going to happen. Sometimes people had premonitions. Heck, I knew how to raise skeletons from the dead. A little premonition wasn't anything shocking.

The victim's screen saver was a picture of a castle in Scotland. In fact, it was The Andarsan—the very one we were staying at. That made me wonder if this had been the first time she'd stayed here. However, she was an author. It was more likely that she'd been using this castle as the inspiration for her next book.

After the second try at the password, I sat back in the chair, afraid to attempt it again. If I did it too many times, the computer might shut down completely. "Either of you know how to magically hack into a computer?"

Drew came to look over my shoulder. Then he moved the computer so he could type. "Let me try something." He winked and typed in some kind of code.

I laughed. He really never ceased to amaze. "Is computer hacking a required skill for hunters?"

Drew grinned and kissed my cheek. "I can teach you to do it. It's a handy skill to have."

Yeah, if you wanted to go to prison for it. Then again, I was married to a sheriff. Drew was pretty tech-savvy, but the computer hacker side gig was new news for me. "What else do I not know about you?" I tried not to sound accusing. We'd only been together for a year. We were bound to continue to learn things about one another for a while, at least.

He frowned and averted his gaze. A spike of guilt rushed through our magical bond, so I touched his hand, forcing him to look at me. "I know you held back your hunter abilities from me, and I'm okay with that because I trust you to fill me in before I actually *need* to know." I trusted him completely. That was the important part. He didn't like talking about his hunter life. In his defense, he'd walked away from the hunter life years ago. It really didn't matter to me what he could do. Besides, I could feel his intentions through our bond.

"You may get a crash course sooner than later," he said flatly.

I knew what he meant. Now that his family had accepted me and all my weirdness, Drew had warned me that they would probably try to pass on missions that were near us. After all, they had recruited Owen to work with them full-time. That was probably really good for my best necromancer friend, though. He needed more purpose in life. To feel helpful and useful.

Drew wouldn't go hunting without me. We'd already agreed that if he did return to doing any hunting, it would be with us as a team.

Instead of returning the laptop to me, he searched through her folders until he found something he deemed interesting—a partial manuscript.

"What's this?" I asked as I started reading it. "Annette was writing a murder mystery."

The victim in the story was described as a beautiful socialite who'd been killed in her room at a castle in the Scottish highlands.

Olivia had come out of the closet by then and she said, "I found something, too. Research notes about a blonde woman falling down the stairs every ten years since the sixties." Olivia handed me a folder. I rifled through it and found newspaper clippings and photos, some of them original, some photocopied. Skimming the dates, I nodded. "Yeah, the first article is in the sixties. This is nuts."

Drew and I exchanged a look. This just kept getting weirder and weirder. What would we find next, that the castle cat was a ghost?

CHAPTER FIVE

THE THREE OF us huddled together in Annette's room to read through the newspaper clippings. One, in particular, caught my attention, about a woman who'd fallen down a set of stairs and broken her neck two days before Halloween in 1961. I picked up a picture of a woman who could have passed for Olivia's doppelganger. It also looked somewhat like the woman who we'd found dead last night.

"Wow," I said, handing her the photo. "She sort of looks like you, Olivia."

"Not all blondes look alike," she said with a roll of her eyes and flipped her hair over her shoulder. She eyed the photo like it was some dark omen or something. "I'm far more attractive."

Once we'd at least glanced at each article, Drew took the photo and the articles and stuffed them back into the folder. Then he pulled out a flash drive from his pants pocket.

"You just carry a flash drive around with you?" I teased, wondering what else he was going to pull out of his pants.

Well, there was one thing I'd like for him to pop out, but not in front of Olivia. Maybe we could find a dark corner of the castle to act inappropriately in later.

Drew flashed me a grin. He knew what I was thinking about. "Get your mind out of the gutter. It's one of my keychains. I took to carrying it around years ago. It helps me sometimes at work." He stuck the drive into the USB port and copied her hard drive.

And here I'd been thinking he'd conjured it. He rarely openly used his magic, and I'd been wondering if he'd start now because his family had accepted me. I hoped he would. Hunters had more magic than Drew used. I was sure about that.

Instead of opening that can of worms, I said, "Let's go downstairs and see if the staff can tell us more about the woman killed sixty years ago. I bet there's at least one or two who have heard the story."

We turned to leave the room just as the sound of a high-pitched scream echoed throughout the room.

Olivia jumped and clung to my arm as the dark-haired woman who'd woken me up in the middle of the night appeared. "Get out!" she screamed and then disappeared.

"Well that was rude," Olivia said, releasing my arm.

I nodded. "She was the ghost who woke us last night. This morning she told me to help them. Whoever them are. I still have no idea."

The last thing I needed was to deal with a bipolar ghost with mood swings. I wasn't a ghost expert but felt obligated to help solve this case.

"She's not scaring us off the case now." Drew opened the door and held it for Olivia and me. "If anything, I'm more intrigued."

Olivia nodded in agreement. "Definitely not. Ghost woman doesn't know who she is dealing with."

I laughed and stepped out into the hallway. "A necromancer, the daughter of Satan, and a hunter. We make quite the team."

On our way downstairs, we stopped by our room to drop off the folder and flash drive. Then we were off to ask the desk clerk about the woman who died in 1961. The one in the articles we found in Annette's room, not the moody dark-haired woman, assuming they weren't the same. I'd ask the ghost myself if I thought she'd actually talk to me, but both times I'd tried she'd disappeared.

The lobby was empty since it was lunchtime, so that gave us some time to ask questions. A place this old had to have stories and legends. The great hall of the castle was a large, open room that had served as a gathering place for the laird and his guests. The walls were lined with tapestries, and I could easily imagine the floor covered in rush matting. A large fireplace dominated one end of the room, and there were several tables and chairs scattered around, empty this time of day, but this morning they'd been full of patrons. The castle cat, a black girl who loved getting belly rubs, was stretched in a chair in front of one of the large windows, soaking in the sunshine.

The hall was lit by oil lamps converted to electric and electric candles, and a large chandelier hung from the ceiling. They were made to flicker, and at night gave the impression they were still oil- and wax-based. The great hall was the most impressive room in the castle.

The desk clerk, an older woman with graying hair, looked up from her computer screen when we approached. "Can I help you?" she asked with a forced smile. I couldn't tell if she was annoyed by the interruption or if her mood was from something else entirely. She definitely didn't have the easy manner of Niko. I wished he was here now.

"Yes, we were wondering if you could tell us about the woman who died here in 1961," I said, giving her my brightest smile. No need to irritate her further by being standoffish.

The desk clerk furrowed her brow. "That was a long time ago. I wasn't even born then."

But she had heard about it from somewhere. There was a glint in her eyes. She knew something.

Drew leaned on the counter and flashed his most charming smile. That devil. "Do you know if anyone here remembers what happened? We're just curious, after the terrible events of last night."

"Looking for good ghost stories, if you know what we mean," Olivia added. She also flashed a winning smile. I didn't have that same sort of charm about me. But I could raise a whole graveyard to my aid if I needed to, so what did I need with charm?

"I can ask the owner. He might remember. Just a moment." The desk clerk got up from her chair and walked to the back office, through a door behind the desk. I really hadn't expected the owner to be here, though I couldn't really say why. She returned a few moments later with an older man who looked like he should have retired a few years ago. He was stooped and wrinkled, with a face that looked as though it had been carved out of an ancient tree trunk. His hair was thin and wispy, and his clothes hung loosely on his frame. He walked slowly and carefully, as though he was afraid of falling.

Despite all of this, he still managed to have a twinkle in his eye as he peered at us through thick glasses. "I'm Peter Tarkin, owner of Andarsan Castle. What can I do for you?"

I repeated our question, and he furrowed his brow, thinking. "Oh, yes, I remember that story. Back then, the Andarsan family still lived here. It was before I lived here. The woman in the photo," he tapped the photocopied picture Drew had set on the counter, "was the children's governess. Two days before Halloween, she took a nasty fall down the stairs and broke her neck. The family sold the place shortly after. Their oldest son became heir to it all. He took on the responsibility of his younger siblings." He shrugged. "I always figured they couldn't stand the stain of death. Or maybe they needed the money."

"Did they ever find out what caused her to fall?" I asked.

The man shook his head as he peered down at the photo. "No. It was ruled an accident. But there were always rumors that she'd been pushed."

I glanced from Drew to Olivia. This was definitely getting interesting. I had to know what those rumors were. If this woman was the ghost of the dead governess, she wasn't staying around because she'd died in an accident. No doubt there was something far more nefarious going on.

Then the man added, "Every year since then, on the anniversary of her death, her ghost has been seen walking around the castle. There was also talk that people felt her presence around the stairs where she died."

"Where Annette was found," I said softly, not meaning for him to hear me. But he did. Oops.

"Yes. There have been incidents where women have fallen and claimed they were pushed, but no one was around to corroborate their stories. No one has died from those accidents." He hung his head. "Until now."

We exchanged a look. Oh, yeah. We were all thinking the same thing. Annette's death was no coincidence. It was no accident. She'd been *murdered*. The question was whether or not her murderer was alive.

"Thank you for your time," I said and shook Peter's hand. "If you think of anything else, my husband, Drew, is helping the police with the investigation."

"I will let you know." Peter's eyes twinkled again before he turned to go back to the office.

"Oh, here," the clerk said. She'd stood to the side while we'd talked, listening and observing. "Don't forget the flyer for our annual Halloween ball. It's an event you definitely don't want to miss." She held out a stack of flyers, so I grabbed one to take back to our room with us. Who knew if we'd have time to go with all this going on?

CHAPTER SIX

I BROWSED the Halloween flyer as I walked up the stairs, but my mind was all on the case. I couldn't focus on the details of their Halloween ball. "So, it sounds like we have a murder mystery on our hands," I said as I sat down on the bed in our room. I had a couple of murder cases under my belt but, obviously, Drew had more experience than me. Olivia was all in, no matter what. She was always up for a good investigation. I could count on her.

Between the three of us, we could solve this case. The supernatural side of it. I was half convinced there wasn't a human bad guy behind any of it.

Drew nodded. "It certainly does. I'd rather us solve this than the humans."

"For sure. It sounds like there is a ghost pushing people down the stairs." She had the same thoughts I had. Olivia took a seat at the desk in front of my laptop. Then she picked up the room service menu. "We should order lunch."

Right on cue, my stomach growled, reminding me we all skipped breakfast. "Food sounds good. While we eat, we could dig more into Annette's research of the castle. Maybe she was on the same track we were."

"And maybe that's why she got pushed down the stairs," Drew said darkly.

Neither of us had any reply to that. He was right. In all likelihood, we were in danger by investigating.

Drew and I gave Olivia our order. We had the menu memorized. She took a few minutes to pick something before she called it in. Then she turned to Drew. "Can I have the flash drive? Might as well see what was on Annette's computer."

He handed her the little thumb drive and she plugged it into my laptop. I moved to the other side of the bed so I could look over Olivia's shoulder. The desk was close enough that I could just see. Drew scooted closer to me.

We spent the entire twenty minutes it took for our lunch to arrive looking through the computer files. There wasn't much information about the castle or the ghost on her computer. It was more the fiction part of her book. "We'll have to read the actual manuscript," I said. "She might've used her theories in it."

As we ate, I thumbed through the folder with all of Annette's research. She'd scrawled notes all over the place, but it seemed likely she had no idea about the supernatural aspect. She thought she was dealing with a serial killer. And her book looked like it was going to be a contemporary, not a paranormal. She'd done the research but hadn't gotten there yet. Or the ghosts hadn't revealed themselves to her.

Munching on a delicious sweet potato fry, I picked up a news article I hadn't noticed before. The article was dated two days after the one about the governess who'd tragically fallen to her death. The laird had killed his wife and then himself in their room right after the governess died in the sixties.

I scanned through the article a few times before turning my attention to the photo to the left of the article. Holy ghoul snot! It was him. The guy, the one who'd been crying over Annette's body. The one who'd been sad in the dining room. He was the laird who'd killed his wife and then himself. And beside him in the photo was none other than the dark-haired woman who'd appeared to Drew and me the night before, asking for help. The lady with the party dress.

Well, well, well. It was all coming together, wasn't it?

"Drew, look at this," I said, handing him the article. With my hands freed up, I took advantage to take a few bites of my huge and delicious sausage.

He read through it quickly before setting it down with his eyebrows raised. "The plot thickens."

Olivia picked it up and began skimming the article, making little chirpy noises of agreement deep in her throat.

I nodded. "For sure. We should talk to the owner again and see if he knows anything about this." Surely, he had. Why hadn't he told us about it? This was absolutely related.

We finished our lunch and then made our way back down to the lobby. The owner was still at the front desk, this time without the cranky woman, and he greeted us with a smile.

"Is there anything else I can help you with?" he asked.

"We were just wondering if you could tell us more about the couple who died in the castle two days after the governess died," I said. "The man in particular. He would've been the laird?"

The owner's smile faded. "That certainly was a tragic incident. We don't like to talk about it too much because it happened in one of our rooms."

"We understand," Drew said. "But we're curious about how it all went down. Do you know which room it was?"

The owner hesitated for a moment before answering. I didn't miss that twinkle in his eye. He thought this was funny. What an imp. "It was the room you're currently staying in."

A chill ran down my spine. We'd been sleeping in the same room where two people died.

Eh, well. It wasn't that shocking. Not to a necromancer. Death was part of life, most definitely for me.

"Thank you for your time," Drew said as we turned to leave. "If you think of anything else, please. Let us know."

"You're welcome," the owner replied. "And I hope you enjoy the rest of your stay." His voice had gone back to that customer service lilt. All business.

As we walked away, I couldn't help but feel like we were being watched. I scanned the lobby, the giant pictures in their gilded frames, and the tapestries that probably hid a dozen secret passages. The fireplace and the tables. As we walked toward the stairs, I spotted a few ghosts lurking around, but they weren't the source of my feeling. They'd been here pretty much nonstop.

"While we're down here, let's mingle with the other guests. I want to see if anyone has heard any stories about the castle," I asked. Something was just bugging me. I had to figure out what it was.

Drew linked his fingers with mine. "Good idea."

CHAPTER SEVEN

"WHAT DO YOU THINK?" Olivia asked as we stepped into the dining room. Lunch was almost over, and people milled about. Some at the tables and some moving toward the great hall. "Split up?"

Drew and I nodded. "We'll go this way." I pointed toward the dining room.

"Okay. I'll head toward the fireplace." Olivia went off to find guests to mingle with to dig up any information she could.

Drew and I walked around the dining room until we found a small group of people who didn't look like they'd hiss at us if we intruded.

"So," I said conspiratorially. "Have you guys heard about the castle curse?" We wanted to know if anyone had seen anything or knew anything that would help. The best way to do that was gossip.

This little group of guests was more than happy to talk about the curse of the castle. "Oh, yeah." A woman nodded her head sagely. "It's been a rumor in this area since I was a little girl." She looked to be in her sixties or seventies, so it made sense.

"Did you grow up around here?" Drew asked.

"I did. I'm back visiting family, and they don't have room for me to stay there. I'd always wanted to stay in the castle as a child, so I figured why not stay here instead of the small inn in town?"

"I didn't grow up here, but someone at the pub in town told me all about it." A man leaned forward, looking way more excited than scared at the prospect of a ghost. "I keep trying to see one of the spirits, but as far as I can tell, this place isn't haunted." He leaned back and puffed up a bit. "I'm a bit clairvoyant, you know. If there were ghosts here, I'd feel them."

The rest of the crowd seemed properly impressed at his declaration. Drew and I exchanged an amused glance, then nodded along with the crowd, seeming to agree that the place must not be haunted.

It seemed that everyone had heard the stories and most believed them. The most popular rumor amongst the people we talked to in the dining room was that anyone who died in the castle was doomed to haunt it forever.

I wasn't sure why the ghosts were all here, but it wasn't due to a curse. I would've felt the dark magic that powered a curse, which I didn't. It was a coincidence, or they just liked hanging out here. The only sure way to ask them was to give them power, but they, for the most part, steered clear of me. And I wasn't about to attempt the massive power surge I'd need to go into the Inbetween to talk to them properly.

As long as they weren't bothering anyone, it wasn't my or Drew's responsibility to do anything with them. The dark-haired woman and the man, on the other hand, we had to do something with because it was likely they were behind Annette's death and the accidents guests had been having on the stairs over the years. Those people who had fallen down the stairs were extremely lucky they hadn't broken their necks.

We chatted a little longer with the dining room guests before leaving to go back to our room, looking for Olivia in the front room to let her know we were headed up, but she didn't seem to be in there.

"Let's go up," Drew said. "I want to see if there's anything else in the folder that we might have missed."

"Okay. I can start reading her book, too."

When we got to our room, we found Olivia waiting for us.

"Find anything?" Drew asked her.

She shook her head and plopped back on the bed. "No, not really. Just rumors and suppositions. Nothing more informative than what the owner told us." She sat back up. "But I *did* overhear a few people talking about something strange that's been going on lately."

"What is it?" I asked and stretched out beside her on the bed. I had to find out where they got their mattresses. This one was heavenly.

"Some of the guests have been complaining about things moving in their rooms," she replied. "Like their clothes or shoes."

I laughed. "I'd rather have things moved around instead of being pushed down the stairs." Sounded like typical ghost activity. Too bad the fella we'd talked to hadn't had any of his stuff moved. That would've made his whole week. Probably his whole life.

Olivia snorted. "Me too, but these are humans who aren't used to dealing with the strange and undead like we are."

Olivia yawned and got up, shuffling toward the portal in the mirror on the wall. "I'm going to take a little nap on your bed at home. Sam's kept me up late at night. I'll see you two later."

That portal Luci created sure was handy to have. "Okay," I said. "If we're not here, we'll be down in the lobby."

She went through, but then stuck her head back into Scotland. "Hey, if you hear anything, text me. I'll come back."

When Olivia was gone and the mirror returned to looking like a mirror instead of a shimmering wave of magic, Drew said, "That portal is handy. We won't need to fly home."

I grinned at him. "I was thinking the same thing. We should cancel our flight and see if we can get a refund or apply the points toward another trip."

He chuckled as he wrapped an arm around my waist and pulled me to him. I ended up falling on top of him, which was exactly what he'd intended for me to do. Straddling his hips, I wiggled my brows. "What do you want to do now?"

With a shift move, he flipped me onto my back. "I have a few things in mind."

Then he kissed me. Oh, yeah. I *so* liked where this was going.

IT WAS early evening when Olivia stepped through the portal. "You could get whiplash from the time difference."

No joke. I did a quick calculation in my head. It was early afternoon in Maine. Sam would be asleep. Olivia would've had to have gotten up really early to be here with us this morning. No wonder she'd wanted to go back for a nap. "You ready for dinner?"

"Yep. I'm starving." Olivia grinned and headed to the door. "This place is amazing." She was not wrong. Even the doors were large, heavy wood, and obviously ancient. Everything about the castle was impressive.

When we got to the restaurant, we sat with some of the guests we'd met earlier in the day. They were in the middle of talking about leaving early.

"I'm not leaving," one woman with a bouffant hairdo said as she smacked the table. "I paid good money for this vacation and I'm going to enjoy it come hell or high water."

"I don't know," another woman said. "I keep thinking I see things out of the corner of my eye." She shivered. "It's freaking me out."

"It's just your imagination," the first woman said. "There's nothing here that can hurt you."

Olivia and I didn't dare look at each other. We would've burst out laughing. Then the jig would've really been up.

It was then I spotted the owner walking towards us. Nudging Olivia, I nodded his way, which pulled Drew's attention that way, too.

Peter had a worried look on his face. When he reached our table, he spoke directly to Drew and me. "Can I speak with you for a moment?" he asked.

"Sure," Drew said and he and I got up and followed Peter—slowly, he was about a hundred—to a sitting area near the kitchen. Olivia looked like she'd swallowed a frog, not going with us. I didn't know why she'd stayed behind. She could've come with us.

Even here, which appeared to be more of an employee area, felt like I was sitting in some historic spot.

The area was decorated with dark, heavy furniture and had an enormous fireplace. A giant portrait of a woman in a white dress with her dark hair pulled back in a tight bun hung over the mantle. She had a stern look on her face, and she looked like she was staring right at me.

Creepy much?

We took a seat, Drew and I crammed onto the loveseat while Peter sat in the armchair in front of us. The fire crackled merrily, keeping the room toasty warm against the brisk October Scottish weather. Peter glanced around before focusing on us. "I take it you *are* investigating the hauntings?"

I glanced at Drew, wondering if Peter somehow knew we weren't human. Was Peter a bit supernatural himself? Drew didn't look at me as he answered the question. "We are now, yes."

The poor man leaned forward with wide eyes and whispered, "Are you hunters?"

I snorted out loud and quickly covered it with a fake coughing fit. But my dear husband said, "Yes, but we really did come here for our honeymoon. Now that we know Annette's death was caused by a ghost, we can't just ignore it."

The owner nodded. "I understand." He paused and we waited. He obviously had something he wanted to share. Finally, he said, "I was a boy when it happened, but I've never forgotten. As if the people here would let any of us forget. The rumor was that the laird of the castle was having an affair with his children's governess. She's the one who fell down the stairs. Everyone always assumed the wife did it but there was no way to prove it way back then." He shrugged. "The sixties didn't exactly have big-time forensics. Then, two days later, the laird killed his wife and himself. Their eldest son, who was of age, quickly sold the estate, having no desire to stay in the castle his parents died in. The new owners immediately started using it as a destination hotel." He sucked in a deep breath. " I got a job here as soon as I was old enough, as did many people in the village. The castle is the largest employer in the area, even still."

I looked around. It made sense that it would take an enormous staff to maintain this place.

"I lived on-site and saved every penny of my paychecks. By the time they were ready to sell, when I was in my 40s, I had enough for the down payment."

"What about the women falling down the stairs?" I asked.

"It happens every ten years on the anniversary of the governess's death. The last time, before Annette's death, the hotel was closed for renovations. We'd actually planned it that way, to hopefully keep anyone from falling." He shook his head regretfully. "But somehow a young woman wandered into the castle while it was locked up tight and fell down the stairs." The owner looked into the fire for a moment, then continued. "We've done seances, called so-called ghost hunters, but nothing has worked. Every decade, another young woman falls down the stairs."

"We'll figure it out and solve the mystery," I said. "It's what we do."

Drew added, "If there is any more information you can give us, that will help."

Peter took out one of his business cards and wrote down the Laird's name, his wife's, and the governess's. Malcolm, Nora, and Holly. "That's all I know about them."

"It's a start. Thank you." I took the card and tucked it into my pants pocket.

Then Drew and I returned to the table. Olivia had turned the conversation around while we were talking to Peter. The group was laughing and chatting about their adventures since staying at The Andarsan. My besty stared at me with questions in her eyes, but I couldn't exactly fill her in now. She'd have to wait till after dinner. No doubt it was going to kill her to wait. I giggled and took a sip of my water. Poor Olivia.

CHAPTER EIGHT

"Whᴀᴛ ɪғ ᴡᴇ do our own seance?" I asked, moving my gaze from Drew to Olivia. We'd just returned from dinner and now that we were alone in our room—the room where the Laird and his wife had died. I'd filled Olivia in on the owner's story as we walked back to our room.

Olivia nodded quietly, a thin smile on her lips. She was loving every minute of this. I hated to remind her this wasn't all fun and games. Someone had *died.*

Drew scratched the back of his neck and lifted one shoulder. "I don't see how it could hurt," he said. "We've done them before."

Of course, there were ways it could hurt, hurt a lot, but I was betting on my necro powers to keep the spirits from harming us or anyone else. I hoped. They were still super wonky. At least now we knew why. My powers had been so strong before because I was the last female descendant on both sides of my family. But now that my son's girlfriend was pregnant with a baby girl. That had to be what was causing my powers to only work when they wanted to. My mother had told me that when she was pregnant with me, she had problems with her powers as well. I never did with Wallie, but I didn't really use my powers when I was pregnant with him. I'd still been denying my abilities at that point.

"Shouldn't we wait for dark?" Olivia asked as I conjured a few candles, matches, and some salt, happy my malfunctioning powers allowed me to do this much.

"Nah, that's not necessary. It's possible that doing them during the witching hour would make them stronger, but there's a large debate about when the witching hour actually is, so, meh." I shrugged.

We needed a larger space to work, so I had Drew move the bed to the side, which ended up being impossible. The bed was a *gigantic* solid four-poster and as strong as Drew was, even with his supernatural hunter strength, there was no moving it on his own. Olivia wiggled her fingers, the bed rose up, drifted off to the side, and sat gently back down on the ground.

I poured salt into a large circle while Olivia placed the candles around the salt line and lit them.

We sat outside the salt circle, and I held out my hands. "I want the ghosts contained in the circle, so don't let go."

Drew and I took Olivia's hands, each of us having to lean a bit to reach. The air felt charged, but it was hard to tell if that was me or the ghosts.

Tension knotted my neck as I fed my power into the circle. A buzz of energy forced me to open my eyes, and a thick silver rope of light wrapped around Olivia's and my hands, drawing us together in a solid barrier. Light from the candles flickered as our circle snapped together. Now the silver rope of light ran down all of our arms and hands.

Drew sucked in a breath. As a hunter, he was bred to hate this sort of thing.

I loved it.

His magic started to rebel against mine and Olivia's, so I waited. It needed time to be comfortable with this, and we had time to be patient. Drew's magic was part of mine, ever since we'd bonded, just as mine was part of his now. However, Olivia's magic was a mix of fae and underworld power, and Drew had never connected with her magic before.

It was freaking him and his magic out.

"Drew?" I arched a brow at him. He had to get himself together.

"I got it." He closed his eyes and took deep, even breaths. I could sense his magic calming down, listening to whatever he was telling it. Or maybe as his heart rate slowed and he got himself under control, the magic followed suit. Sometimes I talked to mine, and sometimes it just did what I wanted. It was a topic of conversation I should bring up another time. It would make for an interesting conversation at the next coven meeting.

Drew smiled shakily. "I'm good now."

Olivia watched us with a worried expression. I quickly explained. "Hunter magic doesn't play well with darker powers. And let's face it. Half of your magic is as dark as it comes."

She snickered and nodded. "True."

We sat quietly for a few minutes to ground ourselves and clear our minds. Then I took the lead by pushing out my necro power, which seemed to be working for the moment. When the salt circle was full of my power, boosted by Olivia's and Drew's, I spoke, also lacing my words with magic. "Malcolm Andarsan, show yourself."

We waited in calm silence for a few minutes. Nothing happened. Talk about anticlimactic.

"Is there anyone here with us?" Olivia asked in a soft voice.

We waited for a few more minutes, then I tried again with a little more magic, really cramming the circle full. This castle was chock full of ghosts. What the heck? There was no response.

"Maybe this isn't going to work," Drew said, sounding doubtful.

I was about to agree when the candles flickered and went out. A few seconds later the candles lit on their own and inside the circle was a ghost. It wasn't Malcolm Andarsan, but this ghost was definitely Scottish and dressed in nothing but a kilt. He locked eyes with me, then Olivia laughed like someone had told him a really good joke, then flipped his kilt up, flashing us his private bits.

Trust me, ghost bits weren't as exciting as the real thing. Or maybe just *this* ghost's bits weren't.

Just then, a noise came from the other side of the room, near the bathroom. It sounded like someone was crying. We all turned to look but there was nothing there. When we looked back, the flasher ghost was gone.

"Did you hear that?" I whispered. Why did this freak me out so much? This was nothing new or strange for me.

Drew and Olivia both nodded their heads, Olivia with wide, startled eyes. We sat in silence for a few more minutes, but we didn't hear the crying again.

"Well, that was weird," Drew said. Then he shot up to his feet and started waving his arms around like he was fighting off an invisible attacker. He bobbed and weaved, grunting. "Help me," he said as he flailed.

"Holy crap, he's possessed!" Olivia scrambled to her feet, and I followed suit, fear bubbling up my throat.

I grabbed Drew's hand, but the invisible force still held onto him with a vice-like grip. I tried to pull back but now he had a hold of me. I couldn't get him to release my fingers.

"Drew, let go of my hand so I can break the connection," I said, ready to fight the ghost or spirit or whatever the heck it was. I gathered my powers, ready to blast this ghost into oblivion.

Drew tried to shake his head, but he was still unable to break the ghost's hold on him. "Help!" He looked seriously freaked out, my big strong hunter. I had to help him!

Tears pricked my eyes as I scrambled to figure out what I could do. "Drew, please. I don't want to hurt you."

Drew nodded his head, then after a deep breath, he let go of my hand. At that moment, the invisible force released him. Drew fell to his knees and started gasping for air.

"Get him some water," I said to Olivia while I searched Drew's body for injuries. Could the ghost have bodily harmed him?

Probably. They could be nasty.

Olivia darted into the bathroom as I used my healing powers to feel if he was injured. Besides a racing heart, I didn't think he was.

A moment later the water turned on, then Olivia returned with a glass and put it to Drew's lips. He gulped down the entire glass. "Are you okay?" she asked, leaning over him.

Drew nodded his head. "That was not fun."

I helped him to his feet while monitoring his emotions through our bond. "Are you sure you're okay?"

Drew nodded but his teal eyes looked a little glazed over. He was emotionally rung out but physically fine.

Olivia and I helped Drew over to the bed so he could sit on it. I walked to the salt circle and used my magic to gather it up in a small cyclone, then directed it to the trash can. One of my little parlor tricks that were so handy. With a wave of my hand, the candles went out.

Just then we heard a dull thumping noise. "What now?" I asked, more than exasperated.

CHAPTER NINE

Ah! There it was again. The hollow thump, thump, thump was coming from inside our wall. What in the world could be in there? I waved at Olivia and pointed at the wall beside the tapestry. She nodded and came closer. "I already checked behind there for a hidden passage," she whispered.

Drew scoffed. "I looked there the first day."

At least it wasn't another ghost ready to possess one of us. Well, it could've been, but I doubted it since the banging sounded like something or someone, possibly, was stuck in the wall. Ghosts could've just gone through it.

Drew, Olivia, and I pushed against the wall where the noise was coming from, poking and prodding on the crown molding, and the baseboards, and tugging on the light sconces. "It would be something old, original to the house," Olivia said. "The secret entrance won't be in a modern electric light.

I eyeballed the fireplace mantle across the room. "Possibly it's not something close?" I hurried over and began prodding away at the intricately carved mantle.

Sure enough, the inner circle of a little flower depressed with just a little bit of pressure. After a couple of seconds, a secret door popped open on the other side of the exit door, several feet away from where we'd been searching.

A stale, dank musty smell, like an airless, damp basement, came with it. We peered into the dark, creepy passage, which went in the direction of the original thumps we'd heard.

I shrieked when something came rushing toward us, and everyone jumped back as Lucy-Fur and Snoozer came running out.

"We've been yelling for you for hours!" Lucy said in almost a growl.

I gaped at my incredibly spoiled, cute-but-so-bad cats. "How in all the heavens did you get in there?"

Lucy tossed her snow-white head back haughtily. "We came through the portal earlier, when you weren't here and decided to have a nap on that amazing bed while we waited.

I felt the urge for a moment of private time, so I went looking for a litter box and found a passage." She glared at Snoozer. "I don't know how he opened it, but I know it was him."

"Was he up on the mantle?" Drew asked.

Snoozer licked his paw delicately. He loved being up high.

"Yes," Lucy said darkly. "Right after I went into the passage, he ran in behind me. Somehow the door shut behind us, and we were stuck."

"What did you find?" I asked. "Where does it go?"

Lucy gave me a disdainful look. "Do I look stupid to you? Do I look like a complete idiot? Do you think for one second that I would stray away from the opening we came in? The moment we went any further down the passage we would've ended up getting lost."

She huffed, and it sounded suspiciously like a hiss. "We stayed right by the door until we heard you lot come back from wherever you'd been enjoying yourselves." Man, her voice *dripped* with venom.

"Well, heck. I want to see where it goes!" Olivia jumped up and down on the balls of her feet.

We followed the passage using the lights from our cell phones and found ourselves in a room with cobwebs draping from the ceiling and dust everywhere. It was so quiet that I could hear my own heart beating.

Olivia conjured an energy ball to light up the room.

"Oh, gosh." It was awesome. I quickly realized that the room was a secret reading room. Everything had been carefully put in place. There was a small lounge with a quilt on it. Nearby, in a wooden case near a window, a stack of books was neatly piled from top to bottom.

To the left of the lounger was a round table. On it, there was a candlestick in the center and an old-fashioned matchbox nearby. Next to the candlestick was a stack of folded papers with a quill and an inkwell. The corners were curled with age and the paper was yellowed.

We searched the room for any clues about who the late Laird Andarsan and his wife had been. What sort of people were they? Had they been kind or cruel, rash or calm? We knew nothing.

After a few minutes, Olivia muttered, "I think I found something." She was splayed out on the floor where she'd been checking floorboards. Grinning from ear to ear, she reached down and lifted a loose floorboard. She reached underneath and pulled out an old, leather-bound book. Its spine was worn from use, but the pages were still in good shape.

"What is it?" I asked, hurrying over to crouch beside her on the floor.

"I think it's an old journal," she said, holding it up for me to see. "Maybe there's something in here that can help us."

I took the journal from her and started flipping through it.

It was Nora Andarsan's diary. Olivia and I sat back, and she conjured another orb to hover.

The woman's handwriting was neat and so easy to read. We skimmed, mainly looking at dates and a few sentences per page. It seemed like it covered her turmoil leading up to the deaths and included the day she shoved the governess down the stairs. The last entry was on October 30, 1961. She'd been getting ready for the Halloween ball and the entry talked about being excited about her dress and that her husband was finally her own. She even described it. "That dress is the one she's wearing to this day," I whispered. "The one her ghostly body adorns." I spoke in a spooky voice and dissolved into giggles.

Once I composed myself, Olivia looked at me with wide eyes.

"That's the day they died," she said, in a low tone.

I nodded, suddenly feeling sad, my giggles disappearing, which was crazy because Nora had killed her husband's mistress and gotten away with it. Did she deserve to die for her crime? Perhaps. Her husband had clearly thought so.

I flipped to the last page, hoping for some sort of explanation, but there was none. No more entries past that night. "That's the last one." It seemed indecent to raise my voice in here, so I kept my tone low.

"Cause she was dead," Drew said ironically. He was studying the books on the shelves.

"Drew," I hissed. "Be respectful."

An answering chuckle was all I got.

Maybe this journal was the key to helping the ghosts move on. But first, we needed to find out why they were still stuck at the castle. What was keeping them here? And not just the three involved with this intrigue. Why was this a hotspot for ghost activity in general?

If I remembered correctly, one of the ghosts on the ghost train had told me there were certain places ghosts just enjoyed hanging out. Maybe this was one. Heck if I knew.

I studied the journal again, flipping through the pages until I came to an entry from the day before the Halloween ball. There was something else here. Scrawled in the margins of the page, hidden under layers of yellowed ink and etchings, were two words: stuck forever. The word forever was underlined several times, and the ink was weird.

Geeeeeeez. "Is that blood?" I whispered, pointing to the words.

Olivia nodded with a shiver. "This place is spooky."

Had Nora bound her husband and his mistress to this castle so they would be forced to relive their deaths over and over again for all of eternity? How had she done it? Had she cast some sort of dark magic spell before her death? The other guests at the castle had mentioned a curse. Was that what they had meant? Or were there secrets buried deep in Andarsan Castle that only the family knew about?

One thing was for sure—our investigation into this mystery would keep us occupied for some time as we desperately searched for answers from beyond the grave.

"Let's get out of here," I said as I took one last look around at all of the old books and artifacts in the secret room.

"As spooky as it is," Olivia said. "This room is so cool. I gotta ask Luci if there are secret passages in his house."

I snorted as I led Drew and Olivia back through the passage. "Knowing your father, there are some that lead to places or rooms that you don't want to see."

"Eww." She drew out the word. "Gross, I bet you're right. I'll definitely *ask* before I go exploring."

We turned right, and I had a vague feeling that we took a wrong turn. My feeling was cemented when we came to a set of stairs going down. We had taken a wrong turn, dang it. I definitely didn't remember there being stairs on our way into the secret reading room. That wasn't the sort of thing I'd forget.

As we came to the bottom of the stairwell, we emerged into the lobby right next to the large fireplace. "This is interesting." As busy as the lobby was, nobody seemed to notice our emergence from nowhere.

"Yep," Drew agreed.

Olivia nodded.

As we made our way through the lobby to the elevators, goosebumps rose on my arms and shivers danced down my spine as if Nora herself was watching me from beyond her grave.

Which was likely, since I now knew she was the dark-haired ghost who'd woken me up to help. But why would she have asked us to help when she was the one who'd trapped Malcolm and Holly there? It made no sense. Either she wanted them freed or she didn't. Maybe she'd just had a major afterlife change of heart.

Despite how unsettled I felt, we were determined to find out what happened to Malcolm Andarsan and his lover, Holly, so they could finally rest in peace once again. Maybe we'd get lucky and find a way to help Nora find some peace, too.

If there was anything left behind by them in this castle or even clues about their deaths elsewhere, then it was our mission to unearth those secrets for good and put their souls to rest forever.

CHAPTER TEN

OLIVIA

I woke with a start like someone had doused me with water. What happened? Blinking rapidly, I waited for my eyesight to catch up with my brain as I checked my surroundings. No wonder it was hard for me to get my bearings. I was no longer in Ava and Drew's bedroom where I'd fallen asleep. I'd stumbled through the portal and collapsed on their bed to get a few hours' sleep. Going back and forth was messing with me, even with Sammie busy with his grandmother Phira and Sam busy with Wade planning the bar. Just the time difference was getting to me. It had still been early evening when I'd fallen asleep back in Maine.

Now I was standing at the top of a set of stairs, with just a sliver of moonlight coming through a window to light the way. Panicked, I turned to rush back to their room when I felt a presence behind me. It did not feel friendly, either.

I sensed her before I saw her. The hairs on my neck lifted, and the feeling of being watched grew stronger.

"Go! And never return!" shouted an angry voice in front of me. A dark-haired woman in a ballgown stared down at me. Her eyes were so dark they looked black, and her face was contorted with rage. She floated several inches off the ground. "You never belonged here!" she shrieked, then she shoved me down the stairs.

I had no time to brace myself for the fall. Pain exploded in my ankles and shoulders as I tumbled down the staircase. It happened so fast, but I had to get out of there.

Before I hit the ground, I teleported myself without really thinking about where I was going. I needed a safe place to land. Like a trampoline. My body disappeared from the castle and reappeared on a trampoline in the backyard of my childhood home. I bounced on the trampoline and held myself still, trying to get the creaking of the old thing to stop. Crap. I couldn't be there. If my *very* human, adopted parents had seen me appear out of thin air, I wasn't sure how they'd react. I certainly couldn't explain myself.

Rolling off of the trampoline, I disappeared underneath it before I quickly teleported myself back into Scotland and Ava and Drew's room.

I stumbled to Ava and Drew's big comfy bed, still clutching my shoulder. My whole body ached, but I was afraid my shoulder was bruised or jammed. It definitely didn't feel good. "Ava, Drew. Wake up!" I cried. Snoozer jumped off the bed and ran under it with a yowl.

Lucy did it with a, "What the fu—"

"What's wrong?" Ava asked, cutting the cranky cat off, her sleepiness quickly forgotten. She rolled out of bed and rushed to me, grabbing my elbow, thankfully the one on my arm that wasn't currently throbbing.

"Someone pushed me down the stairs!" I explained. "It was the ghost, the one you described in the ball gown. Nora."

"Are you sure?" Drew asked, looking just as worried as Ava. He pulled on a dressing gown and helped Ava get me to the bed.

"Positive," I said. "She screamed at me to go away and never come back. Then she hauled off and shoved me."

"Well, we aren't leaving until we find out how to stop her from pushing other women down the stairs," Ava said, moving closer to me. "This will sting a bit."

I opened my mouth to ask her what she was doing when her cool hand landed gently on the bruised, tender spot on my shoulder. A tingle of something warm and soft spread slowly through me as she pushed her healing magic into me. Soon all my aches vanished.

"That's better. Thanks," I said, then asked, "I thought she wanted our help. What gives?"

"Maybe she does," Ava said. "Maybe she can't stop her mood swings. Remember how Phira was an evil black blob in the Inbetween? She was stuck somewhere she didn't belong and had lost her daughter."

I had never considered that, but it made sense. Phira's corrupted father had punished her for falling in love with Luci. Phira had been sent to the Inbetween, which was sort of a hell dimension for witches. Human ghosts also spent a lot of time there. Fae ghosts were not ever meant to go there. Phira's pain and the magic from the Inbetween had turned her into this massive evil blob of black slime. It wasn't until my blood had touched her that she turned back to herself—a fae princess, my biological mother, and a wonderful person.

"Being stuck in the castle is making Nora's ghost go crazy."

Ava nodded. "That's my working theory."

"We won't be scared off that easily," Drew said with a smirk before leaning over and stroking Ava's cheek with the back of his hand. She closed her eyes and relaxed, leaning into his touch like a cat who had just discovered where her bowl of catnip was kept.

Ah, newlyweds. My chest tightened. I missed Sam. I missed the ease we'd had with one another before.

Since he'd become a vampire, our schedules had been off. When he was awake, he couldn't stay away from me for too long. He clung. It was unhealthy to go on as we had been. I had to figure out how to fix that. Fix us. These last few nights with him focused on the bar had been great, but almost too much distance. I'd barely seen him at all. We had to find a nice in-between. A compromise. Middle ground.

But I couldn't do that right at this moment, so I focused on our little ghostly mystery. This was fun. We should start solving mysteries like this more often.

"There's not much we can do right now. It's almost sunrise." Ava groaned. She'd never been an early riser.

I patted her hand sympathetically. "We can go back to sleep for a bit, then go into town tomorrow to see what we can dig up about the Andarsans. Surely someone remembers something important."

Ava crawled back under the covers. "Sounds good to me."

I moved to the portal in the mirror and stepped through to Ava and Drew's bedroom in Maine. Winston gave the floorboards under my feet a little shake in greeting. "Hi, Winston." At least he'd stopped treating me like the black sheep of the family. Six months ago if I'd stepped into the house while Ava and Drew were gone, he would've completely revolted.

Staring at the bed, I debated whether or not to take a little nap. Going back and forth from Scotland to Maine was really screwing with my internal clock. Hmm. I wasn't sleepy. I *should've* been, but no dice.

The familiar rumble of Sam's voice echoed from downstairs. Aww. My bae, as my daughter Jess would've said.

With a smile, I turned and made my way downstairs, following my hubby's voice to the kitchen where he, Wade, and Luci sat going over plans for the new vampire bar. This venture couldn't have come at a better time. It was just what he needed to find some purpose again and to help him acclimate to his fanged lifestyle.

I sat in his lap, and he curled his arms around me, hugging me close while burying his nose into my neck. "I've missed your scent," he whispered.

"I've missed us." I laid my head on his shoulder with a sigh.

"We'll fix it," he said. "We'll get through it. Every marriage goes through ups and downs."

I agreed wholeheartedly and settled in to listen to them talk about location options and plans for the building. Sam seemed at peace and happy for the first time since he'd been turned. That made me happier than I'd been in weeks.

CHAPTER ELEVEN

AVA

IT MADE sense that being stuck in the castle was making Nora's ghost go crazy. What didn't make sense was that it seemed like she was the one who trapped them there, to begin with.

The only thing we could do right now was try to sleep, hoping that when we woke again, we might be able to figure out some way of getting rid of her spirit once and for all. And hopefully without any of us becoming possessed again.

I sighed as I crawled back into bed with Drew and pulled the covers over us both, trying not to think about what would happen if our efforts failed. It was only a matter of time before someone else died. If Olivia hadn't had portaling powers, it could've been her, tonight.

There was nothing else I wanted more at this moment than rid the castle of Nora's ghost.

Just as I started drifting off, a familiar meow startled me awake again. Snoozer. I reached down and scratched his head. As I closed my eyes, I felt another cat jump on the bed. At first, I thought it was Lucy, but when I looked over at the chair by the balcony door, Lucy was curled up sleeping in it. She'd settled there after finally coming out from under the bed. She'd had a few choice words and phrases for Olivia as she went, too.

Um, who else was in my bed?

I sat up and raised my eyebrows as, in the moonlight coming through the balcony windows, I watched the castle cat, Nix, rubbing up against Snoozer like she was happy to meet a new friend. It was sweet. Snoozer let Nix greet him, though he seemed a little on edge. Everything remained relatively calm for a minute.

Until Lucy woke up. The moment Lucy caught sight of the castle cat, she jumped to her feet and glared bloody murder. Yes, cats can glare. I've seen it. I was seeing it right then.

With a blood-curdling cry that sounded like a woman fighting off a monster in a horror movie, Lucy leaped off of the chair and launched herself at the bed and at the castle cat. "How dare you come in here you brazen buddy!" Nix didn't speak people, but she must've understood because she began her own ear-splitting shrieks as tufts of fluff flew. The two felines, one snowy white and the other pitch black rolled around on top of Drew's legs, waking him up with his own yell.

Mindful of all the claws, I grabbed Lucy and pulled her off of the poor black cat. Snoozer was nowhere to be found. As soon as he'd heard Lucy screaming, he'd gotten the heck out of Dodge.

As gently as I could, I pushed Lucy off the bed and onto the floor, where she settled herself with a huff. "Get that bit—"

"Lucy!" I scolded.

"—that *homewrecker* out of here!"

Drew picked Nix up, carried her to the door, and put her out in the hallway. I wasn't even sure how the cat had gotten into our room, to begin with.

Just then, Olivia walked through the mirror portal.

"What's up?" She looked at the two cats, then over to us. Lucy stood glaring at Snoozer while he peeked out from underneath the desk. "Or should I ask?"

I laughed and explained about the castle cat and how she'd just jumped into bed with us.

"I took care of business," Lucy said with a shake of her tail. "That bi—"

"Lucy..." I warned again.

"That *cow* will think twice before trying to get her claws into my Snoozie again."

I finished explaining about the catfight between Nix and Lucy.

Olivia laughed. "Well, it looks like someone is feeling a little left out."

She walked over and scratched Snoozer behind his ears. He purred and crept out from under the desk to let her scratch his back.

Then Olivia turned her attention to Lucy, who was still glaring at the door where the other cat had been moments before. It was like she expected Nix to come back. Or more like wishing she would so she could finish the job. Geez, Lucy could be so dramatic.

"Poor Lucy. You had to defend your man, didn't you?" Olivia said as she picked her up. To my surprise, Lucy didn't protest too much about being picked up. When she started squirming, Olivia sat her on the bed with Snoozer.

Lucy looked at Snoozer. "You're not innocent in this."

He hunkered down in response.

Olivia smirked and looked at me. "Since we're up, let's go shopping for Halloween costumes for the ball. I had a look at the flyer, and I really want to go. Plus, maybe while we're in town we can ask around about the Andarsans and the castle."

We called for a taxi, then headed down to the lobby to wait. By the time I was in the car, squished between Drew and Olivia, I felt much better. Having a different focus besides ghosts and mysteries helped to calm my nerves. It probably didn't hurt to be out of the menacing atmosphere Nora brought to the castle. Plus, going to town to shop brought on a thrill of its own. I did love Halloween and dressing up.

We quickly found a cute little boutique shop with a massive costume section. The racks were filled with everything from biker chick outfits to superhero capes, pirate swords, and beautiful gowns for beauty queens. And everything in between.

"Ooh, look at this one." I held up a hotdog costume. It was cute and would definitely get a laugh.

"I think you should try it on," Olivia said with a grin.

"Why not?" I snagged the costume and headed into the dressing room.

A few minutes later I came out of the dressing room and did a little twirl for Olivia and Drew with my arms spread out.

Olivia laughed and then applauded. "It's perfect for you."

It was ridiculous, but fun too. At least Sammie would have gotten a kick out of it if he were here. I grinned, loving the idea of wearing such a silly costume.

Drew smirked and said, "I think it's hot."

I stared at him, trying not to burst out in a fit of laughter. Through our bond, I felt his amusement. In fact, he was barely holding it together.

"No, I think I need something a little sexier," I teased. "Let's see what they have."

Olivia laughed and rummaged through the rack, pulling out one after another outfit to try on.

After trying on a few more different looks while Drew made appropriately interested noises, we settled on a couple of vintage matching dresses. Olivia's was dark purple velvet with a rose-gold lace overlay at the waist. Mine was black and accented by silver chains at strategic places that made it look like they belonged there. We also picked up a couple of cat ears that clipped into our hair and looked a little too realistic.

Then it was Drew's turn. He opted for a kilt and tartan with a heavy sporran hanging in the front that made him look like he'd stepped out of a historical romance novel. Be still my heart. It was *extremely* difficult to keep my hands off of him.

Happy with our finds, we paid for our outfits and accessories before heading out to grab lunch at a cozy cafe nearby.

As we ate, a middle-aged woman, maybe a bit younger than me, with long black hair peppered with gray approached our table. She seemed excited to talk to us and barely waited for the waitress to leave before starting up a conversation.

"Heard you were in town looking into the Andarsan castle curse," she said with a twinkle in her eye and a thick Scottish accent. A local, for sure. "Oh, I can tell you so many stories about that place."

I glanced at Drew and Olivia before returning my attention to the woman. "How did you know that?" I asked. "It wasn't like we advertised." Maybe she'd talked to one of the guests that we'd talked to the other night.

"I'm psychic," she offered with a smile and a wave of her hand.

Sure. Why not?

"I knew you'd be coming here seeking answers. And that it's important you know Laird Andarsan's son is still alive and lives nearby."

She pulled a piece of paper out of her bag and wrote down an address. "GPS will take you right there. I hope you three can free their spirits."

I took the paper when she held it out. "You're psychic. I assume you're involved with a local coven?" That's how it was in the States. Most all witch-related paranormals belonged to the coven. It was a safety measure, really. "Why haven't you or your coven done anything about it?"

"Oh, we have." Oh, good. It was the same here. She was with a coven. "Or at least we've tried. Nora's ghost is too strong even with the power of thirteen. She blocks us out." The woman frowned and then looked out the window as if in a daze. Then she said, "I have to go." She jumped to her feet and rushed to the door, then disappeared from sight.

This was the strangest honeymoon I'd ever been on.

CHAPTER TWELVE

As we pored over historical records in the public library of the castle, my heart raced with excitement. I hated that someone had died, but Olivia's enthusiasm for solving a mystery had rubbed off on me.

We combed through old maps and documents, searching for clues about where Malcolm, Nora, and Holly might be buried. At first, we'd thought a quick internet search would provide the records, but no such luck. The last thing I wanted to do was bother the son of the laird and dredge all this up for him again, but if we didn't find some information in this library we might have to.

After hours of meticulous research and poring over ancient records, we finally found what we were looking for: a cemetery nestled deep in a forest at the edge of town, near but not on the castle's property. "They must not have wanted to bury murderers and murder victims here on the manor grounds," Olivia murmured as we looked at the cemetery map. "Bad juju and all that." Excitement mounted with every step that brought us closer to our goal.

After bundling up against the Scottish wind, we eagerly followed an overgrown path through dense underbrush towards the graveyard shrouded by looming trees. At least it was secluded. There didn't seem to be a ton of people vying to spend time at this particular graveyard.

We carefully made our way through rows upon rows of mossy gravestones, using a little discreet magic to clean them off enough to read them, until finally reaching three distinct markers bearing familiar names etched into their surfaces long ago by grieving loved ones.

"Why would they bury them side-by-side?" I asked. "That's... weird."

"And wouldn't the laird normally be in some fancy mausoleum?" Olivia looked around. "There isn't anything like that here. This graveyard is super lonely."

It didn't even have large gravestones. Just small, rectangular ones. Most graveyards in Maine held a mixture of large and small, ornate and simple.

"We may never know," Drew said. "Those things were made sixty years ago."

"Let's raise Holly, the governess, first," I said. "She's the only ghost we haven't seen yet. Maybe she's not actually trapped in the castle but can give us some answers."

Olivia used her power to lift the dirt from the grave and cast it aside. Then my powerful friend lifted the lid of the coffin, revealing Holly's skeleton. "That's handy." I didn't have the ability to raise all that dirt, or at least I'd never tried. They generally just clawed their way out of the ground. Bit of a PITA for the poor animated skeletons. Maybe I'd try the dirt thing the next time I had to unbury someone.

I knelt by the hole and pressed my fingers against the dirt, too far away to reach the bones. I wasn't trying to climb in and out of any six-foot holes today.

I focused on Holly's body and urged my power to flow into the bones. Dirt popped and hissed, floating away from the exposed bones draped in a nice dress. Holly shifted, bones that had been dead for sixty years rising up from the coffin, held together by magic and my will.

It'd been a while since I'd dealt with an animated skeleton. I'd forgotten how comical they were. Holly looked around wildly until her gaze fell on me. Don't ask how I knew her skeleton was looking at me. I just knew. Maybe it had something to do with living with Larry as a skeleton for as long as I had. Heavens, don't let me laugh now.

"Why am I here?" Holly asked softly. Her fear vibrated off her. "Who are you?"

"My name is Ava." I motioned to Drew and Olivia and introduced them. "This is my husband Drew and my best friend Olivia. We know what happened to you and Malcolm. We're here to help you move on."

Holly's eye holes filled with tears, and she shook her head vigorously before replying, "No! You can't! If you do, Nora will kill you too."

"We're a little too hard to kill." I didn't go into why.

"Yeah," Olivia chimed in. "You don't have to worry about us."

Once back in her ghostly form, Holly would sense what we were, probably. They always seemed to know what I was, anyway.

"Nora killed me," Holly said matter-of-factly. "And has been holding Malcolm and me in the castle ever since, forcing us to relive our deaths every ten years."

"Why?" I asked. "What does she want?"

"Revenge," Holly replied simply. "Nora is consumed by hate for me and my Malcolm. She wants us to suffer as she did."

Holly sighed and leaned against the side of her grave. "Where did they bury me?" But she kept talking before I could tell her. "Nora blames me for their failed marriage, and we shouldn't have had an affair. We were wrong. But their bond was falling apart *long* before Malcolm and I fell in love."

"How can we help you?" Olivia asked. "We need to know what she did to trap you both so we can set you and Malcolm free."

"I don't know, in this form," Holly said, glancing around as if searching for something or someone. Probably she was looking for Malcolm. "Maybe if Malcolm was with me, we could move on together."

"Hang tight," I said and went to his grave a few feet from Holly's. "Stay right there."

Olivia did the dirt thing, obviously trying to hurry. She was a little sloppy with the dirt moving but got the job done. As soon as the casket was open, I animated Malcolm's bones. He stood, wearing scraps of what looked to be a kilt. It barely hung on by threads around his waist. He looked around, and once he saw his lady love, tried to climb out of his grave.

It didn't go so well.

Drew choked back a laugh as Malcolm fell back into his grave and his arm popped off. "Seems to be a theme with skeletons we know." Larry was always losing his head back when he hadn't had flesh. Heck, sometimes it still tries to fall off.

"Oh, yeah, sorry," Olivia said after elbowing the barely composed Drew. She lifted the dirt from between their graves so they could reach one another.

The skeletons embraced, legs intertwined, and arms wrapped around each other. Without skin and... well, bodies to stop them, their bones intertwined, rib cages going inside each other. It was a few steps past disturbing.

Olivia snorted back a laugh and leaned into me to whisper, "They're boning."

I choked on my spit as I tried valiantly not to laugh, and Drew failed to cover his laugh with a cough.

They held each other for a while, long after we'd composed ourselves, their arms wrapped tightly around each other, until Malcolm finally said, "Thank you."

Their souls rose out of them, two shining white orbs that hovered a few seconds over us before dancing around our heads then shooting straight up into the sky and disappearing.

Their bones rattled down into Holly's casket, nearly perfectly lining up. "Can you adjust them?" I asked. "Let's leave their bones to rest together for all of eternity."

"Aw, I love that." Olivia beamed at me.

At the same time, Drew rolled his eyes. "There's nothing left of them in the bones," he said.

I poked him in the side while Olivia wiggled her finger and the bones shifted so they were fully together in the casket, then she shut both the full casket and the empty one.

Olivia raised her hands, and the air hummed as she willed the piles of dirt to rise up and float above the graves. With a look of concentration, Olivia attempted to shift the dirt over the holes, but she'd tried to do it all at once. Both graves, and the dirt from between them. Instead of neatly repacking the dirt, she lost her grip on her telekinesis and one pile of dirt fell on Lucy and Snoozer, who I hadn't even realized had followed us out here. I was glad the two cats were immortal ghouls, or they would have been seriously injured.

Lucy, in her dramatic fashion, screeched, and even Snoozer yowled. "I knew it!" Lucy screamed as Olivia rapidly moved the dirt again. "You hate me! You've always hated me. You want to see me suffer."

"Oh, Lucy." I picked her up and dusted her off with my own power.

Thankfully, they were both okay, just a little dirty.

When we finished putting the bones to rest, which mainly consisted of Olivia making sure the graves looked normal, repositioning the grass, and patting it all down, we turned to the third grave. Two ghosts down. One to go. I had a feeling the last one wasn't going to be nearly so easy.

CHAPTER THIRTEEN

ATTEMPTING to animate Nora's skeleton, I poured my necromancer magic into the pile of bones. It wasn't working. Darkness fell as I tried, and minutes turned into more minutes.

I closed my eyes and tried to imagine purple light flowing from my body into the bones. Breathing slowly and deeply, I sent the bones all my healing energy, but nothing happened. I tried several times more until Drew finally placed a hand on my shoulder in a silent plea to stop. "It's not my magic this time," I said. "It's actually working properly. It's as if there's an invisible barrier separating me from Nora's spirit." I couldn't call her ghost to me, no matter what I did or how hard I tried.

"What now? I thought Nora wanted us to free her." Despite being a necromancer, I didn't know much about ghosts or why they acted the way they did.

Drew pulled out his phone. "I met a hunter once that specialized in ghosts. Blair Braden. She's retired now, but I'm sure she'll answer a couple of questions."

I didn't know hunters actually retired. Drew had, of course, but his family still called him on occasion to try to pull him back in. Hunters didn't allow their members to leave the ranks easily. Kinda like the mafia, but with a noble purpose. I had a feeling that they would try harder now that they'd met me and were starting up a paranormal liaison division. I wasn't even sure what that all entailed, but it was sure to become a headache for Drew and me at some point.

Drew dialed Blair's number and put her on speaker. She answered on the second ring. "It's never good when a Walker calls me, but *you* are supposed to be as retired as I am."

"When are any of us really retired?" Drew asked.

Blair laughed. "True. What can I do for you, Drew? Wait. Aren't you supposed to be on your honeymoon?"

"News travels fast." Drew rolled his eyes, then said, "You're on speaker. My wife, Ava, and our friend Olivia are here."

Liv and I said, "Hi," at the same time.

"Hello." There was the sound of a male voice in the background, then Blair said, "Don't touch that. It might be cursed."

I raised a brow at Drew, and he explained. "Blair owns an antique store where she looks for cursed objects and other relics and reports them to hunter HQ. AKA Pearl."

"Ah, so she's not truly retired either," I said with a grin. Drew's grandmother had mentioned several times that hunters never retire. Many pretend they are, but they're not.

"I *am* retired," Blair said. "If I keep saying it, it makes it true." Her voice flattened. "What do you want, Drew? I'm busy keeping Lachlan from reorganizing my store."

Drew chuckled. "Say hello to Lach for me. Haven't seen him in years. We have a ghostly matter I wanted to ask you about." He briefly ran through what we'd been dealing with and then asked, "Why would Nora seek us out to help her, then block Ava from animating her bones?"

"Sometimes ghosts want one thing until their rage takes over. Like, they get moments of clarity and seek help to free themselves from wherever they're stuck, even if they're the ones who stuck themselves there. The clarity never lasts long before they're completely taken over by their rage and the need for vengeance." Blair paused as if thinking over our situation. "It sounds like you need to get her spirit out of the castle before she can move on. If she won't come out willingly or by magical force, you'll have to find something she wants bad enough to leave the castle for."

It made sense. We thanked Blair and hung up. All we had to do now was find out what Nora wanted that we could use to lure her out of the castle.

It was late when we got back, dirty and tired, it was to a full-blown haunted house. Dread clotted my throat as the hairs on my arms stood up. Nora had put two and two together. She must've known we'd released her laird and his mistress, and she was beyond mad about it.

The moment we stepped into the lobby, all of the stuff on the walls came alive and tried to attack us. The poor front desk clerk, Niko, cowered under his desk. At least it was late enough that other guests were asleep in their rooms, hopefully *not* being haunted by their wall art. I didn't want any humans hurt by this raging psycho of a ghost.

Boy, was she livid. Nora appeared in the doorway to the dining area. We rushed over to see her go toward the tables, which were already set for the next morning's breakfast. "You ruined everything and I'm going to make you pay!"

The irate ghost swept plates from a table, and they flew in a spinning arc toward Olivia. She screamed and threw up her hands, blasting the plates with her magic. The shards of glass swept on either side of her and fell to the ground. I had to find a way to stop this. Or at least get us out of here.

Suddenly, I remembered the door to the secret passage we'd found the day before. I grabbed Olivia's hand and pulled us toward the bookcase next to the large fireplace, running through the lobby. "Drew, come on!"

Wind whipped around us, and debris flew past us in a blur. Someone screamed as metal objects soared overhead and crashed through windows. We plunged into the hidden stairwell, darkness enveloping us.

With the help of an orb, we ran up three flights of stairs. At the top, I listened as everything fell silent.

When we finally reached our room, via the secret passage, Snoozer and Lucy were lying on the bed. Snoozer looked remotely interested to see us. Lucy was bathing herself, despite the fact that we'd used magic to make sure they were clean.

Figured they'd make it to the room before we did. Ignoring the cats, Drew, Olivia, and I barricaded the door and the windows with salt. Then we plopped onto the bed, against a protesting Lucy's wishes, and tried to catch our breath.

We were in for a long night.

CHAPTER FOURTEEN

THE NEXT MORNING OVER BREAKFAST, which we ate in our room, Olivia, Drew, and I made a plan to get Nora's ghost out of the castle.

We'd gone through the portal and slept in our own beds, coming back occasionally to check on the castle and make sure she hadn't killed anyone. With us gone, she seemed to have calmed down.

Once we had her outside, I could force her spirit into her bones. It was getting her out that was tricky.

After breakfast, we tiptoed through the castle, wary and nervous that Nora would pop out and attempt to behead us again with one of the swords hanging on the wall.

The presence of all the other people must've been calming her, or at least making her wary because we managed to get out the front door without anyone losing as much as a fingernail.

We hopped in a taxi and headed to Malcolm Jr.'s house. The woman from the cafe the day before had written down his address, so I just gave it to the driver. I was hoping that Malcolm Jr. might have some idea about how to draw his mother's ghost out of the castle. He'd been in his twenties when they'd died. He'd known her a while, longer than almost anyone else alive.

Malcolm Jr. met us at the door. He was a small, wiry man, and he looked exhausted, yet somehow not surprised to see three American strangers on his stoop. "What can I do for you?"

"Hello, Laird Malcolm. My name is Ava. This is my husband Drew, and my good friend Olivia." I gave him a sad smile. "We're here about your parents."

With a sigh, he unlatched the screen door. "You mean their ghosts?"

I nodded and Olivia said a little too cheerily, "Yep."

Malcolm's shoulders slumped. "You'd better come in." He led us into his living room without saying much.

Drew, Olivia, and I sat on the sofa while Malcolm eased into the armchair. "I've always known my parents were haunting the place. I could feel them there, like a weight on my chest. Even all the way out here, so far from the village." His home was on the other side of the village from the castle, and a good way up in the hills past that.

He continued, "But I never knew what to do. It was my life's curse, knowing what happened to them, what they did. Besides, who would ever believe me that ghosts were real?"

"Your mother came to me a few nights ago asking me to help them. That's what I plan to do," I said. "The problem is that she refuses to leave the castle. We believe that when her rage takes over, she loses all sense of helping herself. We think, and hope, that if we can get her ghost out of the castle, her power will be reduced. Is there anything that she would want badly enough to leave the castle?"

"Her husband." He frowned and added, "Looking back, I realize she had an unhealthy obsession with my father."

I slouched in my seat and thought about pouting for a nano-second. "We *were* able to help your father and Holly to move on. So his ghost is gone. He's at peace."

I waited a moment while tears filled Malcolm Jr.'s eyes. "That's nice to hear," he whispered. "Excuse me."

He left the room for a few minutes, coming back with red eyes.

"Is there anything else you can think of?" I asked.

He cleared his throat and dabbed his nose with a hankie in his hand. "My grandson, Osker, looks just like my father. Perhaps he could help you lure her out," Malcolm said. "He knows the story. My son thinks I'm an old fool, but Oskar always believed me."

"That could actually work," Olivia said, eyeing me. I plucked the thought right out of her head. Not literally because I wasn't telepathic, but I knew that look. It was the *we'll improvise with magic* look.

"Could you get him to meet us at the castle? We'll explain everything to him when he gets there." I stood and held out my hand. "Tell him not to come inside. We'll come out to him."

Malcolm nodded. "I think he'd do that. And he's off work today. I'll call him right away."

I sighed in relief. "Thank you for your help."

He stood and smiled, taking my hand in both of his. "Thank you for helping them move on."

"Just pray we can pull it off." Even if that didn't work, I wasn't going to give up easily. I couldn't leave knowing Nora was still pushing women down the stairs. If we couldn't get her to move on, I didn't want to think about what she'd do without her husband and Holly there to torment. One way or another, we were getting Nora out of that castle, even if it meant calling in the un-retired hunters. Or the devil himself. He'd probably have a trick or two up his sleeve.

Hopefully, this would work, and we could all move on with our lives.

Drew, Olivia, and I were quiet on the ride back to the castle. We were each contemplating how magic could help get Nora's ghost out of the building. You know, just in case Oskar pretending to be his great-grandfather didn't work.

Everyone needs a backup plan.

When we arrived back at the castle, it was eerily quiet. No one was around, which would make getting Nora's ghost out easier, but also more dangerous because there would be no witnesses if something went wrong. Where was everyone?

"Let's get out of here," Olivia whispered. "I don't have a good feeling." We waited outside for a while, then decided to walk around the castle once to pass the time. When we came around the last corner, arriving in the front again, Oskar was waiting for us.

Wow. He did look just like Malcolm senior. So much so that they could've been twins. For the first time, I started to have a little hope that this plan would work. Maybe we wouldn't have to call Luci after all.

As long as we could convince Nora her husband had come back for her. That'd be the hard part.

After I explained everything to Oskar, he agreed to help us. "My grandfather filled me in on the way." He still looked a little skeptical of the whole thing, but I was glad he was playing along. Even if it was probably only to humor Malcolm Jr.

We led Oskar to a secluded garden in the back, which we'd picked out on our walk just a few moments before.

Olivia portaled to the cemetery and returned with Nora's bones, which, thanks to the practice she'd gotten last night, only took her mere minutes.

She set them on the ground a few feet from us. Then I turned to Oskar to go over the plan again. "You're pretending to be your great grandfather, Laird Malcolm. Just call Nora, using her name." Umm, had he had a pet name for her? I hoped not. We should've looked at earlier entries of her diary to see if it mentioned it. Too late now. "We'll take care of the rest."

Olivia added, "Tell her you've come back for her."

Oskar nodded. "I think I know what to say."

I stretched out my hands and tried to create a protective circle. One that would trap her once she crossed the barrier. The circle formed around us and quickly disappeared. Crap. Stupid faulty magic.

My mom said that my power glitches would go away once the baby was born, and the lineage magic evened out between me and the new girl in the family.

I tried again and it held a little longer. Then Drew moved closer to me and took my hand. "Try again."

I did and the circle slammed closed and stayed. "Thanks," I said and kissed him on the cheek. Then I motioned to Oskar, who was staring at us like we were nuts. He couldn't see the barrier, so it probably looked to him like I was constipated. "Go ahead and call out to her."

He gave a single nod before facing the north side of the castle. "Nora, it's Malcolm. I'm here." He spoke loudly but didn't yell. His accent thickened as well, and his voice did remarkably resemble Malcolm Seniors, or at least how I remembered it had sounded last night.

A long couple of seconds passed in silence. I was about to tell Oskar to try again when I heard a scream that would put a banshee to shame. I jerked my gaze up and watched Nora's ghost careen out of the side of the building. She wasted no time. Her rage was so hot she didn't sense the circle at all. She shot right into the middle of it, to my delight.

Oh, my. She was not happy to see us at all. She studied Oskar's face, squinting and cocking her head. "Malcolm?"

The bright sunlight made it even more apparent she was transparent, but it was clear enough to see that her face was etched in anger as she rounded on me. I reacted instantly, praying to the universe that my powers wouldn't fail me now.

I took a deep breath, pulled the energy from my core, and reached for the necromancer magic that hummed in my blood. It spilled from my hands and flew through the air, tendrils reaching for Nora's ghost. With one gigantic yank, I forced Nora's spirit into the pile of bones on the ground.

Like Holly and Malcolm, Nora's skeleton rose and became animated. It wasn't funny this time.

I'd used so much power to compensate for my faulty magic that I'd really whammied her. Her bones fleshed out so that she looked like before she died. She'd really been beautiful.

She looked down at herself and calmed, then turned to Oskar. Reaching out she asked, "Malcolm?"

Oskar shook his head. "I'm sorry. I'm Oskar, your great-grandson."

Her face softened. "Malcolm Junior's boy?"

He nodded. "Close enough. They say Father looks like you, but Grandfather and I look like Malcolm Senior."

Nora pulled Oskar into her arms for a long embrace, and then she turned to us.

"Thank you," she said. "Thank you for giving me the chance to say goodbye."

And with that, she was gone. Finally free. Her spirit floated, less energetically than Malcolm and Holly had. More peacefully. At the same time, her body turned back into bones in Oskar's arms.

"Ugh," he said and dropped the bones. "I mean…"

"No." I laughed. "Ugh is an appropriate response."

CHAPTER FIFTEEN

It was Halloween night, and Olivia and I were preening in front of the bathroom mirror. Olivia's dark purple velvet gown set off her blond hair. My black one seemed to make my usually too-pale complexion glow in this wonderful castle lighting. Everything was magical here, especially now that the malevolent ghost was gone.

Sam, Wade, Winnie, Alfred, and my parents walked through the portal mirror. They were all dressed up. Sam and Wade went with the 1800s vampire theme. No one but us knew the fangs were real. "I love it!" I chirped.

Mom and Dad were dressed as Gomez and Morticia Addams. "You both look amazing." Mom had glamoured her hair black, so it looked so natural like it was how she always looked.

Winnie and Alfred—I still couldn't wrap my head around them being a couple— were dressed like cave people. Of course, Winnie had gone with her normal state of undress. Her furs barely covered anything. And Alfred, who on his own would've dressed far more conservatively, wore only a loincloth, which he kept tugging at.

"You two look sexy as hell." That was the perfect thing to say to Aunt Winnie, who was obsessed with her new body.

Not that I blamed her.

Luci and Phira had Sammie in Faery for a Samhain celebration. Wally, Michelle, Zoey, Larry, Devan, and Jessica were hanging at the house handing out candy and watching scary movies.

"Oh my gosh, you guys look great." I stepped out of the bathroom and had to squeeze by everyone. The room had gotten smaller with my family there. "Are we ready to head down to the ballroom?" Everyone was in agreement, and so looking forward to a haunting good time now that the ghosts were friendly and not stabby.

The ballroom was filled with tables covered with thick red cloth. Printed on the fabric were the outlines of rib cages with the words Rest in Peace quilted into them. Large skeleton garlands made of paper streamers dropped from the ceiling and waved gently above us.

I looked around and smiled at the others. "They did a nice job, didn't they?" I said. Everyone nodded and smiled back, seeming to agree despite the hard time we'd been through.

We found a table close to the dance floor and ordered drinks. Whether Drew knew it or not, he was dancing with me, frequently.

And as soon as the first slow song came on, I dragged him out onto the dance floor.

Our hips swayed in unison as we held each other. Our eyes closed, our breath felt hot and heavy, and our hearts raced. I felt his as much as my own. Such a wonderful feeling, to be so connected to Drew.

"I love you, husband," I whispered.

He held me tighter and nipped at my ear. "Love you more, wife."

"Oh, not possible."

"It's possible."

"Time will tell," I teased. "We work well together. I'm glad we were able to get Nora to move on."

"If we hadn't, we'd have to come back in ten years and try again." He flashed me a smile before pulling me even closer.

I was about to ask him if he missed hunting when my phone buzzed in my dress pocket. Without breaking our dance, I pulled it out and answered. "Hello?"

"Um, Mom, Drew's grandmother was just here looking for you," Wallie said.

Then Drew made a noise before saying, "What is *she* doing here?"

I looked up in time to see Pearl entering the ballroom. "She's here," I told Wallie. "Thanks for the warning."

I hung up and Drew and I made our way off of the dance floor and to our table. It didn't bode well that the matriarch of the hunters had made her way to the Halloween ball. She certainly hadn't been invited.

Pearl didn't bother with a polite greeting. I hadn't really expected her to. It wasn't her style. "You know that tentacle monster we fought at your rehearsal dinner?"

Oh, no. Please don't tell me he has a brother.

Drew worked his jaw and then said, "Yeah."

"Well, his twin sister was spotted off the coast of Owl's Head." Pearl glanced from Drew to me, then back to Drew. Crap. That was *really* close to Shipton.

My husband picked up his drink, took a sip, and set it down. "And?"

Pearl glared at her grandson. "You and Ava will be going to take care of it."

I had my drink halfway to my mouth. "We're doing what now?"

Pearl turned her glare to me. "You are a hunter now, Ava Walker. You married a hunter. You bonded with a hunter."

I gaped at her. We'd never told his family that we'd bonded.

"Oh, yes." She put her hands on her hips. "If you don't think I didn't see that first thing when I arrived at your house, you've got another think coming."

Super. It looked like I was going after a tentacle monster.

Witching After Forty follows the misadventures of Ava Harper – a forty-something necromancer with a light witchy side that you wouldn't expect from someone who can raise the dead. Join Ava as she learns how to start over after losing the love of her life, in this new paranormal women's fiction series with a touch of cozy mystery, magic, and a whole lot of mayhem.

A Ghoulish Midlife
Cookies for Satan (Christmas novella)
I'm With Cupid (Valentine novella)
A Cursed Midlife
Birthday Blunder (Olivia Novella)
A Girlfriend For Mr. Snoozerton (Novella)
A Haunting Midlife
An Animated Midlife
Faery Odd-Mother (Novella)
A Killer Midlife
A Grave Midlife
A Powerful Midlife
A Wedded Midlife
A Newly-Webs Midlife
An Inherited Midlife: Coming Soon!

READ AN EXCERPT FROM
BITTEN IN THE MIDLIFE

Bitten in the Midlife is the first in a new spin off series featuring Hailey Whitfield, whom you met in this book. The new series is titled, Fanged After Forty and we hope you love Hailey and her friends as much as Ava's.

Get your copy of Bitten in the Midlife Here

Here is the first chapter of Bitten in the Midlife.

Chapter 1

THE DAY HAD FINALLY COME, and I could hardly contain my excitement.

I never knew starting over at the not-so-ripe age of forty would be so freeing. It was like a huge weight lifted off my whole body. And I was *free!*

I didn't have to look at my ex-fiancé's face anymore. Nor did I have to watch him openly flirt with all the other nurses. I didn't have to watch him move on happily with the tramp he cheated on me with.

Jerk.

He was a lot more than a jerk, but I was *not* thinking about him anymore. Plus, karma always got back at people who deserved her wrath. And I was starting my new life in a new city, in my new-to-me house.

The best part of this move was that my best friend since we were in diapers was my neighbor.

We were celebrating this glorious day together with champagne on my front porch, ogling the movers as they unloaded the truck and carried all of my things into the house.

It was a great way to celebrate on a Monday.

See? All Mondays weren't bad.

Another thing that made this move better for my sanity was that I was closer to my two older brothers. One I adored and loved, Luke. The other was the eldest of the five of us, and... the poor guy wasn't everyone's favorite. We all loved him, but we wouldn't walk out in front of a bus to save him. Oliver was just...Oliver. He was a hard person to figure out. Oh, calm down. We'd save him. We might just shove him out of the way extra hard.

Pushing away thoughts of family and ex-jerkface, I went back to supervising the movers. It was a tough job, but someone had to do it.

"What about that one?" Kendra asked.

I hid my smile behind the crystal flute she had brought with her.

My bestie had taken the day off to celebrate with me. She was a lawyer and had just won a big case, so that gave us double the reasons to celebrate.

Good times!

I watched mister tall, dark, and delicious with rippling abs, a luscious tush I could've bounced a quarter off of and one of those cute little man buns carry a large box toward us.

He was young enough to call me mama but still legal. Maybe being a cougar wasn't such a bad idea. Just as long as he left before the sun was up. I had no plans to wake up beside another man, ever.

Did you hear me? *Ever.*

It would give my eldest brother Oliver something else to turn his nose up at and lecture me about why it wasn't a good idea to date a man young enough to be my son.

At least Luke would support a fling with the hot moving man. On second thought, Luke supported orgies and any manner of sexual escapades. That was a little too many hands, arms, legs, and bodies for me.

No, thank you. Although... maybe... Nope.

As the cutie with the man bun walked past, he batted a pair of lashes that looked like someone had dipped them chocolate, and I glanced down at his pants, totally by accident.

No, really. I didn't mean to.

But oh, my. His pants fit like they'd been painted on. Molded to every move of his body, but also like they were begging to be torn off. It'd been a while since I'd had a back to rake my fingers down.

Kendra, my bestie for as long as I could remember, cocked a dark brow, then shrugged. "I have socks older than he is."

I snorted, then giggled. It was probably the champagne, but who cared. "I didn't say I wanted to marry him."

God forbid. One bite of that sour apple was enough for me, and even if spitting out that second bite wasn't my choice, I was over the whole idea. Kendra had it right. Her love 'em and leave 'em lifestyle was my inspiration from now on. New start, new motto.

Broken hearts were a young woman's game, and I wasn't young enough to be willing to risk another. No way, buddy.

"Since when is a little bump and grind enough for you?" Skeptical was Kendra's middle name, while a smile flirted with her lips. The skeptical part sure helped in her budding law career as her last name was Justice, after all. Literally.

Kendra didn't trust easily, which was why she'd stayed single after her divorce almost fifteen years ago.

I shrugged and watched a mover lean against a dolly full of boxes while he rode the truck gate to the ground. Shirtless, muscular, and blond were apparently my new turn-on. Who knew I had a type? "Being left at the altar was eye-opening and threw my entire life in a new direction," I mumbled.

And this direction's sheen of sweat, when combined with the champagne, put thoughts into my head. Fun thoughts. Sexy thoughts. Thoughts a newly single woman with no prospects had no business having. Or maybe every business having them.

The best part was I didn't have to wake up next to anyone or answer to anyone. Ever. Again.

"Have you found a job yet?" It figured Kendra would change the subject to something more serious. What a way to snap me back to reality.

She was such a buzzkill sometimes.

"No, but I put in applications and sent out resumes to hospitals within fifty miles and every doctor's office in the greater Chestnut Hill-Philadelphia area. I also found an agency that offers private nursing. I'm thinking of checking it out." At this point, I had to take what I could get. My life savings had gone into the sanity-saving move.

Kendra nodded. Her approval wasn't essential, but the validation was nice. "Have you met the neighbors yet?"

She knew I'd come to tour the house and talk to the previous owner about a week ago. Kendra had been on some witch's retreat.

Pointing to the house on the other side of mine, she said, "Sara lives there with her 2.5 kids and a husband that is never home. She's nice but on the snobbish side. She is one hundred percent human, like you. But don't tell her anything you don't want the whole neighborhood to know."

Kendra had connections with the neighborhood I didn't yet. There were two reasons for those connections. One, she was a witch. Two, she'd lived in this neighborhood for the past fifteen years. She'd moved right after her divorce to start a new life with her kids. Of course, now she had a great relationship with her ex. They made better friends than lovers, as it had turned out.

It had been the same years ago for me and my ex-husband, Howard Jefferies. Our divorce had been messy and painful, mostly because I hadn't wanted to admit we'd fallen out of love with each other. I was bitter for a long time before we'd finally become friends.

"No. I've been here a couple of times, but always during the day when people are working, I suppose." I hadn't met a single soul besides the previous owner, Ava Harper, who was also a witch, and her extended family that had been with her.

Kendra hid her smile with another drink. "The neighbors across the street are," she leaned closer to me and lowered her voice, "*weird.*"

"Yeah?" I glanced at the house across the street. "How so?"

It was a large three-story, modern brick home with a balcony that wrapped around the top floor. I wondered if the top floor was one large room or a separate apartment or living space.

Black shutters accented the windows, which appeared to be blacked out. The front door was crimson with black gothic-looking embellishments. There was a front porch on the ground level that was half the length of the front of the house. The lawn was perfectly manicured with lush green grass and expertly trimmed bushes.

"You know, weird." Kendra cocked an eyebrow. "*My* kind of weird."

Maybe she'd had too much to drink, or I had because I wasn't following whatever it was she hinted at. Then it hit me. Oh! *Her* kind of weird. "You mean like...." I lowered my voice to a whisper as I looked around to make sure there wasn't anyone in earshot. "Witches?"

She shook her head, and I grinned. A guessing game. Awesome. I so sucked at those.

I kept my voice low enough so only the two of us could hear. "You said there's more than witches out there. Is it one of the others?"

This time, she tapped the left side of her nose and smiled. Kendra so loved her dramatics.

"Werewolves?"

"No."

"Werepanthers?"

"Nope."

"Bears?" I paused for another negative reply then ran through a list. "Dragons? Lions? Cats of any kind?"

"No, no, and no." She kept her brow cocked and her smirk in place. She loved torturing me with these crazy guess games.

"Llama, dog, sock puppet?"

She burst out laughing at the latter, drawing glances from the movers. We laughed together like old times. God, I'd missed her so much. Being around Kendra was soothing after everything I'd been through.

"If we were playing the hot-cold game, I would say you were getting hot, but you're very cold." That helped so much. Not. Cryptic hints were her thing. "Brr." She ran her hands over her arms and faked a shiver. Then cackled like the witch she was.

"Zombie? Something in the abominable category?" Now I was reaching into the tundra. While Philly was cold in the winter, anything of the snow critter variety wouldn't stand a chance in a Pennsylvania summer.

"Warmer with zombie, a little too cold with the snowman."

My tone dropped to reflect my almost boredom. "Ghoul? Ghost? Alien?" She was losing me.

"Oh, come on!" She stood to her full height and leaned against the rail on the porch to stare at me. "You're dancing right around it." She let her tongue slip over her canine.

Oh, snap! No way.

"Vampire?" I whispered that one, too, because somewhere I'd read vamps could hear every pin drop in a five-mile radius. Then again, that article was on the internet, and you couldn't trust anything on the web. At least I didn't.

I stared at the house again after her wink, indicating that I guessed right. Finally. Now, the gothic embellishments and blacked-out windows made a little more sense. However, the home looked normal at the same time.

"Wow." Were they friendly vampires?

"Yeah." She nodded with her lips pursed.

We both shifted to look at the truck, then as one of my boxes went crashing to the ground and the sound of breaking glass tinkled through the air.

I groaned inwardly and hoped it wasn't something valuable in that box. The movers would be getting a bill for it if it was.

Later, after the hotties had left and the sun began to set, Kendra started unpacking the kitchen while I worked in the living room. Thank goodness they'd put the boxes in the rooms they belonged in, thanks to my OCD in labeling each one.

I was knee-deep in opened boxes and bubble wrap when the doorbell rang. "I'll get it," I called to Kendra in the kitchen.

Not waiting for her to answer, I swung the door open and froze.

The most exquisite man I'd ever seen stood in the doorway.

Hellooooo handsome.

This guy was...tall. Well, taller than my five-one height, but then, most people were. He towered over me with a lean, more athletic than muscular form. His deep amber eyes reminded me of a sunset while his pale skin said he didn't spend much time in the sun. Light hair, something in the blond to strawberry variety, brushed the tops of shoulders. Shiny, clean, and begging for my fingers to run through the strands.

Smiling as if he could read my mind, Strawberry Man handed me a basket strongly scented by blueberry muffins. The smell made my mouth water. Or was that him? Maybe he was Blueberry Man. Oh, geez. I hadn't even said a word yet. Had I?

"These are for you." He nodded toward the basket, looking a little uncomfortable.

Oh, yes, they were. His large hand brushed mine as I grabbed it, and I sucked in a short, quick breath. At some point, I'd become awkward. And ridiculous.

And I remembered I hadn't brushed my hair all day since the movers arrived. Damn.

The porch was smaller with him standing on it, somehow it had shrunk, and I couldn't draw in a breath around him. Dramatic, yes, but so true. Or maybe he was too hot, and all the oxygen had evaporated in his presence. Either way, I found it hard to breathe and think.

"Th-th-thank you." I was like a nervous teenager who'd just met her very first pretty boy. I chuckled, hiccupped, and would've fallen out the door if not for the frame I'd somehow managed to catch my shirt on.

He nodded and tilted his head, smiling. Damn if my knees didn't go weak. "No problem. If you need anything at all, I'm Jax, and I live right over there." He pointed to the house across the street. And the back view of his head made my heart pitter-patter and my belly rumble as much as the front.

"You're the...." I didn't know if he, if they, were loud and proud with their creatures of the night status, and I didn't want to take the chance of outing Kendra for telling me. Unfortunately, I thought of it a second *after* I started speaking. "Neighbor."

His grin hit me like sunshine poking through the clouds on a rainy day. Ironic, since vampire meant allergic to the sun in a deathly kind of way.

"Yeah."

I didn't know if I should invite him in. What if there was a Mrs. Vampire? The last thing I needed was to become a jealous vampire wife's main course.

Like the queen of the dorks, I held up the basket, gave it a sniff, then hiccupped again. "Thanks for the goodies."

As I spoke, I wished again I'd taken a moment to brush my hair or put on a clean shirt before I answered the door. Vampire or not, this guy deserved a neighbor who combed her hair.

Get your copy of Bitten in the Midlife Here

SNEAK PEEK INTO A NEW SERIES

A bunny bit me on the finger and everything went sideways after that.

That's just the beginning of my insane life. The Fascinators, the local ladies' club, suddenly are incredibly interested in having me join their next Bunco night, which is a thinly veiled excuse to drink and gossip.

I've been dying to get into that group for years; why now? I'm over forty, my daughter is grown, and all I do is temp work. What's so special about me?

After I shift into a dragon, things become clearer. They're not a Bunco group. The Fascinators are a pack of shifters. Yes, shifters. Like werewolves, except in this case it's weresquirrels and a wereskunk, among others.

And my daughter? She wants to move home, suddenly and suspiciously. As excited as I am to have her home, why? She loves being on her own. It's got something to do with a rough pack of predators, shifters who want to watch the world burn. I hope she's not mixed up with the wrong crowd.

There's also a mysterious mountain man hanging around out of the blue. Where was he before the strange bunny bite? Nowhere near me, that's for sure.

Life is anything but boring. At this point, I'm just hoping that I'll survive it all with my tail—literally—intact.

Preorder your copy today

MORE PARANORMAL WOMEN'S FICTION BY LIA DAVIS & L.A. BORUFF

Witching After Forty https://laboruff.com/books/witching-after-forty/

A Ghoulish Midlife

Cookies For Satan (A Christmas Story)

I'm With Cupid (A Valentine's Day Story)

A Cursed Midlife

Birthday Blunder

A Girlfriend For Mr. Snoozleton (A Girlfriend Story)

A Haunting Midlife

An Animated Midlife

A Killer Midlife

Faery Oddmother

A Grave Midlife

Shifting Into Midlife https://laboruff.com/books/shifting-into-midlife/

Pack Bunco Night

Prime Time of Life https://laboruff.com/books/primetime-of-life/

Borrowed Time

Stolen Time

Just in Time

Hidden Time

Nick of Time

Magical Midlife in Mystic Hollow https://laboruff.com/books/
mystic-hollow/

Karma's Spell

Karma's Shift

Karma's Spirit

Karma's Sense

Karma's Stake

An Unseen Midlife https://amzn.to/3cF3W54

Bloom in Blood

Dance in Night

Bask in Magic

Surrender in Dreams

Midlife Mage https://amzn.to/3oMFNH3

Unveiled

Unfettered

An Immortal Midlife https://amzn.to/3cC6BMP

Fatal Forty

Fighting Forty

Finishing Forty

ABOUT LIA DAVIS

Lia Davis is the USA Today bestselling author of more than forty books, including her fan favorite Shifter of Ashwood Falls Series.

A lifelong fan of magic, mystery, romance and adventure, Lia's novels feature compassionate alpha heroes and strong leading ladies, plenty of heat, and happily-ever-afters.

Lia makes her home in Northeast Florida where she battles hurricanes and humidity like one of her heroines.

When she's not writing, she loves to spend time with her family, travel, read, enjoy nature, and spoil her kitties.

She also loves to hear from her readers. Send her a note at lia@authorliadavis.com!

Follow Lia on Social Media

Website: http://www.authorliadavis.com/
Newsletter: http://www.subscribepage.com/authorliadavis.
newsletter
Facebook author fan page: https://www.facebook.com/novelsbylia/
Facebook Fan Club: https://www.facebook.com/groups/
LiaDavisFanClub/
Twitter: https://twitter.com/novelsbylia
Instagram: https://www.instagram.com/authorliadavis/

BookBub: https://www.bookbub.com/authors/lia-davis
Pinterest: http://www.pinterest.com/liadavis35/
Goodreads: http://www.goodreads.com/author/show/5829989.
Lia_Davis

ABOUT L.A. BORUFF

L.A. (Lainie) Boruff lives in East Tennessee with her husband, three children, and an ever growing number of cats. She loves reading, watching TV, and procrastinating by browsing Facebook. L.A.'s passions include vampires, food, and listening to heavy metal music. She once won a Harry Potter trivia contest based on the books and lost one based on the movies. She has two bands on her bucket list that she still hasn't seen: AC/DC and Alice Cooper. Feel free to send tickets.

L.A.'s Facebook Group: https://www.facebook.com/groups/LABoruffCrew/
Follow L.A. on Bookbub if you like to know about new releases but don't like to be spammed: https://www.bookbub.com/profile/l-a-boruff

Made in the USA
Coppell, TX
04 October 2024

38186329R00292